# FLAMES OF REDEMPTION

## THE OMNI TOWERS SERIES BOOK 5

# JAMIE A. WATERS

Flames of Redemption © 2018 by Jamie A. Waters

Cover Art by Deranged Doctor Designs
Editor: Beyond DEF Lit

ISBN: 978-0-9996647-8-0 (Paperback Edition)
ISBN: 978-0-9996647-9-7 (eBook Edition)

Library of Congress Control Number: 2018907712
First Edition *November 2018

## THE OMNI TOWERS SERIES

### Flames of Redemption

# CHAPTER ONE

THE AIR PRESSURE shifted in the darkened room, indicating the door had been opened. Valentina, pretending to be asleep, continued to breathe deep, regular breaths. The intruder's movements were silent, but she could sense him moving along the wall and toward the bed.

She counted the seconds and anticipated the closing distance, her heartbeat slowing in time with the progression of her would-be assailant. When he was almost within touching distance, she rolled out of bed and threw a scalpel in his direction. It planted itself into the wall with a *thump*, and she dropped to the ground, waiting for retaliation.

"Ah, Valechka, you always did have trouble holding on to your weapons."

Her eyes narrowed at the taunt, and she withdrew her one remaining scalpel. "If I had known it was you, Seryozha, I would not have missed."

"You wish to dance?"

Thankful he couldn't see her smile in the darkness, Valentina slipped under the bed, trying to track his movements. She was better at stealth, but Sergei usually had more patience. Tilting her head, she focused on each of her senses to detect his location. He was moving around the edge of the bed, his confident footsteps painstakingly slow and noiseless. If they hadn't been trained by the same people, she never would've known he was there. She slid out from the opposite side of the bed, determined to approach him from behind.

Palming the second scalpel, she moved forward in the darkness and froze. *How could he be back on the other side of the bed?* She waited, knowing it was a trap but unsure of where he was.

"Behind you," Sergei whispered next to her ear before grabbing her wrist and bending it backward, causing the makeshift weapon to fall to the ground with a clatter. She followed it, using the momentum of her weight to force him to either release her wrist or unbalance him. He let go and jumped backward, narrowly missing her leg swiping out toward him.

Anticipating the move, he grabbed her ankle and yanked her in his direction. She slid along the ground and kicked out, forcing him to unhand her again. Valentina rolled away, pushed off the ground, and sprung back to her feet. The movement pulled at her abdominal injury, and she inhaled sharply.

"Lights on, eighty percent," Sergei ordered, and light flooded the room. Valentina blinked at him and frowned, annoyed he'd curtailed their game too soon. A few more minutes and she would have been able to get the other scalpel out of the wall.

"How badly are you hurt?" Moving forward, he reached for her shirt.

Valentina narrowed her eyes and took a step backward before he could make contact. "I did *not* invite you to touch me, Sergei."

He froze and lowered his hands to his sides. They stared

at each other for several heartbeats, both assessing and considering. The few minutes she'd seen him in Sofia's camp hadn't been nearly enough time to notice all the changes. His blond hair was longer than when she'd last seen him, reaching almost to his shoulders. He used to wear it much shorter, but now he looked much more like one of these Omnis. She tilted her head, wondering if that had been his intention so he could better fit in with them.

His physique had filled out even more too. He'd once been as slender as her, with gray eyes too large for his face. The changes were appealing, though, even if she noticed a few more scars than he'd had before. Then again, they all had more scars. Some were more easily seen than others.

He straightened his body and took another step toward her. "Nikolai wanted me to make sure you were well. Let me see the injury."

Valentina carefully kept her face blank; inwardly, she doubted Nikolai had said any such thing. Sure, Nikolai was probably concerned. After all, what good is a blunted blade? But Sergei needed to be reminded she wasn't his weapon to wield.

Taking another step backward, Valentina lowered herself onto the bed and began unbuttoning her shirt. She shrugged out of it and dropped it beside her casually as if she didn't care she was only wearing a bra. Tracing downward from her collarbone, she moved her hand over her breasts and to her abdomen where Pavel's blade had entered. Sergei swallowed, his Adam's apple bobbing as his heated gaze followed her leisurely movements. There was no outward sign of a wound; only a small line marred the surface of her skin.

But Sergei wasn't particularly focused on looking for a scar.

He moved toward her, and she leaned back on the bed, letting him see the invitation in her eyes. "If Nikolai wanted you to make sure I'm well, then do whatever he wishes. You know I would never refuse any of Nikolai's orders."

Sergei froze, his entire body tensing, and his jaw clenched. He grabbed her shirt and threw it at her. "Get dressed, Valentina. If you wish to whore for him, that's your choice. I'm not interested."

Feigning indifference, she picked up the shirt and turned away from him so he wouldn't see her hands shake when she put it back on.

He dropped something onto the nearby table. "This is Pavel's blade."

Valentina turned, her eyes widening at the sight of the knife Pavel had used on her when she'd gone to Sofia's camp to help rescue Ariana. Unable to suppress her shock and confusion, she reached out, her fingers sliding over the hilt of the blade. For Sergei to be gifting this to her meant he'd declared vengeance in her name, and it was now settled. She lifted her head to meet his eyes, the light gray color reminding her of another blade from long ago.

It was enough to make her turn away, her heart clenching at the memory. She pulled back her hand. "You should give this to Ariana or her lover. They'll want to know."

Sergei paused for a long moment, the weighted silence making it difficult for her to breathe. She forced her body to stay relaxed, mentally chastising herself for revealing too much. If given the opportunity, he'd use it against her, just as she would with him.

"The blade is for you, Valechka."

Her heart thudded in her chest, and she turned around to face him. A hundred questions went through her mind, but she couldn't bring herself to ask any of them. She couldn't even force herself to make a flippant response to drive him away. As though sensing her weakness, he took a step toward her.

Valentina looked up into his eyes, drowning in their gray depths. There was a small ring of gold around his irises as though an internal flame lit him from within. He took another step in her direction, and she swallowed as the heat from his body radiated outward, offering to chase away any lingering shadows of memory.

Almost of its own volition, she raised her hand and rested it against his chest. His nearness seared her skin like a brand, but she couldn't bring herself to push him away. He moved even closer, pinning her against the edge of the bed. His magnetism pulled her in, captivating her, and demanded she surrender to its insistent plea.

Footsteps sounded in the outside hallway, rapidly growing closer. Shoving him away, Valentina snatched the knife from the table, tucked it into the back of her waistband, and slid back on the bed just as the door opened. Sergei had already moved several steps away, pretending to inspect the empty juice container on her table.

Brant, the security agent who had escorted her back to the towers after her injury, halted at the sight of them. She flashed him a genuine smile in greeting, part of her relieved by his timely interruption. The last thing she needed was to get caught in Sergei's web.

Brant eyed Sergei with a frown before turning back to her. "Am I interrupting?"

She shook her head, motioning for him to come in. "No, we're finished catching up." *You have no idea, but you just saved me from myself.*

Sergei leaned against the wall, making it clear he wasn't going anywhere. Valentina glanced at him, doing her best to keep her expression blank but wishing he would take the hint and leave. *Please don't make me try to hurt you, Seryozha. Just go.*

Brant placed a small box and a large covered cup on the

table beside her. "You didn't seem to like the cookies here in the medical center, so I thought you might want to try these."

Touched by the gesture, she scooted over to investigate. "You brought me cookies?"

Inside the box were several cookies that didn't bear any resemblance to the small, biscuit-style offerings the medical center had given her earlier. She picked one up, the heady aroma of sugar and spices wafting toward her nose. They were still warm. Breaking off a piece, she offered it to Brant. Once he'd put it in his mouth and swallowed, she took a bite. Leaning back on the bed, she closed her eyes and let out a soft moan at the explosion of flavors on her tongue. They were heavenly—decadent, rich, and better than anything she'd ever tasted.

Valentina opened her eyes and sat up to reach for the tea, hesitating for a fraction of a second at the realization that both men were staring at her with heated expressions. Well, that was rather unintended, but it might have some benefits. She pulled off the cover of her tea and offered the cup to Brant. He chuckled but drank from the cup before handing it back to her. She beamed a smile at him and took a sip.

The moment the tea passed her lips, she realized she'd found another piece of nirvana. It wasn't only the taste, but the smell too. She inhaled deeply, her senses alighting as she breathed in the light floral scent. There was no comparison between this delicacy and the imitation brew they offered back in her camp on the surface. Was it any wonder Sergei was intent on staying if this was just a sample of what the towers had to offer?

"Brant, these are heavenly. Even my babushka never made anything this divine, and she was a wonderful cook."

Brant smiled, obviously pleased by the praise. "Well, you lost a lot of blood, and the doctor wants you to try to replenish your fluids. Since you refused medical treatment, I thought cookies and tea might be the way to encourage you to keep drinking. There's a small café down a few levels. I can take you there when you're better so you can try some of their other items."

Sergei pushed off the wall, his gaze furious. "You refused medical treatment?"

Holding his gaze, Valentina reached over to break off another piece of the cookie. Shoving it in her mouth, she began to slowly chew, taking her time so he would have to wait for a response. His eyes narrowed, the small throbbing vein on his neck the only other outward sign he was angry. She swallowed the last bite and made a dramatic show of licking a stray crumb off her thumb. Sergei's eyes lowered to her thumb, and he swallowed, his expression suddenly guarded.

"I did," she agreed. "They wanted to give me some sort of blood substitute. You know how I feel about needles."

What she didn't need to say was that she didn't trust these people. The only reason she decided to eat and drink the items Brant brought was because he had shared them with her both times. So far, Brant hadn't given her the slightest hint his motives were dishonest. This would be the way if he were going to do something nefarious though. Those cookies really were divine.

Sergei, however, was a different story. He may be living here with these Omnis, but two of their people had just abducted an OmniLab resident. Even though she'd intervened to rescue Ariana, there was no way in hell she'd allow these Omnis to do any sort of treatment until she knew whether there would be repercussions from Pavel and Sofia's actions.

"This is not acceptable, Valentina," Sergei retorted, clearly not agreeing with her assessment.

She shrugged and picked up the tea again, taking a long

sip. If he wanted to be foolish and trust these people without testing them, that was his decision. She had another scar on her hip to remind her about the dangers in trusting people.

Sergei turned to Brant. "Bring the doctor in here. She will agree to whatever treatment they decide."

Valentina put the cup down. "No. I am not in any danger, and this is my decision."

"You will, or I will strap you to this bed!" he shouted in their native language, all traces of his earlier calm gone.

She pushed herself out of bed and stood in front of him, refusing to back down. "If you so much as try it, I'll pull out Pavel's blade and gut you right here. Then *you* can be the one to receive their treatment. You do not have any right to dictate to me, Sergei."

"I do if you're being foolish. You nearly died today, Valentina. You should not have been anywhere near that camp to begin with."

"You didn't give us a choice!" she yelled, jabbing her finger against his chest. "Nikolai said our alliance was in danger. I was the closest person to Sofia's camp. My life is nothing compared to the thousands of our people at risk."

"Your life means everything!" he roared, grabbing her wrist and yanking her close. "Nikolai promised he would keep you out of harm's way if I took this assignment."

She jerked her hand away and shoved him. "It was never your place to make an agreement on *my* behalf, Sergei."

The door opened, and a vaguely familiar man entered the room. He hesitated for a moment, his blue eyes regarding them both curiously. "Is everything all right in here?"

"Everything is fine, Lars," Sergei snapped, not looking away from her.

Valentina glanced again at the newcomer and tilted her head to study him. So this was Lars, one of the exiles Sergei had rescued. She'd seen him at Sofia's camp but didn't realize he was the one who'd started them all down this path with OmniLab.

*Interesting.*

Brant cleared his throat. "Valentina is correct. She's not in any danger. The doctor merely wanted her to keep drinking to replenish her fluids. She just needs to rest and finish healing."

Sergei's jaw clenched, and he took a step back. "When will she be released?"

Brant hesitated. "She can leave now, but they would prefer to monitor her for a few days to make sure she doesn't reopen the wound. I spoke with Alec, and he wanted to extend the invitation to have her stay in the towers until she's fully recovered."

"Your offer is generous, but I need to return to the surface," she replied, eager to put some distance between her and Sergei.

"No," Sergei said in a clipped tone. "You will remain here for now."

She turned back to glare at him. "I will not. I have responsibilities on the surface."

"They will wait until you are fully recovered," he said in a low growl, edging closer again.

She paused, smiling sweetly at him. "Did Nikolai tell you he wanted me to remain here? Or did he tell you to make sure I was healed up as quickly as possible so I could return to his side?"

Her words had the desired effect. Sergei's expression blanked, and he took a step back. His eyes were once again shuttered, a mask replacing his earlier frustration. He pulled out his commlink, and she knew he was trying to contact Nikolai.

Valentina crossed her arms, not bothering to hide her irritation. She'd contact Nikolai herself, but her commlink had broken during the struggle with Sofia. If for no other reason, she needed to return to one of their camps to get a replacement.

Sergei switched back to their native tongue, speaking rapid-fire to Nikolai's assistant. Annoyed, Valentina held out her hand for the commlink. He ignored her, and a moment later she knew he was speaking directly to Nikolai.

Sergei turned away. "It is finished. They are no more."

Valentina lowered her hand, now more curious than annoyed. He was referring to the end he'd given to Pavel and Sofia. It had been tempting to refuse Sergei's insistence to receive medical treatment at the towers in order to handle them personally, but by accompanying Brant, she hoped she could learn more about OmniLab from one of their security forces.

Sergei launched into an explanation about her injury, how she'd been stabbed and nearly died but was now refusing medical treatment. Valentina's body stiffened, knowing Nikolai would probably go out of his mind. Taking a step forward, she held out her hand. "Give me your commlink, Sergei."

Sergei smirked and dropped it into her hand.

"Valya," Nikolai said, using the nickname reserved for only those closest to her. "What is this I'm hearing about you refusing treatment? How badly are you injured?"

Dammit. She couldn't lie to him. Glaring at Sergei, she admitted, "Sergei is correct. The injury was serious, but I am healing. Additional treatments are not necessary. I can return to the surface tonight."

"No," he ordered. "I will arrange to have a new commlink sent to you. Sergei has assured me they have state-of-the-art medical facilities in the towers. You will not return until you are completely healed."

Her jaw clenched, but she couldn't dispute his orders. "Very well."

"I need you to assess the situation while you are there. Given what happened with Pavel and Sofia, I have concerns about this alliance and our people. You will let me know if Sergei is unable to hold command."

She swallowed, not willing to risk glancing at Sergei again. "I understand."

"Good," he replied. "Be well, Valya, and return to me soon. You're missed."

Valentina ended the transmission and handed the commlink back to Sergei, doing her best to ignore the uneasy feeling in her stomach. Nikolai knew that of all the people she'd ever been asked to investigate, Sergei was the one person she wanted to avoid, and she suspected that's why he was now demanding she do so. Sergei wouldn't allow anyone other than her to get close enough to find out the extent of any problems —or even if his loyalty still lay with the Coalition. She'd heard rumblings from their people about the amount of time Sergei had spent with these Omnis and how his sympathies had possibly even fallen in line with the towers.

Sergei pocketed the commlink. "He's ordered you to remain here?"

"Yes," she snapped, irritated by his meddling.

It was his fault for putting her in the position to spy on him. Though, it might be for the best. She would at least give Sergei a fair assessment, which was more than what he might get if the assignment had been given to someone else. Sergei had never been particularly good at making friends. He had too many enemies and too many people envious of his command.

"If you're going to remain here, I have plenty of room in my quarters. You can have one of the guest rooms," Lars suggested, taking a step forward. "You'll be more comfortable there instead of staying in the medical center. It's the least I can do for the woman who helped save Ariana."

Sergei stiffened. Valentina glanced at him, somewhat amused. He didn't appear to like the idea of her staying with Lars. Good. She always got perverse pleasure out of annoying him.

Valentina smiled at Lars. "That's a very generous offer. I would be honored to accept and stay in your quarters with you."

Sergei glared at her, but she simply smiled sweetly at him.

*Oh, Seryozha, you have no idea what you've just gotten yourself into.*

# CHAPTER TWO

VALENTINA WALKED DOWN THE HALL, escorted by Sergei and Lars. Apparently, Sergei wasn't willing to let her out of his sight just yet. She had mixed feelings about this—she needed to get close to him, but she needed some time to mentally prepare herself. He was a little too good at reading her.

Since her visit to the towers hadn't been planned, Brant had offered to make arrangements to have some clothing brought to her. She was still wearing her uniform, complete with blood stains. Judging by a few of the shocked and horrified looks from other tower residents, they were more than a little sheltered. Besides, she intended to learn as much about these people as possible while she was here, so blending in with the natives would only help to expedite her investigation.

Lars placed his palm on a panel by a large ornate door, which enabled it to slide open. "I'll arrange to have your biometrics added to my quarters so you can come and go as needed."

Valentina nodded. That would make things a bit easier, but it wouldn't have stopped her even if he hadn't offered.

She'd already reviewed some of the security schematics from their original infiltration of the towers. She'd have to familiarize herself with them again once she received her new commlink.

She stepped inside, immediately taking note of the strange and elaborate furnishings. These Omnis didn't know how to utilize functionality over aesthetics. There were dozens of places to hide and more potential weapons than she had imagined. Any of these items—vases, glass, metal rods—could all be used to inflict serious damage.

Lars led her down a hallway past several other empty rooms and opened the door to one of them. "You can use this room while you're here. I'm a bit farther down the hall, so you'll have plenty of privacy."

The bedroom was much larger than the suite of rooms she shared with Nikolai. Once again, the furnishings were elaborate, with a large wooden bed that could easily sleep four people, a dresser, and a desk complete with wall monitors. But it was the ceiling that immediately caught Valentina's attention and held her interest. It was a simulated design depicting the sky outside the towers. Right now, it was darkened with a scattering of stars against the night sky.

"You can turn it off if it disturbs you," he explained, directing her to the controls and showing how they were touch and audio enabled.

She pressed one of the buttons and cycled through the images, enabling the display on the ceiling and walls. With one touch, a wall shifted and became a lush forest. A rich canopy of leaves and branches spread overhead with a smattering of sunlight trickling through. She pressed it again, and the image changed to a beach scene, complete with accompanying audio of crashing waves. She pushed another control and it shifted yet again to a remote, snowy mountaintop. The panel made several recommendations on temperature adjustments and wind speed to maximize the realism of the simulation.

"How many are there?" she asked in wonder, pressing it yet again to see a desert scene. She could easily spend hours staring at the different images without growing bored.

"I'm not sure," Lars admitted, rubbing his chin thoughtfully while he studied the latest image. "At least several dozen. I had a few favorites when I was younger, but it was mainly set to the sky. These are installed in most of the bedrooms in this part of the towers."

Valentina pressed the button to reset it to its default and turned around to find Sergei watching her intently with an amused smile on his face. She narrowed her eyes at him, wanting to wipe the look from his face. Part of her was tempted to throw her blade at him to see if he could still move as fast as he used to. His smile deepened as though guessing her thoughts.

She turned away, prowling around the room, and inspected the rest of the furnishings. "You live alone?"

"Yes," Lars replied. "You won't be disturbed if you wish to explore."

She nodded. It helped that Lars had lived with them for some time. Certain boundaries would be respected without causing offense.

"I'll warn you against exploring the rest of the towers though," Lars informed her, clasping his hands behind his back. "We can set up a profile with our security officers to allow you to move freely throughout the public areas of both towers, but the Inner Sanctum is much more heavily monitored. You should have an escort so you can avoid any unnecessary questions once you leave my quarters."

Pretending to study a small painting on the wall, she glanced at Sergei out of the corner of her eye. He inclined his head a fraction, enough to let her know he'd already discovered a workaround. Good. That would make things easier.

"You have a beautiful home, Lars." She ran her finger over the frame of the forest painting. "It's kind of you to allow me to stay with you."

"It's my pleasure. I owe Sergei and your people a great deal," Lars replied, walking over to open the adjacent bathroom door. "This bedroom is fairly private, but it's close to the common room. I can let you know when Brant arrives. In the meantime, feel free to help yourself to whatever you find. There's food in the kitchen area, and my private rooms are down the hall. I'll let you get some rest or explore, whichever you prefer. Please let me know if you need anything."

When she nodded, Lars turned and started to leave the room. Stopping in the doorway, he looked expectantly at Sergei, who was still leaning against the wall watching her.

Sergei waved him away. "I'll be with you in a moment, Lars."

Valentina didn't bother to hide her irritation. As soon as the door closed behind Lars, she tensed, wanting to draw the blade at her back but not willing to make the first move until she was sure of Sergei's intent. Knowing him, it could go either way.

Sergei pushed away from the wall. "Is Nikolai sending over a commlink?"

"Yes. It will probably be delivered tomorrow," she said, relaxing a fraction. He wanted to talk business. "How is security?"

"Better than our initial reports," he admitted, crossing the length of the room toward her. "You can move throughout this area, but you'll require a cloned keycard. I'll upload copies of the floorplans to you once you receive the commlink. Certain areas are completely restricted, and I'm still working on circumventing their security."

She tilted her head to study him. He'd never been one to overly dramatize the situation. If he said it was good, it was probably better than that. "You have a list of areas which can be used for diversionary tactics?"

"Yes. I'll send it to you and include the key areas to avoid. Do you have any weapons on you?"

She smirked at him. "Come now, Seryozha. You cannot expect me to answer that."

A slow smile spread across his face as his gaze perused her body, making it obvious he was taking the opportunity to not only assess her for hidden weapons but also to appreciate her softer attributes. "Only the blade I gave you?"

Valentina shrugged and leaned against the wall. They both knew she'd never answer, but that was part of the fun in the game. They'd confiscated her weapons when she entered the towers, but that wouldn't stop her for long. Sergei could believe whatever he wanted. She could be just as lethal without a weapon handy.

He leaned in close. "I will enjoy knowing your hands will be wrapped around my blade, Valechka. When you thrust my knife into your target, the pleasure you receive will be mine."

She lifted her hand, trailing it down his chest, noting how he unwittingly tensed at her gesture. Pleased he was still affected by her, she lifted her head, mirroring his movements, and leaned in closer. "Would you like me to return it to you now? One strong thrust and we can see how much pleasure you'll receive."

Sergei threw back his head and laughed, moving away from her. "Tempting, but I shall decline. Until next time, Valechka."

Valentina couldn't help the smile that crossed her face as she watched him leave the room. She'd missed their sparring more than she wanted to admit.

————

SERGEI CHUCKLED to himself as he headed out of Valentina's room and into Lars's common area, where the former exile was mixing a drink at the bar. Valentina was still as formidable and captivating as ever. It was that edge of unpredictable danger that had always drawn him to her, but she was more than a little distracting. That could prove to be deadly in his line of business.

Lars glanced over at Sergei. "Would you like a real drink instead of that swill you favor?"

"I don't believe your people understand the concept of a real drink." Sergei moved toward the bar as Lars chuckled and poured a glass for him.

"So that's the mysterious Valentina," Lars mused, taking a sip of his drink. "I've heard about her ties to Nikolai Berkutov. Is there anything I should know about her?"

"Yes, two things," Sergei replied, sniffing the amber-colored liquor in the glass. "One, she can kill you as easily as she breathes, so I would recommend taking care not to offend her."

Lars frowned. "And the second?"

"And I'll be the one to kill you if you fuck her."

Lars froze and then lowered his glass to the bar area. "Well, that wasn't what I was expecting. I'm afraid that leaves me with more questions than answers, not to mention a lot of sleepless nights in my future."

Sergei smirked and tossed back the liquid. It wasn't bad, but it wasn't his preferred choice. "Your people have much to learn about liquor."

"I'm guessing you're not going to expand upon your comments?"

"No," Sergei replied, investigating the other bottles on Lars's bar.

Lars was quiet for several long minutes while he finished off his drink. "What exactly is her relationship to Nikolai? I've heard rumors but nothing concrete."

Sergei frowned. Nikolai was an unwanted complication, but he wasn't about to admit that aloud, especially not anywhere near Valentina's sensitive hearing. If he had to guess, she was probably already prowling around Lars's quarters and investigating. By the time he visited her next, she'd have a small arsenal stashed in her room. He grinned. It would make their next encounter even more interesting.

"You would have to ask them," he replied, opening a different bottle and splashing it into a glass. "But I would not recommend it."

"I see," Lars said, continuing to study Sergei. "You're being even less forthcoming than usual."

The resounding door chime interrupted them, and Sergei glanced over at the monitor on the wall to see Brant had finally arrived. Lars headed for the door and opened it for the dark-haired security officer.

Brant held up a nearly overflowing bag. "Alec arranged to have some things sent over."

Sergei walked over in a handful of steps and snatched the bag from Brant's hand. Brant's eyes narrowed, but Sergei ignored him and began digging through the bag. His mouth curved upward in devilish appreciation.

*Oh, she will hate this.*

They'd manage to accumulate a rather extensive array of flowing dresses and dainty shoes. The silken undergarments were more than a little intriguing, but it wouldn't do much good to sit there and fantasize about Valentina wearing them while Lars and Brant were watching him search her bag.

"You're either a perverse bastard or you don't trust us either," Brant muttered, grabbing the bag away from him and resealing it. "Valentina wouldn't eat or drink anything in the medical center until I ate and drank first. Now you're searching her bag? Just what do you think we're going to do to her?"

Lars grinned. "She wouldn't eat or drink?"

"Valentina is cautious," Sergei agreed. "I was simply curious."

"A perverse bastard then," Brant acknowledged. "Where is she so I can hand these over?"

"I will take them to her," Sergei declared, hesitant to allow Brant anywhere near her. If Valentina wasn't listening in on their conversation, she was probably getting into trouble that couldn't easily be explained to the suspicious security officer. Besides, Valentina had been a little too friendly with Brant earlier. Granted, it was most likely because he was the equivalent of a soldier for their once-acknowledged enemy and not from any real personal interest.

She'd view Brant as a possible source of intel, but Sergei wasn't willing to take the chance he was wrong. She was a little too curious and far craftier than most people gave her credit for.

"I don't think so," Brant argued, holding tightly to the bag. "Lars? Where is her room?"

Valentina stepped into the room, feigning surprise at the sight of Brant, and gave the security officer a warm smile. Sergei'd been right. She'd been listening. At least one of his concerns was unfounded.

"I heard a strange chime and wondered what it was," she said and gestured to the bag. "Is that for me?"

Brant held the bag up. "Yes. It's a bit heavy though. Would you like me to take it into your room?"

Sergei's eyes narrowed on the security officer. He'd most likely have to give him the same warning he'd given to Lars, especially given the security officer's entranced expression as Valentina tilted her head and blinked her eyes at him. A few wisps of her chestnut hair had escaped from her ponytail and framed the delicate features of her face. She was stunning, and even worse, she knew it. Every gesture, expression, and movement was carefully calculated to disarm. It was no wonder Nikolai relied so heavily upon her.

She beamed a smile at him and gestured down the hall. "Oh, that's very kind of you. I'll show you to my room."

Sergei hesitated. Part of him was tempted to follow them, but he knew it would be a mistake to give in to his urges. Not only would Valentina probably make good on her threat to plant her newly acquired blade in his gut, but it would give her an even greater advantage over him. Instead, he sprawled out on the sofa and gave her a sardonic smirk.

Temper flared in her eyes for only a second before she schooled her expression. His grin deepened. The only outward sign of her lingering irritation was the slightest hint of rigidity in her shoulders. As soon as Valentina and Brant disappeared down the hall, Lars rescued his drink and sat on the couch. "I keep having the feeling I'm missing something when you two are in the same room."

Busy counting the minutes, Sergei shrugged but didn't reply. If Brant didn't reemerge soon, he'd abandon all pretense and go in after them.

Lars took a sip, his gaze gravitating toward the hallway. "She's very attractive."

Sergei arched an eyebrow. "Have you already forgotten my warning?"

Lars grinned. "I'm curious as to why you haven't warned away Brant."

Sergei drummed his fingers on the back of the couch. "I would be disappointed to have to kill you. Him? Not so much."

Lars laughed. Sergei's mouth curved upward, but his smile faded as Brant reappeared in the common room. The security officer looked a little too self-assured to have simply dropped off a bag in Valentina's room. She was definitely up to something.

Brant nodded at them in farewell. "I'll see you tomorrow, Lars. Have a good evening."

Lars frowned. "Tomorrow? Do we have a meeting I don't know about?"

Brant paused. "No. I'm stopping by in the morning to take Valentina out for breakfast. She wants to see some of the towers."

Lars nearly choked on his drink and darted a quick glance at Sergei. "I see. Well, I suppose I'll see you in the morning. Have a good night."

Brant let himself out, and Sergei turned to glare down the hallway toward Valentina's room.

"I'm not helping you hide the body," Lars advised.

"There will not be a body left to hide," Sergei growled, pushing off the couch. He had half a mind to confront the confounding woman and remind her the alliance with OmniLab was tenuous at best, but it wouldn't do any good. Valentina always did as she wished. Besides, unless she had suddenly lost her touch, she'd have the security officer enamored enough that she could steal all the tower's secrets by the end of the morning.

Sergei glanced down at Lars. "I'll return before breakfast."

Lars shook his head, an amused smile on his face. "Of course you will."

# CHAPTER THREE

VALENTINA TOSSED another dress on the bed and resisted the urge to swear. Sure, a little skin went a long way when trying to entice someone into talking, but where the hell was she supposed to keep her weapons? Not one of them had any pockets or enough fabric to hide a knife, much less any of the weaponized objects she'd found in Lars's quarters.

Walking over to the nearby dresser, she dug around in the drawers until she found a belt. It was a start. Tossing it on the bed, she headed down the hallway in search of more items. Sergei had left shortly after Brant, so she didn't have to worry about running into him. Lars was still awake and wandering around, but he might have some idea about where she could locate the objects she needed. She'd look for them herself, but time was an unfortunate deterrent.

The soft sound of movement reached her ears. Based on the direction and cadence of the steps, Valentina surmised Lars was in the common room. Slowing her gait to more of a casual stroll, she entered the room. He turned to look at her, his eyes widening as he glanced down at her bare legs under the long shirt she was wearing. She slowed her walk even further, the slightest swing of her hips making the material brush against her thighs.

He swallowed and held up his glass. "Uh, can I offer you a drink?"

"Actually," she began, tucking her loose hair behind her ear, "I was wondering if you could help me with something."

His face paled, and Valentina bit back a smile. Lars really was taking Sergei's warning to heart. Deciding to put him out of his misery, she said, "I need some heavy, pliable material," she held up her hands to indicate the size, "about this big. I also need some type of thread or twine."

He blinked at her and lowered his glass. "I'm not sure exactly what you're looking for, but I might have something that meets your requirements."

Valentina gave him a brilliant smile and followed him down the hall to his private rooms. She'd explored them earlier but hadn't spent more than a cursory amount of time in them. Lars led her into his closet and opened one of the built-in drawers. "There's some thread in here somewhere."

She approached him, looking over his arm to peer into the drawer as he began rifling through it. He turned to regard her, opening his mouth and then closing it as though he wanted to ask her a question. Valentina softened her gaze to give her an even more unassuming appearance and set him at ease.

After the slightest hesitation, Lars asked, "Would you be offended if I asked why you wanted these things? If I knew what it was for, I might be better able to help you find what you need."

"I'm not offended," she said with a small smile, making it clear she wasn't going to answer his question. "The needle and thread in the back corner of your drawer will work well for my purposes."

Lars frowned, glancing down and spotting the items she mentioned. He picked them up and offered it to her.

Valentina took it and then ran her hand over some of the well-crafted clothes hanging in the closet, admiring their softness and colors. "There are so many. Do you wear all of them?"

He scanned the contents of his closet and shook his head. "No. A few, but I got used to a simpler lifestyle while living on the surface."

Valentina stroked her hand down a long tunic that would be more than adequate for her needs. It even had small buckles she could cut off and repurpose. "This one is lovely."

"That tunic?" His frown deepened, and she nodded, letting a small smile play upon her lips. "Would that tunic work for... whatever you're doing?"

She bit her lip, pretending to consider it. "Why, it just might. It's a little bigger than what I need, but I could always use the remaining material for something else. If you don't need it, I wouldn't mind taking it off your hands."

"You can have it." He pulled it off the rack and handed it to her. "I don't think I've ever even worn it."

"Thank you, Lars." Valentina headed out of the closet, aware his eyes were once again on her legs. Now she just had to get back to her room, cut up the tunic, sew some hidden pockets on a dress for tomorrow and make sure she had a place to stash some of her weapons. Then she'd have to figure out a way to barricade the door so she could get some sleep. It would be a busy night.

————

SERGEI PRESSED the button on Lars's door, mildly surprised when it opened almost immediately.

Lars looked exhausted, his eyes red-rimmed and wary. He waved Sergei inside and then slumped onto the couch. "I've been up all night, and it's all your fault."

Glancing down the hall toward Valentina's bedroom, Sergei arched an eyebrow. "Why is that?"

Lars lifted his head to scowl at him. "You know why."

Sergei grinned and sat on the couch, angling himself so he could watch the hallway from his position. "What did she do?"

"She came out here last night, wearing hardly anything at all. The woman has fantastic legs, by the way. I nearly had heart palpitations. Then she asked me for my help."

Sergei's eyes narrowed. He agreed about her legs, but he decided to focus on the most important part of Lars's comment. "What sort of help?"

"She wanted a needle, thread, and a tunic," Lars said with a frown. "Maybe the clothing didn't fit?"

"Perhaps," Sergei mused, peering down the hallway again. Domestic duties didn't usually interest Valentina. What was she up to now and where was she?

"I had your warning replaying in my head all night. I was half expecting you to come into my room to kill me."

Sergei chuckled. "I will not kill you for looking."

"That's a relief," Lars murmured. "Because as long as she's staying here, I might as well enjoy it."

Valentina still hadn't emerged from her room. Sergei frowned, a smidgen of worry beginning to fill him. The entire reason she was here was to recover from her injuries. He stood, wondering if she could be in worse shape than he thought. "Have you seen her this morning?"

"No," Lars said, shaking his head. "I've only been up for about thirty minutes though. I didn't hear her all night."

That didn't mean anything. Valentina had always excelled at sneaking around, but she should have come out to investigate the door chime. Sergei headed down the hall toward her room, pausing outside the door. He lifted his hand to knock but stopped. If she wasn't injured, it might be more entertaining to surprise her.

He started to open it, but the door held fast. He frowned, pushing against it, but it still wouldn't budge. His eyes widened at the realization she'd barricaded the door. Taking a step back, Sergei lowered his shoulder and slammed into it. He staggered inside, the large dresser falling to the floor with a resounding *crash*.

A dagger swooshed by his head, and he dropped to the ground to avoid any other flying weapons. He peered toward the bed where Valentina was sitting, a large shirt hanging off one of her shoulders and exposing a creamy expanse of skin. Her chestnut hair tumbled in waves over her other shoulder, making her delicate features even more arresting.

"Go away, Seryozha." Valentina yawned and rubbed her eyes. "It is too early to play."

Sergei glanced up at the knife embedded in the wall less than an inch from where he'd been standing. He grinned. Even half asleep, she had exceptional aim. There was no doubt in his mind that if she truly wanted him dead, he would be.

"What was that crash?" Lars stepped into the room and paused, his eyes widening at the sight of the dresser on the floor. He paled when he saw the knife embedded in the wall. Looking back and forth between Sergei and Valentina, he took a small step backward.

Valentina frowned, her lips curving into an adorable pout. "What time is it?"

"Seven," Sergei replied, standing and stepping around the dresser. He doubted even Valentina would kill him in front of witnesses, unless she planned to kill Lars too.

"Already? I just went to bed an hour ago," she complained, slipping out of bed and heading toward a door on the opposite side of the room. Lars was right. She had exceptional legs.

Her comment about just recently falling asleep finally registered, and Sergei glanced around the room to see what had kept her up most of the night. She'd spread out all her newly acquired clothing, and he walked over to a dark tunic she'd started cutting up. Picking up a pile of material she'd sewn together, he grinned.

Lars stared incredulously at the buckles and sewn pieces. "Is that... Is that a holster?"

"Indeed." Sergei chuckled, tossed it back down, and began poking through the rest of Valentina's collection of trinkets.

She'd been busy, managing to find a few more knives, scissors, a portable heating element, a few chemicals that could easily be used to create a rather rudimentary explosive, and a couple other highly entertaining objects.

Lars frowned. "Industrious, isn't she?"

"Mmhmm," Sergei agreed, hearing the sound of the shower in the other room. The thought of her naked under the water was a little too tantalizing. He walked over to the dresser, intent on distracting himself.

Lars stared at the toppled furniture. "She barricaded the door?"

Sergei grunted an affirmative as he set the dresser upright and pushed it back to the far side of the room. How the hell did she move it without reopening her wound? Unless she did. He frowned at the thought and glanced toward the bathroom door. Dammit. Now that he thought about it, her movements had been a little stiff when she'd climbed out of bed.

He headed toward the bathroom door and shoved it open to find her standing in the shower running soap-covered hands through her hair. She blinked at him with those gorgeous blue eyes of hers. A trail of suds slid over her breasts and down her athletic body. He took a moment or two to appreciate the view, although it could have been even longer.

All sense of time and urgency evaporated from his mind at the sight of her naked body in front of him.

She turned away, tilting her head toward the water, and continued to rinse the soap from her body. His gaze followed the sudsy movement and back up again. Her legs were fantastic, but her ass was even better. He was hard-pressed to decide which view was more appealing, the front or the back. Each one had its own set of benefits and very few drawbacks.

At least he was assured she didn't have any more weapons this time. Although, Valentina had always excelled at improvisation.

Valentina glanced at him over her shoulder and arched an eyebrow. "Are you here to wash my back or just admire the view?"

Sergei took a handful of steps toward her. "Turn around, Valentina."

She did as he asked and gave him a saucy little smile that seemed to have a direct line to his cock. "You want to wash my front instead?"

He swallowed, trying to keep his disobedient body under control, and raised his hand to brush against her abdomen. Her mouth parted on a gasp, and she took a small step backward. His eyes narrowed on her. "You hurt yourself again?"

"I am fine," she snapped and slapped her hand against the water control valve to shut it off. She started to brush past him, but he wrapped his arm around her and pulled her against him.

Part of him expected her to fight him, but when she didn't, Sergei wasn't sure if he was more relieved or concerned. "The truth, Valentina."

"Which truth do you want, Sergei?"

All of them, but it wasn't wise to tell her that. "How badly did you hurt yourself moving the dresser?"

She shrugged.

He sighed. "Will you go back to the medical center?"

"No."

"Will you allow a medic to check you out here?"

She paused for a long moment. "Yes."

*Dammit.*

Sergei's jaw clenched. She would never have agreed if she wasn't in a great deal of pain. He released her. "I'll have them meet you here. Get dressed."

"Sergei," she called to him. He turned around, waiting expectantly and trying not to stare at the water droplets trailing over her naked skin. She licked her lips, glancing down at his pants before meeting his gaze. "It would have been more fun if you had offered to wash my front."

Sergei swallowed, his mouth going dry, and debated whether it was too early to start drinking. He turned away and stormed out of the guest room. That woman was going to drive him insane. She didn't need any tangible weapons. Her entire body was one, and she was definitely a master.

Lars glanced up and snorted at the sight of Sergei's damp clothing as he reentered the common area. "You look like you have an interesting story to share."

"We need to call a medic to your quarters," he snapped, irritated at himself and Valentina.

Lars stood, heading over to the panel on the far wall. "How bad is it?"

"She's in pain but will not tell me more than that. I believe she may have reopened the wound. I didn't see anything externally, but she may have caused internal damage."

Lars pressed a few buttons on the panel. "They're on their way. Why would she have moved the dresser? Did she think I would hurt her?"

"It was to prevent me from entering," Sergei admitted. Maybe if he promised not to try to best her until she was healed, she would avoid taking such risks. Although, she'd likely take offense to the suggestion she was too weak to offer much of a challenge. Then she'd most definitely retaliate, and it would likely be without her usual playfulness.

Lars frowned. "Dare I ask why she would be worried about you entering?"

Sergei waved his hand dismissively, not about to explain their complicated history. "That's not important. How long until the medic arrives?"

"A few minutes," Lars confirmed after checking the panel again.

———

VALENTINA ADJUSTED the makeshift holster on her thigh and yanked the knife out of the wall. She glanced down at the blade to make sure it was still adequately sharp. It needed a sharpening stone, but it was still functional. She should probably find something else to throw at Sergei next time though. The knife wouldn't continue to hold up if she had to keep avoiding hitting him. Although, part of her was tempted not to miss next time.

She frowned, rubbing her abdomen and thinking about how she'd let him walk right into the bathroom. She wasn't thinking clearly, and her dizziness was getting worse. Not only had it been a foolish move to leave herself so exposed, but then she'd admitted to possibly reopening the wound. Next time someone stabbed her, she might as well just twist the blade herself.

Valentina sighed. What she wouldn't give for a few hours of sleep. She was so tired, and her injury hurt more than it should. As long as she was in OmniLab's domain, though, rest was out of the question. It was unlikely Nikolai would object if she returned to his camp, but there was no way she'd go back simply because she needed a nap. That was a level of humiliation she wasn't willing to accept.

She slid Pavel's knife into the makeshift sheath, considered it for a minute, and then added another blade she'd found in Lars's kitchen. A girl could never have too many weapons, especially with Sergei around intent on irritating her.

The strange chime from the night before echoed from the common area. Smoothing out the short blue dress, she headed down the hall to investigate.

"She is not going to breakfast with you," Sergei announced.

"I don't believe I asked for your opinion," Brant replied.

Ah. So it was her breakfast date and not the medic. She shook out her hair, letting it fall past her shoulders. It was still slightly damp, but the drying tube had taken most of the moisture from it. With her hair down and wearing this foolish dress, she knew she appeared even more unassuming than usual.

"Good morning, Brant," she called out, stepping into the common area.

"Valentina," he greeted her, his eyes warming in appreciation at her attire. "Did you sleep well?"

Sergei regarded her expectantly, his smirk daring her to tell him the truth. She lowered her gaze a fraction and said in a soft tone, "Actually, I think I may have tried to do too much yesterday. I'm a little sore this morning."

Brant frowned. "I'm sorry to hear that. Would you like me to take you back to the medical center so they can check you out?"

She shook her head. "I appreciate your concern, but I believe Sergei has already called a medic for me. I would rather not go back there unless it's absolutely necessary."

"Ah, yes," he murmured. "Your fear of needles."

Sergei snorted, moving over to lean against the wall. She smiled sweetly at him.

*A flick of my wrist and I could end you.*

His eyes twinkled in amusement, and he inclined his head in a silent challenge.

Brant studied her for a long moment. "Maybe it would be better to reschedule if you're not feeling up to it this morning."

"Oh, no," she assured him. "That will not be necessary. If you don't mind waiting a bit, I would enjoy seeing some of the towers. I am probably fine, but Sergei worries about me. He is... a bit of a mother hen."

Sergei's eyes narrowed, and she bit her lip to keep from smiling.

*Ha.*

Lars didn't bother to stop his laughter. He sprawled out on the couch and waved away Brant's curious gaze. "Ignore me. I just haven't heard Sergei described quite in that manner."

She darted another glance at Sergei, feigning dismay. "I didn't offend you, did I? Would you rather I call you... What is the word for a male hen?"

"A cock," Lars supplied helpfully.

"Of course," she agreed, pleased he'd caught on. "A cock."

"I prefer to be called a falcon, *golubushka*," Sergei purred. "But you may call me whatever you wish."

Valentina's eyes narrowed at the endearment. Little dove, indeed. And he thought he was the falcon who would eat her? She dropped her hand to the sheath on her thigh, prepared to draw a blade and fling it at him. Sergei grinned at her and shook his head a fraction. "You're a little flushed. Would you care to sit?"

She straightened a second before Brant turned back

around to regard her. Before she could reply, the door chimed again.

Lars chuckled. "That must be the medic. Excellent timing."

Lars led the medic into the room, and Valentina nodded politely at the man. She recognized him as the same person who had treated her in the Coalition camp.

"I understand you may have reopened the wound?"

She shrugged. "Perhaps. A few twinges, but nothing overly concerning."

"I'll need to check," he said, glancing around at the audience. "Is there a private area where I can examine you?"

"Yes," she said, turning around and heading back down the hallway toward the guest room. She opened the door and caught sight of Sergei following behind them.

At her irritated glare, he said, "I will hear what he says, Valentina. Nikolai will want to know how badly you are injured."

"I can tell him myself," she snapped.

"Yes, but will you?" he retorted, crossing his arms over his chest.

She turned away, determined to ignore him, and slipped off the straps of her dress. It slid to the floor, and she stepped out of it wearing nothing but her undergarments and weapons. Putting her hands on her hips, she lifted her chin, daring Sergei to make any other comments. The medic floundered for the briefest moment before ducking down and digging through his bag.

Lazily leaning against the wall, Sergei grinned and slowly perused her up and down. "Nice... weapons."

The medic pulled out an imaging wand and ran it over her abdomen. It beeped, and he glanced down at the display readings before reaching into his bag to pull out another small device. He gestured for her to place her hand on it and frowned at the readings. "We need to readmit you to the medical center immediately. Have you had any dizziness? Headaches?"

Her gaze flew down to the medic, and she swallowed. She'd suspected something was wrong but had hoped it was nothing. "Yes. Why?"

The medic nodded, reaching for his commlink. "I'm calling for an emergency transport. You have some internal bleeding, but I don't know how extensive. We'll know more once we get you back to medical."

"You do not need to call for a transport. I will carry her," Sergei declared, moving in her direction.

Her eyes flew to his, and she took a step backward, her body stiffening. "I can walk."

Sergei nodded. "Yes, you can, but I would ask that you please don't fight me on this, Valechka. Allow me to help you."

Valentina hesitated and then inclined her head in agreement. Sergei scooped up her dress from the floor, and she pulled it back on. He bent down, lifting her up into his arms.

She squeezed her eyes shut. This was absurd. She was perfectly capable of walking. Taking a deep breath, she tried to convince herself this would help lend believability to her non-threatening persona. And the fact that she was enjoying having Sergei's arms around her? Well, that was a whole other matter.

Both Lars and Brant were still waiting in the common room with mirrored expressions of worry on their faces.

Lars took a step toward them. "What's wrong?"

"Call Ariana," Sergei said, not stopping. "See if she can meet us back in the medical ward."

Valentina shook her head. "No. You're overreacting. It's not so bad. Ariana's injuries were probably worse. Leave her to rest."

"Enough," he growled. "I am not discussing this with you now. If you weren't already injured, I would bend you over my knee."

"Put me down," she demanded, pushing against him. To hell with her damsel in distress routine. She'd bend him over her knee first.

"Settle yourself," Sergei said, his arms tightening around her. "If I put you down, my next action will be to call Nikolai and tell him about your recklessness. What will he say to you acting like an impulsive child?"

Her jaw clenched, and she looked away before she said or did something she really might regret. Sergei didn't say anything more to her, for which she was thankful. He followed the medic into the priority elevator, and when the door opened, they stepped out into the medical ward.

Valentina swallowed, the first stirrings of worry beginning to set in. She wasn't concerned about dying, or even about the possibility of surgery. The thought of being unconscious and at the mercy of these strangers was what had her suddenly wary and reconsidering this decision.

"Sergei," she whispered, curling her fingers into his shirt, "call Nikolai. I want our doctors to evaluate me."

He frowned, his gaze whipping toward her. "What?"

"Please," she urged. "Give me your commlink, and I will call him myself."

He carried her back into the medical room she'd been in the night before and placed her on the bed. There was a trace of sympathy in his eyes, and he nodded. "Give me a moment. I'll take care of it."

She nodded, and he left the room.

## CHAPTER FOUR

CLOSING THE DOOR BEHIND HIM, Sergei walked down the hallway and waved over the medic. "How serious is her condition?"

"Very," the medic replied. "I'm astounded she's still conscious. We'll know more soon, but I'd say the likelihood of surgery is very high at this point. Without it, she could die. She lost too much blood the night before, and her blood pressure is remarkably low. The surgical team is already prepping."

Sergei glanced at the closed door. "Can you sedate her?"

The medic frowned. "She'll be sedated once we take her into surgery."

"Sedate her now, or she will not make it to surgery. She is demanding to leave the towers."

The medic shook his head. "She won't survive the trip. I don't know what kind of medical team you have in place on the surface, but she may not even have enough time to make it there."

"Then give me the sedative and I will give it to her."

"I can't do that," the medic argued.

"She is one of my people," Sergei snapped. "If you do not give me the sedative and anything happens to her, I will bring a wrath down upon the towers, the likes of which you have never seen. Now give me the sedative."

The medic hesitated and then nodded. "Very well. You'll need to inject it into her upper arm. If Ariana Alivette is able to make it here in time, she may be able to heal her without surgical intervention."

Sergei followed the medic over to a locked console where he pulled out a small syringe. Sergei glanced down at the small device. It would be easy to hide, but getting close enough to use it might be more challenging. He palmed the syringe and headed back inside Valentina's room.

She looked up when he entered, and he noted the shadows under her eyes. How had he not noticed how tired she appeared?

"You spoke with Nikolai?"

"All the arrangements have been made," he lied, keeping his expression carefully blank. She tilted her head to study him, a trace of uncertainty on her face. He sighed. She was far too perceptive. He would have to resort to more drastic methods to distract her and face the consequences later. "Nikolai is very disappointed with you, Valentina. I have not heard him that angry for a long time."

She frowned at him, still wary. "I don't believe you. What did you say to him?"

He walked around the edge of the bed, making his movements casual and timing them with his words. If he could lower her defenses, he could get close enough without her noticing what he was going to attempt. Unfortunately, he didn't have many options. He'd been surprised she'd even allowed him to carry her here. She'd kill him for sure if she knew what he was about to do.

"I told him how you disregarded his orders to rest and

recover. You not only refused medical treatment but you managed to reinjure yourself with your foolish antics. The doctor ordered you to keep drinking, but Lars said you were not. And now you are disregarding Nikolai's orders again and insisting on returning to one of our camps for treatment."

Her face paled. "You told him all that? What did he say?"

Sergei sighed. "You have put yourself in a position where you have jeopardized your life again. He agreed your actions are not seemly for an agent of one of our leaders. I believe he is having doubts about you."

"Why would he say that? I thought..." She squeezed her eyes shut, a look of such heart-wrenching pain on her face. When a small tear escaped to trail down her cheek, Sergei froze. *Oh, God.* He couldn't do this to her. He could handle anyone else's tears but hers.

"Please don't cry, Valechka. I swear I didn't call him."

She blinked up at him, confused and uncertain. "You lied to me?"

Sergei quickly moved forward, pressing his hand against her arm until it beeped. She gasped, jerking away from him, and withdrew her blade in one swift movement. She threw it at him and he dove away, but not before it impaled his shoulder.

He swore loudly, pushing up from the floor, his shoulder feeling as though it were on fire. A nurse rushed in, faltering at the sight of the knife sticking out of Sergei's shoulder. She stuck her head out the door, calling for assistance. Sergei ignored the nurse and the knife, moving to stand beside a now unconscious Valentina. He supposed he should be thankful the sedative was fast-acting. Otherwise, he might have more than just a blade in his shoulder.

Sergei reached down and removed her other weapon before slipping off the thigh holster and tossing it on the floor.

"We need to assess your injury," someone said from behind him.

"Later. Take care of her first," Sergei ordered, not bothering to turn around.

"Ariana Alivette will be here any second. She wants to see her before we proceed."

Sergei nodded and sat in a nearby chair. The doctor hesitated, motioning for the nurse to assist him. They brought over a scanner and proceeded to survey the damage. Sergei ignored them, focusing instead on Valentina's slow, rhythmic breathing. It was strangely soothing, and he found himself timing his breaths to match hers.

The door was pushed open a moment later. Ariana and Alec entered the room, followed by the medic who had diagnosed Valentina and given him the sedative. Ariana's worried gaze met his before turning toward Valentina's unconscious form.

Alec frowned, his gaze sweeping the room. "What happened here?"

"A misunderstanding," Sergei replied, not willing to explain.

Ariana hesitated, glancing back and forth between him and Valentina. Before Sergei could even open his mouth to direct Ariana to attend to Valentina first, she moved toward the bed. "I should have checked her again after we bonded. I was too weak to do more than a cursory healing."

She held her hands over Valentina's abdomen for a moment and called over to the medic, "Paul, I need your help with her clothing. I need skin contact for this, preferably over the wound itself. It's worse than I thought."

Paul stepped over to assist, and Sergei leaned forward, not willing to let Valentina out of his sight. The doctor grabbed his arm. "You need to remain still while we're sealing the wound."

Sergei ignored him. They could damn well figure out how to work around him or do it later. Ariana placed her hands on Valentina's abdomen and closed her eyes. Something in the air shifted. That was the only way Sergei could describe it.

Alec placed his hand on Ariana's shoulder and murmured something in her ear. She nodded but didn't remove her hands from Valentina. Ariana remained that way for almost ten minutes, her eyes closed in deep concentration. When she finally pulled her hands away, she turned around to face him with a soft smile on her face.

"She'll be all right. She still needs to rest, but I don't believe she can easily reopen the wound again. I'm going to recommend the doctor give her a blood substitute though. She's weaker than she should be."

Sergei swallowed, relief flooding through him at her words. "Thank you, Ariana."

Ariana nodded, and Alec wrapped his arm around her waist in a protective gesture. She glanced at Sergei's shoulder and frowned. "How are you feeling? Can I help with your pain?"

Sergei shook his head, not interested. His pain was insignificant compared to what he'd inflicted upon Valentina with his words. He knew the depth of her loyalty to Nikolai, and he'd tried to turn it against her. Maybe it was his frustration with her blind devotion, but he should have tried a different way to distract her.

Alec frowned. "She stabbed you? Why?"

Sergei ignored him. The doctor had finished whatever they'd done with his shoulder, and he got up to move beside Valentina's bed. The nurse came over, attached an I.V. to Valentina's arm and pressed a button to begin transfusing the blood substitute. He glanced over at the medic who had provided him with the sedative. "How long will she sleep?"

"An hour or so, maybe less depending on her metabolism."

Sergei nodded. It would probably be sooner. He gestured to the I.V. "When will this be complete?"

"An hour or two," the nurse replied, checking the levels on the machine. "We'll determine then if she needs any additional amounts. If so, it will take longer."

Sergei shook his head. "You need to keep her sedated until you are finished."

The nurse frowned, looking down her nose at him. "That won't be necessary. This is a painless procedure."

He glared at her. "If she awakens before you are finished, she will rip out the needle from her arm, strangle anyone who tries to stop her with that tube, and disappear from the towers before their body hits the floor." He took a threatening step forward. "Keep. Her. Sedated."

The nurse stared at him in shock.

Alec pulled out his commlink and pressed a button. He turned to the nurse and said, "Do as he says. Security will be here shortly to remain with her."

Sergei knew that whatever security Alec had in mind would be next to worthless when it came to her. He lifted one of Valentina's limp hands, turning it over in his and tracing his fingers over her palm. Her skin was remarkably soft, and her hand so small and delicate compared to his. A small scar marred the outside of her hand, just under her thumb, and he resisted the urge to kiss it. He remembered it well. They'd been scouting a potential facility primed for a takeover, and she'd mistimed jumping over a barbed wire fence. She'd been furious when it happened, more so about the gloves she'd torn and needed to replace than anything else. Another scar on her arm caught his eye, and he frowned.

Brant entered the room, his footsteps tapping lightly on the tiled floor. "How is she?"

"Sleeping," Ariana replied. "She'll be fine."

"I want you to stay with her at all times," Alec ordered. "If you need to leave for any reason, make sure to have another security officer remain here."

Brant raised his eyebrows and glanced down at Valentina. "Is there a problem?"

"Other than the fact she just stabbed Sergei and he refuses to explain why? Or that he's indicated she's a potential danger to the people here in the medical ward?"

"Alec," Ariana chided gently.

"No, Ari," Alec told her. "I'm grateful for her part in saving you, but I will not allow our people to be threatened."

Sergei sighed and gestured to the patched wound on his shoulder. "Her reaction was warranted. I played upon her fears to distract her, so I could sedate her. She demanded to return to the surface and be treated by our doctors. Your medic informed me she would not survive the trip."

Ariana's expression softened, a trace of pity in her gaze. "Oh, Sergei, that must have been difficult for you."

Brant frowned. "You told her she wouldn't survive the trip?"

"No," Sergei replied, releasing Valentina's hand and crossing his arms over his chest. The movement pulled at his shoulder, but he ignored it.

"So she might have actually agreed to the treatment to save her life?" Brant demanded.

"She would not," Sergei informed him. "Until she is confident your people will not seek retaliation for Pavel and Sofia's actions, she will be cautious."

"She saved me," Ariana said quietly. "We don't wish her or any of your people harm."

Sergei's gaze softened as he regarded Ariana. She was far too trusting, and even her unfortunate captivity hadn't damaged her naïve innocence. "Valentina doesn't know you or your people, Ariana. It will take time for her to feel comfortable. Trust does not come easily to many of us."

Ariana nodded in understanding, but her dismay was evident.

"I'll remain with her," Brant said to Alec. "Even if she's not a danger to anyone other than Sergei, I believe she's established some level of trust with me. Perhaps I can help alleviate some of her reservations."

Alec nodded, and Sergei resisted the urge to smirk at the security officer. Valentina viewed him as a mark, nothing more. Sergei paused for a moment, remembering Ariana's words back at the Coalition camp. Could Valentina truly be attracted to the dark-haired security officer? He glanced down at her sleeping form and frowned. He could read her about some things, but other times, she was a complete mystery.

———

VALENTINA HEARD soft voices somewhere nearby, but they were fuzzy as though speaking through a film. She blinked open her eyes to stare at an unfamiliar ceiling. Her body felt sluggish and heavy, and she tried to flex her hands and get her limbs to cooperate.

"You're awake," a gentle voice murmured.

She turned her head, trying to focus on the man standing beside her. His dark hair and hazel eyes were more than a little familiar. She frowned, trying to recall the memory. It was Brant, the security officer from the towers. More memories came rushing back, and with them, a sharp fury. Valentina pushed herself upright in bed, sloughing off her confusion and grogginess for something far more dangerous.

Sergei was standing on the far side of the room watching her. How dare he sit at her bedside after his betrayal? She didn't need to glance down to know she'd been disarmed. Removing her weapons would have been the first thing Sergei would have done after sedating her, but he would do well to remember she was hardly defenseless.

Brant picked up a cup from the bedside table and offered it to her. "Would you like some tea?"

Valentina glanced over at him and nodded, hesitant to take her eyes off Sergei. Brant had proven to be somewhat honorable, unlike other people in the room. Never would she have believed she could trust one of these Omnis over one of her own people.

She accepted the proffered cup, inhaling the highly aromatic floral scent, and took a long sip, murmuring her appreciation for the warm liquid as it soothed the dryness in her throat. Brant took it from her when she finished, placing it back on the bedside table. She pressed her hands on the bed, her body beginning to tense from Sergei's continued scrutiny.

He was leaning against the wall, his expression guarded. His body language was equally tense, which didn't bode well for either one of them. A small bandage covered his shoulder, indicating she'd hit her mark before passing out. Too bad she hadn't had the opportunity to appreciate it when it happened. Valentina made a point to stare at the injury and lifted her chin in a silent challenge. Sergei slowly pushed away from the wall, taking a deliberate step toward her. She caught a glimpse of some sort of small object in his hand, and the sight was enough to kickstart her adrenaline.

She shoved off the bed, grabbing Brant's weapon from his side, and rolled into a defensive position, aiming it directly at Sergei. Brant cursed, ducked down and withdrew a secondary weapon from his ankle holster, aiming it at her.

Sergei froze, lifting his hands to show her he held only a commlink. She caught sight of Brant out of the corner of her eye and had a moment to appreciate his quick reflexes. Brant might be aiming his weapon at her, but she couldn't afford to drop her focus from Sergei except to give the security officer more than a cursory glance. Even though Sergei didn't appear armed, he'd always been the most dangerous man in the room.

"Lower the weapon, Valentina," Brant urged. "You don't want to do this."

"Do not hurt her," Sergei barked at Brant.

"I won't hurt her. Not if she lowers the weapon."

"She will not lower the weapon," Sergei snapped. "You're not to fire on her under any circumstances."

Valentina agreed with Sergei's assessment. She had no intention of lowering her weapon until she'd determined Sergei's intent. Even with Brant aiming at her, the odds were still in her favor. "Why are you here, Sergei?"

"Nikolai had a commlink delivered for you," Sergei said, nodding toward the device in his hand. "I told him you'd been brought back to medical and were sedated. Nikolai ordered me to wait here until you awakened. He wants to speak with you right away."

"Toss it on the bed and step away," she ordered, adjusting her stance slightly so she could hold the weapon longer if necessary.

He did as she asked and moved away from the bed, his back once again pressed against the far wall.

"I mean you no harm, Valentina." Sergei made sure to keep his hands within sight.

Valentina got out of her crouch and approached the bed, picking up the commlink. She pressed the button and put it against her ear. With her other hand, she kept the weapon trained on Sergei.

"Valya," Nikolai's warm voice greeted her. "I see Sergei gave you the commlink. How are you feeling?"

"I am well," she replied, still eyeing Sergei warily.

"Good," he murmured in her ear. "Sergei said you required

additional treatment. I was surprised you didn't want to come back to have our doctors treat you, but he indicated there wasn't enough time. It was too dangerous. Their physicians appear competent, but I do not like placing you in their care."

Valentina swallowed, wondering what sort of game Sergei was playing now. In a soft tone, she said, "Nor I, Kolya."

She didn't use his diminutive often in public, but it was enough to let him know she missed him. There was a long pause on the commlink before Nikolai spoke again. "If you wish to return to me, I can send Yuri to assess Sergei's command and the situation there."

"Yuri?" Valentina didn't bother to hide to her surprise. It was no secret Yuri disliked Sergei, and vice versa. It was unlikely he would determine a favorable outcome for Sergei if she agreed to step aside. Granted, she was currently aiming a weapon at him, but that was beside the point. "I don't think that would be wise."

Nikolai sighed, and she heard something rustling in the background. "You are right, as usual. I suppose I'm just anxious for you to return. Go ahead and rest. Fulfill your assignment, but I would ask that you check in with me more frequently. I will be moving around to some of the surrounding camps to assess the situation firsthand."

"You are here?"

Sergei stiffened, and she narrowed her eyes at him. What was his problem now?

"Yes, I arrived yesterday." There was another pause, and she heard someone else speaking in the background. "Excuse me, Valya, but there is a matter that requires my attention. Rest, and get well. I will speak with you soon."

He ended the call, and she lowered the commlink and weapon. It sounded as though Sergei had been telling the truth about Nikolai ordering him to remain until he'd delivered the commlink. She still didn't trust Sergei, especially after he'd tricked her. She'd take the lesson to heart, knowing she deserved it for lowering her guard with him. She couldn't afford to make the same mistake again.

Sergei frowned at her. "Nikolai is here?"

Now that the immediate danger had passed, Valentina offered the weapon to Brant. The security officer accepted it and lowered his secondary weapon, returning both to his holsters. Although he was now regarding her with a measure of wariness and apprehension, underneath was a trace of admiration. The first two might make it more difficult to extract information from him, but the latter had possibilities.

"Yes. He arrived yesterday," she replied, still trying to figure out the logistics. Nikolai was too valuable to put at risk. That's why she and several other of his representatives would usually handle business for him that required a hands-on approach. Something must have changed for him to move so close to OmniLab. She didn't like it.

"Has he recalled you?" Sergei asked, his tone a little too even.

She studied Sergei closely, but his eyes were shuttered, his expression and body language not revealing anything. He was hiding something. "Not yet."

After a lengthy pause, Sergei said, "Ariana was able to heal you again without the need for surgery. The doctors gave you several units of blood substitute. They still advise you to rest and finish healing the rest of the way. From what I understand, Ariana's healing abilities only work up to a point."

Valentina rubbed her abdomen and stretched, noting how much better it felt. She hadn't had any twinges from leaping out of bed either. "She's very skilled."

"She is," Sergei agreed and then paused. "I would approach, if you do not object."

Her body tensed, but she forced herself to relax and regulate her breathing. "I don't think that's a good idea. Trust hasn't been our friend for a long time, and it's even less so now."

He glanced over at Brant. "I need to speak with Valentina alone."

Brant eyed them both with a small frown. "I'm not sure that's wise."

Sergei's eyes narrowed on him. "If either one of us wanted to kill the other, you wouldn't be able to stop us. Now leave."

Brant crossed his arms over his chest. "That's not a ringing endorsement."

Sergei pushed away from the wall, danger emanating from him, but he still didn't approach. "You were asked to come here to protect the people within the towers. Neither Valentina nor I are part of that description."

Brant hesitated, glancing at her. "Would you prefer that I remain?"

Her eyes widened a fraction, surprised Brant was asking for her permission. She couldn't help but smile in delight. "I will be fine. I appreciate your concern though."

He searched her expression and nodded. With one more warning glare at Sergei, Brant left the room.

"You already have him wrapped around your finger," Sergei stated with a frown.

Valentina didn't bother replying. Instead, she picked up the tea Brant had brought and took another long sip. It really was heavenly. Maybe she could arrange to take some back to camp when she left.

"I am sorry for deceiving you," Sergei said in a solemn voice.

Her eyes flew to his, and Valentina lowered the cup. "I do not like this new game, Sergei."

"It's not a game, Valechka," he admitted. "I have come to know many of the people here. They're different, but some are honorable. I wouldn't have abandoned you to them without keeping watch over you."

She put the cup back on the table, wanting both hands free. "You told Nikolai it was too dangerous for me to return. I would have agreed to stay if I had known this. Why didn't you tell me the truth?"

Sergei hesitated before speaking. "I feared for your safety, and I made an error in judgment. I worried you would make the wrong decision." He paused and added, "I shouldn't have taken the choice from you. I hope you will forgive me."

She blinked at him. He'd never asked for forgiveness for anything in all the years she'd known him. He shouldn't have done what he did, but she was having trouble reconciling his words with the man she knew. Had he changed so much since she'd last seen him? Physically, there were differences, but perhaps the changes also went beyond the surface.

Valentina tilted her head to study him and took a small step toward him. He watched her but didn't make any other moves, seeming content to let her close the distance between them at her own pace. She took another step, but he remained passive. "This isn't a new game?"

"No," he said quietly.

"I do not understand you, Seryozha."

He nodded. "I know. I am sorry for that too."

She frowned, searching his face and body language for some hint as to his motivations. When he set his mind to it, he was almost impossible to read. It might be a mistake to ask, but she needed to know. "Will you explain it to me?"

He closed his eyes and took a deep breath. When he opened them again, they were pained. "Not yet."

Valentina didn't reply. She wasn't sure what she should say to him.

"May I approach you?" he asked again.

She nodded, waiting to see what he would do. He kept his

movements slow, deliberately choreographing his intentions, until he was barely inches away from her. Reaching down, he took her hand in his and ran his thumb over a small scar on the outside of her palm. "I saw this when you were sleeping. I remember when you received it."

His touch was disconcerting and confusing. Valentina resisted the urge to pull away from him, making an effort to keep her body relaxed. She remembered too. It had been many years ago, another time and place.

He ran his hand up her arm, pausing at another scar on her forearm. "I do not know this one though."

Valentina swallowed, his light touch searing her, but she couldn't pull away yet. "Yuri and I were exploring some ruins. A piece of scrap metal fell on me."

He frowned, rubbing at it as though he could erase the injury. "How long ago?"

"Maybe eight months."

"I should have been with you," he murmured.

"Yuri was with me," she repeated.

He looked up, his eyes filled with unspoken emotion. "I should have been with you, Valechka. Not Yuri. Not Nikolai. Me."

She pulled her arm away from him. "What are you doing, Sergei?"

He stared at her for a long moment and took a step away from her. Whatever had passed between them a moment ago was gone. "The doctor said you can be released. I can escort you back to Lars's quarters, or if you prefer to interrogate the security officer, he is outside waiting for you."

She rubbed her arm, still feeling the effects from his touch. "I will go with Brant."

He nodded and started to turn away but stopped suddenly, a warning in his eyes. "Do not fuck him, Valentina."

She narrowed her eyes at him. "I will fuck whomever I want."

He grabbed her arm. "I mean it. Not him."

Valentina laughed and pulled away from him. "I heard you warn away Lars. Is there an approved list of people I'm allowed to fuck?"

Sergei grabbed her again, yanking her to him, and pressed his mouth against hers. He fisted his hand in her hair, yanking it backward, and she gasped. His tongue swept in, thrusting into her mouth, an intense explosion of suppressed desire sparking between them. His tongue mated with hers, his passion devouring her with its intensity. Sergei broke the kiss a second later, leaving her panting and strangely bereft.

"Yes," he replied. "My name is the only one on it."

Without saying another word, he turned and left her still trying to figure out what had just happened.

## CHAPTER FIVE

SERGEI STORMED INTO HIS QUARTERS, furious at himself and Valentina. Always. He always lost control with her. He could launch an entire attack against a facility, putting hundreds of his people's lives in jeopardy, and not lose a shred of his iron-clad control. However, one look into her blue eyes or even a hint of her devilish smile, and all sense of his composure was gone. No other woman had ever managed to affect him this way.

With a muttered curse, he grabbed an unopened bottle of vodka and a jar of pickled vegetables and slumped down in the chair. Pouring a healthy dose into the glass, he tossed it back and immediately poured another. He downed that one and started on his third when the door chimed.

Sergei scowled at the door but hit the button to open it. At the sight of Lars, he turned away and went back to his drinking.

Lars sat at the table across from him. "How is Valentina?"

Sergei refilled his glass before relinquishing the bottle to Lars. Valentina was a pain in his ass, but he knew that wasn't what Lars was asking. "Ariana healed her."

Lars poured a drink and leaned back in his chair. "Alec mentioned she stabbed you."

Sergei snatched the bottle back. "It's none of your business."

"Uh huh." Lars took a sip, immediately grimacing at the taste, and grabbed one of the pickled vegetables out of the jar. "We should talk about you trying to drink something different. This stuff is just foul."

"What do you want, Lars?" Sergei demanded, not interested in petty chitchat. The liquor wasn't doing nearly enough to erase the erotic memory of Valentina's taste. He doubted anything would. Sergei poured another, trying to distract himself so he wouldn't hunt her down. If he kissed her again, he wouldn't be able to stop and would likely end up taking her against the wall.

"Alec wants a complete list of everyone working on the construction tower and their biometrics uploaded to our system. Full surveillance on the construction areas will be installed by the end of next week. He's also insisting that you provide information on the surrounding camp locations, including detailed demographics of the people living there."

Sergei lowered his glass. "I will agree to the first, but not the second."

"Sergei—"

Sergei held up his hand to cut him off. "No, Lars, we will abide by his request to provide information about our people living on OmniLab property, especially given what happened with Ariana. However, we aren't at war with each other. I haven't asked him to share the same information about your tower residents or the abilities of your Inner Circle. Some measure of trust must be established or this alliance will fail."

"I had a feeling you were going to say that," Lars said with a sigh. He took another sip of his drink. "This is going to be a problem. Alec is being pretty insistent."

Sergei poured more of the liquid into his glass and leaned back. "That is his choice, as are the consequences."

Lars frowned. "Sergei, he's watched you infiltrate the towers and take control over them. The woman he loves was just abducted and beaten by two of your people. Now your people are crawling all over the construction site, inside his towers, and hidden in the surrounding areas. Can you not see how this can be perceived as a threat?"

Sergei regarded the contents of his glass for a full minute. "I value your friendship, Lars, but you're overstepping yourself. If Alec wishes to discuss this, I will meet with him. Our agreement was made to preserve life, and that is still my goal. However, the Coalition will not blindly bow down to Omni-Lab's demands. If Alec decides to insist upon it, our alliance will be at an end. As it stands, he's already in danger of not meeting the terms of our original agreement with these repeated delays."

Lars scrubbed his hands over his face. "All right. I'll tell Alec you've agreed to the first part. Will you consider sharing with him at least some of your camp locations that are in proximity to the towers? That might pacify him."

"No."

Lars lowered his hands and shook his head. "You have to give me something."

"Your leaders should have negotiated better if that was what they wished."

"Fine. I'll relay your message." Lars picked up his glass again. "Have you chosen a new second-in-command yet?"

"No," Sergei said, leaning back in his chair again. He had a few possibilities in mind, but he might need to put that on hold. If their alliance fell apart because of Ariana's abduction and the construction delays, choosing a second would be the least of his worries. "Nikolai is here. I will need to speak with him before making a selection."

Lars's eyes widened. "Oh, shit. He's here in the towers?"

"No. On the surface. Valentina spoke with him when she woke up. She seemed surprised he was here." Sergei frowned, remembering the way her features had softened when she spoke with Nikolai. What he wouldn't give to have her look at him like that.

"You're not surprised?"

Sergei shrugged. He was surprised Nikolai had sent Valentina off without him. He used to keep her much closer. The distance between them had given him some hope their relationship might have degraded. He supposed it wasn't much of a surprise Nikolai was now correcting his mistake. "Not particularly. I knew a couple of our leaders would be visiting the area, but I didn't know Nikolai would be one of them. Last I heard, he was on the other side of the continent."

Lars was quiet for a long moment before he spoke. "You mentioned before that one of the chairmen might move to OmniLab once the construction was complete. If Nikolai's here now, maybe we can arrange to have him meet with Alec. Even if he doesn't move here, a face-to-face meeting with one of your leaders could help smooth things over."

Sergei arched an eyebrow, intrigued by the thought. If Nikolai consented to operating from the new tower, Valentina would also remain close. Unfortunately, that simply wasn't a possibility. "Nikolai will not come to the towers with our current level of tensions. It's too much of a security risk."

"What about at a neutral site? Maybe at the underground river location?"

"Perhaps," Sergei mused, tapping his fingers against the glass. "Nikolai wants this alliance to be successful, but I don't know if he'll agree to such a thing. He tends to take a more hands-on approach than many of our other leaders, but unless it's determined he'll take control of this facility, he is just one voice amongst many."

Lars nodded. "Just meeting with him might be enough to get Alec to back off. I don't know Nikolai, but I've heard he can be fair. Ruthless, but fair."

"That's an accurate assessment," Sergei replied, thinking of several other colorful descriptions. Granted, he tended to be more biased than most. "I will speak with Nikolai and ask him about the meet. He'll probably be curious about Alec and the rest of your people."

———

VALENTINA PRESSED the button beside Sergei's door and darted another glance down the corridor. It was clear, but she didn't want to run into anyone she knew, especially not in her current attire. She was dressed too much like one of these Omnis. It would raise all sorts of questions she wasn't quite prepared to answer.

Sergei opened the door, his eyes widening at the sight of her. He stepped aside, and she entered, sweeping her gaze over the functional room to make sure it was empty before walking over to his desk.

"I need a copy of a cloned keycard," she told him, pulling out her commlink and pressing a button to display the maps he'd sent.

"Hello to you too, Valechka," he murmured, brushing against her as he walked past. "I like this dress on you."

She ignored his comment. "Brant said they are planning to use a modified version of their existing security design for the new tower. It should give us more insight into their current security layout and how to circumvent it. Have they provided this to you yet?"

"Only an initial proposal. I have already begun an in-depth analysis." Sergei opened a locked drawer and pulled out a tablet and keycard, placing them both in front of her. "Would you care for a drink?"

"Fine," she said, activating the tablet and syncing it with her commlink to copy all his data, not just the proposal. While it was transmitting, she pulled up his maps and began comparing them with the ones on her commlink. Some of the areas on his display were highlighted in different colors with abbreviated symbols but no indication what any of them meant. He'd always used codes to identify different areas and changed them as time progressed. "These are the areas of the current towers you've mapped?"

He made a small noise of agreement, the sound of glass clinking behind her while he pulled out a bottle. Leaning over the desk, Valentina studied the maps more closely. Part of the reason she'd agreed to come to the towers was to learn as much as possible about the Omnis and their powers. Sergei had provided Nikolai with some information, but it wasn't enough. There was still too much they didn't know. "What are these marked areas on your maps?"

"Restricted zones," he explained, placing a glass in front of her. He splashed some of the liquor into it and placed the bottle beside her. "How was your meeting with the security officer? Did he take you to the café he promised?"

"Yes. It was delightful," she replied, picking up the glass and downing it. Brant had been somewhat forthcoming with information, but it took more than just one meeting to elicit someone's full cooperation. Information gathering was a subtle art, and the most effective tactics didn't raise any suspicions.

"They're planning to eventually connect the construction tower with their primary tower using several breezeways. This will allow their regular residents and ours to pass back and forth. The Inner Circle's tower will not be included in these plans though."

Sergei moved closer and leaned against the desk. "I suspected as much. Their Inner Sanctum has always been closed to their general population. I've had some flexibility in moving about because of my relationship with Lars."

Valentina nodded. It only reaffirmed her decision to investigate the Inner Sanctum while they still had ready access. "Brant indicated they use biometric scanners, facial recognition, and tracking devices as part of their security features. He also mentioned they're in the process of developing some sort of identifying device which can read individual electrical fields produced by the human body. It's scheduled for initial testing later this month."

Sergei raised an eyebrow. "He told you all this over lunch?"

"Mmhmm. I expressed my concern over the safety of our people. He decided to alleviate my fears." Valentina frowned, focusing once more on the maps. Having Sergei this close was throwing her off-balance. She pointed to the areas he'd marked as restricted. "Tell me about these zones."

"We cannot access those areas with OmniLab's current security setup," Sergei began, leaning over close enough she could feel the heat from his body against hers. He pointed out several locations and added, "I was only able to manually map out the surrounding areas. We installed backdoors on their system during our initial occupation of the towers, but they had safeguards preventing access to their higher security areas."

She took a deep breath, inhaling his alluring, spicy scent. Even if she were blind and deaf, she'd still know he was close by his scent alone. Sergei picked up the bottle of liquor, tipping it until her glass was refilled.

Struggling to resist the urge to lean into him, Valentina

focused again on his tablet. "What about using a drone? Could we send one through a vent?"

"Perhaps," he agreed, putting down the bottle and resting his hand on her lower back as he continued to study the map. "I believe there may be ventilation shafts that are accessible, but we may have to drop the drones from different floors. It will require a coordinated effort to maneuver them."

She picked up her drink again, tossing it back. His touch was more than a little distracting. "You know the layout better. Which of these areas would be best to target first?"

Sergei began stroking her back with his thumb through the thin material of her dress, sending a small shiver through her. With his other hand, he tapped the screen and enlarged one of the areas. "This one. I suspect this is where they have one of their classified research facilities. We may be able to get additional information about their abilities or technology from this location. Based on what we discover, we can then perform a risk assessment to determine the next area to target."

Valentina nodded, accepting the validity of his statement. "Do you have a drone here? Or do I need to request one?"

"I will take care of it," he said, his hand continuing to slide downward.

She turned around, pressing her hand against his chest. "What are you doing?"

Pinning her against the desk, he gave her a devilish smile. "I thought it was obvious, Valechka."

"You think I came here to fuck you?" she demanded, her heart thudding in her chest.

"Did you not?" Sergei reached down to run his hands up her thighs and pushed her dress upward. Her breath hitched slightly as he pressed his hardened length against her core. Leaning in closer, he ran his nose against her neck, inhaling deeply. His hot breath fanned against her neck as he whispered, "You could have called me and asked me to meet you, but you came here to my quarters. Why else would you have done that?"

Valentina closed her eyes, tilting her head to give him better access. He pressed a kiss against her neck and nibbled at her earlobe. Biting back a moan, she ran her hands over his muscular chest. He knew her so well. Ever since that kiss in the medical ward, she'd wanted another taste of him.

"I hope you are not fond of these panties," he murmured, hooking his thumbs through the waistband. "Because I intend to rip them off you."

She heard a tear, and the cool air swirled around her most intimate parts. He lifted her on top of the desk, moving between her thighs, and unhooked his pants. Grabbing his face, she yanked him toward her so she could taste him again. He was more than happy to oblige, his tongue entangling with hers as their kiss took on a life of its own. She needed him. Now.

Wrapping her legs around his waist, Valentina pulled him against her. A moment later, he thrust inside her welcoming heat. She gasped at the sudden intrusion and the sense of rightness at having him inside her. It still wasn't enough. She needed more. Whether she said the words or he instinctively knew, it didn't matter. Gripping her hips, Sergei gave into her wordless demand and began pounding into her. She scored her nails down his back, urging him to go faster.

He did, and she became nothing more than pure primal sensation. All coherent thought evaporated, until she only existed in the place between need and desire. He kept his mouth over hers, swallowing her screams, keeping up his relentless pace. When she finally broke apart in his arms, he planted himself deeply, groaning his release.

Sergei dropped his head against her shoulder, turning his head to kiss her neck, and pulled her even tighter against him. She panted, trying to catch her breath, and ran her hands up his strong arms to encircle them around his neck. He lifted his head to look down at her and pressed himself deeper inside her. She inhaled sharply at the movement, and his eyes twinkled in awareness of the effect he had on her. "Do you still want to claim you only came here for a keycard, Valechka?"

Valentina threw back her head and laughed. God, she had missed him. He pulled out of her, reaching for a nearby shirt and cleaned himself off her.

Hopping off the desk, she smoothed down her dress and picked up the keycard and her commlink. She slipped them into one of her makeshift pockets. "The keycard was one of the reasons I came, but not the only one."

Sergei arched an eyebrow, a smug smile on his face. Valentina eyed him up and down, biting her lower lip in appreciation. He really was a gorgeous specimen of a man.

She ran a fingernail lightly down his chest. "But the *real* reason was because I had to see whether or not this list of yours was worth it."

His smile faded, a question in his eyes. "My list?"

"Mmhmm," she agreed with a mischievous smile. "If there is only one name on the list of people I can fuck, I had to see if it was worth it."

"And?" he demanded, taking a step toward her.

She patted his cheek affectionately. "You know I will never tell, Seryozha."

Without waiting for a response, she sashayed out of the room, pleased she'd gotten the upper hand in that round.

# CHAPTER SIX

VALENTINA ROLLED over in bed and continued to read the notes she'd stolen from Sergei's tablet. Most of them were fairly standard, although the additional information he'd gathered about the Inner Circle was interesting. It was easy to understand why so many of the Coalition had difficulty believing their abilities were anything more than exaggerated descriptions or outright superstition. Sergei hadn't been able to discover nearly enough about how their talents worked. Either that, or he simply hadn't committed the information onto his tablet.

She pressed a button to cycle through to the next set of information and groaned. This was even more dull. It was a collection of materials and supplies needed to complete the current construction phase of the tower. How many nails did one tower need? She shoved the tablet aside, thumping her head against the soft mattress. Inactivity wasn't her strong suit. Maybe she should send the supply list to Yuri and try to convince him to look through it instead.

A soft noise caught her attention. She cocked her head to listen, but there was no other sound. Aha. Sergei wanted to play again. He was the only one she knew who could move that silently.

She grinned and slid off the bed, pulling off her dress and dropping it on the floor outside the closed bathroom door to make it appear as though she'd disrobed before going in. Keeping her movements silent, she headed toward the shelving unit on the far side of the room where she'd stashed some weapons. Crouching down, she put her commlink beside her, pulled out one of the knives, and prepared to wait. Her angled position would give her a clear view of Sergei once he approached either the bed or bathroom.

Ten minutes later, she was still waiting. No other sounds had reached her ears, but it was the absence of noise that made her even more confident Sergei was somewhere nearby. That, and an almost surreal awareness of him. She could feel him close, almost within touching distance, even though he hadn't entered the room yet.

The air pressure shifted, indicating the door had opened. *Finally.* Waiting expectantly for him to make a move, her muscles tensed.

A moment later, the room plunged into darkness. Valentina grinned. Now they were both temporarily blind, but she would have the advantage in this scenario. She knew where he was coming from, but he didn't have the same knowledge. Focusing on each of her senses while her eyes adjusted to the dim lighting, she tried to detect any movement, noises, or scents—no matter how minute.

Her commlink buzzed on the floor, and she resisted the urge to swear. Rolling forward, she narrowly dodged his grip and dove to the other side of the room. She scrambled up and over the bed, but he was too fast. He grabbed her, tossing her back onto the bed, and held her wrists over her head.

"You cheated," she accused, not terribly upset by this new position.

"Since when do we have rules?" He chuckled, nuzzling her neck, and placed a small kiss against it. "You should have turned off your commlink."

"Maybe I wanted to be caught," Valentina suggested and hooked one of her legs over him, making his position even more interesting. She arched her back, and he inhaled sharply as she pressed against him. Releasing her wrists, he ran his hands down her arms, and she twisted her body slightly. He rolled over, taking her with him so she was straddling him. His gray eyes darkened with desire as he reached up to cup her breasts through her bra, rubbing his thumbs over her hardened nipples.

Valentina bent down to kiss him, getting lost for a moment in the softness of his lips and the intriguing contrast between them and the hardness of the rest of his body. Sergei gripped her hips, holding her in place as she tasted and explored his mouth. Her hair fell in a curtain around his face, obscuring his vision and she reached out, her hand wrapping around the knife she'd hidden under a pillow. She nipped his bottom lip and flicked her tongue against it. With a groan, he fisted his hand in her hair as he began to consume her mouth.

She kissed him a moment longer and then trailed the flat of the blade lightly down his chest. He froze, and his mouth curved upward against hers. "Ah, Valechka. I suppose you win this round."

She laughed, pressing another kiss against his lips before rolling away from him. "I was hoping you would stop by to play."

He propped himself up on his elbows, watching while she picked up her dress from the floor and shimmied back into it. "I received your... invitation, but it took me longer than I expected to get away."

"Oh?" Valentina arched an eyebrow, unsurprised he'd noticed the data theft from his tablet. After all, she'd been rather obvious in her efforts. But she was more curious about what had delayed him. She paused, biting her lip and considering him thoughtfully. If they didn't need to get to work, she wouldn't mind a few more delays as long as they both ended up naked.

He grinned, the heated look in his eyes making it obvious he was considering the same thing. "Yes. I got called into a meeting. After that, I decided I would punish you by making you read my construction notes."

Valentina wrinkled her nose at him. "How can you read such drivel? Does it not become tedious?"

He chuckled, putting his hands behind his head. "Yes. That's why I had Pavel do much of it. Now that he's gone, I will need to find and train a new second-in-command."

She tilted her head to study him. "Have you given any thought to potential candidates?"

"Some."

Valentina reached down to pick up her shoes and slipped them back on her feet. "With everything that has happened, Nikolai will want to review your list before you make a selection."

"So I assumed," he said in a detached tone.

Her eyes flew to him, but his expression was carefully blank. She narrowed her eyes at him. "What's wrong?"

Sergei sat up. "Valentina, have you ever considered leaving Nikolai's service? You have enough experience to take on your own command. Or there are other options."

Valentina frowned, bending down to adjust the knives in her thigh holster. It was sufficient as a temporary measure, but she might need something a little longer lasting. Maybe she could arrange to have Yuri smuggle in some of her custom weapons and accessories. "Why would I want to do that? You know I have no interest in command."

"I do not like the way he treats you," Sergei said quietly.

Valentina froze, anger whipping through her at his careless words. She straightened, putting her hands on her hips. "Are you finished? We have work to do."

"Valechka—"

She held up her hand to stop him. "No, Sergei," she snapped. "I have enjoyed playing with you again, and I would be sorry to see our games end, but you are crossing a very dangerous line. What is between Nikolai and me is not your concern."

Sergei's jaw clenched, and he pushed off the bed, radiating silent fury. "I brought the drone. We can go whenever you are ready."

"Good," she agreed, turning away from him.

"Valentina, this is not over between us."

She paused, her heart thudding in her chest, but she didn't look back. "It's been over for a long time, Sergei."

———

SERGEI GAVE Valentina a boost into the ventilation system and watched as she disappeared from view. Since she was smaller and could move quieter, they had decided it would be better for her to control the drone from within while he monitored on the ground level. Although he'd never admit it to her, she'd always been better suited for this type of work than him.

He closed the grating behind her and pressed his earpiece into his ear. Leaning casually against the wall, he pulled out his commlink to watch her progress and pretended he was reading through messages.

He was kicking himself for saying anything to her about Nikolai. Considering her reaction in the medical ward, it was obvious she was still deeply tied to him. His only excuse was that having her so close short-circuited his brain. It had always been that way with her, and time hadn't done a damn thing to dampen it. If anything, he was more captivated than ever.

Sergei rubbed the back of his neck as he watched Valentina maneuver through the narrow ducts. Until his slip-up, she'd begun softening toward him and falling back into old patterns. Unfortunately, he was running out of time before she went back to Nikolai. Once that happened, any progress he'd made would be lost. Part of him was surprised the charismatic chairman hadn't already issued the order recalling her yet.

"What are you doing here?"

Sergei lifted his head, mentally chastising himself for not paying more attention to his surroundings. Ever since Valentina had walked back into his life, he'd been in a perpetual state of disarray. He nodded a greeting to Brant, who was eyeing him with suspicion. "I am waiting for Valentina. She wanted to visit the construction tower, but I seem to have lost her."

He heard her snicker in his earpiece, and he straightened, eager for a little payback. If she intended to toy with Brant, well, he'd just have to make things a bit more difficult. The security officer was a little too enamored with her.

Brant frowned, glancing down the corridor. "She's not in Lars's quarters? I was on my way to check in on her."

"No. She can be rather elusive, always getting into trouble and not listening to reason." Sergei made a dramatic show of sighing. "It can be tedious trying to keep track of her and always having to chase her down, but I will relay your message when she reappears."

"Poor Seryozha," she purred softly in his ear. "If you cannot keep up with me, perhaps I shall find someone who can."

Sergei barely resisted the urge to grin at her taunt. Whenever Valentina reappeared, he'd enjoy proving himself to her. *Fuck*. Just the thought was enough to distract him from the distrustful security officer glaring at him.

Brant crossed his arms over his chest. "She didn't seem all that fond of you, either, when I took her out to lunch earlier."

Sergei settled back against the wall again. "Oh? Valentina did not bother to mention your lunch when she stopped by my quarters earlier... to catch up."

"I'm not surprised. I didn't have the impression she confided in you," Brant retorted. "I just got out of a meeting with Alec. I understand you've agreed to invite Nikolai to meet with him."

The silence over his earpiece was deafening.

"Yes," he agreed, making an effort to keep his tone neutral. *Dammit*. Valentina would be furious he hadn't shared that information with her. He should have told her about the meeting right away, but he'd been distracted when she was half-naked and kissing him. Although, if he were honest with himself, he hadn't been in a hurry to tell her. He hadn't wanted to risk prematurely sending her back to Nikolai. "I sent over the request after I spoke with Alec. I am still waiting for a response."

"Good. Alec mentioned Nikolai would probably prefer a neutral meeting place."

"Yes, that is likely," Sergei replied, darting a quick glance at his commlink and resisting the urge to swear aloud. Valentina was definitely pissed. The visual link to her and the drone had been manually disengaged on her end. She could be anywhere right now, and it was unlikely she'd be interested in playing this time.

Brant frowned at him. "I understand Valentina works closely with him. What sort of man is he?"

Sergei pretended to stretch and glanced upward at the grate before leaning against the wall again. He didn't see her, but that didn't mean a whole lot. "Valentina knows Nikolai far better than I do. You may want to ask her when you see her next."

Brant nodded. "I'll do that. Alec also mentioned you agreed to assist us with a risk assessment. We're going to need you to provide us with some additional information about Nikolai, his escort, and what to expect during this meeting so we can finalize the security detail. I believe Alec is hoping to meet with him in the next day or two."

Sergei froze, dozens of scenarios running through his mind about how best to kill Brant for his reckless statements. Of all the things for Brant to say, the foolish security officer had to suggest he would provide OmniLab with sensitive information.

"If you even *think* to betray Nikolai, you will be a dead man," Valentina hissed in his earpiece. "Next time I see you, your heart will be at the end of my blade."

He swallowed, his heart clenching and not because of her threat.

"I will not have much information to provide, only a meeting location and some other minor details. I cannot be of more help than that," Sergei explained, but he knew the damage was already done.

Valentina was gone—back to Nikolai.

## CHAPTER SEVEN

VALENTINA CLIMBED off the borrowed speeder and stormed into the camp. Two armed men watched her approach. Yanking off her helmet, she tossed it on a nearby rack. "Where is Nikolai?"

"He's in the command center," one of the men informed her, stepping aside to let her pass.

Valentina marched down the hall, aware that most people were taking one look at her expression and moving quickly out of her way. Brant's words still echoed in her head, and her anger at Sergei hadn't diminished during her travel to their camp. His suggestion about leaving Nikolai's service came back to her, and she scowled. If he had some vendetta against Nikolai, she really would kill him.

Valentina pushed open the door to the command center, glancing at the rows of monitors and maps displayed on the screens. A few people looked up when she entered but immediately went back to work.

Nikolai and Yuri were standing on the far side of the room, looking over a technician's shoulder. Yuri said something too low to overhear and pointed to an area on the screen. Nikolai replied, gesturing to another location. Out of all the people in the Coalition, these two were amongst the closest to her heart. They'd been peers in the same training class, but over the years they'd become so much more. Nikolai might outrank her, but he and Yuri were her family. She'd do anything to keep them safe. It might destroy something inside her to actually kill Sergei, but she wouldn't allow any harm to come to them.

Valentina pulled off her gloves, shoving them into her pocket. It had been far too long since she'd seen Nikolai, but he was much the same, with the exception of the shadows under his eyes. He'd always told her he slept better when she was near. As though sensing her silent observation, he turned, his blue eyes warming at the sight of her.

Valentina hastened her step as she approached, and he drew her into his arms, wrapping them around her tightly. She leaned against him and returned his hug, his arms a comforting weight around her.

"Valya," he murmured, pressing a kiss against her hair. "I wasn't expecting you to return so soon. You've been missed."

He released her, and she turned to Yuri, who also embraced her tightly. "I was beginning to think we'd need to storm the towers to retrieve you."

"Never," she whispered, hugging him tightly before turning back to Nikolai.

Nikolai gave her a wide smile, the gesture making him appear almost boyish. He put his arm around her. "Come. Let's go somewhere private to talk. Yuri, finish up with this and then join us. We can look over the rest of the plans later."

"Of course," he readily agreed, turning back to the screen.

Valentina leaned against Nikolai's side, walking back with him to the rooms he was currently using. He closed the door behind them and turned around to study her. His eyes roamed over her, drinking in the sight of her. "How bad is the injury? Do you need me to call for a physician?"

She shook her head. "It's not necessary. The woman Pavel abducted is a skilled healer. She was able to repair the damage without relying on traditional medicine."

"Good," Nikolai murmured, taking a step closer to her.

Placing her hands on his chest, she stood on her toes and pressed a kiss against his lips. "I've missed you, Kolya."

His gaze softened, and he took her hand to lead her over to the couch. "I'm pleased to hear it, but I don't think that's the reason you returned."

Valentina sighed and sat beside him. He'd always been far too perceptive. "No, but my place is here by your side."

"Is it?" he asked mildly, resting his arm on the back of the couch.

She didn't answer right away. Instead, she searched his expression. His eyes were infinitely patient, one of the many reasons he was such a respected leader. That, and his diplomatic skills and military experience. A long scar stretching from his nose and across his cheek was a testament to that service, but it didn't detract from his appearance in the slightest. It made him even more appealing but also served as a visible reminder he could be a formidable foe.

He lifted her hand, placing a kiss against it. "Tell me, what has brought you back to me?"

"I learned you were considering meeting with OmniLab leadership."

"Ah," he murmured, leaning back. "Yes. Sergei sent over a meeting request with one of their leaders, Alec Tal'Vayr. He wants to meet within the next day or two to discuss concerns about our presence, given what happened to one of their people."

She scowled, her hands curling into fists. "Sergei did not tell me. I found out from someone else."

Nikolai's mouth twitched in a hint of a smile. He stood and walked over to a small cooling bin, pulled out a couple of hydrating packs, and handed one to her. "I see. Would it have made a difference to you if he had?"

Valentina stood, unable to sit still. Every time she thought about Sergei and his deception, she was tempted to go back and strangle him. He had plenty of opportunities to tell her about this meeting.

"Yes," she snapped, gripping the hydrating pack a little too tightly. "He knows where my loyalty lies, yet he does not share this information with me? I would never allow you to walk into this meeting without having those you trust by your side."

Nikolai opened his hydrating pack and took a long drink. "What of Sergei? Does he have people he trusts by his side?"

Valentina stiffened, suspecting Nikolai was asking an entirely different question. Certain subjects were off-limits, and she wasn't about to discuss this with him. "If you are asking about the investigation, I did not have an opportunity to interview many of our people. I reviewed Sergei's personal notes, but there was nothing within them that hinted at deception. If you wish it, I will go back to finish properly assessing his command."

"Not yet," he said with a sigh, dropping the empty hydrating pack into a recycler. "You will remain here until the situation with OmniLab is resolved. I have need of you."

She paused, considering him for a long moment. "What do you wish of me, Nikolai?"

"Work with Yuri to secure a location for this meet. I want you both to decide upon an escort and to include yourselves in that number. We have another facility targeted for takeover within the next few months. The situation with OmniLab needs to be stabilized before then."

"I don't like the idea of you meeting with them," she admitted, putting down her hydrating pack. "You're too valuable to our cause to put yourself at risk."

"I wouldn't be any sort of leader if I allowed people to take risks I wouldn't take myself," he reminded her, his tone sharp.

Valentina lowered her gaze for a moment and took a steadying breath. When she lifted her head, she took a step toward him. "We don't know enough about their powers, Kolya. Please let us try to find out more before you put yourself in danger. If you will agree to wait, I can return to the towers and continue to investigate."

Nikolai sighed and approached her, lifting his hands to cup her face. She closed her eyes as he brushed a kiss against her forehead. "You know I cannot. Your concern is touching, but we all have a responsibility to our people. Work with Yuri and contact Sergei to find out who will be meeting with us. I want detailed dossiers on each of them." He paused for a moment and then added, "I admit I'm eager to meet their people and learn more about them."

She frowned. She had met Alec briefly, but there was no way to know who else he would be bringing or what sort of powers they possessed. For all she knew, they could influence Nikolai in some way or cause him harm without ever lifting a weapon. Sergei's notes had been intriguing, but not at the risk of endangering Nikolai.

Nikolai lifted her chin to look into her eyes. "Now tell me about Sergei."

Valentina stiffened and pulled away from him, mentally kicking herself for falling into old habits with Sergei again. No one else had ever challenged her as much or gotten under her skin the same way. "There is nothing to tell. He has changed in some ways, but in others, he is much the same."

"Do you still care for him, Valya?"

Valentina shrugged. "I suppose I will always care for him, but it will not prevent me from doing what is necessary. If he is a threat to you, I will handle it."

"You know that's not what I was asking," he murmured, approaching her from behind. He wrapped his arms around her waist, drawing her against him. "I thought you might be happier if you found your own path, but I'm having difficulties with the thought of letting you go."

"I did not ask you to let me go," she whispered, her heart clenching.

"You will always have a place with me for as long as you want it," he said gently, pressing a kiss against her hair. "But you need to decide if you would rather have a place with him."

She turned around to face him. "I don't trust him anymore. You and Yuri have always been there for me. You are my family. How can you think I would want to go to Sergei when he was the one who walked away from all of us? My place is here with you."

Nikolai sighed. "Very well. Go ahead and get started with Yuri. We will figure out the rest later."

———

SERGEI GROANED and threw his arm over his eyes. The pounding continued, but it wasn't coming from his head. At least, not completely. He shoved off the bed and slammed his fist against the door control to open it. At the sight of Lars, he muttered a colorful oath and turned away, stumbling past several empty bottles on his way to the sink.

"You look like shit," Lars said from behind him.

Sergei shoved his head under the faucet, the cold water doing little to combat his headache. He turned his head, filling his mouth with water, and swished it before spitting it out in the sink. It didn't help. His mouth still tasted as though he'd swallowed dirty socks.

The scrape of a chair across the tiled floor had a direct line to the icepick taking up residence behind his eyes. He grabbed a nearby drying cloth and rubbed it over his face.

"What the fuck do you want, Lars?"

"It's nice to see you too," Lars replied in a dry voice. "I'm guessing your condition has something to do with Valentina's disappearance? She never returned last night."

"She is gone," he said, going back over to his bed and sprawling across it. He threw his arm over his eyes to block out the light. "Turn off the light on your way out."

"Did you drink all of these last night?" Lars asked, the clank of empty bottles causing Sergei's head to feel like it was going to explode. "I'm not sure if I'm more impressed by the quantity or by the fact you're still alive."

"Stop. Talking. Or. I. Will. Break. Them. Over. Your. Head."

Lars chuckled, and Sergei cringed at the sound of the recycler being opened and the clatter of the bottles being tossed inside.

"I hate you," Sergei groaned through gritted teeth.

"I imagine you hate yourself more right now," Lars retorted.

Sergei grunted, agreeing with his assessment.

"What happened with Valentina?"

"None of your fucking business," Sergei snapped.

"I'm not leaving until you tell me what's going on. Alec is concerned that her leaving has something to do with the meeting request." Lars paused and added, "If you tell me, I'll get you something for your headache."

Sergei sighed in resignation. "She was on comms with me and overheard Brant mention the meeting with Nikolai. Valentina was... displeased. I hadn't told her about it or my part in assisting you with the preparation. She threatened to cut out my heart next time she saw me. Then she left."

"That response seems a little... dramatic."

Sergei made a noncommittal noise and rubbed his chest, wondering if Valentina would keep pretending to miss when she flung her next blade. "You do not know her. She is naturally suspicious and rightfully so."

"No, I don't know her." Lars was quiet for a minute and then asked, "Did she think you'd betray your people?"

"I believe Nikolai ordered her to investigate me," Sergei admitted. "He is probably concerned after what happened with Pavel. Valentina stole the data off my tablet and broke into my office in the construction tower to snoop. She made a point to leave several traces so I would know. It was her way of warning me they were unsure of my loyalties. Brant's comments did not help my case, and that is why she left."

"Dammit!" Lars said, and Sergei heard another scrape of a chair and then footsteps pacing the floor. "You haven't betrayed anyone. Will she really kill you?"

Sergei grunted. "I was hoping she would come kill me this morning and put me out of my misery."

"I'm serious, Sergei," Lars insisted. "Is she a threat?"

Sergei couldn't help the smile that spread across his face. "Yes, she is, but I don't know if she will kill me. At one time, I would have said no and believed it." He paused and then added, "But things have changed. If Nikolai orders it, she will do it. She may regret it, but she will do it."

"Would Nikolai order it?"

Sergei shifted and winced as a stream of light crossed his vision. He closed his eyes again. "Yes, without hesitation and regret. If I become a liability or an obstacle, he will order it done. But he does not toss aside weapons as easily as others."

"I don't see how you could be seen as either a liability or an obstacle. You've always been steadfast to your cause."

"There is a long, shared history between Nikolai and me," Sergei admitted. "We parted ways several years ago. I would not have thought him capable of many things he has done since then. He is no longer the same man I used to know."

Lars was quiet for so long that Sergei would have thought he had had left if it weren't for his steady breathing.

"This history," Lars began, hesitation coloring his words. "Does it have something to do with Valentina?"

Sergei's jaw clenched. "I am finished answering your questions, Lars. Either get me something for my head or go away."

———

VALENTINA VIEWED the map of the surrounding area they had decided on for the meet. She pointed to two distinct areas. "What do you think about installing two sniper teams here and here? The ground covering will offer some natural camouflage."

Yuri glanced over and nodded, making some adjustments to the map. "That should work. I will arrange to have the cloaking technology installed over those areas. It should blend seamlessly with the rocky surroundings."

She frowned. "Has OmniLab developed a way to detect it? They employed a similar cloaking device during the tower attack."

Yuri lifted his gaze to meet hers. "Can we rely upon Sergei for that intel?"

Valentina hesitated. She wasn't sure of anything anymore when it came to Sergei. She might be inclined to try it if it were just her at risk, but she wasn't willing to risk Nikolai's life on such a gamble. "No. We should use low-tech options to avoid the possibility of detection."

"That will hamper us a great deal, Valya," he said with a frown. "We will need to move our snipers closer to keep them effective, but that will increase the likelihood they'll be detected when OmniLab does their sweep."

She swore and pushed away from the table. "We need another location then. None of these will be sufficient for our purposes."

Yuri sighed and ran a hand over his shaved head. "It's too late to change locations. We must figure out a way to make this one work."

Valentina began pacing back and forth, various scenarios rushing through her mind. The problem was that Sergei had knowledge of most of their tactics. And with Lars having lived with them for several years, he'd have an understanding too. Either of them could be a liability. They needed to come up with a more unpredictable plan.

She turned back to the map. "Move the meet closer to the top of the ridge. We will have our people install electrical wind pulses at all of these locations."

Valentina marked off more than a dozen places along the ridgeline and highlighted two other areas. "We will put the sniper teams here instead, but they'll remain on standby to protect our escape, if necessary. The lower-level outcroppings will make it more difficult to detect them."

Yuri raised an eyebrow, turning the map to view it in three dimensions. "You intend to create a dust storm?"

"Yes," she agreed, flipping the map back toward her and expanding the radius visual. "If things go bad, we will use the dust storm as a distraction. It should give us enough time to relocate Nikolai to a secure area that is more defensible." She pointed to a new location, marking it to have a backup team on standby.

"What's to stop this Alec Tal'Vayr from using his wind talents to knock out the dust storm?"

"Electrical fields," she explained, pressing another button to simulate the effect. "The electrical pulses we're going to plant will react with the wind. If he uses his powers in the vicinity, it will only increase the severity of the dust storm."

Yuri nodded. "That could work. The electrical pulses could be explained as being tied into our UV shield."

"Exactly," she agreed, walking around the table to view the map from a different angle. "Do we know how many people they will bring with them?"

"Only five from their side will be permitted within the perimeter," Yuri said and glanced down at his tablet. "Alec Tal'Vayr, Lars Cerulis, Jason Alivette, Ryan Thomas, and Brant Mason. Sergei will also be there but acting as a neutral liaison."

She frowned. "I have met three of them, but I do not know the other two. Alec and Lars have powers. Brant is one of their security officers. He appears more comfortable with a weapon than the others."

Yuri glanced at the tablet again. "The notes you stole from Sergei's tablet indicate Brant Mason can only cancel out others' talents. He does not possess offensive abilities like the rest. Jason Alivette is the twin brother to Ariana Alivette, the young woman who was abducted. He most likely has some sort of ability, but we don't have details. We also don't have any information on this Ryan Thomas."

Valentina sighed and sat in a chair, propping her feet up on the desk. "I suppose you can ask Sergei if he knows anything more, but I don't know how reliable his information will be. I would not trust it. I am not sure of his agenda."

Yuri lowered his tablet and pulled up another chair. Resting his elbows on his knees, he said, "Does Sergei need to be eliminated, Valya?"

Her gaze flew back to him. "That is not our call to make, Yuri."

"Not yet," he agreed. "But if Nikolai asks your opinion, what will you tell him?"

Valentina dropped her feet to the ground and stood, her heart hammering in her chest. "The same thing I am telling you. That's not our call to make. Do not ask me this again."

## CHAPTER EIGHT

SERGEI PICKED up his commlink and turned it over in his hands. He could try to contact Valentina, but it was unlikely she'd respond. She'd probably be there this afternoon, but he had no way of knowing what sort of reception he'd get. He suspected it wouldn't be a favorable one. Otherwise, someone from Nikolai's team would have reached out to him before now, if only to gather intel.

He knew there were doubts about his continued loyalty, even without Valentina's not-so-subtle warning. This alliance was the first of its kind, and his friendship with Lars and the other exiles was well known. Now that he'd been named ambassador, the rumblings were even louder. His initial orders had been somewhat straightforward: secure OmniLab and then step aside to allow one of the chairmen to manage its operations. But now he was in a position to run this new facility, and many of their people weren't particularly pleased with the idea.

Most of the construction on the new tower had come to a halt, with the exception of a skeleton crew primarily consisting of ruin rats. Orders had been made to recall most of the Coalition forces to some of the outlying camps pending the outcome of this meeting. If things had degraded to this degree, it was possible their leaders, including Nikolai, had concerns about his continued worth to the Coalition. A serious attempt on his life was most likely imminent. He didn't know if it hadn't already happened because Valentina had refused to allow it or because she wanted the privilege of executing him herself.

"Sergei? Are you all right?"

He glanced over to see Ariana walking toward him. Sergei shook off his mood, rising from his seat to press a kiss against her cheek. He inhaled the light floral scent that always surrounded her. "All is well, Ari. How are you feeling?"

"Nervous," she admitted, clasping her hands together. "I don't know what to expect from this meeting, and I'm worried about being away from Alec. He assures me this is the best way to smooth over any tensions and help cement our alliance though."

He gave her a warm smile. "You shouldn't worry. Your people and mine have much to gain from making this alliance work."

"I know," she said with a sigh. "Have you heard anything from Valentina? I was disappointed I didn't have a chance to see her again before she left the towers."

Sergei frowned. "No. She will most likely be there today, but I have not spoken with her."

Ariana took a step closer, searching his expression. "You're worried about her, aren't you?"

Sergei hesitated and then nodded. "I have known Valentina a long time. She is capable of taking care of herself, but..." His voice trailed off as he tried to figure out how to explain.

A small smile crossed Ariana's face. "You care for her, don't you?"

"Yes," he admitted in a quiet voice, unable to deceive Ariana. "But she belongs to another."

"Nikolai?"

Sergei sighed. "It's a long story, and one I do not enjoy revisiting."

Ariana reached over and placed her hand on his arm in a comforting gesture. "Sergei, the moment I met her, she reminded me of you. Other than you, she's the only other non-sensitive I've had difficulty reading. But when I was healing her, I picked up on a few of her emotions. I sensed that she cares for you, but it hurts her."

Sergei stiffened. "I do not believe she would want you to tell me this, Ariana."

"I'm sorry," she said, lowering her head. "I don't like to see anyone suffer, and I can tell you're hurting. I thought my words might bring you some comfort."

Sergei lifted Ariana's hand and placed a kiss against it. "You have a beautiful heart. I appreciate your gesture, but I do not deserve your comfort."

"Ari," Lars's voice interrupted them. "We're leaving in a few minutes. If you want to say goodbye to Alec before we go, he's finishing up with Brant in his office."

She nodded and leaned over to kiss Sergei's cheek. "I'll see you soon."

He watched the door to Alec's office close behind her and then met Lars's gaze.

"I don't have a good feeling about this," Lars admitted with a frown. "Brant's been trying to talk Alec out of going. With the construction being shut down and everyone disappearing, we're all on edge. We've launched drones over the surrounding areas, but there's no sign of your people."

"You know how skilled we are at staying hidden," Sergei reminded him and began heading out of the executive offices.

Lars grabbed his arm, stopping him. "If you knew something or suspected this was a trap, would you tell us?"

"As long as your people remain calm and there are no overt threats, I do not anticipate a problem. Alec and the rest of your people will be safe. My issues with him aside, Nikolai is honorable. He wants this alliance to succeed as much as I do."

Lars nodded. "What about you, Sergei? Will you be safe?"

He sighed and turned away again. "I do not know anymore."

————

VALENTINA HELD on to the handlebar mounted on the ceiling of the caravan. They were only a few minutes away from the meeting point, and as far as she knew, everything was in place. She would have liked to investigate the area personally, but they'd caught sight of OmniLab drones in the area and weren't willing to risk it. Fortunately, they'd been able to get their crews in to bury the diversionary devices before the drone surveillance had been launched.

Nikolai wrapped his arm around her waist and gripped the bar mounted above her head. He looked down at her, his eyes sparkling with anticipation. She couldn't help but smile in response. If they'd been alone, she would have teased him about being as giddy as a child. The daily monotony of his position sometimes bored him. Ever since they'd learned about the Omnis' powers, he'd been eager to discover everything he could about the towers.

Yuri had chosen well in selecting the other two guards to accompany them. Both were well-seasoned and formidable. Valentina had been on expeditions with them before, and she knew they'd do what was necessary to make sure Nikolai was protected. The rest would fall to her and Yuri.

The caravan came to a sudden halt, and the UV shield beeped loudly, indicating it was clear for them to exit. She and Yuri jumped down from the caravan to help secure the meeting point. In the distance, Alec's vehicle was rapidly approaching. She grabbed one of the UV poles and shoved it into the ground to widen the radius around their vehicle. The others did the same and began pulling out some temporary seating.

She'd wanted Nikolai to wait inside the caravan until they determined OmniLab had followed the meeting guidelines, but he'd refused. He was now prowling around under the UV guard, much like a predator pacing the perimeter of a cage. She grinned at the mental image, knowing he'd appreciate the comparison.

The OmniLab caravan stopped, and the doors opened. She moved over to stand beside Nikolai, her hand brushing against the weapon holstered at her side. There had been some arguments back and forth about whether weapons could be brought to the meeting. Alec didn't want them present, but Valentina had put her foot down and convinced Nikolai to refuse the demand. With their well-harnessed supernatural abilities, these Omnis possessed innate offensive talents which would put their people at a disadvantage.

Sergei and Brant climbed out of the vehicle, followed by two others she didn't know. One of them had the same dark hair and gray eyes as Ariana and was most likely her brother. Lars and Alec were the last to exit. Valentina's eyes met Sergei's for a fraction of a second, her earlier anger at him flaring to the surface before she forced it back down. Instead, she turned to the others, noting visible weapons and trying to determine the potential for any hidden threats.

They were all armed, except for Alec and the man she suspected was Ariana's brother. It made sense since she had the impression the leader of the towers didn't have any sort of military training. The concept was rather strange, but then again, many of the things these Omnis did was unusual.

Relaxing her body slowly to give herself a more casual appearance, Valentina rubbed the side of her neck, making sure three of her knuckles were slightly elevated to alert her companions there were at least three energy channelers. Sergei's sharp gaze flew to her, but she ignored him. She'd deal with him if and when it came down to it.

Sergei approached them. "Alec Tal'Vayr, this is Nikolai Berkutov."

Alec inclined his head and held out his hand. Nikolai shook it and gestured to the seating. "Please, join me."

One of their men had pulled out a small table from the caravan and placed it down in front of them. Nikolai placed his hand on Valentina's lower back and led her over to one of the seats while several of the others joined them. To all appearances, it was a chivalrous gesture on Nikolai's part, but it was carefully designed to disarm. Both their weapon hands were kept free, and the small gesture served as a subtle reminder that this was an amiable meeting between allies. Most of the time, especially given OmniLab's culture, a woman's presence could ease tensions.

Brant and the other armed man, whom she suspected was another security officer, remained standing while the others seated themselves. Sergei took the chair directly across from her, which somewhat surprised her. If it was his intention to appear nonthreatening, sitting was a good move. Sergei was still dangerous, but he might be trying to show them he was still one of them.

Valentina would have preferred to stand herself since drawing her weapon would take a fraction of a second longer while sitting, but she was there just as much to calm mounting concerns as to play bodyguard. She'd played this role often enough with Nikolai that she'd become accustomed to the part.

Yuri placed an unopened bottle on the table in front of her and several glasses. She leaned forward to open the bottle and began pouring. She served Nikolai first, and then went around the table offering each of the others a drink, taking the opportunity to study them even more for possible tells. It was easy to read body language for tension if you set them off-guard with a casual question first.

With a tilt of her head and a small unassuming smile, all of them accepted her offer. Sergei made a point to brush his hand against hers as he took the glass and whispered, "Thank you, Valechka."

Stiffening slightly at the contact, Valentina resisted the urge to upend the drink in his lap. Instead, she smiled sweetly at him and sat back down in her chair beside Nikolai. She poured a drink for herself and settled back, listening to the small talk and watching each of the guests.

"Initial construction reports on this new tower are promising," Nikolai began, leaning back in his chair. "Sergei has indicated your people are skilled craftsmen."

"Thank you," Alec said, a trace of pride in his voice. "It's coming along quite well, although progress has been a bit slower than we'd like."

"Yes, I understand there have been issues with acquiring resources."

Alec nodded. "Unfortunately, yes. We have several new plans in place to secure the necessary materials, but it may take longer than we originally anticipated to complete the new tower."

Valentina glanced over at Sergei, who still hadn't taken his eyes off her. He didn't appear surprised by this news. She'd known about the delays, but not that they'd be unable to complete the tower in time. Granted, she'd been tied up on other business for the past few weeks, but that was still no excuse. *Dammit*. She hated coming into situations blind.

"I see," Nikolai acknowledged, placing his hand on her leg. Understanding his silent warning not to reveal her irritation, Valentina relaxed her body and continued to listen. "I'm afraid additional delays may pose a problem. Our agreement stated the new tower would be complete within a year's time."

Sergei's gaze lowered to Nikolai's hand resting on her thigh. Picking up his drink, he tossed it back and placed his empty glass on the table. He leaned back in his seat and resumed watching her. The nonstop scrutiny was beginning to unnerve her, and she returned his gaze in a silent challenge. What was Sergei up to now? He couldn't want to play here and now, especially given their audience. His mouth curved upward a fraction, and she blinked at him in surprise. He did.

"I understand," Alec said, still focused on the conversation with Nikolai and oblivious to the silent communication occurring in front of him. "But the delay is unavoidable. If you would be willing to extend our original timeframe by six months, we would be able to take in another one hundred of your people once the tower is complete."

Even if Nikolai hadn't been touching her, she still would have picked up on his worry. Although he showed no outward signs of stress, pushing their timeframe back to that extent would create a great deal of hardships on their people. They had a thousand people in the vicinity and were already feeling the strain from the lack of supplies. Their nearest facility was too far away to provide more than cursory support.

If Nikolai agreed to Alec's proposal, he'd be putting his position at risk. At the last summit meeting, the other leaders had discussed the possibility of terminating the alliance. They all had concerns about these delays, arguing that OmniLab could be intentionally trying to weaken the Coalition's position in the area by withholding vital resources. And that didn't even begin to broach the argument about this alliance possibly hindering future negotiations with OmniLab.

Once their people began occupying this new construction tower, they would still be at a disadvantage. OmniLab would retain a controlling interest given their population far exceeded the thousand new residents prepared to move into the towers. Essentially, their people could find themselves dependent upon OmniLab's continuing goodwill. There was also some concern about falling under OmniLab's rule and what it would mean to the Coalition's future.

Nikolai had vehemently argued against terminating their alliance, throwing his support in with Sergei and even offering to come here to evaluate the situation. It would cost Nikolai dearly to extend the deadline, both in favors and accumulated supplies, but the alternative could be even more deadly. None of them wanted another war, unless there was no other option.

Valentina placed her hand over Nikolai's and discreetly tapped three times to give her opinion. They couldn't afford to extend the timeframe any more than that. She'd most likely have to take on some additional jobs to pay off the favors Nikolai would need to borrow. He didn't like it when she went off on her own, but there wasn't much of a choice. Yuri didn't have her same skillset or versatility, and one of them needed to remain behind with Nikolai. She might reach out to Peter or Lena's people first. They were two of the other leaders who were supposedly operating in the area.

Nikolai was quiet for a long moment and then said, "Three months, and you will take in another two hundred of our people."

Alec hesitated, glancing at Lars. When the former rene-gade nodded, Alec said, "Very well."

The conversation then temporarily shifted to more

mundane matters, and her attention fell back on Sergei. He lifted his eyebrow in silent challenge, asking whether she intended to play. Valentina had to bite the inside of her cheek to keep from smiling. He'd always been such a troublemaker.

Nikolai squeezed her leg gently, a pre-arranged signal to repour. She refilled the glasses, leaning over a little too far to hand Sergei's drink back to him. The liquid splashed over the front of his pants, and she frowned in dismay at her clumsiness.

"I might have something to... help remove that," she said, making a show of brushing her hand against one of her knives. "Shall I check to see what I can find?"

Sergei's eyes twinkled in amusement. "I do not believe that will be necessary. It will dry."

Valentina gave a small shrug and turned away, putting an extra sway in her hips as she walked over to the caravan. She bent down and reached inside to pull out a small cooler, feeling the weight of more than just Sergei's gaze on her backside.

"Do you need help?" Brant approached behind her and gestured to the cooler. Valentina took a step back, allowing him to carry it over to the table. She gave him a small smile in appreciation.

Careful not to interrupt the conversation at the table, she quietly said, "I wondered if I was going to see you here today."

He returned her smile. "I was sorry to learn you left so suddenly. How are you feeling?"

"Much better," she admitted, tucking a lock of hair that had escaped from her ponytail behind her ear. "Although, I miss those cookies already."

"I have a standing reservation at that café, anytime you want to go," Brant offered with a grin and then gestured to the cooler. "What's in here?"

"Nothing nearly as good as your cookies." She picked up a small covered dish and leaned in close to him, whispering, "Whatever you do, avoid this one. It tastes like old shoes."

Valentina wrinkled her nose, and he chuckled.

"I'll keep that in mind," he whispered back. "What's that other one?"

"Oh," she murmured, knowing he was performing his duties to protect his leader, just as she would have done. It was all part of the game, and Brant was playing it well so far. She glanced over at Sergei, who was ignoring everyone at the table and focusing completely on her and Brant. It would be tempting to pour the whole bottle over him next time. "This is one of my favorites. It is a salted fish, but it's difficult to come by here. We have it shipped from one of our facilities where we have farming tanks." She pointed to another and added, "Those are pickled vegetables."

Brant made a point to brush his hand against hers as he helped place them on the table. She smiled up at him and then turned away to pull out another bottle from the cooler. Yuri caught her eye, his mouth twitching in the barest of smiles. He knew exactly what she was doing and was enjoying the show. She winked at him before turning back to the table. A little harmless flirting now would only help her efforts to get more information out of Brant the next time she stopped by the towers.

Valentina sat back down, uncovered the dishes, and poured herself another drink. She tossed it back and picked up a small bite to demonstrate the items were safe to eat. Brant's eyes danced in amusement, and he followed her example.

Nikolai placed his hand back on her leg and rubbed his thumb against her thigh. Even though he'd appeared attentive to the conversation with Alec, Valentina was sure he was aware of her interactions with Sergei and Brant. The gesture was a clear indication he needed her focus on the conversation.

"We deeply regret any harm that may have come to Ariana," Nikolai said. "These actions were taken by two renegades, and they have been dealt with harshly."

Alec nodded. "Sergei and Lars have both shared with me how they met their untimely end, but that doesn't change my position on the matter."

"Your demand for information about our other camps is unreasonable," Nikolai informed him in a firm, unyielding tone. "We are not at war with each other. My decision to send Valentina to assist in Ariana's rescue should be proof of our goodwill. I treasure her deeply, and she nearly lost her life to protect your fiancée."

Valentina frowned. The whole situation with Pavel and Sofia pissed her off. From all appearances, Ariana was a wonderful person who had nearly given her life to save Valentina's. Even if this alliance fell apart, Valentina would always retain a sense of loyalty toward the dark-haired woman. They had each put their lives on the line for each other, and that wasn't a bond forged lightly.

Alec glanced over at her. "I'm grateful for your intervention, Valentina. Ariana told me about how you distracted them to buy us time."

She nodded. "I owe Ariana a debt that cannot be repaid. If she ever has need of me, I will come to her aid."

Alec's gaze softened, the love he felt for Ariana shining in his eyes. "Thank you. That will mean a great deal to her."

"We all have much to be gained from this alliance," Nikolai reminded him. "Relationships have already been forged between our people."

Alec sighed. "I agree, but this issue has fractured a fragile trust between us."

"The first pancake is always lumpy," Nikolai said, quoting

an old pre-war proverb. "What happened was a regrettable setback, but we are still finding our way. It would not be wise to judge all our people based on the actions of a few."

"You're right," Alec relented. "But if you are more forth-coming with information, it would go far to alleviate our concerns."

"Perhaps. We may share this information in time, but our alliance is still in its infancy." Nikolai squeezed her leg again gently and added, "In an effort to deepen our understanding of each other's cultures, I would like to invite your people to visit one of my camps. You have been gracious in your hospi-tality, and I would be pleased to offer the same to you."

Valentina stood to refill Alec's glass. While handing it to him, a red light on the arm of her jacket caught her attention. She dropped the bottle, reaching for her weapon, but Sergei tackled her to the ground. His body spasmed against her, and she rolled to the side, weapon drawn, searching for the attackers. Shouts echoed throughout the clearing while more shots ripped through the air.

Yuri flipped the table over on its side, using it as a shield to protect everyone. It wouldn't last. The table wasn't sturdy enough to offer more than cursory cover. Yuri and the others began returning fire, more as a distraction than anything else. Their weapons were designed for close encounters, whereas their attackers were using high-powered, long-distance weapons.

A groan caught her attention and Valentina glanced down, her heart nearly stopping at the sight of the bullet hole ripped through Sergei's jacket. Panic flooded through her, paralyzing her for a moment. He was bleeding too much, the wound a sucking, gaping hole in his chest.

"I need a visual, dammit!" Yuri shouted into his commlink as more shots were fired in their direction, pinning them down. "Where are the shooters?"

"Valechka," Sergei began, but she shook her head.

"Shh, Seryozha, do not talk," Valentina ordered, withdrawing a knife to cut open his jacket. She reached over to grab the dropped bottle and pulled off its cooling sleeve. With a snap, she broke it in half and placed one of the thin pieces on top of his wound. Shrugging out of her jacket, she pulled off her shirt and cut it into strips. Holding the cooler piece in place, she tied the strips tightly around Sergei, creating a makeshift occlusion bandage. She pressed her hand against the wound, applying even more pressure.

Another smattering of shots rang out, one of them piercing the table and hitting one of their men in the arm. Nikolai was crouched behind the table, returning fire. A few inches to the right and the bullet would have hit him. They needed to get everyone out of there now.

"Yuri!" she yelled. "Give me your shirt."

Yuri glanced over at her and yanked it off, still shouting instructions over the commlink. One of the Omnis was ordering air support to their location, but it would be too late.

"Lars! Hold pressure on Sergei's wound. I need both hands free."

As soon as he was in position, Valentina quickly cut strips from both shirts. Using a combination of gestures and verbal instructions, she ordered everyone to tie them around their noses and mouth. Leaning over Sergei, she carefully fastened a strip around his face before affixing her own.

"Yuri!" she shouted again and pulled her jacket back on. "Launch pulses four through nine."

She took over applying pressure to Sergei's wound and yelled to Lars and Alec, "Use your wind powers. We need a large dust storm to cover our escape."

They nodded, their eyes widening. A moment later, a strange wind kicked up, spreading dust throughout the area.

The electrical pulses crackled to life, heightening the range of the storm.

Yuri motioned them forward. "Move out. Now!"

Lars and Brant reached down to help move Sergei into their caravan. Valentina curled her fingers into fists, trying to resist the almost desperate urge to go after them. If they managed to get Sergei to Ariana in time, the young woman could heal him. Valentina had already seen her perform miracles. She had to believe Ariana would save him. The alternative was unthinkable.

Nikolai grabbed her arm. "Go with Sergei, Valya."

Valentina hesitated, torn between making sure Sergei would survive and not leaving Nikolai while they were still in danger.

"Now. That's an order," Nikolai snapped.

She gave him a curt nod and ran after Lars and Brant. If they were surprised she had followed them, they didn't say anything. She jumped into their caravan and sat on the bench seat, motioning for them to put Sergei's head in her lap while they laid him across the bench. She pressed her hand over his wound, continuing to apply pressure.

The caravan jerked forward, and Sergei winced.

She frowned, worried about his pallor, and stroked his hair back away from his face. "I do not like this new game, Seryozha."

He gave her a weak smile. "Ah, Valechka, it got you to remove your shirt and now my head is in your lap." He winced again and added, "I win this round."

A small laugh bubbled out of her. "You have always been a troublemaker."

"Mmm," he agreed, closing his eyes.

"Seryozha, you must stay awake," she urged, fighting back panic and scrambling to think of some way to entice him. "If you do, I will tell you either one secret or grant one favor."

He opened his captivating gray eyes once again but had to blink several times before his eyes focused on her. "My choice?"

"Yes," she agreed immediately, running her hand over his forehead. His skin was cold and clammy from losing too much blood. They needed to hurry.

"I want a favor," he whispered, his expression pained.

"Tell me," she encouraged.

"You will forgive me for leaving."

"Seryozha," Valentina whispered, her eyes welling with tears. She hastily blinked them back. Of all the things she expected him to say, that wasn't one of them.

Sergei placed his hand over hers and whispered, "Please do not cry, Valechka. It hurts me more than being shot."

She managed a weak smile and nodded. "Very well. I don't like crying anyway. But you must stay awake, or I will be angry with you all over again."

He squeezed her hand in agreement, but less than a minute later, his eyes drooped and his face went slack. A tidal wave of panic flooded through her, and Valentina lifted her head. "How far out are we?"

"Ten minutes," Lars said, kneeling beside Sergei to check his vitals.

She turned toward Alec, praying to whatever deity might be listening that they weren't too late. "Can Ariana heal him?"

"I've already reached out to her," Alec said, holding on to the caravan handle. "She's heading to the entrance now. A medical crew is standing by."

Valentina swallowed, trying to suppress her fears.

"Seryozha," she whispered, bending down to press a kiss against his forehead, "please stay with me. I cannot lose you again."

# CHAPTER NINE

THE CARAVAN HALTED, and the medical crew rushed in to stabilize Sergei before transporting him to the medical ward. Valentina watched with a strange sort of detachment as though she weren't really in her body. She'd seen countless injuries and had doctored more than a few, but the sight of Sergei like this evoked a powerful, primal reaction within her.

Ariana was leaning over him, doing something with her hands, but Valentina couldn't see anything except for a strange shimmer appearing in the surrounding air. She didn't care what it was as long as it meant Sergei lived. Ariana said something in a low voice, and they rushed Sergei toward the elevator. Valentina ran after them, not willing to let him out of her sight.

Pressing herself into the tightly cramped elevator, she rode it upward and exited onto the floor with them. The medical crew started moving down the hall, but Lars touched her arm. "Valentina, we need to wait here. They're taking him into a clean room to remove the bullet and stabilize him."

Valentina nodded, her heart hammering in her chest. She wouldn't have been allowed into surgery in their camp either, although she probably could have bullied her way in. Looking down at Sergei's blood covering her hands, now drying and turning a crusty brown, she voiced the question that needed to be asked. "Was this done by your people?"

"No," Lars replied, seemingly shocked by her question. "I swear to you, we didn't do this. Sergei is my friend, and I owe him my life." He paused for a moment and then added, "Sergei said you might try to kill him, and I thought he'd been right. But I realized you couldn't be responsible when I saw your reaction and heard what you said to him."

She continued to stare at the door, willing it to open with news that Sergei was alive and whole. "No one in my camp would have dared risk Nikolai's life in such a messy attack. If orders came down to terminate Sergei, it would have been done cleanly and without any fuss. We do not put others in jeopardy when performing sanctioned executions. This was done by a coward."

Lars winced at her description. "Sergei hasn't said anything about someone wanting to harm him. Could it have been done by one of the other Coalition camps?"

She'd considered it while they were in the caravan. It was a possibility and one she intended to explore. It didn't make sense for them to target him though. Besides, they'd trained their weapon on her first. "My position was blocking a clear shot of Nikolai and Alec. It could have been any one of us they were targeting." She shrugged. "Either way, they will not be breathing much longer."

"You're a little scary," Lars said with a frown. "But if you're going after these people, I'd like to help."

Valentina didn't reply because someone finally emerged from the room where they'd taken Sergei. An older woman with tired eyes approached them. "Are you Valentina?"

When she nodded, the woman said, "We were able to remove the bullet, and Ariana Alivette healed the most serious of his injuries. He's been given a metabolic booster, and we're giving him some additional blood units. You can go back to see him now."

A lump formed in her throat and she nodded again, heading toward the door. She needed to see him for herself. Lars went with her, but she ignored him, intent on her destination. Pushing open the door, she noted there were several medical people still in the room, along with Ariana and Alec.

Ariana gave her a warm smile. "He'll sleep for a few more hours, but he'll be okay."

Valentina couldn't respond, her eyes focused on the motionless figure in the bed. Sergei's eyes were closed, and there were machines beeping beside him. She walked over to him and took his hand in hers. His skin was still cool to the touch, but it was better than it had been. Lifting his hand, she pressed it against her cheek. The fire that usually burned so brightly within him was banked, slumbering in the darkness.

A tear escaped, and she blinked, trying to regain control of her chaotic emotions. He was going to be fine, she kept reminding herself. But seeing this strong and powerful man in this state wounded something inside her. He'd been injured before, but something about this time was different.

"I forgive you, Seryozha," she whispered and leaned over, brushing a soft kiss against his lips. "Please get well so we can play again."

Valentina pulled back, her eyes roaming over him one more time before she turned to the other occupants in the room. They were all watching her, different emotions in their expressions. She ignored them and focused on Lars instead. Out of all of them, he had the closest ties to Sergei. She needed to rely on that bond now so she could focus on what needed to be done.

"Will you watch over him for me?"

Lars agreed immediately and then frowned. "You're not staying, are you?"

"No," she replied, refusing to look at Sergei again for fear she might reconsider. Until he opened his eyes, she'd continue to worry. "I must return to Nikolai and find out who's responsible."

"You could be a target," Alec said in a low voice, taking a step toward her. "Sergei thought they were aiming for you. That's why he intervened. You would be safer remaining here."

"Exactly," she agreed, heading toward the door. "If they were targeting me, they will try again. I need to give them that opportunity. It will make it easier to find them."

Without waiting for a response, she pushed open the door and headed out into the brightly lit corridor, leaving Sergei asleep behind her.

———

SERGEI AWOKE amongst the beeping of machines. He groaned and started to sit up, the heavy weight in his chest lending to the idea he'd been hurt worse than he thought.

"You might want to take it slow," Lars warned. "You got shot and your lung collapsed. You almost died before we got you back here. Ariana healed you, but she could only do so much. I've never seen her heal such a serious injury on a non-sensitive. She must have gotten stronger since she bonded to Alec."

Sergei glanced around the empty room and frowned. "Where is Valentina?"

"She left," Lars explained, walking toward the bed.

Sergei cursed and pushed himself upright. He had to find her. The infernal woman would get herself hurt—or worse. He gripped the tube in his arm to yank it out, but Lars stopped him. "Dammit, man, they're still giving you the blood substitute. Just wait. I'll call for someone."

Sergei scowled at him but relented, leaning back against the bed and closing his eyes. "Tell them to hurry. How long ago did Valentina leave?"

Lars's footsteps moved closer to the bed, and Sergei heard the beep from a button being pressed. "She's been gone for a few hours. She stayed long enough to make sure you were going to be okay and then took off."

"Did she say anything?"

Lars hesitated. Sergei's eyes flew open, and he pinned Lars with his gaze.

"Tell me," he snapped.

"You're a fucking lousy patient," Lars grumbled, crossing his arms over his chest. "She thinks she's the target, but I'm not sure. It could have been you, Alec, or Nikolai. I had the impression she thought they were aiming for her. Our drones surveilled the area, but we didn't catch any sign of the attackers. My guess is your people are responsible. Any idea why they'd be targeting her?"

"It's because of Nikolai," Sergei said with a sigh. "He's made it no secret she's his right hand, and Yuri is his left. Without them by his side, Nikolai is not nearly as effective at keeping order. He's come to depend on their threat to enforce his will."

"If that's the case, why wouldn't they have targeted Nikolai instead?"

The attendant finally came in and began unhooking the machines. Sergei studied them to make sure they weren't wearing a translating device before switching to his native language. He might trust Lars to an extent, but not the rest of the residents within the towers. "If something happens to Nikolai, another will step in to take his place. It is widely believed Valentina would be the one to do it, but she has no wish to command. She prefers operating in the background."

Lars frowned. "So she's intentionally made herself into a target?"

The attendant finished with the machines and started to take his vitals, but Sergei waved them off. Once they were gone, he said, "I believe so. It would have been a tactical decision to give Nikolai's people the opportunity to respond and remove the threat. If necessary, Yuri would be the one to step into Nikolai's role. He is even more ruthless and unscrupulous than Nikolai, but he'd be very effective if Valentina remained by his side."

"If they want Nikolai removed from power, I still don't see why they wouldn't target him."

Sergei pushed off the bed, his head swimming from the blood loss. He leaned against the wall for support, taking a moment to allow the worst of the dizziness to pass. "All three of them would need to be eliminated from power. The best way to do that would be to prove Nikolai ineffective or discredit him. If that happens, his territories will be taken away and reassigned amongst the rest of the leadership. They will not trust either Valentina or Yuri to hold command. His entire camp would be put at risk."

Lars took a step toward him. "Sergei, what the hell do you think you're doing? You can barely stand."

"I must find her before she does something foolish," Sergei said, pushing off the wall and glancing around for the rest of his clothing. "Nikolai promised me he would protect her, but he's put her directly in harm's way."

Lars paused, studying him closely. "I'll be damned. This isn't just concern over her well-being. You love her, don't you?"

"Yes," Sergei snapped. "Now hand me my clothes or get

out of my way. I will walk out of here naked before I allow anything to happen to her."

Lars grabbed the clothing and handed them to him. "I'm going with you."

"You cannot," Sergei said, starting to get dressed. "I will have a hard enough time getting in to see Nikolai on my own. They will have increased security after the shooting."

"You're not in any condition to go off on your own," Lars argued.

Sergei ignored him and reached over for the commlink they'd removed while he'd been unconscious. He pressed a button and a woman's voice answered, but it wasn't the one he was hoping to hear.

"Regina, this is Sergei. Has Valentina returned?"

"I cannot give you that information," she replied.

Sergei's teeth gritted. "Fine. I need the coordinates to Nikolai's camp."

"We are not accepting visitors."

"Tell Nikolai who is requesting the information," he snapped, his patience quickly growing thin.

There was a lengthy pause and then she said, "Nikolai is in a meeting. I am connecting you with Yuri."

A moment later, Yuri's voice answered. "What can I do for you, Sergei?"

"Has Valentina returned?"

"I fail to see how that would be your concern," Yuri replied, a trace of boredom in his voice. "Was there anything else?"

Sergei forced himself to take a deep breath. If Yuri were in front of him, he'd be inclined to snap the man's neck. "I must speak with Nikolai in person. If you send me your camp's coordinates, I can meet with him directly."

"You are not in a position to make demands," Yuri

reminded him. "Once we have completed our security assessment, we will consider your request."

The transmission terminated, and Sergei resisted the urge to throw the commlink against the wall.

Lars frowned. "Can you contact Valentina directly?"

"I did. Her commlink is being rerouted because they are on lockdown. Yuri would have asked more questions if she hadn't returned yet. She is most likely meeting with Nikolai right now." He paused for a moment, considering his options. "How did Valentina leave here? She did not have a vehicle."

"I would assume she took one of our speeders," Lars said, his eyes lighting up in understanding. "We should be able to track it."

"Only partially," Sergei said, heading for the door. "She is unfamiliar with the area, so she would have needed to rely on the coordinates to find her way back. Once she got close enough to Nikolai's camp, she would have disabled the tracker. It may be enough to give us an idea of their location. I am familiar enough with her tactics that I believe I may be able to find her."

"I'm going with you," Lars said, following behind him. "I don't care if I can't step foot inside, but you're not in any condition to go on your own."

Sergei was tempted to argue, but Lars was right. If he had any hope of protecting Valentina, he needed whatever help he could get.

———

SERGEI CLIMBED OFF THE SPEEDER, rubbing his chest. Between Valentina stabbing him and getting shot, he was running out of places to get injured. Lars pulled up alongside him and dismounted.

It had taken far longer than he expected to locate Nikolai's camp. Valentina had laid several false trails, and at one point, he'd been convinced they were heading in the wrong direction. Fortunately, one of Nikolai's recruits had gotten sloppy, and Sergei been able to deduce the approximate location. From there, it had been an issue of circling back around until they practically stumbled upon the camp.

Sergei motioned for Lars to follow him. It was impossible to know what sort of reception they'd receive. He'd half expected them to be fired upon for approaching without clearance.

They walked inside and were both immediately slammed against the wall by armed guards. He winced as pain erupted in his chest from his barely healed injury, but he remained silent while they briskly searched him and removed his weapons. When they finished, he turned around, keeping his hands slightly raised.

"I need to speak with Nikolai," he said, not recognizing any of the guards.

"Sergei," Yuri called out and stepped into the room, "I suppose I shouldn't be surprised to see you."

"Yuri," Sergei acknowledged, keeping his tone neutral even though he was tempted to slam the man's head into the wall. The only reason Yuri would have avoided giving him the camp's coordinates was to be a pain in the ass.

Yuri studied him for a long moment. "If it were up to me, I would turn you away or kill you, but Nikolai has agreed to speak with you."

"How fortunate for me," Sergei replied in a dry voice. The head slam was looking even more attractive.

Yuri grinned. "Come along, but your friend must remain here."

Sergei motioned for Lars to stay back and followed Yuri down the hall. As they passed various rooms, he recognized a few people, but most of the faces were unfamiliar. There had been more changes than he realized, but then again, it had been three years since he'd last stepped foot in one of Nikolai's camps.

Sergei walked into an office where Nikolai was standing behind a desk, viewing something on a small tablet. He glanced up as Sergei entered and then went back to studying the screen in his hand. From all appearances, Nikolai hadn't changed in the slightest over the past several years.

"Valentina mentioned you survived," Nikolai observed. "I did not expect you to be up and walking around so quickly. Their healers must be remarkable."

"They are," Sergei confirmed, taking a step toward him. "I am here about Valentina."

Nikolai paused, placing the tablet on his desk. "Is that so?"

Sergei inclined his head, not giving a damn if this ended badly. After seeing her again, he couldn't walk away without a fight. "I want you to release her from service."

Yuri stiffened in his position against the wall, but Nikolai held up his hand. "Yuri, leave us."

Yuri hesitated, but one sharp look from Nikolai had him immediately turning and leaving the room. Once Yuri was gone, Nikolai regarded Sergei for a long moment. "If I recall correctly, you gave her to me. Now you would ask that I return her?"

Sergei's jaw clenched. "I never *gave* her to you. I asked that you protect her. If I had any idea what you would turn her into, I would have never done such a thing."

Nikolai's mouth curved in an amused smile. "Interesting. And what have I turned her into?"

Sergei fell silent, glaring at Nikolai. "She is not the same woman we both knew."

"No," he agreed, "she is not."

Sergei waited, but Nikolai didn't say anything further.

"Will you release her from service and allow her to reclaim her life?"

Nikolai sighed wearily and pinched the bridge of his nose. "Come with me."

Curious but wary, Sergei followed him out of the room, down the hall, and past the barracks area. Nikolai opened a door which led to a rather large suite with a living area and secondary office off to the side. More doors were closed, which most likely led to bedroom areas.

Nikolai tapped on one of the doors. "All is well, Valya, but would you mind joining me?"

A few moments later, one of the doors opened and a sleepy Valentina emerged. Her disheveled hair tumbled loose over her shoulders, and her shirt barely reached the top of her thighs. Sergei caught a glimpse of black panties underneath, reminding him of the pair he'd ripped from her body the day before. It was the sight of her sleepy and barely dressed in Nikolai's quarters, though, that made regret surge hot and deep within him. He never should have left her.

Valentina rubbed her eyes and yawned. In a voice husky from sleep, she murmured, "Are you all right, Kolya? Did Yuri finish the analysis?"

Nikolai walked over to her, wrapped his arm around her waist, and pressed a kiss against her temple. "I am fine. Sergei is here though."

Valentina blinked and lifted her head, staring at him for a moment as though not comprehending he was there. When recognition cleared the sleep from her eyes, a small smile traced over lips. She took a step toward him, looking him over and searching for any injuries. "You are better? Already?"

He swallowed and nodded, not quite trusting himself to speak. God. Had she always been this beautiful? When she looked at him with those gorgeous eyes filled with happiness at seeing him, every thought evaporated from his head, except for an intense desire to take her back to bed.

"Valya," Nikolai said gently, "Sergei has asked that I release you from service."

She stiffened, shock coloring her expression as she looked back and forth between them. When Nikolai nodded, she turned back to Sergei but not with any of her earlier warmth.

"You do not have any right to ask this," Valentina snapped, fury making her blue eyes even more striking.

"He was supposed to protect you, not put you in more danger," Sergei accused, glaring at Nikolai. "I would never have left you with him if I had known what would happen."

"You know nothing about my relationship with Nikolai!" she shouted, clenching her hands into fists as though resisting the urge to take a swing at him. Sergei supposed he should be thankful. In addition to the knife strapped to her forearm, she was probably also wearing another weapon somewhere under that shirt. Even when asleep, she was rarely unarmed.

"Can you not tell he is using you?" Sergei argued, taking a step toward her, determined to make her see reason. "I have heard many rumors about your relationship, Valentina. I have seen some of it for myself. You were a decorative trophy at the meeting today, and you have made yourself into a target to protect him."

"It is a game!" she said, throwing up her hands. "You used to play it with us."

"I never asked you to whore yourself," he said in a low voice.

Valentina fell silent. Nikolai took a step toward her. "Valya, you must tell him."

"It is none of his business."

"Valentina," Nikolai admonished.

She sighed and lifted her head to regard him. "Nikolai and I are not lovers. We decided to play the part because it allowed me to stay close to him without arousing suspicion. I can go places with him that Yuri cannot. He has never asked me to do anything I did not wish to do."

Sergei froze. Every thought suddenly evaporated from his mind. He stared at them, wondering how he could have possibly missed the truth. She'd always been affectionate with Nikolai, but the small touches, the intimate looks... it had all been so convincing. People had been whispering for years about them.

"You put her in danger just to keep a foothold on your power base?" Sergei roared, leaping forward and tackling Nikolai to the ground. Sergei reared back to swing at him, but a sharp blade pressed against his neck.

"Release him," Valentina ordered, her dispassionate voice like a cold bucket of water over him. "I would rather not slit your throat, but I will if you force my hand."

Keeping his movements slow and deliberate, Sergei did as she instructed. Nikolai stood and moved away, but Valentina still didn't lower the knife.

"All of this has been my choice," she said in a low voice. "Out of all of us, Nikolai is the best leader. Neither Yuri nor I have Nikolai's patience or skill at diplomacy. We all have our strengths and played our little parts."

"Then this has all been another facet of your game to keep Nikolai in power?" Sergei glanced at Nikolai out of the corner of his eye. "Why didn't you tell me?"

"You have been gone a long time, Sergei," she said with a sigh. "The rules have changed, but the game remains the same. Your loyalty has not been with us for many years. We could not trust you with our secrets."

The truth in her words hurt, but he couldn't argue it. "Why are you telling me now?"

"Nikolai believes you are still one of us," she admitted. "But Yuri does not."

His heart thudded in his chest, hope unfurling inside him. "And what do you believe, Valechka?"

Valentina pulled the knife away and took a step back from him, her expression shuttered. "It does not matter what I believe. Nikolai wished you to know the truth, so now you know." She gestured to the door and added, "Go away, Sergei. It is late, and I am tired."

She handed the knife to Nikolai and headed back into her room, the door closing softly behind her.

# CHAPTER TEN

SERGEI STARED at the door for a long time, warring between the desire to go after her and to give her space. If he went in there now, there was only a small chance he'd walk out with all his body parts intact. Even with that threat hovering in the forefront of his mind, he took a step toward the door.

Nikolai's voice broke through his thoughts. "Join me for a drink, Sergei."

Sergei turned to regard him, and Nikolai shook his head in warning. Nikolai was probably right, but having her so close and out of reach was another kind of torture. He gave another last longing look at the door before turning around to follow Nikolai down the hall.

Nikolai led him into his office, motioned for Sergei to sit, and pulled a bottle from a small cooler in the corner of the room. He poured two glasses and sat in a chair across from him. Sergei picked up one of the glasses, holding it in his hand but not drinking.

"She needs time," Nikolai advised, reaching for his drink.

"She's had three years," Sergei said, looking into the glass and wishing it held the answers he sought. "In all that time, she never hinted your relationship was a lie. Neither did you."

"Would you have believed it?"

Sergei hesitated and then swallowed the cold liquid. In all honesty, he wasn't sure. He'd known for years about Nikolai's attraction to her, but she'd never reciprocated. "I've always known she loves you. I thought it had turned to more once I left."

"She does love me, just as she loves Yuri," Nikolai agreed. "We have always been family to her."

Sergei lifted his head to regard his former friend. "Why did you not tell me? If you believe my loyalty still lies with you, why keep this from me?"

Nikolai sighed and leaned back. "It was not my place. You hurt her when you left, Sergei. If I had told you the truth back then, she never would have forgiven me."

"I had to leave," Sergei said, reaching over to refill his glass. He downed it, the warmth from the alcohol doing little to alleviate the chill inside him. It was a poor substitute for what he really wanted—she was asleep a few rooms away.

"I agree. You had your orders and your reasons, but your choice in timing was poor. Valentina woke up, and you were gone. You owed her at least an explanation."

Sergei lowered his gaze to the glass again, remembering how pale and lifeless Valentina was the last time he'd seen her. He'd carried that image with him over the years. Even now, the thought of a world without her in it filled him with despair. The memories from that night would forever haunt him, and not just because he'd walked away from her.

"You know why I did it," Sergei said with a sigh. "You had just been appointed to your position. I thought she would be safer remaining behind with you than accompanying me on another takeover. I couldn't risk anything else happening to her."

"That wasn't your choice to make," Nikolai reminded him. "Our Valentina has always been strong-willed. You treated her like a fragile doll, and she's spent the last three years proving you wrong."

Sergei put the empty glass on the table. "Am I too late to fix this?"

Nikolai shrugged. "I don't know. She still cares for you, but she is not the same girl we grew up with."

Sergei knew that, but she still possessed that playful spark that had always intrigued him. It had a darker, sharper edge than when they were younger, but for some perverse reason, that thrilled him even more. He wanted her, as much as he ever had, maybe more. "I will not leave her again, Nikolai."

"It may not be up to you," Nikolai replied, leaning back in his chair. "It's her choice now, as it should have been back then."

Sergei studied him, wondering about Nikolai's motivation in all this. "Will you interfere if I try to win her back?"

Nikolai was silent for a long time. "No, but I will not help you either. I have already done too much. She will not forgive more, and I will not risk losing her."

Sergei nodded. It was fair, less than what he hoped, but he could understand Nikolai's position. "If I am successful, this will affect your subterfuge."

Nikolai waved off his warning and leaned forward to pick up his glass again. "Valentina will probably come up with some other ruse. We all knew this plan wouldn't last forever."

"She always has enjoyed a challenge," he agreed, wondering what inventive idea she'd come up with next. At least with Nikolai not opposing him, he might have a chance to convince her—a challenge in itself. "And what of Yuri? Will he interfere?"

Nikolai frowned. "Yuri has not forgiven you, and I do not know if he will. We don't speak much about you, but he is protective of Valentina. They have always been close, but the first year without you was particularly bad. Their fights got more than a little heated, especially when your name was mentioned. He was furious when I ordered Valentina to accompany you back to OmniLab."

Nikolai fell silent for a moment and then added, "To answer your question, yes. I believe he will do what he can to warn her away from you. She values his opinion in most things, but I don't know how she will react to his interference when it comes to you."

Sergei nodded. Most likely, she wouldn't react well. At least he had that going for him. "What do you know about what happened earlier at the meeting with OmniLab? Do you know who attacked us?"

Nikolai's eyes narrowed, revealing a trace of the dangerous man Sergei knew lurked beneath the surface. It was a stark reminder that under the polished veneer, Nikolai was just as deadly as any of them. "No, but we *will* find out. We sent a team back to the area after it had been cleared. They determined the weapons used in the attack were ours. I have reached out to the other chairmen and facility managers to determine who is operating within the area. Unfortunately, we have over a thousand people nearby with too many different agendas."

Sergei frowned. "I would offer my aid, if you are willing to accept it. Valentina was the shooter's target, and I do not want to see her harmed any more than you do."

Nikolai nodded. "Your assistance would be welcome, especially if you can act as a liaison with OmniLab. Their surveillance may have picked up on additional clues. I will also need the names of all our people within the area who have been working under your direction, especially those who have raised objections in the past with either my leadership or with Valentina."

"I'll send over the information right away," Sergei agreed. "Lars accompanied me here, and OmniLab is also determined to find out who is responsible. It would help deepen our alliance if we work together to accomplish our goals."

Nikolai leaned back, regarding Sergei with a calculating gleam in his eyes. "Interesting. I did not know you had political ambitions."

"None of us are the same as we once were," Sergei reminded him with a small smile.

Nikolai chuckled and stood. "Come. Let me show you and your companion to a bunk. You can remain here tonight and begin helping us tomorrow."

———

VALENTINA WAS YANKED out of sleep by a hand covering her mouth. Before she could draw a weapon, another hand grabbed her wrists, yanking them up over her head. A heavy body came down on top of her, pinning her with its weight.

"Shh, Valechka," Sergei's voice whispered in her ear. "You do not want to wake anyone."

Valentina jerked her wrists, but he held her tightly. She glared at him, mentally kicking herself for not barricading the door. Although, she'd assumed he would have been tossed out of camp on his ass. She'd strangle Nikolai and Yuri for letting him stay and not giving her fair warning.

He slid his leg between hers, resetting his weight over her body. Trailing his nose against her neck, he inhaled deeply and placed a small kiss behind her ear. "You smell like cookies. I haven't been able to eat one in three years without thinking of you." He flicked out his tongue, tasting her skin. "You taste as sweet too."

She swallowed, her heart thudding in her chest. These

were not words she wanted to hear from him. Maybe she had once upon a time, but things were different now.

Sergei nipped at her earlobe, and she quivered. He chuckled and murmured, "I have missed you, Valechka. You have always been so responsive."

She started to move, trying to upset his weight, but he pressed his body even deeper on top of hers. "I am not leaving. Not until you talk to me."

Valentina's eyes narrowed at him, asking with her glare how she was supposed to talk when he was covering her mouth. He grinned and kissed her nose. "If I remove my hand, will you call for anyone?"

Ha. As if she needed anyone's help to exterminate a rat. She shook her head, making her intentions clear. His grin deepened at the implied threat, and he removed his hand but didn't release her.

"Get off me, you oversized oaf," she hissed.

"I thought you appreciated my size," he teased, shifting slightly to make his meaning clear.

"Release me and I will show you how much I appreciate it," she suggested.

"I think you are far too dangerous to release just yet." Sergei ran his free hand along her arm to the knife strapped against it. He removed the arm sheath, tossing it aside on a nearby chair, and slid his hand downward along her side, and then up, under her shirt.

His movement was a sensual caress, trailing along her skin until it found another of her knives. He removed that sheath as well, tossing it into the chair with the first. Grabbing her wrists with his other hand, he stroked her other side, looking for any other hidden weapons. It was a slow, seductive exploration, and her breathing became a little more rapid. Each of his movements was intended to stimulate, and he was most definitely a master.

"We are getting closer," he murmured, pressing a kiss against her jawline. "Shall I see what else I find?"

Valentina closed her eyes. His scent and the feel of him pressing against her was its own form of sensual torture. He continued running his hand along her body and cupped her breast. Her breath hitched, and she whispered, "I do not think you are still looking for weapons, Seryozha."

"Is that what I was doing?" he murmured, nuzzling her neck again as he gently pinched her nipple. "You have distracted me again."

Her mouth curved upward. "You have always been distracted easily."

"Only with you," he said and kissed her.

His lips were gentle, a teasing exploration, both tasting and sampling. She could taste the hint of liquor on his tongue, and underneath was a richer, deeper flavor belonging only to him. It was one she craved, a dangerous addiction, and she wanted more. She pulled her wrists downward, and he released her.

Valentina reached up to draw him closer, running her fingers through his hair. He found her breast again, and she whimpered, arching into his hand. Deepening their kiss, she hooked one of her legs around him and pulled him tighter against her. It still wasn't enough. She broke their kiss, panting softly and looking up into his passion-filled eyes.

"Take off your clothes, or I will cut them off you," she warned, the threat not an idle one. He'd taken the knives she had on her but not the ones she'd hidden *in* the bed.

Sergei chuckled and sat up enough to pull his shirt over his head. When he tossed it aside, she sat up with him, running her hands over his muscular chest. She frowned at the sight of the bandages marring his skin. It had been too close. A few more inches, and he would not be with her right now.

Valentina leaned forward, pressing a kiss against the place where he'd been shot. He inhaled sharply and threaded his fingers through her hair. She lifted her gaze a fraction to meet his eyes and ran her fingers over the bandage on his shoulder where she'd stabbed him. Leaning forward, she pressed a soft kiss against that one too. He swallowed, looking down at her with eyes filled with longing and some other unnamed emotion.

"Valechka," he whispered, "I have missed seeing this look in your eyes." She started to pull away, but he stopped her. "Please don't turn away from me. We don't have to speak of this tomorrow, but I want to see you. No games. Just for tonight. Let me love you."

She shook her head, panic rushing through her. "No. You should go. I cannot do this with you again."

He squeezed his eyes shut, a look of agonizing pain on his face. "I shouldn't have left you. I have regretted it every day."

Valentina lowered her gaze, memories from the past rushing back. Before she could stop herself, she asked the one question that had been plaguing her for years. "Why didn't you ask me to come with you?"

"I thought it was my only choice. I wanted to protect you, but I never dreamed how much it would hurt."

"I don't want to love you again," she admitted, wrapping her arms around herself to protect against the rush of emotion. "Please do not ask it of me."

"Valechka," he murmured, lifting his hands to cup her face, "I will try not to ask for more than you are willing to give."

"Then what do you want from me?" she whispered, her heart aching all over again.

Sergei was quiet for a long moment, searching her expression. "Will you let me love you?"

Wasn't it the same thing? Valentina lowered her gaze

again, taking a deep breath. She wanted him. She missed what they used to have, but it wasn't possible to recapture the past. There was only the future, and it was wild, unpredictable, and just as full of potential heartache. But if she didn't try to grasp this small amount of happiness, the regret of what might have been would always plague her.

"Yes," she whispered.

Sergei's eyes shone with unmistakable elation, that flame around his irises even more brilliant in the dim lighting of the room. He placed a kiss against her lips and pulled her shirt over her head. Tossing it aside, he allowed his eyes to roam over her body. "I did not believe you could get any more beautiful. I was wrong."

She leaned back on the bed again, watching as he trailed his hand over her stomach. He brushed against her hip, tracing over the scar she'd received before he left. The injury had been bad, but it paled in comparison to the pain of his leaving. He lifted his gaze again, an apology in his eyes before he bent down to place a kiss against her hip.

Valentina reached down, running her hands through his hair again. It was much longer than he used to wear it, not altogether unpleasant but different.

He cocked his head, studying her thoughtfully. "You don't like it?"

"I am not used to it."

"It was a means to assimilate into OmniLab," he admitted, lying beside her and looking down into her eyes. "I will cut it if you prefer it shorter."

She ran her fingers through the blond strands. "It is soft."

"Not as soft as you," he said, placing another gentle kiss against her lips. He rested his hand against her hip, holding her in place while his mouth leisurely teased hers.

She ran her hands down his chest, his strength and unyielding hardness a tantalizing contrast to his kiss.

Lowering her hands to his belt, she started to unbuckle it, but he grabbed her wrists.

"If you do that, I will not be able to take my time with you. I am already at the edge of my willpower being this close to you."

Valentina leaned forward to nip at his bottom lip. "I want you now, Seryozha. Stop teasing me."

Sergei chuckled and allowed her to yank off his belt. She unhooked his pants, and he assisted, shifting himself so she could pull them off. "Always so impatient, Valechka."

"Only with you," she whispered, repeating his earlier words.

His gaze became smoldering, and he lowered his head, claiming her mouth once again. All earlier traces of leisurely tenderness were gone and replaced with scorching desire. No one else had ever brought her close to this insatiable need. His scent and taste clouded her mind until nothing else existed but him.

She wrapped her arms around him, wanting more. Each fervent touch only heightened her already unbridled passion, and she hooked her leg over his in a wordless demand. His hardness pressed against her, and she arched into him. He gripped her leg, hiking it even higher as he sought entrance. With one hard thrust, he penetrated deeply. She gasped and grabbed his face when he froze.

"Do not stop or I will kill you," she swore.

"Always so bloodthirsty," he admonished with a grin. Gripping her hips, he began moving slowly at first and then built up speed until he was pounding into her. She clutched the bedding tightly, throwing her head back as the sensations overcame her.

His mouth found hers again, swallowing her screams as she erupted in a wave of sensation. He didn't stop, but instead shifted his angle, deepening his penetration even more. She gripped his arms, her body once more building toward an exquisite release. It was too much. She couldn't do it.

"Again, Valechka," he ordered.

Unable to resist his verbal demand or her body's response to his, Valentina complied and shattered into a thousand pieces. A moment later, he followed her over the edge of the precipice and exploded inside her.

Her heart thudded in her chest, too spent to even lift her hand. He had utterly and unabashedly destroyed her. Gathering her into his arms, Sergei rolled over, taking her with him so she was sprawled on top of him. His breathing was as rapid as hers, his heart thundering in time with hers, and she wasn't sure she would ever be able to move again.

They laid in each other's arms for several minutes, each of them relearning how to breathe. He reached down and leisurely began stroking her naked back. She made a small noise of contentment, her eyes beginning to drift shut as a long-elusive peace began to settle over her.

"Are you falling asleep on me, Valechka?" Sergei whispered.

"Mmhmm," she agreed, nuzzling against his chest.

He tightened his arm around her. "I have missed you, little dove. I will not leave you again."

She made another small noise of agreement and closed her eyes, almost immediately slipping into a deep slumber.

# CHAPTER ELEVEN

VALENTINA WOKE up the next morning alone. If it weren't for the faint scent of Sergei on her blankets and the memory of his touch on her body, she would have sworn she'd imagined the whole thing. It was just as well that he'd disappeared during the night. Otherwise, she might linger in bed, and there would be countless questions she wasn't quite prepared to answer. She stretched and walked into the bathroom to shower.

When she emerged, she still wasn't quite awake. With a yawn, she grabbed a pair of pants and pulled a tank top over her head before turning to the weapons Sergei had removed the night before. She hesitated and then grabbed a few more, attaching her arm and leg sheaths while an electrolaser gun went into the holster at her side. It wasn't her preferred weapon, but it gave her an advantage in some situations.

Grabbing a hair band, she pulled her hair back into a ponytail and headed out into the common area of Nikolai's suite. Yuri was leaning over the table looking down at a tablet and glanced up as she entered.

"Good. You're awake," he said, studying her thoughtfully. "You're wearing more weapons than usual."

Valentina glanced down at herself and frowned. He was right. She must be feeling more insecure than usual. Not wanting to examine the reasons too closely, she shrugged. "It makes sense given the attack."

He arched an eyebrow but didn't call her on it. Instead, he glanced toward Nikolai's closed door. "Is Nikolai still asleep?"

"I don't know. He was still awake when I went to bed last night, but I haven't seen him this morning. I only got up a short time ago."

Yuri nodded and handed her the tablet he'd been studying. "I put a team on trying to trace the weapons used at the ambush. We have a few leads so far, but we will need to investigate further."

She looked at the tablet, reviewing the types of weapons they suspected of being used in the assault. Some of the ones listed were the same type that coincided with another active investigation in the area. It could be related, but she wasn't willing to jump to conclusions without any proof. "Perhaps we should go back out to the ambush site today. We may find something the others missed."

Yuri nodded. "I agree. We can put together a team at breakfast. Are you hungry?"

She handed him the tablet and stretched. "I need caffeine more than anything. But I should probably eat something if we will be offsite today."

Yuri chuckled and put his hand on her back to lead her toward the door. "You and your tea addiction. You will most likely never be a morning person."

She grinned at him. "You know me too well."

"That I do," he agreed as they headed down the hall. "Did Nikolai tell you Sergei stopped by last night to meet with him?"

"I know," she murmured. "I saw him."

Yuri gave her a sharp look. "I see. I would be interested to know how he found the location of our camp."

She shrugged. "Sergei has always been resourceful. But with this new threat, we may want to find out. If he was able to locate us, others will too. We should consider moving Nikolai to one of our secondary locations."

Yuri opened the door to the noisy dining hall and led her inside. "I changed the parameters of our security assessment. We're running a new one now. Once it's finished, I'll explore alternate campsites. Unless there's an urgent need, I'd rather move to a completely new location. We can relocate either this afternoon or tomorrow."

"Good," she agreed, halting as her eyes fell on Sergei who was sitting at a table with Lars. He was watching her, and his eyes warmed. He gave her a small nod in greeting, a smile playing upon his lips.

"What the fuck is he doing here?" Yuri demanded, taking a step forward.

She grabbed his arm. In a low voice, she warned, "Do not engage. If he's still here, it's with Nikolai's approval."

Yuri stiffened and whispered, "This is unacceptable, Valya. Nikolai goes too far."

"It's not our call to make," she reminded him and smiled politely as a woman approached. "Regina, how are you this morning?"

The brunette beamed a smile. "Wonderful. I take it you've seen our gorgeous guests?"

Yuri scowled, and Valentina shot him another dark look before turning back to the woman. "Yes, but I don't think that's why you're talking to me before I've had a chance to have any caffeine."

Regina laughed. "No, but it's always fun to appreciate a fine specimen of a man."

Valentina murmured an agreement and said, "I will join you in a moment Yuri."

He nodded and headed over to collect his food while she followed Regina to the drink station. Valentina poured herself a large cup of tea, adding her preferred amount of sweetener while she waited for Regina to tell her what was going on. Something had the young woman on edge. There was a forced cheerfulness about her, but Valentina caught an undercurrent of worry below the surface.

"We received the new weapon shipment yesterday," Regina said, reaching over to fix her drink.

Valentina stirred her steaming cup, noting that Regina's hands were slightly unsteady. "How does it look?"

"Better than expected, but the numbers were off," Regina admitted in a low voice.

Valentina frowned. "How far off?"

"We're missing at least a hundred. I'm trying to trace the disappearance, but this will be a problem if we cannot locate them soon."

"Send me the list of scheduled recipients," Valentina ordered and started making a mental list of what needed to be done to get ahead of this possible disaster.

Regina's nerves suddenly made sense if she was worried about being blamed for the disappearance. Valentina would need to talk to Yuri about checking their other weapon stores to see if they could cover the deficit. Dammit. Between this and Nikolai's agreement to extend the deadline for the tower construction, they couldn't afford any more problems.

Focusing on Regina again, she added, "Pull off three senior officers from our acquisition team to help trace the shipment, but keep it quiet. I want the names of everyone who was involved from the manufacturing point up until we received the shipment. Cross-check everyone on the list with their facility alliances and send me the report right away. Has anything else gone missing?"

Regina hesitated. "I'm not sure. I'll start looking into it immediately."

"Look at ammunition numbers first," Valentina suggested, her intuition telling her this was linked to yesterday's ambush. It was too much of a coincidence otherwise. They were going to need to run a complete inventory of all their assets to find out if anything else was missing. "I'll speak with Yuri about the rest."

"Very well," Regina agreed. "I'll let you know what I find out."

Valentina nodded and scanned the room for Yuri, who was now seated at the table with Sergei and Lars. She inwardly cursed and hurried over to collect a tray. The last thing she needed this morning was to play referee, especially given all these new headaches. She scooped up some food and headed over to the table.

Yuri was sitting directly across from Sergei, both of them glaring at each other over the table. She forced a smile and slid into the seat across from Lars, placing her tray and tea on the table in front of her.

"Good morning," she said, making an effort to keep her voice light and friendly.

"Good morning, Valechka," Sergei murmured, eyeing her appreciatively.

Lars also said good morning, but she didn't reply to either of them right away. After all, she had priorities. She lifted her cup, closed her eyes, and inhaled deeply before taking a sip of the artificial beverage. It wasn't nearly as good as the tea in the towers, but it was caffeine. She had a feeling she was going to need more than one cup to get through today.

"So, Sergei," Yuri began, taking a bite of his food, "how did you manage to locate our camp?"

Valentina opened her eyes to find Sergei's gaze still on her. The intensity made her stomach do a neat little somersault, and she took another sip, willing the caffeine to work faster.

"Not easily," Sergei admitted. "I traced Valentina for part of the way, but she cut off the transponder sooner than I would have thought. We circled around for a few hours until we picked up another trail. One of your other recruits didn't clear his path, so I was able to determine the approximate location of your camp."

Valentina frowned. Some careless recruit would be having an unpleasant morning once Yuri was finished with them.

"Why are you still here?" Yuri asked, using a bit more force than necessary to stab his food.

She took another sip. Yep. The recruit was in for a very bad morning.

"A few reasons," Sergei said, still focusing on her.

Valentina's eyes narrowed over the rim of her cup. She'd enjoyed last night and would always treasure the memory, but that's all it was. He needed to accept she wouldn't fall back into old patterns with him. They might enjoy each other here and there, but what was once between them was over. It had to be.

Apparently, Yuri felt the same way. He leaned forward and said, "You need to be careful about those reasons, Sergei. If I suspect they are for any reason other than business, you may stop breathing sooner than you expect."

"It would be a shame for you to die," Sergei said as casually as if he were commenting on the weather. "Nikolai and Valentina both think highly of you."

She took another sip, hiding her smile behind her cup. Only Sergei could get away with threatening Yuri and still walk away. As though sensing her appreciation, Sergei grinned at her, his eyes lighting up with mischief.

Sergei was far too appealing for his own good and too

dangerous to keep around. Valentina lowered her cup and took a bite of her breakfast, the bland flavor not doing much to help with her appetite. "How long are you staying, Sergei?"

He paused for a long moment. "I offered to help Nikolai find whoever was responsible for the attack yesterday. I will stay as long as you wish."

She lifted her gaze to meet his, the promise in his words clear.

"Then you should leave after breakfast," Yuri suggested. "You can help far more by keeping your distance."

"Yuri," Valentina warned, pushing away her barely touched tray. They were beginning to attract curious looks. And with them, gossip and rumors would follow. It wasn't just her heart at risk.

Yuri sighed but relented. "Very well. How do you intend to help?"

"I have a few thoughts but would like to review your progress first. OmniLab is conducting their own analysis, and Lars has agreed to offer his assistance."

She smiled at Lars. "Thank you. That's very generous."

"It's my pleasure," Lars replied. "The meeting between Alec and Nikolai seemed to be going well until the interruption. I know Alec would like to resume discussions once the situation is resolved. He's extended the invitation to meet in the towers, if Nikolai is open to it."

"We will mention it to Nikolai," she offered, but Valentina had no intention of allowing him to step foot inside the towers until they learned more about their people.

Sergei eyed her abandoned tray with a frown. "That's all you're going to eat, Valechka?"

She took another sip of her tea. "I'm not hungry."

Yuri pulled her tray over to him and started working on her food. "She never eats in the morning."

Valentina shrugged, but her mouth curved in a smile. They

both knew she only kept up the pretense of filling her tray because he would eat it. She didn't even like whatever that grayish jelly thing was. Nothing edible should ever look like that.

Yuri picked it up and waved it at her, knowing she hated it. "You sure you don't want a taste?"

She wrinkled her nose at him. He chuckled and shoved it into his mouth.

While Yuri was eating, Valentina picked up his tablet and began scrolling through the data. She needed to review her notes from her other investigation to confirm, but it was clear someone was stockpiling weapons. The only question was whether the attack yesterday was a result of her investigation or if they were trying to target Nikolai through her.

Sergei leaned forward. "You've discovered something?"

Valentina glanced over at him, mildly disconcerted with how easily Sergei could read her.

"A possible connection," she admitted, focusing again on the tablet. "We're going back to the meeting site after Yuri is finished stuffing his face. I want to check a few things out."

"Lars and I will join you," Sergei announced, pushing away his tray.

Yuri scowled. "No."

"I was not asking you," Sergei retorted, his shoulders tense and unyielding.

Yuri stood and leaned over the table. "Nikolai may have allowed you to stay, but you are not part of this investigation except by my leave. I will not bring a potential liability along with us."

"I will not allow Valentina to go back there without suffi-cient protection," Sergei argued, standing to meet Yuri's threat.

"Enough." Valentina pressed her hands on the table and pushed herself up. "Sergei, you do not have any rights here beyond those which Nikolai has extended to you. If he has ordered you to accompany us, so be it, but this is Yuri's investigation. You *will* follow his orders. Otherwise, you know where to find the exit."

Sergei's jaw clenched, and she knew he was inwardly battling the urge to argue Yuri's competency. Sergei and Yuri had always been in competition with each other, and she was relying upon that now. Even if part of her wanted Sergei to remain, he needed to leave. There was no way he'd agree to remain and fall under Yuri's command.

He held her gaze. "If that is your wish, I will do my best to follow Yuri's orders."

Valentina stared at him, completely stunned. Her mouth opened, but she immediately closed it, unsure of how to respond. Surely, what happened between them last night wasn't the reason for his agreement. What in the world had Nikolai said to him?

Eyeing him warily, she snatched up her cup. "I need a refill."

Without waiting for a response, she escaped from the table and Sergei's all-too-perceptive gaze.

———

SERGEI WATCHED Valentina hastily retreat to the drink station. He'd surprised her, but then again, he'd expected that. If her intent was to drive him away, she was in for a lot more surprises. Holding her in his arms last night had only reinforced his decision. No matter what happened, he wasn't going to walk away from her again. Last night had been the first few moments of happiness he'd had in three years. He had to believe she felt it, too, or she never would have fallen asleep in his arms. Part of her must still trust him. He just needed to find a way to get her to admit it, and for that, he needed time.

Sergei had no intention of following Yuri's orders if they countermanded his primary objective, but he'd go along with it for now. He was going to have to do something about Yuri though. His former friend had gotten a little too close to Valentina over the past several years. Just watching their brief interaction at breakfast had shown him that much, even without Nikolai's comments.

"Stay away from her, Sergei," Yuri warned in a low voice. "If you play this game with her, I will end you."

"I am not leaving," Sergei replied, determined to make his position clear. "Nikolai told me the truth last night."

"Truth is only a matter of perspective," Yuri snapped, pushing away from the table. "You don't know any of us anymore."

Sergei watched Yuri walk over to Valentina and press his hand against her back in an obvious gesture of affection. He leaned in close and whispered something in her ear. She nodded, and they headed out of the room together.

Lars blew out a breath. "Well, that went well. Looks like you pissed off both of them."

"Only Yuri," Sergei replied.

Valentina had been too confused by his presence to really get angry. She was always so pliant when she was sleepy. Her reaction last night was proof of that. He'd most likely need to rely on as many devious tricks as possible if he was going to win her back. Valentina still cared for him; she just didn't want to. The game between them was about to shift dramatically, and her reactions were always so stimulating.

Lars frowned. "You look far too pleased about something."

"An intriguing possibility, my friend," Sergei murmured.

"Something tells me I don't want to know," Lars

muttered, taking another bite of his food. "I don't think Yuri's going to agree to your help. How do you want to handle this?"

"Valentina did not openly object," Sergei said in a quiet voice. "She is wary about me being here, but she didn't outright refuse. I'm still learning their dynamic though. It's far different than what I expected. I need to see the three of them interact more to figure out how to handle the situation."

"You know, I see the allure," Lars admitted. "Valentina wearing all that weaponry was pretty damn hot."

"You have no idea," Sergei said with a grin and clapped him on the back. "Come. We need to visit Nikolai and cause more trouble."

Lars sighed and pushed away his tray. "I'm not going to be happy if that was my last meal. This little visit has reminded me why I enjoy living in the towers."

———

VALENTINA PICKED up Yuri's tablet again and walked over to the couch. If he was determined to have this out here and now, she could at least get a little work done. She sprawled out across the length of the couch and placed the tablet in her lap.

"Nikolai," Yuri called out, banging on his bedroom door.

"If you break it down, you'll be the one to repair it," she reminded him, taking another sip of tea and pulling up the surveillance videos from the day before.

"You both sleep like the dead," Yuri retorted, still banging on the door.

She shrugged, knowing he was right. If she wasn't such a sound sleeper, Sergei never would have caught her unaware last night. In all fairness, though, he was one of the few who could. "With you nearby, why should we not? I sleep lightly enough when I must. A girl needs her beauty sleep."

Yuri snorted but continued pounding. "Nikolai, if you do not get out of bed, I will drag you out."

"I'm coming," Nikolai replied, his voice muffled. The door opened a moment later, and Nikolai staggered out, shirtless and fastening his pants. "What the hell do you want? I just went to bed two hours ago."

"You did not tell us Sergei remained here," Yuri snapped, crossing his arms over his chest.

Nikolai walked over to the couch and motioned for Valentina to scoot over. He sat down and pulled her back over until she was sprawled halfway across his lap. She cuddled against him, enjoying their morning ritual. Yuri had always been the annoying older brother type, whereas she enjoyed a more intimate relationship with Nikolai. He was far more affectionate, which only helped to reinforce their subterfuge.

She settled back and offered him her tea, and he took a sip before handing it back.

"It was late. I was hoping we could have this conversation after I had a chance to get some sleep." Nikolai wrapped his arms around her. "Did you sleep well, Valya?"

"Somewhat," Valentina admitted, taking another sip and continuing to study the air surveillance on the tablet. She wasn't about to admit her interrupted sleep was because of Sergei. They both probably knew, but they wouldn't dare ask her directly.

Pressing a button to switch to the thermal imaging view, she started to watch the feed again. The attackers must have used technology to camouflage their movements because nothing was showing up.

"This is unacceptable, Nikolai," Yuri declared, pacing the length of the small room. "We agreed we would all decide who would be brought into our circle. Sergei has proven to be unreliable."

Nikolai sighed. "We've had this conversation before. I do not believe as you do. Sergei left for his own reasons. I do not agree with them, but he has never betrayed us."

"We have different opinions of what constitutes betrayal," Yuri argued. "He also said you agreed to allow him to work with us on the investigation. Tell me he is lying."

Nikolai traced his thumb along her side, a nervous gesture she chose to ignore. Valentina was determined not to get involved in this argument unless she had no choice. As it was, she had mixed feelings about the whole thing.

"I agreed to accept his help," Nikolai said, shifting her slightly and reaching for her tea again. "He has contacts within OmniLab who can facilitate our investigation into the attacker's identity. I would not leave Valentina a target longer than necessary."

"Valentina will be protected," Yuri declared.

She stiffened. "I can protect myself."

"Indeed," Nikolai murmured, pressing a kiss against her shoulder. "I also believe it will do much in the way of good-will between our people and theirs to work together."

Yuri paused in his pacing. "It has possibilities, but Sergei does not need to be involved. We can coordinate with his companion instead. Send Sergei back to the towers to count nails."

Valentina bit her lip to keep from smiling. Apparently, Yuri hadn't enjoyed reading Sergei's construction notes any more than she had.

A knock at the door interrupted them. Yuri walked over to the door and opened it, his shoulders tensing. She sighed. Of course it was Sergei. As long as he was in their camp, he'd cause trouble. At least there was a small measure of comfort knowing he got under Yuri's skin too.

Nikolai leaned in close and whispered, "We could both go back to bed and leave them to it."

She grinned and took her tea back from him. "Do you really think we'll be able to sleep through a battle between them?"

"I suppose not," he agreed with a sigh. "Let him in, Yuri."

"He is not alone," Yuri said, his voice a low growl.

"Let them both in," Nikolai snapped. "We have accepted their help. We might as well make use of it."

Yuri stepped aside to allow Sergei and Lars to enter the room. Sergei reached over to grab a chair, flipping it around, and sat down on it backward so he was facing her and Nikolai. She glanced over at him, noting the way his uniform fit over his muscular body. His sleeves were rolled up, showing a hint of his strong forearms.

His eyes warmed at her perusal, and he nodded toward the tablet in her lap. "You mentioned you discovered a possible connection. What was it?"

Valentina glanced down at the tablet again. "Regina said some weapons are missing from a recently delivered shipment. She's trying to trace it down, but they match with Yuri's list of possible weapons used in the attack."

Yuri frowned and reached over to take his tablet from her. He scrolled through the information, studying it.

Nikolai squeezed her waist. "What else, Valya?"

"I was near Sofia's camp the other day investigating a rumor about another missing shipment of weapons. That's why I was able to get to Ariana so quickly when she was abducted." She paused, wishing she'd had an opportunity to fully debrief her contact. Unfortunately, he'd gone back underground to avoid suspicion and she wouldn't be able to reach him for at least a few more days. "It cannot be a coincidence that two shipments have gone missing so close together. I need to reach out to my contacts in different camps to find out if there are others, but it will take time. Peter, Lena, or one of the other chairmen in the area may be conducting their own investigations and trying to keep it quiet."

Sergei frowned. "Are you suggesting a mutiny of sorts?"

She shrugged. "I don't know. The number of missing weapons isn't small. If other camps are missing weapons too, that could indicate a larger problem. To start, I need to go back and trace down that rumor. If there is a planned rebellion, I don't believe it's originating from our camp."

"Do what you can to reach out to your contacts and find out what they know," Nikolai said, his arm tightening around her waist. "I am all for being cautious, but we cannot afford an all-out rebellion or another incident like the one yesterday. I will keep your investigation quiet, but I intend to reach out to Peter and share some information about our theft. I have a better relationship with him than Lena, and if he knows anything, I'll find out."

Yuri continued studying the tablet. "It's our best lead for now, but we need to consider other possibilities. I am not willing to write off our camp's involvement completely."

Valentina lifted her head to regard him. "What do you mean? Did the security analysis reveal something else?"

"Not yet. We simply don't have enough proof either way. Our camp knew about the meeting location because they prepared the site. Who else knew?"

She frowned, and Nikolai stroked her side again. Sergei's gaze lowered to Nikolai's hand and then met hers. From the meaningful glint in his eyes, Sergei was telling her he would be touching her again—soon. She took a long drink of tea, debating whether to switch to something stronger. How was she supposed to concentrate when he was this close and looking at her like that? Maybe it had been a bad idea to admit she and Nikolai weren't lovers.

"My people knew," Lars admitted. "I don't believe they were responsible though. We tend to use energy attacks against each other. Our stores of weapons aren't as extensive as yours."

Valentina shook her head. "It wasn't OmniLab. Our people collected empty casings from the site yesterday. The tactics and weapons were ours."

"That may be another avenue to explore," Sergei mused and drummed his fingertips on his arm. "If we study their tactics and approach, we may be able to detect similarities."

She tilted her head, intrigued by the idea. "What are you thinking?"

"We were trained by the same people," Sergei explained. "Ariana mentioned that when she met you, she was reminded of me. It's possible we may get some clues to the attacker's identity by studying how they approached the site, set up their ambush, and escaped."

Valentina stood and walked over to the large monitor on the wall. She turned it on and pulled up the map they had used to develop their plan.

"You may be on to something," she acknowledged and pointed to a few areas north of the clearing. "The shooters were firing upon us from here."

Sergei stood and approached her, placing his hand against her back. With his free hand, he pressed a few areas of the screen, shifting the view. "Why did you choose to meet up on the hill? Your sniper teams were at a tactical disadvantage."

"Because you know our tactics and we needed a low-tech solution," she confirmed, highlighting the areas where they'd originally planning on meeting. "We had first placed them here but moved them when we decided to plant the electrical wind pulses."

"The dust storm was clever," he admitted, tracing a small pattern against her back with his thumb. The movement brought back memories from when they'd been in his quarters. She couldn't help the small shiver that went through her, his nearness once again scattering her thoughts. He gave her a knowing smile but didn't pull his hand away.

"Our Valentina is very clever about *some* things," Yuri said with a scowl. He reached over to press a button on the map, reverting it back to the ambush view. "The shooters would have needed to know about our location change, get into position without alerting our people, and arrange an exit strategy before our surveillance aircraft moved into the area. That's not an easy feat to accomplish without leaving a trace."

Valentina stepped away from Sergei, needing the distance to focus her thoughts.

"If I had been the one to set up the ambush, I would have placed my people here," she said and highlighted another area further to the west. "There is more cover, and it would be easier to escape without detection. Why did they choose the other location?"

Yuri frowned. "They must not be as skilled with a long-distance weapon. Your location would be better tactically, but not as many would be able to take the shot."

She took Yuri's tablet from him and pulled up the list of names in the area. There were simply too many suspects and not enough concrete evidence to point them in any particular direction. If their attackers had chosen a more challenging location for their attack, she could eliminate some of these people based upon their skill level. As it was, they had no way of knowing if their location choice was based upon their lack of skill or simply a diversionary tactic to redirect attention elsewhere.

Nikolai stood and walked over to her. "Yuri, you should head back out to the meeting site and attempt to recreate the ambush with Sergei and Lars. We can run scenarios based on your findings to determine if there are similar tactics described within our databases. I will reach out to Peter while you are gone. Valentina can remain here and work with Regina to trace the missing weapons."

"I will do no such thing," Valentina declared and turned away. She knew what Nikolai was up to, and she wasn't going to put up with it. Not from him or anyone else.

"Valya," Nikolai began, placing his hand on her arm to stop her, "they were targeting *you*. Going back out into the open is not the wisest course of action."

"No," she argued, pulling away from him. "Do not start with me on this, Nikolai. I am going with Yuri. If my presence draws them out, we can have this resolved by lunchtime. I will not sit here in camp hiding from these people. We have the advantage right now because they have already shown their hand. I intend to use it."

Nikolai swore under his breath, but she ignored him and headed to her room. She grabbed her bag, tossing in some of her gear and a few more weapons for good measure. Yuri walked into her room, and she flung a knife in his direction. It hit her target with a *thunk*, embedding itself into the wall. He glanced at it and grinned. "You could not even wait until we started arguing?"

"I was trying to save time," she said, turning away to find her UV-protective gear.

Yuri laughed. "Valya, Nikolai has a point."

She unsheathed another blade, balancing it in her hand. "I can show you my point, if you wish."

He held up his hands but didn't stop grinning. "I told him I would talk to you, but I did not say I would commit suicide."

She laughed and sheathed her knife. "Fine. Hand me my weapon."

He yanked it from the wall and walked over to her, holding it out hilt first. "Nikolai and I both wish to keep you safe, but it's your choice. If I were you, I wouldn't want to sit in camp either. Besides, if you decide to come along, you will most likely keep me from killing Sergei." He paused and added, "I am not sure if that is a good thing or not. Maybe you should stay here after all."

Valentina checked the tip of her blade. If people kept irritating her, she'd have to get new knives soon. "Sergei's perspective may be valuable. He's worked with many of the people in the area. He may recognize something."

"Perhaps," Yuri relented. "Do you mind if I play with him though?"

She arched an eyebrow. "What do you have in mind?"

He walked up to her, wrapped his arm around her waist, and bent down to kiss her neck. "We could see how long it takes for him to lose his mind."

She laughed and pushed him away. "You changed your mind about committing suicide already?"

"Ah, but Valya, some things might be worth dying for," he teased.

"You are a horrible flirt, and the answer is no," she retorted, zipping her bag closed. "Come. Let's go find some people to kill. Then you can play with them."

# CHAPTER TWELVE

VALENTINA FINISHED WALKING the ambush site, her eyes gravitating toward the ground where Sergei had nearly lost his life. She glanced at him across the clearing where he and Lars were searching for clues. He must have sensed her gaze on him because he lifted his head and turned in her direction. Even from this distance, the energy between them was magnetic. Forcing herself to turn away, she headed up to the area where Yuri was crouched and began to study the ground. She couldn't think about Sergei now or she might fall into his arms again.

She spoke into her headset, "Find anything?"

Yuri shook his head. "Not yet."

Valentina scanned the length of the clearing again. It was all a matter of perspective and shifting her viewpoint to a different one. She walked away from the clearing, determined to recreate the scenario in her head.

Sergei jogged up to her, slowing his pace to match hers. "Did you think of something?"

Valentina glanced over at him and nodded, not altogether

surprised he'd picked up on her intent. "Play this out with me. Where would we hide our vehicles if we were going to ambush this site?"

Sergei's gaze swept over the area. He motioned for her to follow before climbing up some rocks. She started up after him, testing each rock for stability before moving to the next one. At their highest point, Sergei stopped and studied the area. He pointed to an area in the distance where some abandoned buildings had collapsed, creating a convenient place to hide. "It would be a hike, but that would be my top choice. It's outside the range of our immediate surveillance."

She frowned. "Our people should have checked it out when they placed the pulses."

"We should take another look," Sergei suggested and held out his hand to her. She accepted it, following him down the rocks and toward the ruins.

Yuri spoke over the headset, "Where are you going?"

"Sergei and I are going to check out the abandoned ruins."

"Lars and I will meet you there," Yuri replied, not bothering to mask the irritation in his voice.

Sergei grinned at her. "He does not want you to be alone with me."

"I heard that," Yuri snarled. "And no, I do not."

Valentina sighed and shook her head. If Sergei kept provoking Yuri, it would soon get ugly. She pulled her hand out of Sergei's grasp. He glanced at her but didn't make any other moves toward her.

They walked in silence the rest of the way, slowing their pace as they approached the ruins. Valentina kept her eyes cast downward, scanning the ground and looking for any sign someone had been there. She walked around one of the buildings which appeared to have once been some type of two-story commercial outpost. The entire top floor was mostly gone and collapsed inward. The bottom floor didn't appear to be faring much better.

She was about to move to the next building when she noticed a piece of scrap metal leaning against a wall. Its placement was a little too convenient.

Crouching down, she peered between the metal and wall to find it blocking a doorway. The room behind it would have enough space for at least a person to hide, if not a speeder.

Valentina started to reach for the large piece of scrap metal to move it, but a hand grabbed hold of it. She glanced up at Sergei.

"I have it, Valechka."

She moved away, and he lifted the deteriorated metal easily, placing it to the side. Pulling out a flashlight from her utility belt, she shined it around the room. It was larger than she had expected. This might be what they were looking for.

She gripped the edge of the wall and stepped down into the building. The neighboring walls had collapsed, but there was enough room to hide several people and their speeders. Sergei crouched down, studying the floor.

"These markings are recent," he stated, trailing his light over the pattern. "There were at least two speeders here. The tire marks belong to our vehicles—not OmniLab."

Valentina walked over and picked up an empty hydrating pack. It was the same type the Coalition produced. She tossed it to Sergei, who caught it easily with one hand.

"This was definitely left by our people, but this was very sloppy," she said, looking around the room again. "The scrap metal was too convenient, they left trash behind, and chose a poor shooting location. How could someone this disorganized have evaded our air surveillance?"

Lars's voice came over the headset, "What exactly did you use to create the dust storm?"

"Why? What are you thinking?" Sergei asked, his tone more curious than suspicious.

"Could whatever you have used made the dust heat enough to affect the thermal imaging? Maybe it wasn't their technology that masked their retreat."

Valentina frowned. She hadn't even considered the possibility. "You suspect our own devices worked against us?"

"It's a thought," Lars said.

"If that's the case, we may be able to discover more by viewing earlier or later surveillance feeds," Yuri suggested, moving into the room with Lars right behind him.

Valentina could kick herself for her stupidity. She'd been so focused on the potential threat from the towers, she'd ignored other dangers much closer to home.

She calculated the distance in her head. "If they moved quickly, it would have taken them less than ten minutes to get into and out of their firing positions from here. Once the dust storm kicked up, that would have been more than enough time for them to retreat."

Sergei frowned. "You had no way of knowing, Valentina."

"I should have," she snapped, moving to climb back out of the ruins. She studied the ground outside trying to search for any indication of the direction they'd gone. If they had moved in after their crew planted the pulses, they wouldn't have been detected. "Not only did I manage to cover their retreat, but the dust storm removed all traces of their vehicles."

"Valya," Yuri began, grabbing her arm. "Your plan was a good one. Our scouts should have located this hideaway."

She pulled away from him. "No, Yuri. This is unacceptable. Neither one of us would have tolerated such a mistake from any of our people."

"I did not catch it either," he argued. "Stop kicking yourself and focus."

Valentina nodded, recognizing the wisdom in his words. She could beat herself up later, but they needed to find these people. She closed her eyes and took a steadying breath, trying to put herself into the attackers' mindset.

"Let's assume they did not have the skill to make a long-distance shot," she began, the words clarifying what they knew about the shooters. "They also lacked the discipline to do more than make a cursory attempt at hiding this location and did not bother cleaning up after themselves."

"Keep going," Yuri encouraged.

She opened her eyes and began to pace the length of the building, the movement helping to sharpen her thoughts. "They were not experts at infiltration, but they were able to put a competent plan into place after we changed our meeting site at the last minute. Our people should have noticed them or their tracks when they came out to bury the electrical wind pulses, so they must not have been here yet."

Yuri nodded. "We did not come back out to check the devices because OmniLab already had drones in the air. That left them with a very narrow window to get into position."

"We know at least two people were involved in the shooting itself," Sergei added, "which means they would have needed additional support from a remote location for the plan to work."

She nodded at him, a sick feeling in her stomach. "Someone from our camp must have been involved, either on the pulse crew or by providing information about the meeting site. We didn't share information with any other camps. Nikolai wanted to keep the details quiet until after the meet."

The potential implication struck her, and she swore. They'd left Nikolai unattended. If they had someone in their camp with a vendetta against Nikolai, this would be the perfect opportunity for them to act upon it. Without another word, she turned and ran in the direction of the vehicles. If anything happened to him, she'd never forgive herself.

———

VALENTINA RACED into the camp with Yuri and Sergei right behind her. Nikolai hadn't been answering her calls, and she was in a near panic. She threw her unwieldy helmet to the side and headed directly for their quarters, knowing Yuri would check Nikolai's office first. She shoved open the door to find Nikolai wiping his hands with a cleaning cloth, a look of irritation and disgust on his face. His eyes widened in surprise at the sight of her, but she ignored it and threw herself at him.

"Valya," he murmured, taking a small step back to brace himself as her weight crashed into him. He wrapped his arms around her and pressed a kiss against her hair.

"You idiot," she grumbled against his chest and then peered up at him. "Why didn't you answer my calls?"

He frowned down at her. "I must have left my commlink in my office. Why didn't you call dispatch?"

"I see you're still alive," Yuri acknowledged.

"Yes, but Regina is not," Nikolai replied, gesturing behind him. "She's in my room."

Valentina pulled back to peer into Nikolai's bedroom. Regina's body was sprawled face down on his floor, a large puddle of blood pooling beneath it. She gripped Nikolai even tighter and snarled, "That *suka* tried to kill you?"

"While I was trying to get back to sleep, no less," Nikolai muttered, which explained his annoyance. Nikolai didn't enjoy being woken up any more than she did. "Between Yuri pounding on my door and people trying to kill me, I might as well forget sleep and get on with my day."

"That's why she made it a point to tell me about the missing weapons this morning," Valentina said, resting her head against Nikolai's chest again and listening to his heartbeat. She wasn't willing to let him go just yet. "She would have seen Yuri's initial security assessment, which mentioned the type of weapons used in the shooting. She must have suspected I would go out with Yuri to the ambush site to investigate and leave you here unattended. We didn't call dispatch because we didn't know who was involved." She lifted her head to look at Nikolai and added, "I am sorry, Kolya. I failed you."

He chuckled. "That's not possible, Valya. I can still take care of myself. I just prefer having you around."

Valentina cupped Nikolai's face and stood on her toes to press a chaste kiss against his lips. "You are the most important of all of us."

"I disagree," he whispered, leaning down and resting his forehead against hers. She smiled up at him.

"Well, it's too bad we can't question her," Yuri muttered, nudging at Regina's lifeless body with his boot.

Sergei sprawled out on the couch, seemingly unmindful about the dead body in the other room. "Did she say anything to you?"

"No," Nikolai said with a frown. "I hadn't yet fallen asleep. I heard a noise and saw the gun. My knife was already in the air before I thought about it." He sighed and added, "It's too bad. I would have taken my time killing her."

"That is a shame," Sergei agreed, reaching over to grab an unopened hydrating pack from the table. "Maybe next time."

Valentina wrinkled her nose. She hated that Sergei was right. There would always be another assassination attempt, especially as Nikolai's power increased. This one had been too close, and she was more than a little shaken. When the world around you became crazy, interjecting a bit of dark humor could keep you sane. "I am not cleaning up the blood this time. It's Yuri's turn."

"I did not kill her," Yuri argued. "Nikolai can do it. He made the mess. Or better yet, have Sergei do it."

"Have a grunt do it," Sergei suggested, taking a swig from the hydrating pack. "Is there anything stronger to drink around here? Some food might be nice too."

"There are a couple of bottles in the cooler," Valentina offered. "Are the rest of you hungry? They probably finished serving lunch, but I can see what I can find."

"Food would be good," Yuri agreed. "You know what I like."

"I'm also a bit hungry," Nikolai admitted. "Yuri, stop kicking at her. You might damage my knife. That blade is one of my favorites."

"I keep forgetting how scary you guys can be," Lars said from the doorway.

Valentina and the rest of them turned to stare at him. Her mouth curved upward in a smile. If her brief glimpse into life in the towers was any indication, it was a wonder he'd adapted as well to living on the surface with them. "Does that mean you're not hungry?"

Lars chuckled and shook his head. "I must have lived among you guys for too long. I'm hungry too."

She pulled away from Nikolai and winked at Lars. Sometimes, witnessing the precariousness of life made you cognizant of your most basic human needs. "I thought so."

———

VALENTINA SPREAD out lunch for everyone on the table and picked up an open-faced sandwich. They had gotten a couple of their newer recruits to clean up Regina's body.

Other than a slight disinfectant smell, they hadn't done a bad job.

Sergei wrapped his arm around her waist and planted her in his lap. He grinned at her and said, "Nikolai got to hold you earlier. It's my turn."

She swatted at his hand but didn't move away. There wasn't enough seating in the room as it was, and she didn't particularly mind. This had been a frequent game between them when Sergei had lived with them.

Yuri scowled at him but didn't object. Instead, he sat beside them on the couch and reached over to grab some food.

She took a bite of her sandwich. Before she could put it down, Sergei leaned forward and wrapped his hand around her wrist. Pulling it toward him, he took a bite of it and winked at her. She rolled her eyes.

"You are getting a little too comfortable over there, Sergei," Yuri warned.

"Yes, I am very comfortable," Sergei retorted, squeezing his arm around her midsection.

Valentina reached over to pick up another sandwich from the table and handed it to Sergei. "Eat and stop provoking Yuri."

"It's more fun to watch his face turn red," Sergei said with a grin before biting into his sandwich.

"We need to discuss our next steps," Nikolai began. "Obviously, we cannot discount the possibility of more traitors within our camp. Since I would rather not torture those who are loyal to me, I am open to suggestions."

"We don't have to torture all of them," Yuri suggested, swallowing another mouthful. "Pick one or two. If we make it memorable enough, the guilty parties will show their hand."

"Random torture, Yuri? We need to find you some new hobbies," Valentina said, reaching for her tea. She leaned back against Sergei and mused, "Speaking of which, you never told me how you handled Pavel and Sofia."

"Ah," Sergei murmured, running his thumb along her side. "Let's just say I made it clear I wouldn't tolerate anyone laying a hand on you again. Lars killed Sofia before I had a chance to make an example of her."

She glanced over at Lars. The blond man shrugged and said, "I'm not a fan of torture."

"It's a trait of many Omnis," Sergei explained. "They have more delicate sensibilities in the towers than those of us on the surface."

"That is a shame," Yuri acknowledged, taking another bite.

"It is," Sergei agreed.

"Scary motherfuckers," Lars muttered, shaking his head.

Valentina grinned. "Then how do your people extract the truth? It's too easy to trick technology."

"We use truth barriers," Lars explained. "It's an energy field our kind can hold. You can't lie when you're standing within it."

"Interesting," Nikolai murmured, leaning forward. "I would love to see this in practice. Would your people be willing to provide a demonstration?"

"Possibly. Not all of us can do it, and it can be difficult to hold the shield for long periods of time. From what I've seen, you have over a hundred people here in this camp alone. If you could narrow down the suspect pool, we might be able to help you question them. I would suggest doing it back at the towers, however. My people will be wary about traveling to the surface, especially considering your camp's ties to the attack."

"I understand," Nikolai said, drumming his fingers on the arm of his chair. "Alec was kind enough to meet us in a neutral location. Your people have shown they are honorable, and the attack was clearly not their doing. I do not seem the harm in visiting these towers."

"No," Valentina declared, putting her sandwich and tea aside. "You will not go to the towers, Nikolai."

"I agree," Yuri said. "It is too risky."

Nikolai ignored their outburst. "Sergei, what are your thoughts?"

Valentina spun around to glare at Sergei. If he encouraged Nikolai to do this, she'd cut off his balls with her bluntest knife. Sergei searched her expression for a long moment and then sighed. "Do not ask me this, Nikolai."

"I need to know the dangers," Nikolai prompted.

"No!" Valentina stood and put her hands on her hips. "Nikolai, one of our own tried to kill you today. That was a threat we understood. We do not have the ability to protect ourselves from these powers. I will not see you walk into danger simply because you are curious."

Nikolai rose from his chair. "There is more to this than simple curiosity. I wish to know more about them, yes. But if we have an opportunity to include them in our investigation, it will do much to ease tensions. It was our people who fired upon theirs too. They have as much right to know the truth."

"Figure out another way," she demanded. "I cannot lose you."

"Valya," Nikolai began, his expression softening. He took a step toward her, but she backed away from him.

"I mean it, Nikolai," she said in an unyielding tone. "I will not play this game with you. Do not push me on this."

She turned away and went into her room, slamming the door behind her.

———

SERGEI FROWNED at the closed door, startled by Valentina's

unexpected outburst. She'd always been headstrong and passionate, but something more was going on.

"This is your fault, Sergei," Yuri said in a conversational tone and took another bite of his sandwich.

"What are you talking about?" Sergei demanded, irritated all over again. He was tempted to shove that sandwich down Yuri's throat. "I did not take sides."

"She has been all over the place since you reappeared," Yuri said, his mouth still full of half-eaten sandwich. He finished chewing and swallowed, reaching for another one.

Lars cleared his throat. "I think this is probably a good time to check in with the towers and grab another hydrating pack. I'll just... leave you to talk." He stood and slipped out of the room before anyone could say anything else.

Nikolai sighed and sank back down into his chair. "I'm afraid Yuri is correct. Valentina is more concerned about my welfare than usual."

"Explain," Sergei demanded.

Yuri gestured at Nikolai. "You tell him. If I do it, I might end up taking a blade to him."

"Valentina is worried about losing more of her family," Nikolai explained. "She already lost you once. Your reappearance has brought all those concerns back to the forefront of her mind. Regina didn't help matters either."

"I see," Sergei said quietly. "That is regrettable, but I am not going away again."

Yuri snorted. "You fuck her again last night and suddenly you are here to stay?"

Sergei's eyes narrowed. "Watch it, Yuri. What may or may not have happened between us is none of your business."

Yuri tossed his sandwich down. "You don't think we all know? She was wearing a small arsenal this morning. I thought it was because of the ambush until I saw you in the dining hall. Then it all became very clear."

"Yuri," Nikolai warned. "Sergei is right. This is not our business."

"Fuck that," Yuri declared, standing up. "I warned you against this. You invited him here knowing this could happen."

"You know why I did it," Nikolai retorted.

"And look what has happened!" Yuri gestured to Valentina's closed door. "If your actions drive her away, Nikolai, our agreement will be at an end. I will go with her. Choose your side quickly because I am done with this."

Without waiting for a response, Yuri headed out of the room.

Nikolai gripped his glass tightly and threw it against the wall, shattering it into a thousand pieces. Sergei frowned, watching the normally stoic man swear loudly while pacing back and forth. He finally turned to Sergei, pointing at him. "You *will* fix this with her or get the hell out of my camp. I thought this might be a chance to correct the past, but they are both right. I will not lose them because you were an idiot three years ago and broke her heart."

Sergei stood up. "I still love her, Nikolai. I am not leaving her again."

"We *all* love her!" Nikolai shouted. "The only difference is that she loved you best, and you fucking left her. Fix it. Now." He turned and stormed out the same way Yuri had gone.

Sergei sighed. His time had run out. It wasn't ideal, but he didn't have much of a choice.

Sergei walked over to her bedroom door and hesitated. If he walked in, she'd likely throw a knife at him. Maybe more than one if her temper was hot enough. If he knocked, she'd probably ignore it. He lifted his hand, deciding to try the more conventional method first.

"Valentina? May I come in?" he asked through the door.

There was no response.

He pressed his back against the wall and reached over to push open the door, waiting for an attack that never came. A muffled sob sounded from her bed. His heart dropped into his stomach, and he rushed into the room to find her curled up on her side, clutching her pillow.

"Valechka," he murmured, crawling onto her bed and pulling her into his arms. "Shh. Please do not cry."

She turned her head against his chest and curled her hand into his shirt. He ran his hand over the silky softness of her hair, completely at a loss. He'd dealt with weeping women in the past, but Valentina was stronger than anyone he'd ever known. She was proof that women weren't the weaker sex, just the prettier one. He didn't know if her tears wounded him so deeply because it contrasted with her strength or if it was because of his feelings for her.

"What can I do to fix this, little dove?"

"I am not your little dove anymore," she grumbled against his chest.

He smiled, continuing to stroke her hair. "You have always been my little dove."

She sat up, wiping the tears from her eyes. "Go away, Sergei. I do not want you here."

He reached over to brush his hand against her cheek. "If you wish me to leave, I will go into the other room, but I am not leaving you again, Valechka. If you wish me to abandon my post at OmniLab to remain here with you, I will do so. If you wish to join me in the towers, I will make it happen."

"I do not want your promises," she said, pulling away from him.

"You have them anyway. I love you, Valechka."

"Do not say such things," she snapped, turning away and climbing off the bed.

"I will keep saying them until you believe me," he replied, standing and taking a cautious step toward her.

"Do not come near me, Sergei. I mean it," she threatened.

He ignored her and took another step in her direction. If he couldn't reach beneath the walls she'd built, she'd never allow him close enough again to try. "I have loved you since we were teenagers, Valechka. I love your insatiable curiosity and tendency to always get into mischief."

"Stop it," she ordered.

"I love your passion, your loyalty, and even your stubbornness," he said, advancing another couple of steps. "You are fearless, strong, and the most beautiful woman I have ever known."

"Stop saying these things!" she yelled.

"No," he told her, inches away from her and knowing she was about to snap. "I will always love you, and I know you still love me."

With an anguished cry, she withdrew a dagger and brought it down toward him. He grabbed her wrist, yanking it to him, and pressed the blade against his chest over his heart.

"Do it," he taunted. "It will change nothing. I will still love you until my last breath."

She gasped and opened her hand, allowing the blade to drop harmlessly onto the floor. Her eyes grew haunted, and she pulled away. "Why are you doing this?"

"I hurt you," he acknowledged. "I promised you once before that I would always be here for you, and I broke your trust. I understand why you don't want to believe me now."

She backed away from him again. "Please, stop. Don't do this to me, Sergei."

He continued to advance slowly, refusing to retreat. "I love you. I will keep proving it to you until my last breath."

Valentina continued to back up until she was pressed against the wall. Her eyes were wild, their stark panic wounding him even more. "Stop saying that! I cannot give you what you want!"

"You can," he urged, cornering her until there was nowhere else for her to run. "Say it, Valentina."

Sobbing into her hands, she dropped to her knees. "I do. I still love you, Seryozha. I've always loved you. But it hurts. It hurts so much. I don't *want* to love you anymore."

With a relieved sigh, Sergei dropped down beside her. He wrapped his arms around her once more, and she buried her face against his shirt, tears streaming down her face. He threaded his fingers through her hair and said, "I know, little dove. That's my fault. I broke your wings when I left you."

She continued to cry, and he murmured quiet reassurances against her hair. Her pain was heart-wrenching, and he was furious at Nikolai and Yuri for forcing him to push her to this point. None of this was necessary. He'd hurt her enough. If he thought he could survive without her, he would have done as Yuri wanted and left again. But the past three years had been empty without her in it. After having a taste of her again over the past few days, he couldn't go back. He needed her in his life. He always had.

Valentina sniffed and wiped away her tears, looking up at him with eyes that were more green than blue from her tears. He stroked her cheek, brushing away strands of chestnut hair that had escaped from her ponytail. He hadn't been lying to her. She was extraordinarily beautiful, and without doubt, the most sensual woman he'd ever known. But it was her passion for life, her mischievous and curious nature, and the tender heart she guarded so carefully that had made him fall so deeply in love with her.

In a voice that was quiet and unsure, she asked, "Why do you keep pushing me?"

Sergei pressed a gentle kiss against her lips. He wanted to erase all traces of sadness and uncertainty from her face, but that would take time. As it was, he needed to tread carefully or she would pull away from him even more.

"I ran out of time. I'm sorry I pushed you, but I needed you to admit how you still felt about me. You don't open up easily, Valechka. It was the only way I could get you to lower your guard and talk to me."

She frowned. "What do you mean you ran out of time?"

"Nikolai and Yuri are worried you may turn away from them," Sergei admitted, drawing her closer. She leaned against him, and he tightened his arms around her. She'd always felt so right in his arms, as though she'd been made for him. "Nikolai told me to fix things with you or leave his camp. I was worried if he forced me out, it would be even more difficult to convince you. I don't want to live my life without you in it, Valechka."

Valentina placed her hand directly over his heart and whispered, "I don't think I could truly kill you, not even if I were ordered. You have always been my weakness, Seryozha."

Hope surged within him, and his mouth curved upward. "I'm glad to hear it. You had me worried a few times."

A small smile played upon her lips, that mischievous glint entering her eyes once more. She moved her hand to the shoulder still covered by a bandage where she'd stabbed him. "I don't have a problem hurting you, though, especially when you are annoying."

Sergei wrapped his hand around her wrist and lifted her hand to brush a kiss against it. Her eyes softened at the gesture, and he said, "You could hurt me easily without weapons. You are the only one who has ever possessed that power."

She frowned. "Did you mean what you said about abandoning your post?"

"Yes," Sergei said immediately. He'd put duty first for too long, and he was determined to correct his mistake. He wanted his family back, no matter the cost. "If you wish me to remain here, I will turn over my position to someone else. I don't care where I am, so long as you are by my side."

"You enjoy commanding," she said, searching his expression. "I think too much has changed between all of us to fall back into old patterns. How can you think to share control with Nikolai and Yuri when you've been on your own for so long?"

"We were a family once," he reminded her gently. "And you have always been the heart of our family. We can find a common ground again. None of us are willing to lose you."

Valentina rested her head against his chest once more, lacing her fingers with his. Sergei knew she was still wary, but at least he was one step closer. He inhaled deeply, the subtle scent of her hair and skin teasing his nose like an intoxicating perfume. She always smelled of spices and something sweet, like the cookies she loved.

He placed a kiss against her hair. "Do you remember when we were still in training and you convinced Yuri to help break into the storeroom to get into the cookies? I believe you called it a 'training exercise'."

She smiled at the memory and nodded. "You helped me convince him. Nikolai didn't want any part of our scheming."

He chuckled. "Nikolai has always been a righteous bastard. He would have covered for us, though, if we had gotten caught."

"He would have," she agreed, glancing up at him again. "Why did you bring that up now?"

"We were taught to work together as a unit," he explained, determined to convince her they could make this work between them. "We each have our own strengths and weaknesses. Nikolai has always been the politician and negotiator. Yuri and I are more suited to strategy and tactics, doing whatever needs to be done to accomplish our goals. You, my dear Valechka, are a chameleon. You work in the shadows, taking on whatever role is necessary and helping all of us blend in. Without you, our group does not work."

"All of the parts are necessary to form a whole," she argued with a frown.

"To an extent, yes," he agreed. "But I believe the success of our unit is the reason our leaders have tried to select similar group dynamics to make up other units. What they failed to understand is that we are more than a unit. Your love turned us into a family, and that made us stronger."

Valentina fell silent for a long moment. "What if Regina was part of a similar unit?"

"What?"

She sat up a little straighter. "None of us suspected Regina, and we know she was working with others. What if she was part of a similar unit? She didn't have my exact same skillset, but we had a few similarities in our ability to blend in and avoid suspicion."

Sergei paused, surprised by the unexpected turn in the conversation. "That wasn't exactly where I was going with this, but you could be right. The two speeders we found may belong to soldiers, more like myself and Yuri. Which means there is at least a third person involved we don't know about."

"Someone with similar traits to Nikolai," she mused. "A politician or someone else making decisions. Regina was not a planner. She would have followed someone's orders."

"*You* are a planner," he reminded her, playing devil's advocate. "But I see your point. Trying to attack Nikolai was foolish and desperate. Regina should have known he was more than he appeared. Anyone in this camp would have, if they paid close enough attention. If Regina had been under orders to kill him, she may have attempted it without arguing the point."

"Unless the order was also a way to clean up loose ends," Valentina said with a frown. "The chances of the shooters surviving the ambush were slim. I had wondered about that. They had no way of knowing we would use the electrical wind pulses to cover their escape. What if someone sent Regina after Nikolai knowing she wouldn't be successful?"

Valentina stood and began to pace. Sergei couldn't help but grin. She was magnificent when she got like this. Determination and confidence emanated from her, and there was no mistaking her intelligence and drive. Too many people viewed her as little more than a decorative trophy. He was continuously amazed by her ability to transform into whatever role she wanted to play. Few people had the opportunity to see the real Valentina, and for those who did, well, it was usually the last thing they saw.

Sergei got to his feet, continuing to watch her. Her movements were brisk, but there was an underlying sensual grace to them that tempted him into trying to seduce her again. There was no way to know if she'd attack him if he tried, but her unpredictability always made things more interesting. Right now, he was definitely a fan of interesting.

Valentina paused and arched an eyebrow at him, her expression wary. His grin deepened, and he prowled toward her, wrapping his arms around her and pulling her against him. "You are irresistible when you get like this."

She huffed in exasperation. "We can play later. There are people to hunt."

He bent down, nuzzling her neck, and felt her tremble in his arms. Her neck had always been so sensitive. He nibbled on her earlobe and whispered, "We can make it quick, Valechka."

"I do not believe you," she retorted but tilted her head, giving him better access to kiss along her neck.

He slid a hand under her shirt and against her flat stomach, caressing the softness of her skin. Sergei heard her sharp intake of breath, and he smiled against her skin. He'd never get enough of this woman. Reaching down to unhook her belt, he said, "I am willing to try."

"You're a lousy liar," she whispered, running her hands up his chest and winding them around his neck.

"Only with you," he agreed, bending to claim her lips with his, intent on making her his all over again.

# CHAPTER THIRTEEN

VALENTINA WAS SPRAWLED on her stomach, her body deliciously sated. As she suspected, Sergei was a lousy liar. He was propped up on his arm looking down at her, his expression a little too smug. Once she managed to work up enough energy, she'd have to find a creative way to wipe that smirk off his face.

He ran his hand down her naked back. "There is something to be said for taking your time." She made a small noise of agreement. He chuckled and added, "You are quite agreeable when you are relaxed. I rather enjoy it."

"Keep talking," she murmured. "I will make you pay for it later."

He laughed, bending down to kiss her temple. "I rather enjoy that side of you too."

Despite herself, her mouth curved in a smile.

Someone pounded on the door, and she groaned, burying her face in her pillow.

"Who the fuck is that?"

"Yuri," she mumbled into her pillow. "He will keep banging until I come out."

"He can wait," Sergei said and kissed her shoulder. "I'm not finished with you yet."

Yuri kept pounding and called out, "Do not make me come in there and drag you out."

"If you wish to die, be my guest," Sergei shouted back and pushed off the bed. He grabbed his pants and began pulling them on.

"Great," she muttered. "You had to issue a challenge."

Before Sergei could respond, the door flung open. There was a brief pause and then Yuri said, "I will be happy to escort Sergei out of our camp if you are finished playing with him, Valya."

"I think Yuri has gotten more irritating over the years," Sergei stated casually, still fastening his pants. "Why haven't you killed him yet?"

Valentina yawned. All three of them had been walking in on her often enough over the years that it no longer phased her. She stretched, guessing it was time for her to get up and let them work out their issues. "Do what you wish, but do not get blood on my floor."

She climbed out of bed and headed toward the bathroom. The sound of a crash echoed from her room, but she ignored it and climbed into the small shower enclosure. Even though their water was recycled, distribution was timed to minimize resource consumption. She started lathering soap, holding off on pressing the button to activate the water while her thoughts drifted back to Regina again.

Yuri had probably already started tracing Regina's correspondences and known associates. Most likely, Regina would have hidden her tracks, or her accomplice would have done so. Yuri was good, but Sergei was better with network security and electronics. Maybe she should ask him to take another look.

In the meantime, she wanted to approach things from a

different direction, perhaps by identifying those who had the most to gain by taking Nikolai out of commission. It was possible they were targeting her directly in conjunction with an investigation, but it was much more likely that discrediting Nikolai was their ultimate goal.

Nikolai was one of more than a dozen chairpersons who comprised their leadership. He wasn't even close to being one of the most powerful, but that was largely due to his lack of experience. He was still fairly new to his position, but he garnered more allies and additional influence in their political arena every day.

There needed to be some benefit in eliminating Nikolai, either politically or from a personal standpoint. Otherwise, it didn't make sense. The trick would be narrowing down the list of suspects.

She could put together a list of possibilities, but sometimes plans could take years to come to fruition. If this was part of a long-term plan, it might be harder to detect the culprits. She wasn't willing to wait around, not when Nikolai's life was at stake. If each of them worked different angles simultaneously, something had to shake loose.

Valentina pressed the button, enjoying the relaxing sensation of the water cascading over her skin. That was one thing she'd enjoyed about her time in the towers: they had exceptional showers. Lifting her head to let the water rinse away the soap, she started considering who would be at the top of her list of suspects.

Another loud crash interrupted her thoughts, and she scowled. If the two idiots didn't kill each other, she might have to take matters into her own hands and do it for them. She shut off the water before her time expired and stepped out of the shower, wrapping a towel around herself before heading back into the bedroom.

Her trunk had been knocked over, along with a chair. The

small table she frequently used while working had been destroyed. Yuri and Sergei were rolling around on the floor, taking swings at each other. Yuri's shirt was torn, and Sergei was completely bare-chested. She paused for a moment to appreciate the view and then stepped over them to grab some clothing from her toppled trunk. Some things never changed.

"Enough!" Nikolai shouted from the doorway.

They all froze.

Nikolai stepped into the room, pointing at them. "Sergei, Yuri, get out. I want a word with both of you in my office."

The two men shoved away from each other. Sergei reached down to grab his shirt from the floor and pressed a quick kiss on her lips before heading out of the room.

Nikolai walked over to her, his expression wary. "Are you all right, Valya?"

She nodded, surveying the destruction in her room. "My furniture has seen better days. I had forgotten how messy the two of them could be when they worked out their issues."

"I'll have them clean it up," he offered. "I'm more concerned about you."

Valentina shrugged. "There is nothing to say."

Nikolai frowned. "You're still angry."

"Yes," she admitted, reaching down to find some clean clothing from the pile on the floor. At least they had enough sense not to touch her weapons. "I still don't want you to go to the towers, and I'm not happy about you giving Sergei an ultimatum. It wasn't your place to interfere, Kolya."

"I understand your concerns about going to the towers," Nikolai said, stepping around the fallen chair. "But if going there is the fastest way to resolve this threat and cement our alliance with OmniLab, I must do it."

She tossed her clothing onto the bed and turned to face him again. "You don't know if it'll resolve anything. It could cause more problems. You know what's at risk."

Nikolai sighed. "I spoke with Peter while you were busy working things out with Sergei, and he confirmed your suspicions. Additional weapons have gone missing from at least two other shipments, but he didn't have any details about the types or numbers. He suggested you work with Viktor to trace these shipments."

She wrinkled her nose. "I don't like Viktor's methods. He doesn't understand the definition of subtle. Besides, he spends more time flirting than focusing on business. I'll find them faster without his help."

"I would appreciate it if you considered it. Viktor is Peter's right hand. Working with him again would help deepen my relationships with Peter's contacts, especially if we're going to be here for any significant amount of time. Besides, Viktor will most likely provide you with information Peter hasn't shared with me."

"Fine," she agreed with a sigh. "I'll contact him later and set up a time to meet with him."

"Thank you," Nikolai said, his shoulders relaxing a fraction. "I'm concerned about the number of missing weapons. Even with the two shipments we already knew about, whoever is responsible has amassed a large arsenal. If some of our people are planning a rebellion, we must do what we can to suppress it immediately."

Valentina frowned, considering the implications. She'd hoped all of this was a result of a small group looking to branch out on their own, but if something larger and more sinister was at work, that could be disastrous. The idea that so many weapons were missing made her wonder if the culprits were better connected than she first assumed. "All of these missing weapons were taken from shipments in this area?"

"I believe so. If we move to the towers, it will be another opportunity to investigate the work crews to determine whether there's any truth to the possibility of a rebellion. The bulk of our forces in the area have ties to the new tower, either on the construction crew or harvesting resources. Between Pavel abducting Ariana and now these missing weapons, we need to clean up the mess quickly. Perhaps you can arrange to have Viktor meet you at the towers."

She blew out a breath. "You've already made up your mind about going."

Nikolai cupped her face and pressed a kiss against her forehead. "I'm sorry. Will you be able to do your duty even if you don't agree with me?"

"I need to get dressed," she said and turned away from him, hating that she didn't have a choice.

"Valya," he murmured, stepping up behind her and wrapping his arms around her. "If you were in my place, would you do any different?"

She didn't reply. Instead, she asked a different question that had been plaguing her. "Did you ask me to stay in the towers because you wanted me to work things out with Sergei?"

His arms tensed around her, but he didn't release her. "Yes."

"Then you never suspected him of betraying our people," she said, having already guessed the answer.

"No."

She pulled away from him. "Get out, Nikolai."

"Valya—"

She spun around to face him. "No. I am done. I told you things in confidence, and you used them against me. You manipulated me by playing upon my emotions."

"You still love him," Nikolai said, taking a step toward her. "He loves you too. Would you deny all of us a chance to have our family back together?"

"The end does not justify the means!" Valentina shouted,

her hands curling into fists. "I made peace with the past, Nikolai. You had no right to drag me back through all of this. Sergei and I are different people now."

"You can't tell me you're happy without him," he said in a quiet voice. "You will barely even look at another man."

"I do not need a man to be happy," she snapped. "Is that what this is about? Because I didn't jump into bed with either you or Yuri, you think I've been pining for Sergei all these years?"

"Are you telling me you haven't?" he retorted, beginning to show a faint sign of his usually tightly controlled temper. "Sergei left, and you retreated from both of us. You hold us at arm's length. Sergei comes back into your life, and you fall back into bed with him."

"I love all of you!" she yelled. "Sergei left, and my world fell apart. Do you think I would risk the same thing happening with either you or Yuri? How many more people do I need to lose before I learn my lesson? I wasn't willing to risk looking at either of you that way. You two matter to me more than anyone else. It would destroy me to lose you."

At Nikolai's startled look, she took a steadying breath and added, "I already lost Sergei. I knew I could handle losing him a second time if I didn't allow him back into my heart. It was just sex at first, but now I'm back where I was three years ago. I'm scared, Nikolai. If he didn't stay before, why would he stay now? I'm not strong enough to go through this again."

Nikolai fell silent, and he squeezed his eyes shut. "I am sorry. I erred badly. I didn't consider the ramifications or how this would negatively affect you. I only saw an opportunity to heal our family and bring Sergei back to us."

Valentina sat on the edge of her bed, suddenly weary. She hated arguing with him. "If you go to the towers, I will do my duty. I won't leave you without people you trust by your side."

He nodded and approached her. Reaching down, he took

her hand in his. "Please don't leave us, Valya. I know we don't always agree, but we all love you. I'm afraid if you left, you would leave a hole in all our hearts that we would never recover from."

Valentina looked up into his eyes, her heart clenching at the raw pain she saw. She'd seen that same hurt in her own reflection for years after Sergei had left, and she wouldn't allow him to suffer the same way. "I promise. I will not leave you, Kolya."

"Thank you," he whispered and bent down to press a kiss to her forehead before leaving the room.

———

VALENTINA LEANED BACK against the bench seat inside the caravan. It wasn't her preferred way to travel, but their group was too large to use faster modes of transport. In addition to Sergei, Nikolai, Yuri, and Lars, they'd brought five additional guards with them to the towers. They'd gone back and forth about which five were best suited, and Lars had offered to have each of them submit to the tower's version of a lie-detector test upon arrival. Nikolai was eager at the opportunity to get a closer look at these Omni abilities.

They'd kept their destination secret from all but the people within the caravan. Lars had made a secure transmission directly to Alec, with the express understanding their arrival needed to be kept quiet. The accompanying soldiers hadn't even been told where they were headed until they sat down in the caravan. Even so, Valentina couldn't shake the sense of foreboding that had come over her.

Nikolai wrapped his arm around her shoulder, drawing her against him. He kissed her temple and whispered, "Thank you for coming with me."

She rested her head against him. It was impossible to stay

angry at Nikolai for long. "If we don't arrive soon, I might be tempted to get out and push."

Nikolai chuckled, giving her a slight squeeze. "We're only a few minutes away now."

Sergei leaned forward in his seat directly across from them. He glanced at Nikolai and then back at her, his expression unreadable. "The entrance area will be mostly cleared, except for necessary personnel. Alec will be meeting us there, along with the others we discussed. Lars has agreed to act as your host. You'll be staying with him instead of in the construction tower."

Nikolai turned to Lars. "We appreciate your generosity."

Lars nodded. "It's the least I can do. As Valentina can attest, I have plenty of room. That portion of the towers is more secure than many others, so it should suit your needs."

"I will be staying there as well for the duration of this trip," Sergei said, his eyes focused on her and making his intent clear.

Valentina lowered her head, gazing up at him through her lashes. "Wouldn't you be more comfortable in your own quarters, Sergei? I am sure Nikolai, Yuri, and Lars will have everything well in hand. I do not imagine your... services will be needed."

"I will have to provide you with a demonstration," he replied, the faintest trace of a smile on his lips as he slowly perused her up and down. "I have many... *skills* that may come in handy. Besides, after spending the past several years on a hard cot, I am looking forward to enjoying a softer place to sleep."

She made a great show of sighing. "Very well. But I must warn you, Yuri snores. I have heard many complaints from people sharing a room with him."

Yuri grinned and stretched out his long legs in the cramped space. "Ah, Valya, if he complains, so much the better. You know I tend to kill those who cause trouble. We shall see whether Sergei makes it through the night."

"Perhaps I will find a different bunkmate," Sergei suggested with a wry grin. "Otherwise, Lars will have to help me dispose of a body."

"Scary motherfuckers," Lars muttered.

Valentina lowered her gaze again and bit her lip, practically shaking in silent laughter. Nikolai squeezed her shoulder, and she lifted her head to see he was equally amused. It had been too long since they'd all been together like this and teasing each other.

The caravan halted a moment later, and their humor faded away as their training kicked in. Yuri and the guards exited first, followed by Lars and Sergei. Valentina stood, keeping her weapon hand free as she jumped out of the caravan. Nikolai followed behind her, placing his hand on her back as he led her toward Alec and the small group that had assembled.

"Welcome to OmniLab," Alec greeted them with a warm smile. "I wish the circumstances were better, but I'm pleased you could join us."

Nikolai nodded and replied in kind, but Valentina was only partly listening. She'd gone into sentry mode and was busy identifying all points of egress and evaluating each of the individuals in the room, looking for weapons and assigning them a point value according to their potential threat level.

In addition to Alec, the same individuals who were at the original meeting site were present, along with several other people. At least five of them most likely had some sort of supernatural talent, while the others appeared more comfortable with traditional weaponry. She placed her non-weapon hand on her leg, lifting all five knuckles to mark her count. Yuri gave an almost indiscernible nod, indicating he'd identified the same ones.

Alec gestured to two of the men she didn't recognize. "This is Marcus Staghorn and Devan Alivette, two members of our High Council. They have agreed to provide you with the demonstration you requested."

One of the men regarded Valentina for a long moment. "You're the young woman who saved my daughter."

Valentina blinked at him, taking a fraction of a second to note some similarities between him and Ariana. "We saved each other."

The slightest trace of a smile crossed his features, making him appear much younger. She had the impression it wasn't a gesture he was used to making. "Ariana doesn't tell the story quite the same way, but whatever the truth, I want to thank you for your efforts in rescuing her."

Valentina nodded.

The two men moved to stand beside the wall, and Alec gestured to a small mark etched on the floor. "Once someone stands here, we will activate the truth barrier. They won't even notice it, and the entire process is completely painless. You can ask them whatever questions you wish, and they won't be able to lie. I would suggest making your questions as specific as possible to make sure they aren't able to circumvent the truth."

Valentina studied the mark on the ground. It appeared fairly innocuous, but so was a weapon if you didn't know its true purpose.

Sergei glanced over at Alec. "How far will this barrier extend?"

"We'll keep it contained to just the person standing over the mark. No one else in the room will be affected."

Nikolai nodded and started to take a step forward, but Valentina grabbed his arm. Switching to their native language, she whispered, "What are you doing?"

He arched his brow, letting her know he wasn't about to

ask his men to do something he wasn't willing to do himself. She narrowed her eyes and released him, walking over to the mark herself. There was no way she was going to allow these people to use their powers on him.

"Valya," Yuri began, but she cut him off with a wave of her hand. Nikolai couldn't afford to lose either one of them, but she would have the most latitude. If Devan Alivette was truly grateful she'd helped rescue his daughter, she was about to find out.

Her eyes met Sergei's from across the room. He didn't look pleased with having her stand there, but after a brief hesitation, he gave her a small reassuring nod. She relaxed a fraction, suspecting he'd be one of the first ones to drag her off if there was a threat. It was a little disconcerting how quickly she was starting to trust him again.

Alec glanced over at the two men along the wall. "Go ahead, gentlemen."

A moment later, a strange sensation flowed over her skin, reminiscent of static electricity. Valentina frowned and flexed her fingers, trying to resist the urge to rub her arms to rid herself of the strange current.

Sergei straightened, his expression growing concerned. "Are you all right?"

She nodded, glancing down at her hands. They didn't look any different, but the strange crawling sensation was unsettling. It wasn't painful, but it was definitely noticeable. The fact she could feel it at all wasn't a ringing endorsement of Alec's honesty.

Nikolai frowned and took a step toward her. "Do you wish to stop?"

Valentina started to say no, but something held her back. She might want to stop, but she didn't need to. It was interesting that the truth barrier was able to discern the difference. She shook her head and was able to do that without any difficulty. "I'll be fine. The truth barrier appears to function, but it's limited to verbal responses. You'll need to be very specific in your questions."

Alec hesitated, cocking his head and studying her. "Can you feel it?"

She blinked at him, the question setting her even more on guard. Dammit. She needed to be careful. Making an effort to keep her body relaxed, she frowned and pretended to be confused by his question. "I thought you said I would not. Was that wrong? Should I feel something?"

"You shouldn't be able to," he admitted with a frown.

Sergei's jaw clenched as he started to move toward her, but she held up her hand to stop him.

"I do not feel any pain," she stated before one of them decided to yank her off. None of them looked happy with her being there. She turned back to Nikolai. "Your questions?"

"Very well," he agreed, but the rigidity in his shoulders didn't lessen. "Did you have any part in the ambush yesterday?"

Valentina opened her mouth to say no, but nothing came out. She paused for a moment, considering how to answer. "I was present during the meeting but did not conspire in the ambush."

"Interesting," Nikolai murmured. "You're unable to say no because you were there?"

"It will not allow me to say anything that can be construed as a lie," she replied. "Narrow the parameters of your question and try again."

Nikolai nodded. "Did you have any part in *planning* the ambush yesterday?"

"No."

"Do you know who helped orchestrate the attack?"

Valentina opened her mouth and closed it again when she couldn't respond. Realizing her knowledge of Regina was tripping the truth barrier, she suggested, "Try asking that differently."

"Do you know who masterminded the attack?"

"No," she replied.

"Do you know who shot Sergei?"

"No, but I will find out and return the favor," she promised, meeting Sergei's gaze from across the room.

Nikolai hesitated and then grinned. "It appears to be working."

The strange sensation faded away, and Valentina walked away from the mark to stand beside Nikolai once more. Nikolai motioned for one of the guards to come forward. He did so immediately, no reservation in his stance. Valentina nodded at him in approval.

Each of the guards who escorted them took their turn standing within the truth barrier and answering Nikolai's questions. Once they were finished, they all stepped back into formation. The two Omnis who had been holding the truth barrier in place moved away from the wall, and the strange sensation that had filled the area was gone. Valentina glanced over at the guards, but none of them had shown any signs of being affected.

She needed to try getting into the towers' restricted areas again. There had to be something in OmniLab's records that could help shed some light into their strange powers. If Sergei was willing, she'd get him to help her.

Nikolai rubbed his thumb against her back to get her attention, and she automatically leaned into him. He smiled down at her affectionately. "Lunch would be fine. I am sure Valentina would also enjoy seeing Ariana again."

"Yes, I would," she agreed but inwardly was about to strangle Nikolai. The potential risks of having him enter the busy commercial district where she'd gone with Brant would be a security nightmare. "Although, I am a little tired after such a long trip. Perhaps we could have a quiet meal instead?"

"I'll make the arrangements," Alec offered, clasping his hands behind his back. "We can either join you in Lars's quarters or one of the private dining rooms near there. Once things settle down and you both get some rest, I'd be happy to give you a tour of the towers."

Valentina relaxed a fraction and nodded. "That sounds lovely."

"Excellent," Alec replied. "I'll see you all a bit later."

Alec and several of the others headed out of the room while Yuri coordinated the retrieval of their belongings. Now that they'd been cleared from any involvement in the ambush, Nikolai wanted their guards to stay in the construction tower under the guise of additional construction support. After the initial meeting, Nikolai had lifted the construction ban and their people were back at work, so they should be able to blend easily with the others.

Sergei gave them detailed instructions on what they needed to be listening for as they engaged with the residents and workers. He then provided them with maps to their quarters and other key areas. In order to keep Nikolai's presence as quiet as possible, she and Sergei were going to be visiting the construction tower to check in with them and conduct their own investigations.

Valentina grabbed one of the bags, but Sergei took it from her with a grin. "Allow me, Valechka."

She smiled sweetly and gestured to the almost half-dozen bags still in the caravan. "Thank you, Seryozha. I don't know how I would have been able to manage such a heavy bag on my own. Would you mind taking care of the rest too?"

"Of course," he agreed, his eyes twinkling with amusement. He shoved the bag into Yuri's gut with a little more force than necessary. "Yuri and Lars will help me."

Yuri scowled at him but threw the bag over his shoulder. He whispered something to Sergei in a low voice, but Valentina didn't need to hear it to know it was a rather creative threat. She bit her lip and shook her head in exasperation.

"Come, Valya." Nikolai placed his hand on her back. "We should head to our rooms before these two get into trouble."

They divided up the rest of the bags between them before heading into the priority elevator. Lars programmed the floor, and the elevator shot upward. She couldn't help but smile at Nikolai's visible excitement about the expansive view from the elevator. The elaborate gardenscape was breathtaking, and even though it was necessary to keep him safe for the welfare of their people, part of her was glad he was getting this opportunity.

The elevator stopped a few minutes later and they filed out, following Lars down the familiar corridor to his quarters.

"Valentina left her belongings in the room she used before," Lars said, opening the door and leading them down the hallway. He pushed open the door to Valentina's room and then gestured to the one across from hers and another further down the corridor. "I thought you all might want to be close to each other, and these rooms are right next to each other. You can divide them up however you see fit. My private rooms are down the hall a bit."

Nikolai nodded. "I appreciate you allowing us to stay here with you. The privacy will be welcome while we're coordinating our investigation."

Lars inclined his head. "It's my pleasure. I believe Alec's going to have some people stop by shortly to set up for lunch. Other than that, no one else is here. Feel free to make yourselves at home."

Nikolai glanced at her room and the one across from her. They typically shared a room when outside their camp—to keep up appearances and for security reasons—but she knew he was hesitating because of Sergei. She took a step toward Nikolai and placed her hand on his arm. "Do you wish to share my room, Kolya?"

Sergei's body tensed.

Nikolai bent down to kiss her cheek. "I believe it would best to give you some privacy, Valya. Besides, I have a feeling we will be intruding on you often enough."

Valentina nodded and gestured to the door across from hers. "If you stay in this room, Yuri can stay in the one next to you."

"Lars," Yuri called out to Lars's retreating figure. "Do you have a room farther away for Sergei? Perhaps even in the other tower?"

Sergei arched a brow and strolled into Valentina's room, dropping the bags on the floor. "I believe I just claimed my roommate."

"Over my dead body," Yuri snarled, taking a step forward.

Valentina slapped her hands against Yuri's chest. "Not now. We'll figure this out later. We have work to do."

Yuri glared at Sergei but didn't go after him. Sergei smirked at him, grabbed her wrist and, in one swift movement, yanked her inside before slamming the door in Yuri's face.

"What is wrong with you?" she hissed at Sergei as Yuri started pounding on the door, threatening to break it down. A sharp word from Nikolai curbed Yuri's pounding, but she barely heard it.

Sergei pushed her up against the door and lowered his head, claiming her with his mouth. Unable to resist, she curled her fingers into his jacket, holding on tightly as the heat between them erupted. Pulling her against him, he let her know with his body how much he wanted her. She started to unzip his jacket, but he grabbed her wrists to stop her. He broke their kiss, breathing heavily, and pressed his forehead against hers. In a low voice, he whispered, "You drive me to the edge of all self-control, Valechka. I've been wanting to kiss you for hours, and I could not wait another moment."

She blinked up at him, wondering if he expected her to object. "I am not complaining, Seryozha."

He grinned and released her wrists. Pressing another brief kiss against her lips, he murmured, "I fully intend on finishing this later with you, little dove."

Without waiting for a response, he flung open the door. A furious Yuri was leaning against the wall, arms crossed over his chest, and glaring at him. "If you seek to separate me from Valentina again, I will toss your broken body off the top of these towers to see if it bounces."

Sergei shook his head, his expression puzzled. "How have you managed to stay alive all these years? I was sure someone would have ended you before now."

"If you would like to try, be my guest," Yuri retorted.

"I may have to do that," Sergei agreed with a grin.

Valentina rolled her eyes and walked over to one of the bags. She yanked it open and began pulling out weapons, laying them side by side. Yuri grabbed one of the bags from outside and brought it into her room. He opened it and started pulling out pieces of computer equipment.

She began checking the weapons for any damage incurred during the trip. "Where is Nikolai?"

"He's in his room making some calls, but it's nothing important if you need him, " Yuri said, glancing around the room. "We will need another table or something to set up our equipment."

"I will take care of it," Sergei offered, heading out of the room. Valentina admired his retreating figure and bit back a smile, thinking about what she'd like to do with him later.

"Be careful, Valya," Yuri warned in a low voice. "I know you care for him, but I'm worried about you."

She sighed, finished inspecting one of her preferred throwing knives, and slid it back into its case. "I'm trying. The more time I spend with him, the more I forget the past several years."

"He's always had a way of getting under your skin," Yuri muttered. "Like a bad rash or fungus. Perhaps we should see if they have a cream for that."

She arched an eyebrow. "I dare you to try to apply it."

"Like this?" He grabbed her and pushed her to the floor, tickling her sides. She shrieked with laughter, kicking at him, but he pinned her down and continued to tickle her mercilessly.

"I yield," she squealed, trying to wriggle away from him.

He chuckled and released her. "Aha. Now we just need to find a cream that works to get rid of him."

Still laughing, she rolled onto her side to look up at him. "I don't think it will be that easy."

Yuri sighed. "Probably not."

———

SERGEI HEARD Valentina's laughter as he walked down the hall and couldn't help but smile. It had been years since he last heard her laugh like that. The fact that Yuri was the one who brought it about was just another reminder of everything he'd missed. He'd been the one who used to make her laugh more often than not, teasing or tickling her until she begged him to stop. Yuri had slid into that role a little too comfortably, but Sergei couldn't exactly blame him. They all had a soft spot for Valentina. He hadn't been exaggerating when he called her the heart of their family.

Sergei entered the living area to find Lars pacing back and forth while speaking on a commlink call.

"An hour's fine," Lars said, glancing over at Sergei. "I believe it'll just be the five of us here." He paused for a minute. "Great. I'll take care of it."

Sergei arched an eyebrow. "Lunch arrangements?"

"Yeah," Lars said, closing his commlink and slipping it back into his pocket. "They're sending someone to set everything up. Alec doesn't know how to do anything simple. It'll be Alec, Ariana, and Brant joining us. I told Alec everyone would be more comfortable if we limited the number of people."

Sergei nodded. "That would be best."

Lars darted a glance down the hall. "I was surprised Nikolai even agreed to come here. I think it's helped ease some of the tensions though."

Sergei shrugged. "We'll see. I believe Alec's decision to bring Ariana along will do much to help pave the way."

"I think so too," Lars agreed. "Alec says she's excited to meet everyone. She wants to get to know Valentina better."

Sergei made a noncommittal noise. That would be an interesting friendship pairing, if it happened. Ariana was all naïve innocence, whereas Valentina was... not. "I came out to see if you had a table they can use to set up their equipment."

"Sure," Lars said, motioning for him to follow. "They can set it up in one of my empty rooms, if that's easier."

"I think just placing a table in one of their bedrooms would be sufficient," Sergei said as they entered a large storage area where several furnishings had been pushed along one of the walls. Lars gestured for him to pick something out. Sergei stepped forward and began pulling out chairs to get closer to the tables.

"Now that we're alone, I wanted to ask you something

about Valentina," Lars began, moving aside a small nightstand.

Sergei picked up another chair. "You may ask. I may or may not answer."

"Did she say anything about the truth barrier?"

Sergei glanced over at him. "What do you mean?"

"She shouldn't have been able to feel anything," Lars explained. "Alec was wondering if she might have some trace abilities. Only our people tend to feel energy manipulation. When Alec asked her, he thought she might have dodged the question. She didn't outright deny it."

Sergei turned back to the furniture. "She is not one of your people."

Lars frowned. "Are you sure about that? I've wondered about you too. You never told me how you found us on the surface after we were exiled. I have a hard time believing it was sheer luck that made you come out to our location in the middle of nowhere. OmniLab tried to trace as many of our bloodlines as possible before the war, but it wasn't possible to test everyone. We ran out of time."

Sergei didn't reply, intent on pulling a dresser out into the center of the room. Of course the tables had to be buried toward the back, forcing this asinine conversation to last even longer.

Lars grabbed the end of the dresser and helped move it to the side. "Out of all your people, you were the most willing to accept and embrace our abilities. Most of them are still suspicious of us or don't believe in our talents."

He glanced at Lars briefly. "I have done much over the years, but I have never been able to move the wind as you do."

Lars shook his head. "No, but you could have other talents. Maybe they're not as well-developed or strong, but they might be there. Valentina might have them too, especially if she felt the truth barrier. We could give both of you a simple DNA test to find out."

"No," Sergei said, bending down to inspect one of the tables to make sure it was sturdy enough to support their equipment. "And you will not speak of this to Valentina."

"We wouldn't do anything to hurt her," Lars said with a frown. "But if either of you share our abilities, we could help you develop your talents."

Sergei stood upright and turned to face Lars. "I will not tell you again. You will not say a word of this to her or to anyone else."

Lars was silent for a long moment, considering him thoughtfully. "Fine. For the sake of our friendship, I won't say anything to her. I can't guarantee Alec won't though. I'm sure he's already told Ariana his suspicions."

"If you have any hope of this alliance working, you will encourage Alec to leave this alone."

"I'll tell him you refused, but Alec can be stubborn," Lars said, bending down to help lift one end of the table while Sergei grabbed the other end. "But you should still think about it. The whole premise of the towers was to help preserve our people and way of life. If Valentina's part of that, we'd do everything possible to protect her."

Sergei didn't respond. He had no intention of telling her any of this. Valentina was too unpredictable, and there was no way to know how she'd respond. Most likely, she'd be curious enough to agree so she could obtain more information. That was worrisome enough, but it was Nikolai's response that could prove to be disastrous.

They carried the table out of the storage room and down the hallway toward Valentina's room. Yuri was still there, connecting their equipment. He glanced up when they entered and gestured to an area against one of the walls. "Put it there. Valentina wants to keep the monitoring equipment in here so she can track our people in the construction tower."

Sergei pushed the table against the wall. "Where is she?"

"Busy," Yuri retorted, not looking up from the equipment. "Three years without her, and now you cannot handle being away from her for five minutes?"

Sergei glanced at Nikolai's closed door. He could barely make out the soft sound of voices from within. "Jealous, Yuri? That after all these years she still prefers my company over yours?"

Lars's eyes widened, and he backed away a step.

"You are nothing more than a temporary plaything," Yuri said, lifting the equipment off the floor and putting it on the table. He smirked and added, "Her appetites have changed over the years. I know far more than you can imagine."

Sergei crossed his arms over his chest and leaned against the wall. There was no way in hell Valentina had slept with him. Nikolai, perhaps, but not Yuri. And she'd flat-out denied being lovers with Nikolai. "Do not deceive yourself, Yuri. She is too much woman for you to handle."

Yuri scowled. "You are the only one deceiving yourself. She will not be taken in by you again, and I will not let her."

"Since when does anyone *let* Valentina do anything?" Sergei retorted.

"Talking about me?" Valentina swept into the room, followed by Nikolai. She gave Lars a brief nod and went over to the weapons spread out across the floor. "I would have thought you two would have found more interesting things to discuss. After all, we have people to hunt."

"I have always excelled at multitasking," Sergei murmured, his gaze roaming over her figure as she bent down to pick up her throwing daggers.

She tested the balance of her knives in her hand and arched a brow. "Are you sure you wish to have this conversation now, Seryozha? I can always test out your multitasking abilities in finer detail."

Yuri snorted. "As much as I would enjoy seeing that, we need to mount an antenna somewhere for this equipment."

Sergei grinned at her. "I would be happy to provide a demonstration in private, Valechka." He glanced over at Yuri. "Come. I will help you set up your antenna, and perhaps you can try your luck at throwing me off the towers. Or perhaps you shall take a dive instead."

"Done," Yuri agreed.

Lars frowned at them. "I guess I need to go with you. I have a feeling you two are going to raise a whole lot of questions."

———

VALENTINA WATCHED THEM LEAVE, listening for the entrance door to close behind them. As soon as they were gone, she and Nikolai sprang into action. They'd brought their surveillance equipment directly into Nikolai's room and now proceeded to unpack it. She pulled out her toolkit and pried off the cover to the electronic panel that displayed the mural on the ceiling. Once the room was dark and the panel deactivated, they divided the room in half and began scanning for any other electronic devices.

The display lit up as she moved beside a nightstand. She paused, bending down to inspect the underside. "I'm more tired than I expected after that trip."

Nikolai glanced over at her. "I am too. We can spend the rest of the day relaxing and then you can explore the construction tower tomorrow with Sergei."

The device was no bigger than her thumb, but it was just a listening device. Until she was sure there were no cameras, she'd keep scanning. Their equipment was designed to temporarily scramble any visual surveillance, but they didn't want to cause any alarm by interrupting both audio and visual feeds. One could be explained as a technical malfunction, but both might be a bit more difficult to explain. "What will you do while I'm gone, Kolya?"

"I have some calls in the morning," he said, scanning the other half of the room. "Perhaps when I'm finished, we can take a small tour."

She held up one finger to him, tapped her ear, and pointed at the table. He shook his head, indicating he hadn't found anything else. She reactivated the mural and replaced the panel cover. "I suppose. Would you mind bringing my other bag into my room? If we're going to stay here awhile, I should unpack."

"Of course," he agreed, picking up the bag and following her over to her room.

She pried off the panel cover and repeated the same procedure. "Brant, their security officer, took me to a lovely café the other day with the most delicious cookies."

He chuckled, scanning his half of the room. "I should have known. You mentioned you liked him. Now I see why."

"He has excellent taste," she agreed, pausing at the night-stand. Someone had planted another bug here as well, but no cameras. It would be easy enough to get rid of it. They needed at least one secure room. She dropped the equipment back into the bag and pulled out their own listening devices. "Excuse me for a moment, Kolya. I need to use the facilities."

"Of course," he agreed and headed toward the bathroom where he would operate the water and finish scanning while she darted down the hall.

Keeping her footsteps as quiet as possible to avoid detection by any other devices, she slipped into Lars's bedroom. She planted her device under his bed and quickly exited the room. Her commlink buzzed in her pocket, and she glanced at the message from Yuri as she raced back to the living area. She had only a handful of minutes. They were on their way back now.

She placed one of the listening devices in the living area before moving into a room that appeared to be a study. Another device was installed along the back of the wall panel. She'd have to wait for another opportunity to try to hack into their communication system. Although, knowing Sergei, he'd already figured a workaround. She ducked back into her room just in time to hear the front door open.

Valentina nodded at Nikolai to let him know some of the devices were planted. He walked over to her and said, "Do you need any help unpacking?"

"Perhaps," she agreed, glancing again at the nightstand. "Did you see the dresses they loaned me?"

He chuckled. "I have not seen you in a dress for a long time, Valya."

"Don't get used to it," she warned with a small smile. "But I will wear one after I shower. I believe that sort of attire is more acceptable here."

Sergei and Yuri entered the room, but Lars was nowhere to be seen. Good. She tapped her ear and pointed to the nightstand. "I see you two didn't kill each other."

Sergei's eyes narrowed, and he nodded in understanding. He walked over to the nightstand and glanced it over. "Not yet. I couldn't find an open window to throw him out of, and I wasn't sure they would appreciate me breaking one. After all, destroying their tower is not the best way to cement our alliance."

"There are no windows in this room," Yuri retorted.

Sergei barked out a laugh. "You have never been able to take me. I have seen children who offer more of a challenge than you."

Yuri grinned and charged toward Sergei, who neatly side-stepped and crashed into the nightstand. The two of them fell into it, taking the opportunity to swing more punches than necessary and using their combined weight to completely destroy the piece of furniture.

"Enough," Nikolai ordered, nodding his approval. "Clean this mess up. We will have to reimburse our hosts for this destruction."

Valentina made a great show of sighing and stepped over to the broken table. She spotted the bug on the floor and said, "That was a lovely piece too."

Sergei looked up at her from his place on the floor. "Very lovely."

Yuri elbowed him in the side, and Sergei grunted. She grinned and shook her head at them. "While you two are cleaning up this mess, I'm going to shower and get ready for lunch. Please try not to break anything else while I'm gone."

They both murmured their agreement, and she headed into the bathroom. Now they just needed to make sure no one else came into the room to plant another bug. She hadn't worried about such devices during her last trip since her arrival had been so unexpected. Part of her was surprised they hadn't also installed cameras, unless this was their way of giving them a modicum of privacy. If it had been her, she would have wired up the very walls with audio *and* visual surveillance.

Now that she had a moment to herself, she pulled out her commlink and contacted Viktor, Peter's second-in-command. He answered almost immediately, leading her to believe he'd been waiting for her call.

"Valentina," he greeted her. "It's always a pleasure to hear from you."

"How are you, Viktor?" she asked, making an effort to keep her voice light and friendly.

"Busy lately, but never too busy for you. I understand we may be working together again?"

"Yes," Valentina agreed, slipping off her dusty clothes and dropping them onto the floor. She started pulling off her weapons and laid them carefully on the counter. "I would be grateful for your help. Nikolai's troubled by these reports about missing weapons. I want to reassure him, but I'm afraid I don't have your extensive contacts in the area."

"Of course," Viktor acknowledged, a trace of pride in his voice.

She resisted the urge to roll her eyes, worried it would carry over into her tone. Viktor was a lecherous irritant, but he wasn't stupid. It would have been easier to handle him if he were.

"I am planning to visit the construction tower at OmniLab tomorrow. Would you be willing to meet with me?"

There was a lengthy pause on his end. "You are going to OmniLab?"

She sighed. "Unfortunately. I'm sure you're aware our alliance is in jeopardy. Nikolai wants me to meet with Sergei at the towers to see how far along we are with the construction."

With the faintest hint of annoyance, he said, "Sergei is still at the towers?"

Well, that was interesting and rather unexpected. Sergei had managed to annoy Viktor or Peter somehow. She'd have to ask him about it later. Although, throwing a potential irritant in Viktor's path might be beneficial and make him reveal more than he intended. "Yes, I'm meeting with him in the morning. Perhaps you would like to join me for the tour? We could find a quiet corner somewhere and compare notes."

"I am surprised Nikolai would send you to deal with Sergei," Viktor stated.

Valentina paused. Viktor knew something, but she wasn't sure what. At least she didn't have to feign ignorance.

"I was surprised too," she admitted, allowing a trace of her vulnerability to filter through her voice. "Nikolai doesn't always share his reasoning with me. Is there something you know that I don't?"

He didn't answer right away. She waited, hoping he would eventually fill the silence. Viktor finally sighed and said, "I think Nikolai's making a mistake sending you there to deal with him. It would have been better if he had turned this whole matter over to Peter. Even Yuri would have been a better option. What time are you meeting him?"

"Around eleven," she said, trying to give herself enough time to follow up on their own investigation before the meeting.

"I will meet you there. Oh, and Valentina?"

"Yes?"

"Do not meet with Sergei alone," he warned before disconnecting the call.

Valentina frowned, staring at the commlink and wondering what in the world that was about. Resisting the urge to swear at this latest intrigue, she dropped her comm-link on the counter and stepped into the shower.

Between the cookies and the showers, she was hard-pressed to say which of the two she liked more. Even so, she couldn't linger. As soon as she dressed, she needed to work out a tactical plan with Nikolai for this luncheon. Everything related to Viktor, Peter, and the missing shipments needed to wait. They couldn't afford to be distracted when dealing with these Omnis.

She finished cleaning off the travel grime, shut off the water, and wrapped one of the drying cloths around herself. There was a special drying tube in the wall off to the side, but she'd never liked using those things. Maybe it was a luxury, but she'd rather use the old-fashioned method whenever possible and let her skin dry naturally.

When she emerged, Yuri was busy working on configuring their monitoring equipment. Sergei, on the other hand, was lounging against the wall watching over Yuri's shoulder. He lifted his head to regard her, slowly scanning her up and down. "If that's what you're planning on wearing to lunch, I'm not sure I have any intention of letting you make it there."

She smiled and shook her head, walking over to the pile of clothing she'd received from Brant. "Very funny, but no."

Sergei followed her and reached over to pick up a red dress. He glanced at it and then back at her, a wicked grin on his face. "What about this one?"

She tilted her head, considering the garment. It was very short and clingy, not to mention it just happened to be Sergei's favorite color. Wearing her weapons might require some creativity, but she'd managed more in far less. "Do you intend to pick out my undergarments too?"

"I would rather take those off you," he offered.

Yuri cleared his throat. "I am still here."

"You can leave," Sergei suggested without looking away from her and still holding out the dress, a challenge in his eyes.

She'd never been able to resist a challenge, especially from him. Holding Sergei's gaze, she released the drying cloth and let it fall to the floor. His eyes darkened with desire as he slowly perused her body. With a sly smile, she reached over and took the dress from him. She admired the material for a moment, draping the rich, red color over her skin. "Maybe I will just go without undergarments instead."

"Leave, Yuri," Sergei ordered, taking a step toward her and putting his hands on her bare hips.

"Not a chance," Yuri retorted, adjusting one of the controls on the equipment.

Valentina gave a small shrug and looked down at the dress, debating how long it would take Sergei to lose his mind. If the heat in his eyes was any indication, Yuri would be evicted from her room in less than three minutes.

Sergei leaned in close to her and whispered, "I know what you are trying to do."

She gave him a coy smile. "Who? Me?"

He grinned, trailing his hand along her hip, and murmured, "Oh, yes. I know exactly what you are trying to do."

"What do you intend to do about it?" she teased.

"Last chance, Yuri," Sergei threatened. "Or I will throw you out and the equipment with you."

"Try it," Yuri snapped without looking away from the controls. "And Valya, you better get dressed before we get blood on this floor too."

She grinned at Sergei and bent down, making a show of slowly shimmying into the dress. Once she pulled the straps over her shoulders, she placed her hands on Sergei's chest and pressed a light kiss against his lips. With a shrug, she said, "Maybe some other time."

He grabbed her and pulled her close, capturing her mouth and kissing her as though she was the very air he needed to survive. When he broke away, he whispered next to her ear, "No, Valechka. You either get rid of Yuri before you go to bed, or I will do it for you. If it's me, someone will be cleaning his blood off the floor in the morning. Either way, I *will* have you later tonight."

He turned and headed out of the room, leaving her grasping the dresser for support, her knees weak. She had the feeling he'd won that round, although she wasn't entirely sure anymore.

# CHAPTER FOURTEEN

SERGEI HEADED into the common area and directly for the bar. He grabbed a bottle, not particularly caring what was in it, and poured himself a drink.

Lars spoke from behind him. "Problem?"

Sergei paused and then added a bit more, capping the bottle and putting it on the bar. He grabbed the glass and tossed it back. Nope. It wasn't enough. He inhaled deeply and poured another glass. "I am fine."

"Uh huh," Lars agreed with a trace of humor in his voice. "I think I've seen you drink more in the past few days than I have in the past year."

Sergei glanced down the hall, tempted to go back in there and physically remove Yuri from the room. For the rest of the day, he was going to be thinking about what Valentina wasn't wearing underneath that dress. Except weapons. She'd have several weapons, but God only knew where she'd put them. If that wasn't one of the hottest things he'd ever imagined, well.... He downed the liquor and considered pouring another.

"And I don't think I've ever seen you touch my liquor before," Lars volunteered.

"You talk too much," he grumbled, putting the bottle back. "How long is this lunch supposed to last?"

Lars chuckled. "Who knows? They're setting up the room now. Alec and Ariana will be here in a few minutes." Lars paused for a moment. With a wicked grin, he added, "They'll probably want to talk. A lot. Maybe for hours. Who knows? It could last all night."

Sergei glared at him, knowing Lars was baiting him. If he didn't need help getting rid of Yuri's body, he'd put Lars on the list too.

Lars made a show of glancing down the hall. "Where is Valentina?"

"Getting dressed," Sergei snapped, beginning to pace the length of the floor as he imagined searching her for weapons again.

"Maybe you should have another one," Lars suggested. "You seem a little more on edge than usual."

Sergei took a steadying breath and tried to clear his mind, encouraging his body to relax. He needed to get his emotions under control before Ariana arrived. She was far too perceptive with her ability to read emotions and.... He paused and then swore under his breath. His former comrades needed to be warned about Ariana's other talents.

Ignoring Lars, Sergei headed back down the hall. He pushed open the door to Valentina's room to find Yuri still working on the equipment. Nikolai and Valentina were standing close together and talking softly. Sergei closed the door behind him and announced, "Ariana is an empath."

Nikolai turned toward him. "What are you talking about?"

"Ariana can read emotions," he explained. "You need to keep tight control of all your emotions. She cannot read body language well, but she can pick up traces of how you are feeling. I believe she can also sense some deception."

Valentina's eyes narrowed. "You did not think to mention this before now?"

Yuri swore and got up from his chair. "How skilled is she?"

Sergei shook his head. "I don't know. To my knowledge, Ariana has always had difficulty reading me. She has difficulty reading Valentina too, but she hasn't spent much time with her. I suspect it may be our training that prevents her from accurately reading us, so we must stay on guard."

"I see," Nikolai murmured. "What about Alec? Can he do the same?"

"Possibly," Sergei admitted. "Lars once told me that when two *Drac'Kin* bond, they can sometimes share abilities. I believe they must be in proximity to each other for this to work. If they are both here together, it is possible."

Valentina grabbed Nikolai's arm. "We cannot risk it, Kolya."

"It will be fine, Valya," he murmured. "We are here at their invitation, and we have done nothing wrong. They have no reason to suspect anything."

"Yet," Yuri added with a scowl. "Valentina is right, Nikolai. The risk is higher than we expected. I do not know if this visit is worth it."

Valentina looked up at Nikolai. "If they even perceive something is off, they could use it against us. These are just powers we know about. What about their other abilities that we cannot detect?"

Nikolai glanced over at him, but Sergei shook his head. "I don't know, Nikolai. Lars only knew Alec was a wind talent, but he didn't know how his abilities manifested themselves. They do not discuss these things openly, not even with each other."

Nikolai frowned. "It's not ideal, but it's too late to do

much about it. I will just suggest we all keep our thoughts as focused on today's events as possible. Keep your emotions tightly controlled."

"Fine," Valentina agreed and then glared at Sergei. "You should have told us earlier, Sergei. If anything happens to Nikolai or Yuri, the only blood you will have to worry about on the floor will be yours."

Yuri grinned and clapped him on the back. "Guess I don't need to worry about you getting into her bed anymore, do I?"

Sergei scowled at him but didn't respond. Instead, he turned back to Nikolai and Valentina, determined to salvage his blunder. "Ariana is honorable. She has a gentle heart and is far too trusting. I believe that's why Pavel was able to take her from the towers to begin with. Alec would not have agreed to bring her here if he considered the situation to be dangerous. She cannot handle violence."

Nikolai frowned. "You know her that well?"

"I do," he admitted. "Ariana will try not to intrude on your emotions intentionally. She has some difficulty with control and may pick up on some things if you are not guarded. Alec is the one you should be concerned with, especially if he can use her abilities."

"I see," Nikolai murmured. "We will keep that in mind."

Sergei glanced over at Valentina, who was regarding him thoughtfully. He couldn't tell what she was thinking and that had him more than a little concerned.

He met her gaze. "My omission was not intentional. There is too much we still don't know about them. Every day I spend here, I learn more. But even the most trusted among their people don't know everything. I would never keep such information from any of you."

Valentina took a step toward him, the short, red dress leaving even less to the imagination than he'd first thought. "Do you have access into their network?"

"Partial," he admitted, burying his surprise at the change in subject. Although, nothing should surprise him anymore when it came to her. "They have several blocks up, but we were able to install a few backdoors during our takeover. Unfortunately, we cannot access their restricted files remotely without triggering their alarms. They heightened security after another breach several months ago by Kayla, the young woman I told you about. I'm still working on a solution."

Valentina nodded. "If we cannot access their files remotely, we need to get into those restricted areas in this tower as soon as possible. I want to do it this evening or tomorrow morning. We need to be in the construction tower by eleven for a meeting with Viktor."

"Viktor?" Sergei asked in surprise and then narrowed his eyes. "That *mudak* who works with Peter and has never been able to take his eyes off your ass?"

Yuri snorted. "You remember him well."

"Yes," she agreed, watching him carefully. "He seems even less thrilled with you. I want to know why."

"Valya," Nikolai interrupted before Sergei could respond, "let's wait to see how the rest of today goes. We can discuss these matters later. I don't want you to break into any part of the tower until I give authorization. We need to proceed cautiously."

She shook her head and placed her hand on Nikolai's arm. "Please, Kolya. If I can review their files and learn more about their ways, I will feel much more comfortable about you remaining here."

Nikolai sighed, looking down at her. "I have a difficult time refusing you anything."

Valentina smiled up at him and stood on her toes to press a light kiss against Nikolai's lips. Seeing them like this made it easier to understand why most people believed them to be lovers. But Valentina had always had an easy affection with

Nikolai and Yuri. It was just part of who she was, but he'd kill anyone else who dared put their hands on her, including Viktor.

Nikolai glanced over at Sergei. "You will keep her safe if she does this."

"You don't even have to ask," Sergei replied, crossing his arms over his chest. He wouldn't let anything happen to her, and Nikolai knew it.

Nikolai nodded. "Very well. Do what you both must. If you obtain any other information on these people, let us know right away. I do not wish to be blindsided again."

Sergei nodded.

A chime sounded from the living area, indicating Alec and Ariana's arrival. Valentina frowned. "I suppose it's showtime."

Nikolai leaned down and kissed her cheek. "It will be fine."

"I hope so," she murmured.

Sergei followed them out, hoping for Alec's sake that he kept his mouth shut about Valentina and the truth barrier. They were all already on edge. Alec's interference would just add more kindling to the fire. Sergei had enough flames to try to put out on his own.

———

VALENTINA SLOWED HER GAIT, adjusting her movements to make them appear more casual. Nikolai placed his hand against her back, leading her into the common area. Alec and Ariana were there, along with Lars and Brant. The limited number of people made her relax a fraction, and Brant appeared to be the only one on the Omni side who was armed.

Ariana's eyes lit up in welcome, and Valentina couldn't help but respond with a genuine smile. She walked over to

Ariana and kissed her cheek on the left, the right, and the left again. "It is wonderful to see you again, Ariana."

Ariana beamed at her. "I was thrilled when Alec told me you had come back to the towers."

"I wanted to thank you again for everything you have done, for me and for Sergei," Valentina admitted, lowering her gaze and unable to hide the emotion in her voice. "If it weren't for your healing, I don't believe either one of us would have survived. I owe you a debt that can never be repaid. From now until my last breath, I want you to know that you are my sister in all ways but blood. If you ever have need of me, I will be there for you. All you ever have to do is ask."

Ariana's eyes welled with tears and she reached out, hugging Valentina tightly. "I feel the same way. If it weren't for you, I don't even want to think about what could have happened. You saved me."

Valentina shook her head. "No, you saved yourself. I may have helped you take advantage of an opportunity, but you decided to pick up my weapon and use it. You are much stronger and braver than you believe."

Ariana blinked back tears and nodded. "I can't tell you how much your words mean to me, Valentina."

She reached over to squeeze Ariana's hands lightly. "We will talk more later."

Alec stepped forward and put his arm around Ariana. "Ari, I'd like you to meet our other guests."

While Sergei stepped forward to introduce Nikolai and Yuri, Valentina moved beside Nikolai once more. He placed his hand on her back again, the weight a comforting gesture.

After what Sergei had said about bonding, she was curious about the interaction between Alec and Ariana. It was clear they were a matched pair, entwined together in a way that wasn't simply physical. His reactions seemed to mirror her emotions, and vice versa. She couldn't help but wonder if that was a result of their bond or if they'd always been this way together.

Either way, Ariana was extremely easy to read. Every emotion reflected on her expressive face. Alec was slightly less so, and he was the one who would need more careful handling.

Lars gestured toward the bar. "Can I get anyone a drink? The meal is going to be a few minutes yet."

"I believe we may have something for our hosts," Nikolai replied, motioning for Yuri to retrieve the items in question. He reappeared less than a minute later carrying two bottles and a small box. He handed the box to Valentina and passed the bottles over to Lars, who eyed the liquor warily.

Lars glanced at Sergei and held them up. "Are these what I think?"

Sergei merely grinned at him. Lars sighed and took the bottles over to the bar, muttering under his breath.

Valentina walked back over to Ariana and held out the box. "These are considered a delicacy by our people. It is a sample of several different types of sweets."

Ariana's eyes lit up as she opened the box. "They smell wonderful. Are they all different?"

Valentina nodded and pointed to two of them. "Yes. Those two are my favorites, but you really cannot go wrong with any of them."

"You're going to have to share them with me later," Ariana suggested, closing the box again.

Sergei chuckled. "Be careful making such an offer, Ari. Valentina *really* enjoys them. She might end up eating your entire box."

"Only yours," Valentina teased with a small smile. "And that was because you were irritating me. I thought it was fair payback."

Sergei nodded and told Ariana, "I cannot deny it. I have always found annoying her to be highly entertaining."

Ariana looked back and forth between them. "You've known each other a long time, haven't you?"

Valentina hesitated and then nodded. They didn't typically volunteer information about their past or group dynamic with others, but there were ways to share information to maintain a friendly atmosphere without revealing too much. "Since we were little more than children."

"Please have a seat," Alec said, gesturing to the couches.

Ariana sat beside Alec, and he immediately put his arm around the back of the couch in a somewhat protective gesture. Ariana smiled over at Sergei. "I have a hard time imagining you as a child. What were you like?"

"A bit of a troublemaker," Sergei admitted, sitting on the edge of the couch.

Valentina sat beside Nikolai, and he rested his hand on her knee, just a few inches away from one of the knives strapped to her inner thigh. She smiled over at Sergei and said, "Nothing has changed. You are still a bit of a troublemaker."

Yuri leaned against the wall, appearing somewhat casual, but Valentina knew he wouldn't relax while they were in this situation. Brant was obviously emulating his behavior and remained standing as well, a subtle reminder he wasn't there to simply socialize either.

Lars handed several glasses to everyone, with the exception of Brant and Yuri, and then took a seat.

Nikolai raised his glass and said, "A toast to a meeting of friends and a promising alliance in our future."

They all raised their glasses and drank. Valentina took Nikolai's empty glass and put it on the table beside her.

"Lars has been telling me a bit about the time he spent with your people," Alec volunteered.

Lars chuckled. "It was an enlightening experience. I learned far more about basic survival techniques than I ever thought possible. I wish I had some of that knowledge when I was first exiled from the towers."

Nikolai nodded, placing his hand back on her knee and rubbing it with his thumb. "We teach all our people such things. We begin when they are children, and each person learns a wide range of skills based on their aptitude, interest, and our need."

Valentina tilted her head, intrigued by the differences between their cultures. "Your people don't usually teach such things? What sort of lessons do you give your children?"

"Math, science, literature, history, and the arts," Alec explained, leaning back and draping his arm over Ariana's shoulder again. "Those are general subjects taught to all children who live here. The subject matter differs slightly between the towers."

Valentina leaned forward slightly. "Because of your powers?"

Alec nodded. "Indeed. Our children learn to control their powers from an early age, although the more specialized abilities don't emerge until we're teenagers or even later. But up until that point, we focus on general subjects and more rudimentary explanations about energy usage."

"I find this subject fascinating," Nikolai admitted. "Many of our people still don't believe these abilities exist. Have you had similar issues with your other residents?"

Alec shook his head. "Not exactly. We typically don't discuss details with outsiders. Over the centuries, our people have been persecuted and attacked because we're different. We may share a home, but we don't share much information with non-sensitives. We prefer our privacy, but rumors still have a way of making themselves known."

"I see," Nikolai murmured. "Our pre-war records indicated OmniLab was only a medical center. We were not aware your facility still existed until several years ago."

Alec nodded. "That was our intention. OmniLab was created under the guise of a medical research facility. Thousands of people sent in their DNA samples to have us research their ancestry and to receive detailed health information. One of the things we were looking for were certain genetic markers that identified them as being one of our kind. Once we had a list of names and families, we conducted additional testing and extended an invitation for them to join us. Our goal was to preserve as many of our people as possible in the event things progressed the way they were heading."

Nikolai rubbed her knee with his thumb, the absent gesture indicative of his enthusiasm regarding the subject. She placed her hand over his in a subtle reminder they needed to be careful not to allow Ariana or Alec to pick up on any of their emotions. Nikolai didn't remove his hand, but he leaned back and asked, "So your people differ genetically from everyone else?"

Alec glanced over at Valentina. "Yes. A simple DNA test can show us whether someone carries the same genetic markers. Unfortunately, we were not able to test everyone, so we know some of our people slipped through the cracks."

Nikolai nodded. "How different are you?"

"We can still intermarry and have children with others who are not like us, although we tend to prefer staying with our own kind to preserve the potency of our bloodlines." Alec paused for a moment and then added, "If you'd like, we can provide you all with a DNA test and show you the markers we're looking for."

"No," Sergei declared, standing from the couch and walking over to the bar area.

Valentina stared at Sergei's retreating figure, surprised by his outburst. He usually had better control of his emotions than this. Dammit. If he lost his cool now, it could put them all in danger.

"I'm afraid I must agree with Sergei," Nikolai admitted, squeezing her knee a fraction. She took it as an indication for her to diffuse the situation with Sergei. "While I would enjoy a demonstration, this is still very new to us. I would be open to viewing these markers, but I must decline allowing any of my people to participate just yet."

Valentina picked up the empty glasses beside her and carried them over to the bar area. In their native tongue, she said, "Pour it."

Sergei's mouth curved upward, and he refilled her glass before filling his. In a low voice, he advised, "Be careful, Valechka. Do nothing that will allow them the opportunity to take your DNA."

She tapped her glass with his and swallowed the liquor. "You know me better than that."

"That I do," he murmured, briefly placing his hand over hers. "We need to speak after lunch."

Curious, but cognizant this wasn't the time or place, she nodded.

A man emerged from another room and bowed briefly. "Lunch is ready."

Sergei turned and put his hand on her back to lead her toward the dining area. He leaned in close and whispered, "I will enjoy taking this dress off you later."

"There is not much else for you to take off."

He muttered a colorful oath under his breath, and she grinned in delight. At least his earlier mood had been diffused and a different sort of frustration was now plaguing him.

They filed into a large dining area with an elongated table set with several place settings. Large windows were partially shuttered, but she could still see the expansive and mostly barren landscape outside. Valentina took a seat between

Sergei and Nikolai, with Yuri on the opposite side of Nikolai. The Omnis were in similar form across the table, so she was seated directly across from Ariana. The server began bringing out dishes, placing them in front of each of them.

The conversation around the table primarily focused on the construction, the planned features of this new tower, and potential security concerns in adapting to life within the towers. Apparently, there had been a few conflicts between their people and the Omnis, most likely from cultural differences and expectations. Ariana mentioned a friend of hers had created a new club to merge all the different groups in an effort to alleviate these problems.

Overall, it was mostly small talk, and Valentina found her focus on the large windows behind Ariana. It must have been beautiful once.

Valentina took a sip of her soup, the rich flavor much better than anything they had in their camp. When there was a lull in conversation, she gestured toward the glass. "How do your people manage to keep these windows so clean?"

Ariana smiled at her. "Water energy channelers. We create storms to wash away the dirt and grime from the towers. We still send people out periodically to perform maintenance, but we do much of it with our abilities."

"I had wondered how the towers managed to withstand the surrounding destruction," Nikolai commented. "Would that be a result of your talents too?"

Alec nodded. "Yes. It was a group effort to withstand the changes. We had earth channelers who were able to secure the ground below us. We created windstorms and clouds to battle against the more harmful environmental effects. Our fire energy channelers were able to keep our power and generators running. All of our people worked together around the clock to make sure our home withstood the destruction. Even so, there was still damage, but we were able to repair it."

Valentina stared out the window again, remembering all the ruined buildings and obliterated cities she'd seen over the years. The cumulative powers these Omnis possessed were more than a little daunting. "I had wondered. Most of the other surviving facilities are underground bunkers or built into mountains. Your towers are very exposed."

"This area was selected because it was remote and unlikely to be a direct target for an attack," Alec said, raising his wine glass to take a drink. "Fortunately, our gamble worked."

"Have you seen much of the world?" Ariana took another sip of her soup.

Valentina shrugged. "Some. There are still some places that are too dangerous to travel. We send our drones to surveille these areas, testing for contamination levels first. If they are relatively safe, we send a small ground team to assess the area."

Ariana sighed wistfully. "I've only been to the surface once. Alec has promised to take me back to the underground river, but I'd love to see some of the other places in the world."

Valentina nodded in understanding. She loved the adventure of discovering new places, but sometimes it could grow tiring. Every now and then, she thought of trying to talk Nikolai into establishing a more permanent base.

Nikolai was one of the few leaders who went to different facilities to check on things. Because of his hands-on approach, he had made far more alliances within these communities than many others. Since he was still so new to his position, these contacts were critical to securing his powerbase. It was probably too soon for him to consider the alternative.

"Valentina," Alec began and placed his spoon beside his

place setting, indicating he was finished. "I wanted to speak with you about the truth barrier."

"Oh?" she questioned mildly, noting that Sergei had tensed beside her.

Alec leaned forward. "Only someone with a sensitivity to energy channeling would have been able to feel anything."

"Yes, you mentioned that." She took another sip of her soup. "The entire thing was a rather remarkable experience. Lars explained your people use that method instead of relying upon technology."

Lars cleared his throat. "Alec, it may be better to discuss this later."

Alec held up his hand to stop Lars's objections and continued to study her. "Yes, we do. Some of our talents are only effective on our kind, but some of our skills work on everyone. The truth barrier is one of those, but unlike other non-sensitives, only our kind can feel the energy."

"Ah," she acknowledged, making an effort to keep her body relaxed even though her heart was pounding in her chest. "That explains why you said we would not feel it."

"Indeed," Nikolai added. "Tell me, Alec, how exactly does this truth barrier force someone to only tell the truth?"

Alec paused for a moment, clearly not wanting to abandon his line of questioning but unable to ignore another leader's pointed inquiry. "It is difficult to explain since my type of energy typically isn't used in holding a truth barrier, but the mechanics of it are that certain types of energy coincide with the truth. By creating an energy field around a person, you ensure that only certain audible resonances can pass through the field."

Valentina nodded in understanding and took a sip of her drink. Alec's explanation made sense as to why she was able to make certain gestures but hadn't been able to speak. Even so, Alec's insistence on asking her about the truth barrier was concerning. He'd likely try to bring the conversation back around to her again. This could get bad quickly.

Her skin pebbled as a cold wind passed over her, and she resisted the urge to rub her arms. She carefully placed her spoon beside the bowl and dropped her hands in her lap, itching to draw her weapon. Dammit. Extricating themselves from this mess was going to be challenging.

Sergei pushed away from the table. "If you are doing something, you will stop immediately."

Alec turned to him, his expression mildly surprised. "What do you believe we are doing?"

"I have spent enough time with your people to know when you are channeling energy," Sergei snapped.

Valentina slid her blade from its sheath, keeping it under the table and out of sight. Once she brought out the weapons, she usually had to use them. She'd give them a chance to resolve this peacefully, but she didn't have much hope. Alec had made a serious error in using his powers against them. Yuri had probably already drawn his weapon under the table too.

Nikolai stood, his expression hard and unyielding. "I was under the impression you were interested in having this alliance succeed. If you are using your abilities against us, this can be construed as an act of war."

Alec's body stiffened. A moment later, something else overcame the room, and Valentina's body unwillingly relaxed a fraction. Everyone else's tension lowered a bit too, but something still wasn't quite right. It wasn't a natural softening. Valentina tightened her hand around the hilt of her blade, trying to figure out what had shifted. She had the sensation that whatever it was originated from Ariana.

The dark-haired woman laid her hand over Alec's. "We apologize to all of you. It's sometimes difficult to remember not to use our abilities around others. No offense was meant.

I'm sure Sergei must have shared with you how many times I've fumbled around him since we first met."

"That is different," Sergei said, but not with any of his earlier force. Valentina studied him, curious about his gentler tone. He really did seem to like Ariana, and Valentina had the impression he was protective of the young woman too.

Ariana focused on her. "Valentina, would you mind if we spoke privately for a moment?"

"Ari," Sergei warned, "this is not a wise course of action."

Ariana stood and dropped her napkin on the chair. "Please trust me, Sergei. I just want to speak with her for a moment."

Valentina glanced over at Nikolai, and he nodded at her. He was curious and wanted her to find out what was going on. She slipped her blade back into its sheath and stood. Sergei's jaw clenched, but he didn't make any other objections.

Valentina followed Ariana into the other room. Once they were alone, Ariana turned around to face her. "I'm sorry. I tried to tell Alec it wasn't a good idea to bring this up at lunch. He has good intentions, but I'm afraid we sometimes forget our ways aren't the same as yours. I know you don't really know any of us, but we don't mean you any harm."

Valentina didn't respond. She'd found silence was sometimes the best motivator at making people talk.

Ariana sighed and clasped her hands together. "I can sense you're suspicious. I don't know if Sergei told you, but I'm an empath. I can pick up on other people's emotions. You and Sergei are more difficult for me to read than most others, but a few things filter through here and there."

"He mentioned it," Valentina acknowledged.

Ariana nodded. "What he probably hasn't told you is that I can read everyone, both my kind and humans. Humans are the easiest to read because they don't usually have any ability to block energy." She paused, her face flushing slightly. "I know it's rude, and I don't mean to do it. It's background noise for the most part, but I have to make a special effort not to pay attention to it."

Valentina paused, considering this new information. If Ariana could pick up on everyone's thoughts and intentions before they could choreograph their intent, she could easily turn the tides of any negotiation. "I would imagine this is not information you share with many people. Why are you telling me?"

"I want you to trust me," she said, meeting Valentina's gaze with clear, gray eyes that held no hint of deception or artifice. "Alec told me he believed you felt the energy field earlier today. The only way that could be possible is if you share our same traits. It would also explain why I have trouble reading you and why I was able to heal you so well. It's nearly impossible for me to heal non-sensitives if they weren't injured in an energy attack, but I healed you."

Valentina tapped her fingers against her leg and then forced herself to remain still. She wouldn't draw a weapon against Ariana, but the urge to hold one in her hand was nearly overwhelming.

"Sergei said you have healed several other humans," Valentina pointed out, trying to find a flaw in the young woman's explanation.

"Not exactly," Ariana admitted. "Minor injuries, yes. But for major injuries, I've only been able to heal you, Sergei, and one other human who was injured during an energy attack. If energy isn't involved in some way, it's much more difficult."

Valentina blinked at her. "You are suggesting Sergei is one of you?"

Ariana nodded. "He felt the energy channeling at the table. Even those non-sensitives who have some knowledge of our ways can't usually tell when we're using energy."

Valentina didn't reply. This wasn't good. She didn't even know where to begin. This must have been what Sergei was trying to warn her about.

Ariana held out her hand. "Will you allow me to channel energy toward you? I promise not to hurt you or do anything to break your trust. If you're one of us, you should be able to feel it. If you're not, no harm will be done."

Valentina stared at Ariana's outstretched hand, part of her curious and wanting to explore what this woman offered. But another part of her was wary and somewhat fearful. Everything would change if she took her hand, and while that wasn't necessarily a bad thing, it could act like ripples in a pool of water and have widespread repercussions.

When she was younger, she'd been taught during her training that fear was natural. But it was important to identify your fears and your body's response to them. Only then could you decide whether to reject those fears outright or renegotiate with them. Either way, you did not allow your fear to govern your actions.

She eyed Ariana's hand but didn't touch her. "What happens if it works?"

Ariana paused. "What do you mean?"

Valentina gestured to her outstretched hand. "If I do feel it, what happens with your people?"

"You'd be one of us," Ariana explained, hope shining in her eyes. "We all share the same origins. In some way, we're all family. So many of our people were lost in the last war. If we manage to find even one more of our kind, it'll give us so much hope that others might still be out there."

Valentina didn't bother to hide her disbelief. "They would trust a stranger's word so easily? If I say I feel something, they will believe I am one of you?"

Ariana frowned and lowered her hand. "The only way to tell conclusively is with a DNA test or through you actually using energy. I figured this might be an easier way to find out without involving anyone else."

"If we do this between us, will anyone else know?"

Ariana shook her head. "I'm bonded to Alec. I can't lie to him, but I can ask him not to invade my thoughts until you're willing to tell him."

Valentina's eyes widened. "He can read minds?"

Ariana smiled. "Don't worry. He can't read everyone. He can communicate telepathically when he's touching someone, but he can only hear my thoughts when we're out of touch because of our bond."

"He can hear this conversation?"

Ariana shook her head. "No. I'm blocking him so we can speak privately. I can't feel him, and he can't feel me either."

Valentina was quiet for a long moment, weighing the pros and cons. If she could help her family, she owed it to them to find out the truth about these powers. There was no guarantee she and Sergei could access the restricted areas of the tower in the timeframe they had allotted, and this would definitely speed things up. Besides, if the Omnis considered her to be one of them, they would lower their guard even more.

"You do not need to channel energy to me," she admitted. "I felt it during your truth barrier and at lunch."

Ariana's eyes widened, and a huge smile spread across her face. "You're one of us! I knew there was something about you. This is wonderful!"

"You should not have done this, Ari," Sergei spoke from behind her.

Valentina spun around to find Sergei and Nikolai standing in the doorway. Everyone else was standing right behind them. Based on their shocked expressions, they'd heard enough. She resisted the urge to swear.

"Valentina," Nikolai snapped, walking over to her in a handful of steps. He grabbed her arm and dragged her down the hallway toward her bedroom. She was so startled by the uncharacteristic action, she didn't even think to object. He pulled her into her bedroom and slammed the door behind him. He locked it and withdrew his weapon. "Pack. Now."

She stared at him, trying to get her head around what he was saying. Things couldn't have deteriorated that much in the short time she and Ariana left the room. They would have heard raised voices from the other room. "No one was in jeopardy, Nikolai. I made a tactical decision to obtain information from them. Did something else happen?"

"Pack," he demanded, walking over to the surveillance equipment and yanking it apart. "That's an order."

She frowned but immediately picked up the weapons and began putting them in a nearby bag. He wasn't acting normal, but she'd go along with it for now until they got to a more secure location. Nikolai rarely did anything without good reason, but she had every intention of getting to the bottom of it once they were alone.

Someone pounded on the door, and she heard Sergei yell, "Do not do this, Nikolai."

Valentina paused, lifting her head to stare at the door. Nikolai walked over, grabbed the rest of the weapons out of her hands, and shoved them into the bag. He threw the bag over his shoulder. "Good enough. We're leaving."

There was a loud *thud* against the door. A moment later, the door splintered and broke down. Sergei stumbled into the room. "Valentina, do not leave with him."

"Enough, Sergei." Nikolai pointed his weapon at him. "If you interfere, I will end you."

Valentina gaped at Nikolai. She'd expect this from Yuri, but not Nikolai. Gone was the calm and infinitely patient man she knew as well as herself. In its place was a barely controlled fury, the likes of which she hadn't seen in years. "Nikolai, what are you doing?"

"Tell her why you are leaving," Sergei demanded.

"You are no longer welcome in our camp, Sergei," Nikolai declared, grabbing her arm and pulling her toward the door.

Valentina's eyes widened, and she looked back and forth between the two men. Yuri jogged up from behind them carrying several bags.

Nikolai glanced over at him. "Take only what you have in your hands, Yuri. We need to leave now."

Yuri nodded and headed toward the exit with them.

"He does not want to lose you!" Sergei yelled after them. "He would risk damning this entire alliance to keep you by his side."

She halted in her tracks. "Nikolai, is this true?"

"Later," he snapped, his hand tightening on her arm as he pulled her forward. "Do not force me to pull rank on you, Valentina."

"Trust us, Valya," Yuri urged. "We have never abandoned you. We will explain everything later."

She glanced back at Sergei one last time and wished she hadn't. The regret and longing in his eyes matched the same emotions in her heart.

# CHAPTER FIFTEEN

THE DOOR CLOSED BEHIND THEM, and Sergei leaned back against the wall. He closed his eyes and slumped down onto the floor. He'd known this would happen. If he'd made time to talk to her as soon as Lars brought up the subject, maybe all of this could have been avoided. Although, if he'd never left her in the first place she wouldn't have automatically trusted Nikolai and Yuri without also talking to him. There had to be a way to salvage this. He couldn't lose her again.

"Sergei," Ariana whispered, kneeling beside him and placing her hand on his arm. "I'm so sorry. I had no idea they would take her away."

Sergei didn't reply. He would have done the same thing in Nikolai's position, but it didn't make it any easier. Valentina had always been too curious for her own good, and she probably justified her admission by telling herself she could protect the people she loved by getting more information. She just hadn't counted on the lengths they'd all go to in order to protect her from herself.

"We might be able to talk to her and convince her to

return," Alec suggested. "It sounded as though she was interested in pursuing discussions about our abilities."

Sergei opened his eyes, pinning Alec with his glare, and pushed up from the ground. "Do you have any idea what you have done? I told Lars not to let you push this. Our alliance is over because of your actions."

Alec stiffened. "This alliance can still be salvaged. We can speak with some of your other leaders and explain we don't mean Valentina any harm. She's one of us."

"She is not," Sergei snapped. "She cannot belong to our Coalition and to your people. There cannot be any split loyalties among us. If they believe her loyalty lies with you, she'll be executed."

Ariana gasped, and her hand flew to her mouth. "Why would they do that?"

Sergei swore. "Valentina is not just a pretty face. She is one of our highest-ranking field operatives, a senior officer in our military, and only a few steps away from the seat of power. She knows too much and holds too much influence. They will not risk allowing her to live if they suspect her of playing both sides. Contrary to what Valentina may believe, I do not believe even she could talk her way out of it. Nikolai took the only course of action he could to save her life."

Brant shook his head. "I had no idea. All her questions... she seemed so innocent and curious. She was working me for information the whole time and I had no idea. I'd normally be furious, but I'm actually rather impressed."

"She must be a water channeler," Alec mused. "They can be as fluid as water, changing personas with ease, depending on the situation."

Ariana nodded. "Yes, and Sergei is a fire channeler. It explains why they're drawn together, and why my healing abilities work so well on them."

Sergei shrugged. "It does not matter anymore. You will

not see her again. None of us will. Nikolai will most likely have her off this continent by morning."

Ariana frowned. "You can't go after her?"

"No," Sergei muttered, running a hand through his overly long hair. "Nikolai meant what he said. He will not risk losing her, and I am too much of a threat due to my association with OmniLab. He will not chance any further contact."

Ariana's shoulders drooped, and she clasped her hands together. "She loves you, Sergei. I thought she loved Nikolai, but it's not the same. She cares for him and Yuri, but it doesn't even come close to what she feels for you."

He squeezed his eyes shut, Ariana's words gripping his heart like a vice. "It does not matter, Ari. I broke her heart three years ago. I had another chance to get her back and make it up to her, but that is now gone. Nikolai will not allow her anywhere near the towers again, and he will not allow me anywhere near her. I would do the same if I were in his position."

Lars frowned. "I've seen what you're capable of, Sergei. Can't you break into their camp?"

Sergei crossed his arms and glared at Lars. "They will be mobilized by morning, if not by the time they return to camp."

"Leave now," Lars suggested. "You know where their camp is, you know their tactics, and you have our technology behind you. We can get in long enough for you to talk to her."

"And then what?" Sergei demanded. "You think she will just leave the only family she has left? You think she will turn her back on a lifetime of service because she loves me? The four of us were a unit for many years. We trained together and conducted operations together. We were insep-arable, but then I made a mistake. I left her three years ago, and Nikolai and Yuri picked up the pieces. If I walk back into their camp, I will be asking her to leave her family for the one person who abandoned her. I cannot do that to her."

Ariana took a small step toward him. "Why did you leave her?"

Sergei sighed. "She had been badly injured during a takeover. I lost control and caused a fire to break out in the facility, trapping twenty-six people in a service wing. They were burned alive before Nikolai and Yuri managed to stop me. Some of them were innocent civilians."

Ariana gasped, but Sergei turned away and began to pace. He could still see their faces and hear their screams every time he closed his eyes. "Nikolai hid the truth of what happened that day and claimed it was intentional on my part. Our leaders thought my tactics were brutal yet effective since it was the quickest surrender in our history. They offered me my own command on a trial basis. I wanted to bring Valentina with me once she healed, but I worried if something happened to her during OmniLab's takeover, I would lose control again. Nikolai had just been promoted to his position, and I thought it was a safer option for her. He promised to protect her, so I left before she ever woke up."

"A rage," Alec mused, rubbing his chin in thought. "A blinding rage overcame you, didn't it?"

Sergei swallowed back his shame and nodded. "Yes. I could not risk it happening again. Too many innocents died."

Ariana frowned and put her hand back on his arm. "Sergei, what happened was truly horrible, but it wasn't your fault. If you're an untrained fire channeler, your rage makes sense. You view her as your mate, and her life was threatened."

Sergei squeezed his eyes shut and shook his head. No excuse could ever justify what he'd done. "I cannot afford to lose control in my position. If I let her go now, Nikolai and

Yuri will keep her safe. They will not tell anyone what was discussed here tonight."

Ariana's voice was gentle as she said, "You're wrong, Sergei. If you're struggling to cope with your abilities, she is too. Both of you need to be properly trained. These rages can be held in check, and we can help her as well."

Sergei frowned. "It is different for Valentina. Even when I was shot, she still maintained her control. You would never have known about her abilities if she had not admitted it to you."

Lars shook his head. "I don't know about that. You didn't see her because you were unconscious, but she was definitely shaken by the thought of losing you. Even back at Nikolai's camp, Yuri mentioned she's been acting erratically. The fact that she's untrained might be part of the reason."

Ariana nodded. "Valentina's abilities would be different than yours, particularly because you're opposing talents. If I had to guess, I'd say both of you help balance each other out. Many water channelers are quick to anger, impatient, or even irritable if they don't have enough contact with their element or with their opposing counterpoint. She's probably experienced at least some of that, especially with not having you by her side."

"Ariana's right," Alec admitted, walking over to Ariana and putting his arm around her. "I was eager to discover whether you two had talents, but it's even more important we make sure you both survive and are protected. We don't have to share this information with anyone. Many of our people don't discuss their talents with each other. If Valentina agrees to return to the towers, we can train you both in secret."

Lars nodded. "If you can speak with Nikolai and convince him to return with Valentina, we can pretend this never happened. Both of you can remain here, train, and continue to conduct your investigation. You'd still have a chance to win her back." He frowned and added, "Besides, Valentina's still a target. We need to get to the bottom of whoever attacked her. You'll have our full backing to do whatever is necessary to make sure she's protected. And if your control issues are tied to her, having her with you while you train will speed things up considerably."

Hope unfurled inside him. Everything they were saying made a strange sort of sense, and it was the best chance he had to convince Nikolai to stay. It wasn't a guarantee, but short of abducting Valentina and forcing her back here, he was out of options. Besides, it was doubtful he'd survive Valentina's anger if he attempted such a thing.

Sergei pulled out his commlink and pressed a button to call Nikolai. When he didn't answer, he tried to reach Valentina. Nothing happened. He swore loudly. She'd either left her communication device here or Nikolai had ordered her to shut it off too. Either way, he needed to find them. He shoved his commlink back into his pocket and lifted his head. "Do you know if they've left the towers?'

Brant pulled out his commlink and pressed a button. "Not yet. They're in the priority elevator. Do you want me to stop it?"

"Do it," Alec ordered.

Sergei interrupted and said, "No, just slow it down or they will exit and find another way out." He mentally recalled the maps he'd previously downloaded of the towers and the direction they'd traveled to get to Lars's quarters. They would have retraced their earlier steps to get to the exit. His best chance of catching up to them was while they were in the elevator. "I need access to the elevator shaft."

Brant nodded, pressed a few more buttons on his commlink, and headed for the door. "I'll take you. I've overridden the elevator adjacent to theirs. We can take that one to catch up with them."

Sergei ran down the hallway to the priority elevators with Brant and Lars following right behind him. The door was already open and waiting for them.

Brant swiped a keycard over the control panel. "Open the access panel in the ceiling. I'll try to match speeds when we get close to their floor. They've got a big lead on us, though, so hold on."

The elevator shot downward, and the car vibrated from the rush of speed. Undeterred, Sergei reached up to open the ceiling hatch. Lars interlaced his fingers and Sergei pushed off Lars's foothold, climbing into the elevator shaft.

"We're twenty floors away yet," Lars yelled up to him.

He nodded, gripping one of the handholds and scanning the shaft. Fortunately, the glass viewing walls and emergency lighting allowed a great deal of light into the shaft. Ladders ran along the wall and disappeared down below, but their car was moving too fast to even try to grab them. He only hoped his former companions were willing to listen before firing on him.

Their elevator car came into sight, and Brant slowed down until they were keeping pace. Sergei gripped the handhold tightly and called down into the car, "Stop the cars between floors so they can't exit."

A moment later, both elevator cars came to a screeching halt. Sergei let out a breath and jumped across the shaft toward their car. He landed hard with a *thump* and rolled to the side just as a weapon fired at him from below.

"Hold your fire!" he shouted. "I mean you no harm. I just want to talk."

———

AT THE SOUND of Sergei's voice, Valentina lowered her weapon. Yuri yanked open the hatch in the ceiling and a moment later, Sergei dropped into the elevator. Yuri lifted his weapon, aiming it directly at Sergei.

"Do not shoot him!" Valentina shouted, jumping in front of the electrolaser gun.

"Move, Valya," Yuri demanded.

"No," she retorted. "Stand down, Yuri."

"Valentina," Nikolai snapped. "Move."

She shook her head, glaring at them and refusing to budge. "I followed your orders to leave, Nikolai. I listened to you, too, Yuri. But if you hurt Sergei right now, I will not forgive either of you."

"He is working with them," Yuri said, still refusing to lower his weapon. "They slowed the elevator down to keep us here. Do not allow your feelings to blind you."

"I do not believe that," Valentina insisted, still blocking the shot. She glanced toward Nikolai, hoping he'd be the voice of reason. "Please, Kolya. You brought him back to us. Do not do this."

"Allow me to speak with you," Sergei said in a calm voice and put his hands on her waist, drawing her against him. "If you refuse my offer, I will leave and you can return to your camp. I will do nothing to cause harm to Valentina or to anyone else. My loyalty is still with you."

Nikolai's jaw clenched, but he nodded. Yuri lowered his weapon with a look of disgust and turned to pull the panel off the elevator wall. Valentina relaxed and turned around to face Sergei. Whatever reasons he had for being there, she had to believe he wasn't there to harm any of them.

"You're an idiot," she declared. "I could have killed you when you jumped on top of our elevator."

He grinned and shook his head. "You knew it was me or you would not have missed."

She shrugged but didn't bother denying it.

His eyes softened as he gazed down at her. He lowered his

head and pressed a gentle kiss against her lips. "Please don't jump in front of any more weapons, Valechka. I don't think my heart can take it."

She placed her hand over where he'd been shot. "I can do no less for you than what you did for me."

"Maybe we should both avoid jumping in front of weapons for a while," he suggested with a grin and placed his hand over hers.

Valentina smiled up at him, too pleased he was there to argue. Yuri finished disabling the elevator surveillance system and leaned against the wall, crossing his arms over his chest. "They are no longer monitoring us. Now talk. Why are you here?"

"They have agreed not to tell anyone what was discussed tonight," Sergei announced. "If you wish to stay in the towers, Valentina and I will be trained in secret."

"No," Nikolai snapped. "I will not trust her life in their hands. You're a fool to trust them so blindly."

Sergei hesitated. "I do not trust them blindly, but they did say something that interested me and makes me want to learn more."

"What?" Nikolai asked, his tone more curious now.

"They said the rage I experienced when Valentina was injured was because of my abilities. They believe she is my mate, and I reacted to her being threatened. If they can help me learn to control this and prevent more deaths, it may be worth it."

Valentina blinked at him. "What are you talking about?"

Sergei frowned, searching her expression. He glanced over at Nikolai and asked, "You never told her?"

"No."

"Told me what?" she demanded.

Sergei swore. "I never wanted to leave you, Valechka, but I kept losing control every time you were injured. Nikolai and

Yuri were barely able to stop me before too many innocents died in the fire. It was getting worse. I had no idea if you would be the one trapped in the flames next time. I couldn't take that risk. I thought I could do my duty without losing control if I knew you were safe and protected."

Valentina stared at him in shock, trying to get her head around what he was saying. Sergei had always had a temper, especially when it came to her, but she hadn't realized *that* was why he'd left. She'd thought the brutality of the fire had been out of character for him, but she'd been unconscious by that point. She only found out later when she'd read through the reports.

Some of their leaders had been thrilled by his expediency in securing their last facility. The majority had won out even if others were shocked and horrified. Sergei had always been ambitious, so when they'd offered him his own command, she'd believed he'd left for a better opportunity.

"The fire was an accident? Why didn't you tell me?"

Sergei reached up to cup her cheek. "I could not look into your beautiful eyes and still walk away from you, little dove. I had to leave before you woke up, but it was the hardest thing I have ever done."

She laid her hand over his heart. "You hurt me, Seryozha. I thought you no longer loved me."

"Never," he swore. "I have always loved you. That was the problem. I couldn't handle the thought of losing you. I thought Nikolai or Yuri would have told you."

"It was not our place to tell her," Nikolai said with a sigh. "She was different after you left, Sergei. The few times Yuri brought up your name, she took a knife to him. When I tried, she'd disappear on assignment for weeks at a time. After a while, we gave up and left it alone. You made the mess. It was your place to clean it up."

"Nikolai is right," she said, irritated by the whole thing.

"All of this could have been avoided if you had waited to talk to me. It's been three years, Sergei. Three years!"

"And I have felt your loss every single day," Sergei acknowledged, tightening his arms around her. "When I met Lars and realized there were others, I thought I might be able to learn how to control these powers and return to you. After that, I heard rumors from several people that you and Nikolai were together, and I thought you had chosen him instead. I wanted you to be happy, even if I had to lose you in the process."

Valentina pushed away from him, the walls of the elevator far too restrictive for her tempestuous emotions. "How did I not know any of this?"

"You didn't want to look too closely, Valya," Nikolai said gently. "Sometimes it's easier to think the worst than to believe the best, especially when we're hurting."

She stopped, taking a steadying breath, and wrapped her arms around herself. It wasn't fair to blame him. She was just as much at fault as Sergei. "I'm supposed to be able to assess situations without emotional involvement."

Nikolai shook his head. "You excel at that when it involves anyone else, but your emotions have always been too close to the surface when it comes to Sergei or any of us. You're not objective, and it's not practical to expect that from yourself."

She lifted her head and frowned. "Then how am I supposed to maintain my effectiveness? I cannot just turn off my emotions."

"No one wants you to," Sergei said, taking another step toward her and putting his arms around her again. "Valechka, you're the heart of our family. If you didn't love all of us the way you do, we would be nothing more than any other assigned unit. We would have gone our separate ways years ago."

Yuri sighed and ran a hand over his shaved head. "As much as I hate to admit it, Sergei is right. I told Nikolai I would follow you if he drove you away from us. You are what makes us a family."

Valentina swallowed, her eyes burning with unshed tears. "Kolya, you cannot afford any liabilities right now. It's too dangerous. Your position isn't yet secure."

"Valechka," Sergei began, turning her in his arms to look down at her, "do not take the blame on yourself. I knew what would happen if I told you my reasons for leaving."

"I would not have let you go," she whispered, curling her fingers into his shirt.

"Exactly," he agreed. "Avoiding another hostile takeover and agreeing to a peaceful resolution with OmniLab was my way of trying to make up for my mistakes. I can't bring back those who died, but this alliance has the potential to save thousands of lives. I owe it not only to our people but also to the families of those who died in the flames to see it through."

Valentina looked up into his eyes, her heart aching from the pain she saw in them. It was impossible to fault his reasoning, but she desperately wanted him back. "Have you finished punishing yourself?"

He smiled down at her. "Yes, Valechka."

"We need to find a way to prevent anything like this from happening again. It would have helped if we had all talked about it, but that's only a small part of this."

"I agree," Nikolai said. "I am sorry for my part, Valya. I could have forced the issue, but at first, I was angry with Sergei too. I knew you were hurting, but as long as we never brought up his name, it was manageable."

Yuri snorted, rubbing his hand over a scar on his arm that she'd given him. "That was because, other than throwing a few small items at you, she mostly just stormed out if you brought him up. Her reaction to me was a little more enthusiastic."

Nikolai chuckled. "There is that."

Sergei tilted her chin up to look into her eyes. "I'm sorry I hurt you. The last three years have been torture without you. I don't want to live my life without you in it."

She placed her hands against his chest, his warmth radiating against her palms. "I feel the same way."

A trace of a smile played upon his lips. "Will you forgive me?"

"Will you leave me again?" she retorted.

He grinned and shook his head. "No, Valechka, I will not leave you again."

"Then I forgive you." She wrapped her arms around him and rested her head against his chest. His steady heartbeat was a reassuring comfort in her ear. He held her close and pressed a kiss against her hair.

Sergei glanced over at Yuri. "What about you, Yuri? I would like to have all of my family back, if possible."

"No," Yuri said, crossing his arms over his chest. "I will not forgive you. Valentina has always had a sensitive heart, especially when it came to you. You were not here to dry her tears, or to fight with her when she needed a distraction, or to hold her when she was hurting. I don't care what you claim, I don't trust you. I will not just sit by and wait for you to do this again."

Valentina frowned. Everything he said was true, but it was only part of the truth. Releasing Sergei, she went over to Yuri. "I've never thanked you for always being there for me. I knew you would fight with me, even when Nikolai would not. You always knew what I needed, even before I did. I love you, Yuri. Thank you."

He hugged her tightly. "I love you too, Valya. Don't do this to yourself again. I cannot bear to see you hurt."

She lifted her head, cupping Yuri's face in her hands. "I love him, Yuri. I want to be a family with all of you again. Please don't ask me to choose sides. It will break my heart all over again. I don't want to lose any of you."

Yuri sighed. "You don't know if he will stay this time."

"No, but how can any of us know? I don't know if you or Nikolai will stay with me, either, but I'm willing to take that risk. You both gave me the courage to try." She traced the scar on his arm and looked up at him. "You showed me you were willing to stay by my side through the worst. If my heart breaks again, I know you will still be there for me just as I would for you."

He pressed his forehead against hers. "I will kill him if he hurts you again, Valya."

She grinned up at him. "If he does, I will clean the blood off the floor for you."

"Deal," he agreed and pressed a kiss against her forehead.

Valentina turned to Nikolai. "And you?"

Nikolai sighed. "I have wanted to bring Sergei back to us for a long time, Valya. We have always been stronger together."

She beamed a smile at him and walked over to embrace him. "Thank you for bringing him back to us, Kolya."

"You were the one who brought our family back together," Nikolai admitted, putting his arms around her.

"And you were the one who believed it enough to make it happen," she whispered, laying her head against his chest. "I love you as well, Kolya."

"Yuri may not have a chance to kill you if you hurt her again," Nikolai warned Sergei over her head. "I will do it first, and I don't give a damn about the blood."

"That will never happen," Sergei swore and held out his hand toward her. Valentina went to him, a sense of rightness filling her at once again being in his arms. "I love you,

Valechka. I will spend the rest of my life proving it to you, if you will let me."

She nodded, wanting to believe his words more than anything. After being apart from him for so long, it was almost surreal having him hold her once again. She'd always loved him—from the moment they'd first met until the day he'd walked out on her. If she was honest with herself, she'd never stopped.

Even after Nikolai and Yuri told her Sergei was gone, she hadn't believed it. She'd gotten angry with them for trying to convince her otherwise. It wasn't until she accessed the reports from the takeover that she'd realized it was true and he wasn't coming back. Seeing Sergei's signature on the order accepting command to lead the OmniLab takeover had destroyed something inside her. After that, she'd been too angry with herself and hurt to even consider any alternatives.

She'd spent the past three years trying to bury her feelings for him. Sometimes it worked, but more often than not, she tried her best to ignore it. His loss had been a constant ache, and she'd spent more time than she wanted to admit reading his progress reports. Several times, she'd even considered tracking him down to demand an explanation, but her stubborn pride had refused to allow it. She hadn't wanted him to know how deeply he'd wounded her.

Reaching up to touch his face to reassure herself this was real, she looked up into his eyes and let him see how much she'd missed him. His eyes softened as he gazed down at her, telling her without words how much he loved her and how wrong she'd been. Valentina swallowed, tracing the line of his strong jaw with her fingertips.

"I love you too, Seryozha," she whispered.

"You will not regret giving me another chance, little dove." He bent down to kiss her, his lips gentle in a whispered promise. When he pulled back, he looked over at

Nikolai but didn't release her. "Are you willing to consider Alec's proposal?"

"I don't know about staying in the towers," Nikolai said, glancing out the glass elevator wall into the courtyard area below. "Their offer is generous, but we have no way to guarantee their silence on the matter. It will also take longer than we can spare for Valentina to be trained. If we are to support Alec's request for additional time on the construction, I will need her *and* Yuri to help make it happen."

"Would you consider establishing a permanent base in the towers?"

Her eyes widened, and she looked up at him. "That is your command, Sergei."

He shrugged. "We can work something out. We've done it before."

She turned to look at Nikolai, who was regarding Sergei thoughtfully. Nikolai was most likely intrigued by the idea, but it was the implementation of the plan that had the most challenges. Either way, it was a discussion best tabled for another day.

"I think we should stay," she began. "For now, at least. If they believe I'm one of them, they will most likely share some information with me about their powers. This could be one of our only opportunities to get this type of information from them."

Nikolai frowned. "And what happens when our people believe the same? I'm not willing to put your life in jeopardy for this information, Valya."

She gestured to herself and said, "I appreciate your concern, but our Coalition trained me to blend in and adapt. I blended. I adapted. I have never given our people any reason not to trust me."

"You are too close to the line," Nikolai warned, that hardened glint coming back into his eyes. "If you give them reason to suspect you, it will be over."

Yuri nodded. "It's not worth it, Valya. Let someone else investigate. You were too obvious when you stood on the truth barrier. There were too many witnesses."

She huffed. They were sometimes a little too protective. "I can claim it was a ruse. Besides, we still have an investigation to conduct. I'm supposed to meet with Viktor tomorrow morning to tour the construction tower. If I don't show up, he and Peter will take it as a slight. We cannot afford to offend them."

Nikolai waved off her concerns. "I can handle Peter."

Valentina nodded. "You can, and you frequently do. But if any of us are a target, we are safer here than back on the surface. Our people were responsible for the ambush. The Omnis didn't have a hand in the attack."

Nikolai frowned. "You spent all of yesterday trying to talk me out of coming here, and now you're trying to convince me to stay."

She shrugged and gave him a small smile. "Circumstances changed my mind."

"Or Sergei's arms around you did," Yuri muttered.

Those same arms tightened around her as Sergei said, "If you decide to leave and return to the surface, I will join you. I meant what I said about not being parted from Valentina again. However, I agree with her. I think remaining in the towers, at least temporarily, is the best place to launch your investigation. I will go with her to meet Viktor, so she'll be protected no matter what. But in the meantime, can you afford not to take advantage of the possible intel Valentina can obtain by training with them?"

"I do not need protection from Viktor," she reminded him.

Sergei grinned and pressed a light kiss against her lips. "Very well. I will protect him from you."

She rolled her eyes. Nikolai glanced at Yuri, and the other man shrugged to indicate he would defer to whatever Nikolai decided.

Finally, Nikolai sighed. "Very well. We will stay until the meeting with Viktor has concluded. After that, we will reevaluate."

Valentina lifted her head to stare up at the open hatch in the ceiling. "Yuri, do you want to fix the elevator? I would rather not climb while wearing this dress."

Nikolai raised an eyebrow, but Yuri sighed and opened the panel. "She's not wearing any underwear."

Nikolai coughed and said, "Somehow, I don't want to know how you know this."

"I have a much easier solution," Sergei said with a chuckle and pulled out his commlink. He pressed a button. "Lars, tell Brant to activate the elevator again. We are heading back to your quarters."

Valentina leaned back against him. "You cheated."

"Since when do we have rules?" he murmured, running his nose along her neck and pressing a small kiss against it.

# CHAPTER SIXTEEN

VALENTINA EYED the pool with trepidation. When they had told her what she'd be doing, she had imagined something much... smaller. "You want me to get in that?"

Ariana nodded. "The water is shallow in this area, so you can stand without a problem. I can teach you to swim eventually, although you shouldn't have much trouble if you're a water channeler like I suspect."

Sergei leaned in close and teased, "Don't tell me you're afraid, Valechka. Shall I show you how it's done?"

Her eyes narrowed, and she shrugged him off, but his words had their desired effect. Valentina stepped into the cool water, mildly surprised at how quickly her earlier tension began to drift away. She moved down lower until the water was almost to her shoulders. Taking a deep breath, she released her inhibitions and submerged herself completely.

Peace.

An exquisite serenity unlike anything she'd ever known filled her. The only time she'd ever felt anything remotely similar was when she was in Sergei's arms. It was the sensation of belonging somewhere, as though something missing had finally clicked into place. It was a feeling of home.

Sergei's hand on her shoulder interrupted her daze, and she broke the surface with a gasp. He'd joined her in the pool and now his worried gaze met hers. "Are you all right? You were under for a long time."

She blinked and brushed the water out of her eyes, and Ariana smiled at her knowingly. "You feel it, don't you?"

Valentina frowned. "I don't understand."

"You're a water channeler," Ariana explained. "The water is your element. I would imagine you haven't had many opportunities to spend much time in a pool like this one. But those with our elemental alignment tend to be drawn to the water. This is the source of your power and where you're most at home."

Valentina nodded, cupping her hands to fill them with water. It was a little strange to be floating in a pool like a turnip in a pot of soup, but she couldn't deny the sense of rightness. "That's exactly how it feels."

Ariana dipped her hand in the water and spread her fingers, causing water droplets to cascade through the air in a surreal demonstration of her power. "Water channelers can have different talents. We don't know exactly how your abilities have manifested themselves, but we can explore them to find out. Most of us can freeze water, pull moisture from the air, make it rain, or redirect the flow of water. Some of us are healers, some can direct dreams... the list is endless."

Valentina frowned. All those powers sounded more than a little far-fetched, but Ariana's display was proof of the veracity of her words.

Ariana swam closer to her. "Will you try something with me?"

"What?"

Ariana stopped when she was only a foot away and held

out her hand. "If you take my hand, I can form a small connection with you. With it, I can show you some basic water manipulation skills."

At her hesitation, Sergei said, "I have seen her do this with Kayla."

Valentina looked up at him, and he gave her an encouraging nod. She turned back to Ariana and took the young woman's outstretched hand.

"We normally begin training a little bit differently, but I think you might learn better through a demonstration."

A moment later, a strange sort of awareness filtered through Valentina. Before she could fully explore the sensation, a jolt of electricity shot through her. She jerked her hand away. "What was that?"

Ariana gasped, flexing her hand as though it pained her. "I-I don't know. That shouldn't have happened. What did it feel like?"

"It was like an electrical current shooting up my arm," Valentina said, rubbing her hand and still feeling the tingles.

Alec burst into the pool area a moment later. "What happened? I felt your distress. Are you all right, Ari?"

"I'm not sure," Ariana admitted, a frown on her face. "They both have energy, but it's blocked somehow. I thought I had felt Sergei's energy before, too, but I couldn't reach his either. That might be why I was only able to partially heal them."

"Maybe they aren't *Drac'Kin*," Alec suggested.

Ariana shook her head. "No, I know they are. I feel it, Alec."

Sergei wrapped his arms around Valentina, pulling her against him. "Perhaps you should explain what you tried to do just now."

"I tried to form a connection, just like a thousand other connections I've made over the years," Ariana said with a frown. "I was looking for some of Valentina's loose energy so I could connect with her. Most of her energy threads are very tightly bound, which is unusual for someone who is untrained. But when I tried to coax one to separate, that's when there was an electrical shock."

Valentina lifted her head to meet Sergei's gaze, asking him with her eyes if they should tell them. Sergei shook his head a fraction.

"You know something," Alec accused from where he was standing beside the pool.

"Perhaps," Sergei admitted, tightening his arms around her. "A suspicion more than anything."

"Sergei," Valentina said gently, switching to their native tongue. "We need to explore this."

"I know, but we must consider the ramifications," he reminded her.

She squeezed her eyes shut, the water helping to focus her thoughts enough to give her a small measure of patience. Sergei was right, even if she didn't want to wait. She opened her eyes. "I am truly sorry, Ariana. I cannot train with you right now. I'm willing to learn whatever you're willing to teach, but there are boundaries that must be respected."

Sergei took her hand and started to lead her to the edge of the pool. "Come, Valechka, we should get some rest before tomorrow. Thank you for your time, Ariana."

"Wait," Ariana called out, moving toward them. "I can try to walk you through a brief exercise without forming a connection. It will make things a little more difficult for you to learn, but it's still possible. Will you try?"

Valentina hesitated and then nodded. If there was even a chance they could learn something, they needed to take it. Sergei frowned at her but didn't object.

"Hold out your hands like this," Ariana instructed, cupping her empty hands in front of her. When Valentina did as she indicated, Ariana continued, "Now close your eyes and focus on the water around you."

Valentina closed her eyes, feeling the cool water lapping against her skin. Every rhythmic motion siphoned off more of her tension until a soothing peace filled her.

"Imagine in your mind's eye that you pull a thin stream of water from the pool. Now direct it to fill your hands."

Valentina visualized the water arcing upward and gasped as water splashed over her hands. Her eyes flew open, and she gaped at the water in her outstretched hands. Ariana was watching her with an approving expression. "Welcome home, sister."

Sergei placed his hands on Valentina's shoulders in a protective gesture. "You must not say such things, Ari."

Ariana's smile faded a little, and she nodded. "I know. But as a water channeler, we share the same origins. This is a basic water talent."

Intrigued by the possibilities, Valentina concentrated again but with her eyes open this time. When the water filled her hand again, she couldn't hide her wide smile. "How do I find out what else can I do?"

Ariana hesitated. "You learn quickly, but we won't know your more specialized talents until we get much further into your training. It would help if we could form a connection. Some of us have the ability to gauge talents but it requires a connection."

Valentina shook her head, trying to bury her disappointment. "For now, I must decline."

"If you know about more of our kind, we need to reach out to them," Alec said, taking a step closer to the edge of the pool. "We can keep their talents secret, too, but it's too risky to have our people out in the world without any form of training."

"We cannot answer your questions," Sergei said, heading out of the pool.

"Dammit, Sergei!" Alec's frustration was evident by his rigid body language. "Valentina is one of us, and so are you. Only a true fire channeler could be as stubborn as you."

Valentina ducked her head, biting back a grin. That explained a lot.

Sergei frowned. "What is your point?"

"If there are others of our kind out there, these abilities can be confusing or difficult to manage without help. We can provide an environment where their powers are fostered and allowed to grow."

Sergei grabbed a drying cloth off a nearby rack. "We cannot discuss this with you."

"Alec," Ariana interrupted. "I know you want to protect our people, but Sergei and Valentina haven't refused. Maybe we should give them some time."

Valentina sighed and climbed out of the pool, already missing the water. Outside the towers, it was unlikely she'd ever get a chance to experience such a thing again.

Sergei handed her a drying cloth, and she wrapped it around herself. She squeezed some of the excess moisture from her hair and said, "Ariana is correct. I am curious and would like to learn more, but there are things you do not understand. We cannot share them with you yet."

"Valentina," Sergei began.

She put her hand on his arm in a reassuring gesture. "Sergei risked a great deal to convince Nikolai to remain here. We are already skirting the line of what may be permitted. I understand you have concerns, but so do we. Our people have made a study of your culture over the years, but yours have not done the same. You don't understand the ramifications of what you are asking."

Ariana climbed out of the pool, taking the drying cloth

Alec offered her. "Sergei told us you could be executed if they thought you were one of us."

Valentina's body stiffened, and her eyes narrowed at Sergei. He winced and gave an apologetic shrug. "They didn't understand why it was dangerous, so I explained your position."

"You should be thankful I don't have any weapons handy," she snapped.

He grinned. "That wouldn't be much of a deterrent."

"You have compromised me, Sergei," she retorted, furious with him for revealing that information. In less than a day, these Omnis knew more about her than her own people did.

"All is well, Valechka," he murmured, taking a step closer to her. "I would do nothing to put you at risk. They know only your military status and Nikolai's position."

"It's not your place to share even that information," she argued, poking him in the chest.

He grabbed her finger, his eyes twinkling with amusement, and bent down to kiss her. "I will have to come up with a way to get you to forgive me."

"You are impossible," she murmured against his mouth but wound her arms around his neck. He pulled her against him, his heated skin contrasting with the cool air in the room. For a long moment, she was lost in his kiss and in him.

Sergei placed another kiss against her lips but didn't release her. It was so easy to lose track of everything when he was touching her, and based on the heat in Sergei's gaze, he felt the same.

When she turned to look at Alec and Ariana, they were watching them. Ariana smiled. "Your energy complements each other. I've never seen such a perfect pairing of energy before."

Sergei's arms around her tensed. "What do you mean?"

"Your energy is closed off somehow, but when you two are

together and unguarded, it flares. It's almost as though you're already bonded."

Valentina exchanged another uneasy look with Sergei. This wasn't good.

Sergei turned back to Alec and Ariana. "Have you seen this before?"

Ariana nodded. "Yes. Some of our kind can detect energy bonds, but I'm not very good at it. My ability is tied more to emotional connections, which is usually part of a bond. I can pick up on those sometimes, especially in an unguarded moment."

Sergei frowned. "How many of your people can see such things?"

Alec's eyes narrowed, his expression becoming somewhat suspicious. "We don't track that information. I wouldn't say it's a rare ability, but it's not exactly common either. Why?"

"Call it simple curiosity," Sergei said, grabbing Valentina's hand and heading for the door. "If you'll excuse us, we need to take care of a few personal matters."

She reached down to grab her clothes and weapons on the way out. As soon as they were outside, she whispered, "You're being ridiculous. How much more obvious could you get?"

"I had no idea they could see that, or I would never have taken you there," Sergei argued, scanning the corridor for anyone within earshot. "We have no idea what else they can see, but we have already shown them too much."

"So they saw something," she said with a shrug, putting on her arm sheath while they walked.

"Do *you* want to explain everything else to them?"

She frowned and gave up on her other weapons. It was enough to have them in her hands. "No, but they already know we have powers. What they saw between us doesn't make much difference."

"I'm not willing to risk them knowing more yet," Sergei

said, stopping outside Lars's door. He placed his hand on the panel, and it opened a moment later. Leading her down the hallway, they walked into her bedroom to find Nikolai and Yuri working on the surveillance equipment.

"That was fast." Nikolai glanced back and forth between them. "What's wrong?"

Sergei closed the door behind them. "We have a problem."

Nikolai straightened. "Tell me."

She sighed and dropped her weapons on the bed. "They can see the energy between Sergei and me. Ariana said it appeared as though we were already bonded."

Sergei started to pace. "She called it complementary energy. They haven't seen anything else. It was an unguarded moment between us."

Nikolai frowned, his expression growing concerned. "You're sure they haven't seen anything else?"

Valentina shook her head and shrugged. "I don't know. I agree with Sergei's assessment that Ariana is honest, but omission is different than lying. I don't believe the truth is something they will naturally consider." She frowned, part of her somewhat disappointed but not entirely surprised. "I don't believe they would understand, Kolya."

"We never thought they would," Nikolai reminded her gently. "Our intention was never to stay here, but only to learn and assess. I told you I wanted to see Sergei in person to determine what he hadn't been putting in his reports."

"I don't think they can properly train us," Sergei admitted, continuing his pacing. Tension radiated off him and increased with each pass he made across the floor. "Ariana tried to create a connection with Valentina, but it didn't work. I suspect the same thing will happen when they try to train me."

Valentina stopped him, putting her hands against his

chest. Panic was starting to fill her at his unspoken words. "You promised not to leave me again."

Sergei grabbed her, pulling her tightly against him and held her as though worried she could slip through his fingers if he relaxed his hold. "We *will* figure this out, Valechka. I will not lose you again."

She wrapped her arms around him and glanced over at Nikolai. "What do you wish to do?"

Nikolai sighed and sat on the edge of the bed. "If we could harness these abilities fully, it could prove beneficial."

Yuri ran a hand over his shaved head and muttered, "And give us a whole new host of problems by telling them the truth."

"They already know about me and Valentina," Sergei murmured, still not releasing her. "It is up to you if you wish to tell them the rest."

Yuri shook his head. "I say no. Perhaps in time, but not now."

"I'm afraid I must agree with Yuri," Nikolai admitted. "It would also be safest if we left the towers tomorrow after your meeting with Viktor. I don't know what this means for you, Sergei. That's something you must decide for yourself."

Valentina gripped Sergei even tighter. If she knew it was only temporary, it wouldn't be that bad. But if he couldn't be trained, he'd run the risk of losing control again as long as she stayed by his side. She knew it would destroy something inside Sergei if anything like the fire ever happened again. She loved him too much to allow that to happen. There had to be a solution.

A light knock on the door interrupted them. Yuri got up, keeping his hand on his weapon, and opened the door to find Lars standing outside.

"I'm sorry for disturbing you," Lars said, glancing at them.

"Alec and Ariana just called. They were worried you were going to leave again."

"Not yet," Nikolai said. "We will leave tomorrow afternoon."

Lars frowned. "I won't try to convince you to stay, but are there any questions I can answer? Alec told me to tell you whatever you wish to know, and he offered to come here to answer your questions as well."

Nikolai was quiet for a long moment, his gaze resting on Valentina and Sergei. "Tell me about these bonds between your people."

Lars's eyebrows rose. "We form small connections with each other to share energy, but we also have the ability to form permanent bonds with each other. Did you want to know about both?"

Valentina bit her lip and looked up at Sergei. "I'd like to know about your permanent bonds. Ariana said she could detect energy between me and Sergei. I want to understand more."

Lars grinned, the expression making him appear much younger. "Did she? Well, you two must have a connection of some sort. Those are fairly common among our people, but we typically only form permanent bonds when we're in a relationship. It requires a total energy commitment by each person and binds them together for the rest of their lives. It allows them to share energy and power from great distances, and often times, it enhances the other's abilities."

She nodded, leaning against Sergei. "Can you have this connection with more than one person? If a relationship doesn't end well, can you enter a bond with another?"

Lars shook his head. "Not with a permanent bond. You can form connections with multiple people, but a permanent bond can only be with one other person. That's one of the reasons we're cautious about entering into such an arrangement and usually have a courtship period."

Sergei ran his hand over her back and frowned. "I thought you said you were able to share a bond with Kayla during the duel. How was that possible?"

Lars nodded. "Yes, but that was only temporary during..." His voice trailed off, and he straightened, studying each of them. "Holy shit. You're *all* bonded, aren't you?"

Valentina tensed, and Sergei's hand on her back froze. Nikolai slowly stood while Yuri tightened his grip on his weapon.

Nikolai's expression was hard, a ruthless danger radiating from him. "Be very careful what you say next, Lars."

Lars stared at him and then looked at each one of them. A thousand thoughts flitted over his face before he swallowed. "I've never heard of anyone being able to share a permanent bond for any length of time. I suppose anything is possible, but I don't know how it would work or even how it could be maintained."

"Kolya," she said softly, "Sergei trusts him."

Nikolai held up his hand to stop her. "How much is your silence worth, Lars?"

Lars glanced over at Sergei. "I will not reveal your secrets. I owe Sergei and your people more than that."

"He is trustworthy, Nikolai," Sergei said. "Out of all their people, he is the only one with whom I would consider sharing this information."

"I suppose we need some answers," Nikolai relented, sitting on the edge of the bed. "Can you detect bonds?"

Lars relaxed now that his life wasn't in immediate danger and shook his head. "No. I have some abilities to detect types of talent, but it requires touch."

"Yet you never knew about Sergei?" Nikolai prompted.

"He never gave me any reason to suspect," Lars admitted.

"I had moments where I wondered if he might have some latent talent, but it didn't even dawn on me that the bond thing was possible. I had no idea about his connection between you three until Valentina came to the towers."

Valentina rested her head against Sergei's chest and relaxed against him as he began running his hand down her back again. The rhythmic motion of his caress and heat from his body was better than anything the pool had offered.

Lars studied them for a moment. "Fire and water are frequently drawn together." He turned to look at Nikolai and Yuri. "If I had to guess, I'd say Nikolai is an earth-based talent whereas Yuri is air-based."

Valentina glanced over at Nikolai and Yuri, mildly curious by Lars's assessment. "What makes you think that?"

Lars frowned. "Just a guess. Nikolai is usually very even tempered with a focus on politics, so he would be better suited as an earth- or water-based talent. The only way I could see the four of you forming a unit for so long would be if you represented each of the four elements."

Nikolai nodded. "Can you still form connections with other people when you are already bonded?"

"It's possible, but it's not typically done. Most of the time, we're protective of our bondmates. It's against our nature to allow such an intimacy unless absolutely necessary." Lars glanced at Valentina and added, "For example, and I'm not making the offer, but how would you feel if I asked to make a connection with Valentina?"

"It will not happen," Sergei declared, tightening his arms around her.

Lars nodded as though Sergei had just proved his point. "You threatened to kill me if I slept with her. I don't think that was an idle threat. But you were more tolerant when you thought she and Nikolai were lovers. If you four already share a bond, that's why."

Valentina frowned. "But Nikolai and Yuri have both had other lovers. I didn't have a problem with that."

"I doubt their lovers were *Drac'Kin*," Lars pointed out. "There's a level of intimacy with energy sharing that usually goes beyond mere physical attraction. Even though it might not be an issue if they take a human lover, I don't think any of you would be willing to share with another energy channeler outside of your bond."

Valentina bit her lip. What he was saying made sense, but it didn't explain what had happened earlier. "When I tried to form a connection with Ariana, she received a type of electrical shock. Do you know why?"

Lars frowned. "I don't know for sure. If I had to guess, I'd say Sergei may have been okay with it because he knows Ariana well enough to know she wouldn't hurt you. But if Nikolai or Yuri felt it through your bond, they may have subconsciously issued a warning."

Valentina lifted her head to regard Sergei. "Is that what you suspected?"

He nodded. "I thought it was related to them, but I didn't know how."

"If you don't mind me asking," Lars began, darting a quick glance at Nikolai and Yuri, "but how did this even happen? I've never heard of anything like this being done before. The fact that you all found each other and managed to form a bond is incredible."

Nikolai nodded at Sergei, indicating his permission to tell him.

"I told you before that we were assigned as a unit," Sergei explained. "But it was a bit more than that. Our class had almost two hundred students, and our instructors tasked us with forming a four-person team with three others who complemented our skillset. I found Valentina almost immediately. I didn't care who else was in our unit as long as she was in mine."

She smiled up at him, remembering it a bit differently. "I thought *I* found *you*. You were cocky even then, leaning against the wall and looking down on everyone else."

"Except you," he said, his eyes softening as he gazed at her.

"Except me," she whispered, lifting her hand to trace her fingers over his jaw. "I recognized you, too, and knew you were supposed to be mine."

Sergei turned his head to kiss her fingertips. "Valentina was the one who found Nikolai and Yuri. Or they found her." He shrugged, indicating it didn't matter either way.

"A bit of both, I think," Nikolai admitted with a small smile.

Valentina nodded. "We had a connection immediately, each of us with different strengths that complemented each other. But it was during some of our training that things between us changed."

"How?" Lars prompted.

Nikolai sighed. "We cannot go into details because many of the training exercises are classified, but we were subjected to extreme stressors. These exercises were designed to push us beyond all normal limits and work together to accomplish our goals."

"So your bond formed out of a necessity for survival," Lars mused.

"Eventually, yes," Nikolai agreed. "At first, we merely exceeded expectations, but then our trainers wanted to see how much we could possibly handle. One of these exercises went... wrong. That's when our bond was formed."

Valentina frowned. Even now, it was still one of the most harrowing experiences of her life. She didn't think any of them wanted to revisit those memories. "I don't think any of us would have survived without it, especially me."

"That was the beginning for me," Sergei said, lifting his hand to cup her face and run his thumb across her cheek. "I've never been able to handle seeing her in pain, but I almost killed one of our trainers once we returned to camp. Every time after that when Valechka was hurt or threatened, I lost a little more control. "

Valentina wrapped her hand around his wrist, holding her to him, and looked up into his steely-gray eyes with the small flame around his irises. In a soft voice, she whispered, "I love you, Seryozha."

Sergei squeezed his eyes shut and lowered his forehead against hers. "I cannot tell you how much I've missed hearing those words from you, little dove."

Lars's expression turned thoughtful. "These rages started right after you bonded?"

Sergei glanced over at him and nodded. "Yes, but they became worse over time and depending on the severity of her injuries."

Lars glanced at the others. "None of you experienced anything like that?"

Nikolai considered it for a moment. "Not to the degree Sergei did. We're all protective of Valentina, but Sergei has always been closest to her."

Lars hesitated, eyeing all of them warily. "I know this is a delicate subject, but other than Sergei, have any of you been intimate with her?"

Sergei's jaw clenched. "There had better be a point to this line of questioning."

"I'm going to assume not," Lars said quickly and held up his hands in surrender. "Our kind can deepen a bond through an emotional connection or a sexual one. Sergei, if you're the only one who has been intimate with her, you hold a stronger connection."

Valentina stiffened, alarmed and worried all at once. "You mean, if I slept with Nikolai or Yuri, they would have the same thing happen?"

Yuri grinned. "Perhaps we should go in the other room, Valya. I can kick Sergei out of the running."

Sergei snorted. "As if that would ever happen."

"Behave." Valentina turned back to Lars.

Lars nodded. "If you are intimate with Nikolai or Yuri, then yes. It might manifest differently based on their talents, but their reactions to you being injured or threatened would be just as intense as Sergei's response. In their minds, they'd most likely view you as their mate, and it would be instinctive to want to protect and defend you. One of the reasons you were so distraught when Sergei was injured was because of the depth of your connection to him. I suspect if we'd been in a location where water was readily available, it would have been a problem."

Valentina started to pull away from Sergei, but his grip on her tightened.

"No," he declared, holding her in place. "Valentina, you are mine. If you think to lessen our connection by walking away, you can forget it."

"If I have a choice between keeping you by my side or fucking you, I have already made my choice," she argued. "I will not lose you again, Sergei."

"It won't do any good," Lars said gently.

She turned to look at him. "What do you mean?"

"Your connection won't diminish. If you truly have a permanent bond, it can't be removed," Lars explained and then paused. "At least, as far as we know. There's only been one case of a permanent bond being destroyed, but we don't fully understand how it happened or if it's possible to duplicate it." He glanced over at Sergei's scowl and added, "Or even if you'd want to."

"What Lars is saying makes sense," Nikolai said, taking a step toward her. "I've had great difficulties in being parted from you when you've left camp to pursue various investigations. You've also been much more concerned over my welfare than you used to be, and I suspect it's because we've played the part of lovers in public."

Yuri nodded. "We've all noticed it, Valya."

She paled. "I didn't realize..." Turning to Lars, she demanded, "Is this possible?"

Lars hesitated and then nodded. "I believe so. Affection and touch are all tied together in deepening an emotional connection."

Valentina squeezed her eyes shut, wondering how they could have been so stupid. None of their lives were safe, and harm could come to any one of them in a thousand different directions. She was openly affectionate with all of them, and they'd always encouraged it. She didn't want to hold back with them, but she'd already lost Sergei once over this.

Nikolai's sharp tone broke through her thoughts. "Stop, Valentina. Whatever you are thinking, just stop." She opened her eyes, and he sighed. Nikolai walked over to her and pressed a kiss against her forehead. "This isn't a bad thing. Our connection makes all of us stronger. None of us are willing to walk away from each other. Why do you think I wanted to bring Sergei back to us?"

"You missed him too," she murmured.

He nodded, lifting his hand to brush his thumb over her cheek. "Yes. Sergei is like a brother to me, and our family has been incomplete since he left. Even Yuri would agree with me, if he weren't so stubborn."

Valentina smiled and glanced over at Yuri, who shrugged but didn't dispute Nikolai's words. She looked up at Sergei again. Even though she knew Sergei wanted to come back to them, too, she didn't want him to suffer either. "Can we stop these rages from happening?"

Lars nodded. "I believe we can, or at least get them under control enough so they won't consume him. We'll need to find a fire channeler beyond reproach to train him, but it's possible."

Sergei frowned. "How will that work if we're unable to form connections with anyone?"

Lars sighed and ran his hand over his head. "Honestly, I'm not sure. You would all most likely need to be in the same room initially and feel completely comfortable with the training. Even then, there's a chance whoever is training you might realize you're bonded. It depends on the scope of their talents."

Valentina tilted her head. "You have that ability, correct? Can you tell us what talents we have?" When Lars nodded, she took a step toward him. "We're all in the same room now. Will you form a connection with me?"

Lars's eyes widened. "No offense, Valentina, but I would rather not die today."

She frowned. "I will not hurt you."

"On the contrary," Lars began, looking decidedly uncomfortable. "I'm an unbonded *Drac'Kin* male in my prime who can wield a great deal of power. While on the surface it would be innocent, I'm not willing to form a connection with a woman I'm attracted to with three very large, very possessive, and very deadly men in the same room."

"I suppose we don't have to kill the Omni after all," Yuri mused, leaning against the wall. "He's smarter than I thought."

She huffed. "Then one of you form a connection with him and try it."

Sergei walked over to Lars. "I will do it."

Lars nodded and held out his hand as though offering a handshake. Sergei slipped his hand in his. Valentina bit her lip, hoping this would work.

Nikolai moved to stand beside her and put his arm around her waist in a comforting gesture. Grateful for his presence, she leaned into him before focusing again on Sergei and Lars. Nothing appeared to be happening though.

Lars frowned. "I need all of you to try to relax your guard. You're all shielding so hard it's impossible for me to even find the energy connections."

Valentina took a deep breath to center her thoughts and slowly began to release the intricate citadel of protective energy layers in her mind that guarded her thoughts and emotions. She could feel the rest of them do the same, until they were once again all interconnected.

She nearly swayed at the sensation. It had been so long since she'd felt all of them so intimately. They were each right there, Sergei's burning energy that always warmed away any shadows from her mind, Yuri with his sometimes sharp and acerbic wind that could also be as gentle as a caress, and Nikolai with his steadfast patience, offering peaceful stability. She loved each of them, and together, they completed one another.

Lars was suddenly thrown into the mix, a softer, more tenuous grip than the other three, but she could sense him in their web.

Lars stared at them all in wonder. "By the gods, this is incredible. You're all perfectly matched and in tune with each other. I might be able to reach each of you through Sergei to look at all of your talents."

Her eyes widened. "You can do that?"

"I believe so," Lars said with a trace of awe still in his voice. "Will you give me permission to explore the bond you share?"

"Go ahead," Sergei agreed.

Lars reached out first, testing the strength of Sergei's energy connection, and then prompted him to channel energy toward him. After a long moment, Lars said, "I'll be damned. You can hold a truth shield, and not just a basic one either. I think you may be able to isolate even disingenuous gestures and paralyze someone. It's rare enough that I've never seen it in practice, but a fire channeler would know more about the mechanics. That's a highly coveted ability, and it explains why you're so good at reading people."

Sergei made a noncommittal noise, and Valentina knew he was already considering how best to put such a talent to use.

Lars's brow furrowed again in concentration. "You also have an affinity for electronics and can generate your own electrical field. Those are highly-specialized talents. I can't tell more without a fire channeler's assistance though. We may need different people to help you develop those abilities. I've never seen them in one person before."

Lars turned to Nikolai. "May I explore your energy next?"

"What do you need from me?" Nikolai asked, and Valentina could sense his curiosity through their connection.

"It would be easiest if you're willing to take my hand," Lars admitted. "Otherwise, we can try it through Sergei, but my interpretation may be skewed since it'll be funneling through him. Touch can strengthen my link to you."

"That's fine," Nikolai agreed and released her. He held out his hand, and Lars grasped it.

"You need to send some energy in my direction," Lars instructed and waited while Nikolai's strong energy flowed outward toward Lars. Valentina found herself fascinated as she watched their interaction through their open bond and how Lars assessed Nikolai's energy.

"Yes, you're definitely an earth-energy channeler," Lars mused. "I believe you may also have more than one specialized talent, Nikolai. You have the ability to reshape the earth, which appears to be quite strong, but there's also something..." He frowned and then his eyes widened. "You can predict future events. At least, you have the ability to see a few minutes into the future. I believe there's only one other individual in the towers with that ability, but we have documentation on it in our archives. I'll make sure you have access to the records."

"I'd appreciate that," Nikolai said, releasing his hand. "Ariana is also an earth channeler, correct?"

Lars nodded. "I'm sure she'd be happy to show you how to use your basic talents and explain your more specialized ones too. I suspect you all may be able to tap into your bond with each other to develop even more abilities. If your pairing wasn't so evenly balanced, you wouldn't be able to do such a thing."

Yuri approached him and held out his hand. Lars grimaced and said, "This is going to be more difficult since we share the same element. It's hard to avoid the competitive nature of our kind, but I'll do my best."

Yuri arched an eyebrow. "A little competition might make this entire ordeal more interesting."

"Yuri," Nikolai warned.

Yuri grinned, and Valentina could feel him channeling energy in Lars's direction. The other man flinched and said, "Enough."

Yuri cut off the flow of energy abruptly, and Lars withdrew his hand. "Definitely wind. Interestingly enough, I believe you can communicate with creatures of the sky. I've heard you were an exceptional scout. I can't help but wonder if that's also tied into your talents. I believe you may also have the ability to affect and influence people. It will probably require touch to be effective. Alec possesses that talent, and I'm sure he'd be willing to walk you through it."

Yuri smirked. "Now that may prove to be interesting. I would not mind influencing Sergei to do a few painful things."

"I have often said you were full of hot air," Sergei said with a grin.

Lars turned toward Valentina and hesitated, glancing around at the others. "Will you all kill me if I touch her?"

Her eyes narrowed at them. "Not if they wish to keep breathing."

Without waiting for a response, she walked up to Lars and offered him her hand. He took it, and she was momentarily taken aback. His skin was cooler than she expected, and with her natural defenses lowered, he reminded her a little of Yuri. She tilted her head to study him, comparing and contrasting her sense of him through their connection.

"Go ahead and channel some energy toward me," he encouraged, his voice gentler than it had been with the others.

It had been years since she'd explored this side of herself. They spent so much time suppressing their abilities, it was strange to actually embrace it. Focusing within, she withdrew her energy and sent it in his direction. He inhaled sharply, placing his hand over hers, and took a step toward her. Sergei grabbed him and yanked him away, breaking their contact. Yuri and Nikolai surrounded her, each of them scowling at Lars.

"Stop it," she snapped at them. "What's wrong with you?"

Lars shook his head. "It's not their fault, Valentina. I shouldn't have approached you."

She huffed in exasperation. "Nothing happened."

"Valechka," Sergei said, approaching her warily.

"No, do not *Valechka* me," she retorted, putting her hands on her hips. "If he can tell us more about our powers, we need to know. We all suspected some of these things, but now we have confirmation."

Sergei's fingers flexed as though battling to regain control. "I didn't think it would be this difficult. I do not want him touching you."

Valentina lifted her chin and approached Sergei. "Do you think I'm unaware of what happened between you and Ariana?"

Sergei blanched.

She nodded. "Exactly. There is only one reason you would be so protective of her."

"I did not sleep with her," Sergei declared, his eyes narrowing.

"I did not ask, nor am I offering to sleep with Lars," she argued, crossing her arms over her chest. Although, secretly, she was glad to hear nothing had happened between him and Ariana. Maybe Lars was right about this bond thing affecting them differently when it involved others of their kind. "Do not try to stop me from doing this, Sergei. There is no connection, except through you. He is only touching my hand."

Lars frowned. "Sergei's reticence makes sense, Valentina."

She paused, something about his tone catching her attention. "Why?"

"It's your energy," Lars began. "It's different than what I expected. There's a quality to it I've only experienced twice before, and that was with Ariana and Kayla. I don't know what it is, but I think the reason Sergei was drawn to Ariana in the first place was because her energy reminded him of you."

She tilted her head, curious about his explanation. "What do you mean?"

"Your energy is... very potent and highly desirable. I can't say with absolute certainty, but I suspect you're the common thread holding your bond together. If something happened to you, the bond linking all of you would dissolve."

She frowned, her thoughts unwillingly going back to when they'd first forged their connection. It had been done during a high-intensity test of their endurance and skillsets. Being air dropped into hostile and dangerous territory without any method of communication or their usual equipment would have been bad enough, except she'd mistakenly switched bags with Sergei.

Their trainers had secretly doctored his and Yuri's hydrating packs in an effort to temporarily incapacitate whom they believed to be the strongest members of their team. Unfortunately, the poison had been designed with Sergei's larger body weight and faster metabolism in mind. Yuri hadn't been able to take more than two steps without collapsing, but she'd almost died from the effects. When a freak storm suddenly kicked up, it had prevented their extraction team from reaching them. They'd been trapped in the narrow valley for over a week. From there, the situation had gotten even worse.

She swallowed, pushing aside the memory. "I was the one who did this?"

"No," Lars said, shaking his head. "You all had to do it willingly, but you're the common element. Yuri may be able to reach Nikolai's energy and vice versa, but only through you."

"You are the heart of our family," Sergei reminded her.

Lars considered it for a moment and nodded. "That's probably the most apt description I could imagine. I can try to read you again, but it'll take an extraordinary measure of self-control for them to back off. Your energy is very desirable, and I'm an interloper."

Valentina lowered her head for a moment and took a steadying breath. "I think we need to take this opportunity to better understand these powers, but I will go along with whatever you all decide. If it hurts you that much, I will not do it. But I wish you would trust me in this."

They all exchanged a look and then Nikolai said, "We will not interfere unless he crosses a line."

Sergei frowned. "Will it affect your reading if I am too close? I would prefer holding her while you do this."

"That should be fine," Lars agreed. "It affects you more since you're her chosen mate."

Sergei walked over to her and slid his hands around her waist, drawing her against him. He bent down to kiss her neck. "Do not be angry, Valechka."

"I'm not angry," she said in a soft voice, unable to feel anything but comforted by being in his arms again. She held out her hand, and Lars took it once more. Without waiting for a prompt, she went ahead and began channeling energy in his direction.

His eyes closed and he took a deep breath, and she knew he was exploring every nuance of her energy. "You're definitely a water-channeler, but there's something different about it. It's that same quality I've only felt with Kayla and Ariana. You draw energy channelers to you." He paused again, letting her energy wash over him. "I think... Yes, I was right. You can tap into everyone else's energy. They're all connected through you, so you've essentially inherited all the abilities of a spirit channeler."

Lars opened his eyes, staring at her in wonder. "You're a healer too. Not an empath like Ari, but you have a tremendous amount of healing skill." He glanced around at the others. "Do all of you heal faster than normal?"

Sergei squeezed her midsection lightly. "Yes, but more so when we're around Valentina. It's one of the reasons we've been so successful in our endeavors. It's also one of the reasons I was curious about Ariana's healing talent."

Lars nodded. "She's emitting a low-grade healing wave to each of you through your bond right now. It's not focused, but I would imagine she can do considerable healing if properly directed. There's some other quality I sense, but I've never felt anything like it before. It's almost as though your energy has a different resonance. I can't say with certainty what it is, but I would guess you have at least one other rare specialized skill. Whatever it is, it's very strong."

She frowned. "Would Ariana know?"

Lars withdrew his hand. "I doubt it. What I sensed from you wasn't anything like a typical water-energy talent. Part of my training was to expose myself to as many different powers as possible, and I've never encountered anything like this. We can ask Ariana, but I don't think she can test abilities. She can train your healing skills and show you general water skills though. It may take some experimentation to determine the exact nature of that particular talent. In the meantime, I'd like to do some research in our archives to see if we have any records of anything similar."

When she nodded, Lars added, "It would probably benefit all of you to sit in on each other's training. You may be able to draw on each other's talents through your bond."

"If you develop your healing ability, you can practice your knife-throwing skills more regularly on Yuri," Sergei suggested in a whisper loud enough for Yuri to overhear. "A blank canvas can be difficult to find."

"I vote for practicing on Sergei," Yuri retorted, crossing his arms.

Valentina rolled her eyes and sighed.

Lars studied them thoughtfully. "Have you guys practiced with your abilities much? It's obvious you're aware of them, but I'd imagine it's difficult to use them around the rest of your people."

Valentina shook her head. "Not much. We have to keep them suppressed whenever others are around."

"We experimented when we were on assignment together, but that was many years ago," Sergei said with a shrug.

"You're all much stronger than I expected," Lars admitted. "All of you have at least two highly-specialized skills, which isn't common. I can't believe none of us realized how much you were hiding. I suppose I shouldn't be surprised you all found each other."

Nikolai rubbed his chin in thought. "What are the chances we can learn what we need without revealing ourselves to your people?"

Lars hesitated. "It's not impossible, but there are going to be a lot of challenges. We typically form small connections with people during training, but that's going to be difficult in your case. If Valentina wasn't even able to connect with Ariana, I suspect you will all need to be involved. But they'll be able to sense your bond, like I did, the moment a connection is forged. "

"Kayla was able to train with Ariana without Alec being present," Sergei pointed out. "Why is this different?"

"Alec was bonded to Kayla, but they weren't truly mated," Lars explained. "Their connection was weaker, which was why I was willing to duel him for her bond. Yours is extraordinarily strong. I don't know if it's because you needed it to survive or if it's because four of you are supporting it. The only reason I was able to form a connection with you at all was because all of you consented to it. I don't think you're going to easily allow just anyone near the bond you share with Valentina. You are all too interconnected."

Valentina sighed. "I don't see any other option though. I don't want to lose Sergei again or such a valuable resource by keeping our abilities suppressed. We will need to share this information with some of them and hope they keep their silence."

Nikolai frowned. "How many people would need to know?"

Lars considered it for a moment. "With your permission,

I'd like to discuss this with Alec and Ariana. I've been away from the towers for a long time, so I can't vouch for a lot of the more specialized trainers. Alec and Ari would have a better idea about who can train you and who we should avoid."

Nikolai glanced over at Yuri. "Your thoughts?"

He shrugged. "I don't like the idea of sharing this information with them, but Valentina brings up a good point. We have a duty to use and train with whatever weapons are at our disposal. We can try to safeguard your position as best as possible, but we haven't been successful learning the full scope of our abilities on our own."

Nikolai was quiet for a long time. Finally, he nodded and said, "Very well. Ask them to join us."

# CHAPTER SEVENTEEN

VALENTINA WAS CURLED up on Sergei's lap, his hand on her knee in a position vaguely reminiscent of the one she'd shared with Nikolai before lunch. Only this time, there was no pretense. Ariana and Alec were sitting on the couch across from them, wide-eyed, and staring at the four of them in shock as Lars finished telling them what happened.

Valentina trailed her hand down Sergei's arm, marveling at the heat from his body and how it always seemed to run a few degrees hotter than hers. As soon as they were finished here, she wanted to take him into the other room and see just how hot she could make him. He turned to meet her gaze, his mouth curving upward.

"I intend to keep my promise, Valechka," he whispered close to her ear, placing a kiss against her neck. "I *will* have you later tonight." She shivered, and he kissed her neck again, a little lower this time. "And the night after that."

Yuri leaned over the couch. "I will take her away from you if you do not behave."

"Try it, and you will be missing a hand," Sergei said in a pleasant tone, pressing a kiss against her shoulder.

Another delicious shiver went through her at his touch, experiencing not only the effects on her skin but also through their bond. They hadn't clamped down on it since they'd admitted the truth to Lars. Everything was so much more vivid, and her senses were magnified. She knew they were all experiencing some of the same effects.

Alec stared at the four of them in astonishment. "And the whole time you lived with them, you had no idea?"

"No," Lars admitted. "I only spent time with Sergei though. I had a few suspicions about him, but he never said anything. I didn't have an opportunity to meet Valentina, Nikolai, or Yuri until recently."

Ariana was watching them with a small smile on her face. "Now that you're not shielding, I can see the strength of your emotional connections. It's as strong as the bond I share with Alec. How were you able to stay away from each other for so long?"

"With great difficulty," Sergei said, tracing his thumb over her knee. He hadn't stopped touching her since they'd been in the elevator, but she wasn't about to complain. She'd been equally starved for his touch.

"The biggest problem," Lars said, gesturing to them again, "is how to train them without being able to form a connection. Theory and explanations are only going to take them so far. We need to be able to work directly with them, so they can see how we use energy."

Alec frowned. "If you were able to reach each of them through their bond, we could have Brant temporarily suppress their abilities while we form a connection with one of them."

"No," Sergei and Yuri both said simultaneously.

"Or not," Alec said with a sigh. "I am aware of Brant's interest in Valentina, and that would be a problem. She would be the easiest to train since her abilities are most likely closest to Ariana's. But it sounds as though Sergei needs the training more than any of them, especially if he's going to remain close to her."

"I always knew you were hot-tempered," Yuri muttered.

"I think you should call Hayden," Ariana suggested. "He understands the special circumstances of my talents, and I believe he will keep quiet."

Sergei frowned. "I do not think that would be wise."

"I'm afraid I have to agree with Sergei, love," Alec said in a dry tone. "He's definitely skilled enough, and you may have some affection for him, but he doesn't think very highly of me or Sergei."

Ariana sighed. "Kendra, then. But that'll have a whole other set of problems. I love her dearly, but I'm not sure how well Valentina will take to another woman creating a connection with Sergei."

Valentina turned to Sergei. "Will you fuck her?"

"No," he said with a grin.

"Then I don't care," she said with a shrug.

"Are you sure?" Ariana questioned. "Forming a connection when you're already bonded can be rather intimate. Even if the connection is a small one, you may still be able to sense her. It can be very uncomfortable."

Nikolai shook his head. "I do not believe it will be a problem. Valentina rarely says things she doesn't mean. But just in case, we will take away her weapons."

Valentina rolled her eyes. "As if that would stop me."

Sergei lifted her hand and kissed her knuckles. "With you back in my life, I could never be interested in anyone else. She is only a means to fulfill my desire to stay close to you. That's all I have ever wanted."

Valentina ran her other hand down his shirt and whispered, "You should not say such things until we are alone, Seryozha."

He gave her a knowing smile and pressed a soft kiss against her lips. "I'm making up for lost time."

Lars interrupted. "Sergei, you know I share similar views of Hayden, but I think he might be the better option. Kendra is a little flighty, and I suspect there will be some issues if she tries to train you. Hayden will take the severity of the situation much more seriously."

Ariana nodded. "I think he would be the better choice too. The only reason Hayden was previously involved in questionable behavior was when he was trying to develop that serum to save me."

"You might be right," Alec admitted but didn't look entirely pleased about it. "There are many other skilled fire channelers within the towers, but few I would trust with this sensitive of a secret. I'm not sure I would even rely upon our High Council not to reveal you if they thought it would benefit them or OmniLab. Hayden doesn't have a problem with keeping secrets, which can be one of his more infuriating traits."

Valentina placed her hand on Sergei's arm. "You don't trust this Hayden?"

Sergei shrugged. "I don't know him well enough to say, but I'm willing to speak with him if it will keep me by your side."

"Very well," Alec agreed. "We can make the arrangements and have Hayden meet us here in the morning. Ariana and I will work with the rest of you while he trains Sergei."

Nikolai stood. "We appreciate your discretion in this matter. Sergei has informed me he explained our particular challenges with regard to our people. We cannot risk this information getting out to anyone from the Coalition."

"I understand," Alec agreed, glancing over at her and Sergei again. "We're going to do whatever is necessary to make sure you're all trained and kept safe. If you don't mind me asking, do you know if there are more of us living among the Coalition?"

Valentina frowned, unwilling to tell them the truth. "It's possible, but it's not something that would ever be openly discussed. It was more or less an accident we found each other."

"Sometimes, a perceived accident is Fate in disguise," Alec suggested with a small smile.

"I do not disagree with that assessment," Sergei said, interlacing his fingers with Valentina's. "But as far as the rest of our people are concerned, it may be possible to identify them."

Alec cocked his head. "How?"

"No," Nikolai interrupted. "We can explore this eventually, but not now."

Sergei shrugged as though he didn't care either way. Valentina rested her hand against his bare arm again in a reassuring gesture. Sergei wouldn't argue the point with Nikolai in front of the Omnis, but she knew the truth. All four of them had talked about ways to identify others with similar powers. Nikolai wanted to bring them under his protection, but it wasn't possible without alerting other members of their leadership.

Alec turned back to Nikolai. "But you have a way?"

Nikolai sighed. "We require medical testing before accepting applications to various facility assignments. If we allow our people to be run through your DNA test before processing their application to join the towers, you may be able to look for these markers. However, there are many potential issues that need to be considered."

Valentina nodded. "Our testing goes through several different camps for processing. If you claim some of our people as yours, our leaders will begin running their own tests to search for commonalities. It'll only be a matter of time until they isolate those markers and begin performing their own search amongst our people. It's unlikely they'd allow those individuals to join our ranks here and risk losing a potential asset, especially if they have a chance to neutralize any advantage your Inner Circle holds over us. Those who believe in your abilities are wary of them."

Alec frowned. "Would this put our people in danger?"

"It depends," Nikolai admitted, rubbing the back of his neck. "There may be ways to avoid unnecessary risk, but we'll need to consider this carefully. I'm not willing to chance the possibility of having anyone alienated or used as a pawn. Right now, our leadership is divided upon whether these abilities truly exist. Rumors have begun spreading, so it's only a matter of time before it's widely accepted. There will come a point where we must address the issue, if for no other reason than to alleviate our people's fears."

Sergei sighed and leaned back on the couch. "I've already begun having problems with people requesting reassignment. They're afraid of what they saw or experienced during our infiltration. Not only were our people knocked off their vehicles with strong gusts of wind, but an earthquake nearly collapsed the towers. Combined with what they witnessed at the underground river when Ariana saved her brother..." Sergei shook his head. "Some of our people already had concerns from their time living with Lars and the other exiles, but things have only escalated. It's become a rather serious issue, and the rumors are only continuing to grow with each retelling. Pavel was one of those who allowed his fear to consume him, and it was his misguided actions that caused you to be harmed, Ariana. For that, I am truly sorry."

Ariana gave him a soft smile. "I appreciate your efforts in rescuing me. I knew Pavel was afraid, but I thought I might have gotten through to him. I still have hope for the rest of your people. Given everything they've witnessed, I can understand their feelings."

"Nikolai," Sergei began, "Alec requested that all our people who are working or living on OmniLab property have their biometrics uploaded into their security database. Given Ariana's recent abduction, I authorized this procedure to begin in the next week."

Nikolai arched an eyebrow. "Clever. If it's not already a standard requirement, OmniLab could make a reasonable request to include a DNA sample in their processing." He turned back to Alec. "I trust you have a secure laboratory where these samples can be processed?"

Alec's eyes lit up, and he inclined his head. "Absolutely. I can arrange the highest security clearance to process the results separately and restrict access to them. If we can identify any individuals with our DNA markers, perhaps one of you would be willing to reach out to them."

Nikolai gestured to Valentina. "She is best suited for this type of work. If you provide me with the names, I can conduct a discrete inquiry into the person's history and familial ties. From there, Valentina can reach out to them." He paused for a moment and then added, "I will warn you though. Even if they possess these markers, they may not be willing to risk exposure or leave their families."

Alec nodded. "I understand. If nothing else, I want to be able to at least identify them and offer them a haven. Hopefully, in time, your people will trust us more and we can develop a deeper understanding of our respective cultures."

Nikolai held out his hand to Alec. "That's my hope as well."

Alec smiled and shook his hand.

———

SERGEI LOWERED his head to press another kiss against Valentina's bare shoulder. She was lying on her stomach, still fast asleep. He moved her hair aside, marveling at the silky texture, and kissed her neck. Other than making a small noise, she didn't stir. He ran his hand down her back, smiling to himself. There could be an impending invasion outside and she'd most likely sleep through it. He'd always envied her ability to sleep whenever and wherever was convenient.

"Valechka," he said gently. "Do you want to wake up and train this morning?"

She mumbled something that sounded like a complaint, but he couldn't be sure. Sergei ran his hand over a barely noticeable scar on her shoulder blade. It was another one she'd received while they'd been apart, and he promised himself it would be the last. He'd spent hours last night cataloguing every inch of her body, wanting to hear the stories about each mark and making a mental note about where to assign the blame for her injuries. She'd answered the first few times and then refused to give him any more information when she realized what he was doing.

It didn't matter. He'd find out.

Sergei traced the scar on her hip again, the mark forever signifying one of the darkest periods of his life. Although, if he hadn't left to take on this new command, maybe they wouldn't be here like this now.

Someone pounded on the door, and his eyes narrowed. He could fully understand Valentina's penchant for throwing knives at people if that was what she had to deal with on a daily basis.

"Get up, Valya!" Yuri shouted from the other side of the door. "Sergei, shove her out of bed."

Valentina turned her face into the pillow and mumbled a

rather creative objection. Sergei grinned. "Would you like me to kill him for you, Valechka?"

She reached under her pillow and withdrew a knife, shoving it in his direction. Sergei threw back his head and laughed. Valentina turned her head, her blue eyes still sleepy, and smiled up at him. "I've missed your laugh, Seryozha."

He brushed her chestnut hair away from her face and kissed her nose. "I haven't had much reason to laugh until recently."

She placed her hand on his cheek, and he closed his eyes from the rush of emotion that went through him. Just that one touch from her was enough to bring him to his knees. He swallowed as she trailed her fingertips over his face and brushed them against his lips.

"It's been a long time since I woke up beside you. Will you kiss me good morning?"

He opened his eyes, letting her see the depth of his love for her. "I will kiss you every morning for as long as you allow it."

Sergei lowered his head to kiss her. When she made a small noise of desire, he pulled her closer, the soft curves of her body molding perfectly against his. This woman owned him, body and soul. There had never been anyone who evoked this depth of emotion or passion from him. He'd spent most of the night making love to her, and he wanted her again just as fervently as the first time. She wound her arms around his neck in a wordless demand, telling him with her body she felt the same.

Another pounding on the door interrupted them, and he broke their kiss with a curse.

"You have ten minutes before training!" Yuri shouted. "Quit playing with him, Valya."

Sergei looked down into the clearest blue eyes he'd ever seen. He cupped her cheek, and she closed her eyes, leaning into his hand. Ten lifetimes with Valentina wouldn't be enough. "If this training were for any other reason than to stay by your side, I'd say to hell with it. Even knowing its purpose, it's nearly impossible for me to leave this bed with you in it."

She smiled and looked up at him. "I love you, Seryozha."

He groaned and buried his face against her neck. "You are not making it any easier, little dove."

Valentina ran her fingers through his hair. "Yuri lies. He will only give us five minutes before he barges in."

Sergei picked up the knife she'd pushed toward him. "Would you like to kill him, or should I?"

She laughed and took her blade from him. Leaning forward, she kissed him lightly on the lips. "We'll need him for training, but sometimes it's a tempting thought."

She stood and walked over to the clothes on the dresser, and he took the opportunity to admire the lines of her athletic form. Her mouth turned downward in an adorable pout as she studied the dresses. He couldn't help but grin. "Do I get to pick out your dress again?"

She scrunched up her nose. "No. I need to shower first, but I don't understand how their women wear these every day. There are no pockets. What sort of clothing doesn't have any pockets?"

Sergei chuckled and climbed out of bed. "And no place to put your weapons."

"Exactly," she agreed, reaching into one of her bags to pull out her toiletries. "Besides, if we are meeting with Viktor later, I need to dress in my own clothing."

Sergei froze, having forgotten all about Viktor. That wasn't a conversation he was eager to have, especially without witnesses. He grabbed his pants and quickly pulled them on. "I'll go see if Lars has any tea for you."

Valentina paused, lifting her head to regard him suspiciously. Before she could interrogate him, he grabbed a shirt, pulled it over his head, and leaned forward to kiss her. "Do you still take it the same way?"

"You're hiding something," she accused, a trace of temper in her eyes.

"Extra sweet," he remembered and headed out of the room before she reached for a nearby weapon.

———

VALENTINA'S EYES narrowed at the closed door. It was tempting to go after him, but there wasn't enough time. After she finished her morning routine, she grabbed a tank top and pants from her bag and pulled them on. Whatever Sergei was hiding had to do with Viktor. They'd all been in the same training class when they were younger, but Valentina hadn't had much interaction with Viktor back then. It was only over the past few years that she'd had reason to work with him. There must be some shared history she didn't know about between Viktor and Sergei because they were both being cagey.

She buckled her belt and started strapping on her weapons. It was too early to deal with this nonsense. Someone tapped on the door, and she snapped, "Come in."

Nikolai opened the door, his expression worried. "Are you all right, Valya?"

She sighed and lifted her pant leg to equip another weapon. "Annoyed. Sergei is hiding something."

"About what?"

"It has to do with Viktor," she replied, testing the strap to make sure it was secure. When Nikolai didn't reply, she lifted her head to regard him. "You know something?"

He hesitated. "It's probably not what you're thinking. I should let you talk to Sergei about it."

"Viktor warned me away from Sergei," she said, watching his reaction. "He even suggested Yuri would have been a better option for this meeting. Why would he say that?"

Nikolai's face remained carefully blank. "Did you have any tea? I told Lars your preference, and he promised to have some available this morning."

Valentina curled her hands into fists to keep from strangling both of them. She couldn't believe they were going to make her drag the information out of them. With a huff, she grabbed her electrolaser gun and slid it into the holster at her side.

"I *will* get my damn tea, and then you *both* will answer my questions," she declared and stormed past him.

Sergei, Yuri, and Lars were all out in the common room. A small table had been brought out and was covered with a variety of different foods. Sergei smiled warmly at her and held out a cup. She scowled and stomped over to him, snatching the tea from his outstretched hand.

Yuri arched a brow and swallowed whatever he was chewing. "I count at least four weapons on her. I'm impressed, Sergei. I didn't think you would piss her off so quickly."

"Five," Sergei said, studying her intently. "You didn't see her walk over here. Her stance is balanced. She has knives on both ankles."

Yuri glanced down at her pants and reached for another muffin. "Ah, you are correct."

"Six," Nikolai said from behind her. "She has a knife strapped to her back too."

Valentina glared at them and sat on the couch, holding her cup as though it could ward against the stupidity in the room. She took a sip and leaned back, automatically closing her eyes at the exquisite flavors on her tongue. It was tea. Real, potent, and not even close to the imitation beverage they frequently drank in camp. It was even better than the tea she'd had at the café with Brant. Her earlier tension started to melt away in the face of such a heavenly cup of caffeine, and she sighed dreamily.

Sergei cleared his throat. "Lars, I need you to get me a case of that tea."

"You might want to get a few cases," Yuri suggested.

"Good point," Sergei agreed. "Lars, get me a few."

She ignored them, intent on savoring every last drop of the ambrosia in her cup. Nikolai walked over to her and sat beside her, placing his hand on her knee. "Are you sure you wish to do this, Valya? It will affect you more than us."

She nodded. "I'll be fine, Kolya. We have a duty to learn about these talents, and this is our best opportunity."

Lars's commlink beeped, and he glanced down at it. "Alec and Ariana will be here shortly. There was another incident at Hayden's club last night. He's running a few minutes behind."

Valentina put her tea aside and looked over where Sergei was standing. "While we're waiting, you can tell me about Viktor."

Sergei frowned. "Are you sure you wouldn't like more tea first, Valechka?"

Her eyes narrowed. "Later."

Sergei sighed and leaned against the wall. "Viktor and I have never gotten along."

Valentina tapped her foot impatiently. "I'm aware of your history, Sergei. Why did he warn me away from you?"

Now it was Sergei's turn to narrow his eyes. "What exactly did he say to you?"

"He didn't want me to see you alone. Why would he say that?"

Yuri chuckled and went back to perusing the breakfast table. "Viktor has always wanted to fuck you, Valya. Sergei is competition."

"Viktor would fuck anything with two legs," she retorted,

watching while Yuri shoved almost an entire muffin in his mouth and began to chew. It was rather impressive how much food he managed to put away.

Nikolai leaned back on the couch, draping his arm behind her. "Perhaps, but Sergei has always been more protective of you than either Yuri or myself. He handled the situation a bit more forcefully than we expected, especially after he overheard a few things Viktor said about you."

Valentina looked up at Sergei. "What did you do?"

Sergei shrugged. "I warned him away from you."

She crossed her arms. "How?"

Sergei hesitated. "I may have sent him to the infirmary." He paused and added, "A few times."

Yuri coughed. "Four times."

Sergei scowled at him. "You helped me with one of them."

Yuri shrugged but didn't deny it.

Valentina tilted her head to study Sergei. This might have possibilities. If there was that much tension between the two of them, she could definitely take advantage of the situation to keep Viktor off guard. "When Viktor gets here, I don't want him to know we've reconciled."

Sergei's eyes narrowed. "No, Valechka. I *will* kill him if he touches you."

"Then you cannot accompany me," she replied with a shrug. "I need information from him, and he will be more inclined to talk if he doesn't believe I'm sharing your bed."

Sergei's jaw clenched, and he looked as though he was ready to argue.

Nikolai sighed. "She's right, Sergei. You cannot interfere in this. I'm not fond of him, either, but Viktor has always been more forthcoming with her."

Valentina stood and walked over to Sergei. Resting her hands on his chest, she said, "You will be the one in my bed tonight, Seryozha. Never him. I need you to trust me to do what is needed."

"It's him I don't trust, especially with you," Sergei admitted with a sigh. "You're precious to me, Valechka, and he is not a good man. But I will do my best to go along with your plan."

She stood on her toes and pressed a kiss against his lips. He fisted his hand in her hair and pulled her closer, deepening their kiss.

"Didn't you do enough of that last night?" Yuri asked with a full mouth.

Sergei broke their kiss but didn't release her. "No."

Valentina looked up at him, debating whether they had time to slip back into her room. Judging by Sergei's heated expression, he was wondering the same thing.

Lars cleared his throat. "They should be here any minute."

Nikolai picked up her tea and offered it to her. "You should try to eat something before they arrive, Valya. You may not get another opportunity this morning."

She nodded, and Sergei released her. Wandering over to the table, she took a sip of her tea and eyed the selection. Sergei brushed his hand against her back. "Will you trust me?"

Valentina looked up at him and nodded. He reached over and picked up one of the muffins. "It's a blueberry muffin. I think you'll enjoy it."

Curious, she put down her tea and took a bite of the muffin. It was rich, sweet, and almost as good as the cookies she'd had the other day.

Sergei chuckled. "We may need to get some of the muffins to go along with your tea and cookies."

"I can understand why you like living here," she admitted, licking a crumb off her finger.

Sergei leaned in close and whispered, "If you keep licking

your finger like that, we will forget about training, and I will drag you back into your bedroom."

She gave him a sultry smile and whispered, "Maybe it will not be my finger I lick when you do."

Sergei muttered a curse and took another step toward her just as the doorbell chimed. Lars walked over to the door, and Valentina picked up her tea again, smiling over the rim of her cup. Sergei was too much fun to tease.

Alec, Ariana, and a very attractive dark-haired man entered the room. Valentina studied their body language carefully, noting there was a small amount of tension between the two men.

Alec walked over to them. "Hayden, I'd like you to meet Nikolai, Valentina, and Yuri. You already know Sergei."

Hayden gave them all a brief nod, his eyes lingering on her for a long moment. "It's a pleasure to meet all of you. Although, I'm a little confused as to why you asked me to meet you here this morning, Alec."

Alec clasped his hands behind his back. "I need your word that whatever we discuss will not be repeated."

Hayden arched a brow. "I'm intrigued, but I won't make any promises."

Ariana took a small step toward him and placed her hand on his arm. "Please, Hayden. Bringing you here was my idea. You're one of the few people in the towers I trust implicitly. We need your help with a rather sensitive matter."

Hayden's amber eyes softened, and he nodded. "Very well, Ari. You have my word I will not reveal anything. What do you need?"

Alec gestured to Sergei. "We need you to help train a fire channeler."

Hayden's eyes widened, his expression shocked. "You're one of us?"

"He is," Ariana agreed with a small smile. "So is Valentina, but I'll be training her. She's a water channeler."

Hayden's gaze flew to her, and he studied her for a long moment, his expression warming. Something about him reminded her of Sergei, and she felt her body automatically respond. His mouth curved upward, and he held out his hand to her in greeting. She slipped her hand in his and gasped at the almost erotic sensation of heat that flowed through her at his touch.

Sergei slammed Hayden into the wall, a knife at his throat before anyone could react. Nikolai and Yuri jumped forward, trying to pull him off. Hayden's eyes were wide with shock and fear.

Lars shouted, "Sergei, you don't want to do this."

"Valentina!" Nikolai barked.

She jumped into action, moving forward and placing her hand on Sergei's arm to let him know it was her approaching him. Sliding between the two men, she placed her hands on Sergei's chest and in their language, she urged, "Look at me, Seryozha."

Sergei glanced down at her but didn't remove the knife from Hayden's throat. She could feel the blade heating in his hand, and she suspected Sergei was just barely keeping a tenuous grasp on his usual tight control. She ran her hands upward and wrapped her arms around his neck. Keeping her voice soft, she tilted her head and asked, "Will you leave me again?"

"Never," he swore.

"Show me."

Sergei lowered the weapon and put his hands on her backside, lifting her up and against him. Wrapping her legs around him, she nipped at his bottom lip. He complied with her unspoken demand, continuing to kiss her as her cooler water energy extinguished the flames of his anger. She broke their kiss and glanced over to see Hayden watching them warily. Sergei lowered her back to the ground but didn't release her.

The dark-haired man turned to Alec with a scowl. "You could have warned me she was his mate."

"I didn't think you'd be stupid enough to try such a thing without learning the situation," Alec retorted, crossing his arms over his chest. "You're lucky he didn't actually cut your throat."

Hayden rubbed his neck where the knife had pressed against him. "You have my apology, Sergei. I had no idea she was claimed."

Sergei inclined his head but didn't respond. He relaxed his arms around her a fraction though. Valentina bit her lip and leaned against him. If she had any hope in staying by his side, it was imperative they get this situation under control. When Hayden had channeled energy toward her, she'd felt Nikolai and Yuri's anxiety skyrocket as well. Sergei had only acted upon it first.

"I'm afraid that won't be the only challenge we have in training them," Alec admitted, glancing at Nikolai. "Is it all right if we tell him the rest?"

Nikolai frowned. "I'm afraid we don't have much of a choice, especially given what just happened."

Alec gestured to Sergei. "Hayden, try to create a connection with him. I don't think you'll believe me until you experience it for yourself."

Hayden's eyes narrowed on Alec. "Is this a trick?"

Alec shook his head. "Not in the way you're thinking."

Hayden approached Sergei cautiously and held out his hand, making a point not to even look in Valentina's direction. He was smart, she'd give him that much.

Sergei released her and took Hayden's outstretched hand. When nothing happened, Hayden frowned.

Lars cleared his throat. "You need to lower your guard so he can form a connection like we did yesterday."

Valentina swallowed. They'd all gotten so used to keeping everything so tightly contained, it was much more difficult to relax their mental shields. For the second time in as many days, all four of them released their reservations and embraced the bond they'd formed years ago. Awareness filled each of them, and she felt the moment when another fire channeler entered the fray.

Hayden's mouth dropped open as he released Sergei's hand, staring at each of them in disbelief. "All four of you? How is this even possible?"

Nikolai and Yuri approached her. Nikolai put his arm around her waist and drew her against him. "It's a long story, and one we may share with your people one day. But right now, we need to know if you can you train Sergei."

Hayden swallowed, his gaze landing on her briefly before moving back to Sergei. "I need to test your strength. I'm assuming you have some rudimentary knowledge if you managed to form a bond. Is that correct?"

Sergei hesitated and then admitted, "Our bond was formed out of necessity. Unfortunately, we haven't been able to explore our abilities in depth. Our people are not as understanding about such things. It was my hope to learn something of your ways by integrating with OmniLab."

"I see," Hayden said with a frown. "Can you send a small amount of energy toward me?"

Sergei did as he requested, and Hayden nodded. "Good. You're stronger than I expected. I can definitely show you a few of the basics."

Sergei frowned. "I'm more interested in learning how to control my temper. The rest can be learned later."

Hayden's brow furrowed. "Your temper? What do you—"

He paused, and his eyes fell on her again. "I see. You're falling into a rage whenever she's threatened."

Sergei nodded. "Valentina can handle most threats without my interference, but if she's hurt, I lose control."

"Yes," Hayden mused. "I can see how that could be a problem. Very well. We'll work on that first. I have a feeling your discipline will come in handy for this part." He gestured to the couch. "Have a seat with me, and let's talk."

# CHAPTER EIGHTEEN

VALENTINA HAD BEEN SITTING on the floor working with Nikolai and Ariana for almost an hour. Sergei had spent that time training with Hayden, while Yuri was doing exercises with Lars and Alec. She and Nikolai had far more in common than she first realized, with some of their skills overlapping. Ariana was a patient and understanding teacher, and Valentina had learned far more than she ever thought possible in such a short amount of time.

Her commlink beeped, and she reached into her pocket. It was time to meet with Viktor and focus on discovering who was responsible for the stolen weapons. She glanced over at Sergei, who met her gaze and nodded in understanding.

Valentina turned back to the young woman training them. "Thank you for your help, Ariana. I have a meeting, but I would enjoy working with you again another time."

Ariana beamed a smile at her. "I'd like that. You've all done remarkably well."

Nikolai placed his hand on Valentina's arm. "Yuri and I will monitor you from here and review the security feeds from yesterday. If you have any issues, we can be there in minutes."

"It will be fine, Kolya," she assured him, not the slightest bit worried. "Sergei will be with me, and I've handled Viktor before."

He nodded and leaned over to kiss her cheek. "Be safe, Valya."

Sergei walked over to them and held out his hand to help her up. "Are you ready?"

Valentina nodded and grabbed her UV-protective jacket before heading out into the hall with him. As they walked toward the priority elevator, she said, "We cannot go in together. I will wait in the reception area and pretend I just arrived, and you can come down to get us after Viktor arrives."

Sergei frowned but didn't argue. The elevator shot downward, and she watched the numbers display on the screen overhead. She pulled a small microphone out of her pocket, activated it, and attached it to the inside of her arm sheath. Once it was secure and out of sight, she pulled on her jacket. "Testing notification requested."

Her commlink beeped a moment later, and she glanced down at the message from Yuri. Good. Everything was functioning. She glanced over at Sergei, knowing he'd hate this next part. "I need you to give me some time alone with Viktor."

His body tensed. "How long?"

"If I'm unable to get information from him in thirty minutes, it's unlikely he'll give it to me at all," she said, watching the numbers again as they continued to descend. "Yuri can advise you if there's a problem, but Viktor is more of a nuisance than anything else."

The elevator door opened to the floor where Sergei's quarters were located. He turned toward her, a worried look in his eyes. "Be careful, Valechka. A great number of our people are in the construction tower, and we don't know who was responsible for the ambush. While I'm waiting for Viktor to show up, I'll reach out to Nikolai's people to see if they've learned anything."

Valentina grabbed his shirt and pulled him down toward her, kissing him soundly. "I'm always careful, Seryozha. Now go away and let me work."

He grinned and walked out of the elevator, turning around and watching as it closed between them. She lowered her head and smiled. Having him back in her life again was more than she ever dreamed, not to mention a little distracting. But she wouldn't trade it for anything. Taking a deep breath, she tried to focus her thoughts and get into the proper mind-set. She couldn't afford to have her attention divided if she was going to coax information from Viktor.

She was ready once the elevator doors opened again. Valentina headed out into the reception area and walked over to a desk area where a young man was seated. She leaned against it and said, "My name is Valentina. I believe Sergei, the Coalition's ambassador, is expecting me."

His brow furrowed, and he glanced toward the priority elevator she'd exited, but he didn't ask any questions. "Of course. I'll contact him right away and let him know you're waiting for him."

She murmured her thanks and studied the monitors surrounding the desk. Some of them appeared to be security feeds, and she wondered how much they were tied into the restricted areas. Alec would probably share some information with them, but they'd most likely still need to access those areas to find out what they weren't being told. At least some of the urgency was gone and they could take more time to explore the towers once the missing shipment issue was resolved.

The young man glanced up from his screen. "The ambassador will be down shortly. I believe he's expecting someone else too?"

She nodded, gesturing toward the main doors. "My friend will be here soon. Tell me, what is your normal procedure when someone arrives?"

He glanced at the door, but before he could say anything, someone spoke from behind her. "I'll take it from here, Melvin."

Valentina turned around, smiling at the sight of Brant. "Well, hello."

He approached her with a warm smile. "Alec said you might need me for a meeting."

Valentina considered him for a moment and then nodded. She hadn't been anticipating it, but it would make sense for him to be present. "Yes, your assistance would be appreciated. I need to know your normal procedure for an arrival."

"Well, since you just arrived," he began, obviously guessing her intent, "we took your helmet, jacket, and logged in your credentials."

She pulled her jacket off, and he eyed the weapons on her. "Well, that should raise some rather interesting questions."

Valentina glanced down at herself. "Is it a problem?"

He hesitated. "If I say yes, will it make much difference?"

She shook her head. "I cannot go into this meeting unarmed. If it'll make your people uneasy, I will keep my jacket on."

"It's fine. You're going to be staying in the construction tower, so it shouldn't be an issue. I'm assuming your friend will also be armed?"

She nodded, and Brant took her jacket. He handed it to Melvin, who went over to put it in a nearby locker. Brant turned back to her, leaned against the counter, and smiled again. "I'm glad you changed your mind about leaving. I had a feeling those cookies might have convinced you."

"In part," Valentina agreed with a laugh. "Although, I had a blueberry muffin this morning. It wasn't quite as good as your cookies, but close." She leaned toward him and whispered, "I admit I'm now curious to learn what else your towers have to offer."

"I'll take you on a tour of my favorite restaurants," he promised just as the doors opened.

Viktor strode in, the energy within the room immediately swirling with an undercurrent of danger. He wore the typical protective gear distributed throughout their camps, although his were in much better condition due to his ranking within the Coalition. Pulling off his helmet to reveal his short dark hair, he scanned the room for potential threats.

Valentina watched him immediately write off Melvin, but his eyes lingered overly long on Brant before meeting hers. She offered him a smile, and his brown eyes warmed in response. Melvin scampered out from behind his desk to take Viktor's helmet from him.

She walked over to Viktor, stood on her toes, and kissed his cheek. Before she could move away, he wrapped an arm around her and hugged her tightly against him. She returned the embrace, taking the opportunity to catalogue each of the weapons he had equipped.

"You're still as beautiful as ever, Valentina."

"And you are still a flatterer," she teased lightly and then gestured to Brant. "This is Brant Mason, a security officer here at OmniLab. Brant, this is Viktor, an old friend. Viktor's agreed to join me on a tour of the new tower this morning."

Brant gave Viktor a curt nod, his earlier friendliness now gone and a cool businesslike persona in its place. It didn't take a body language expert to realize Brant had some serious reservations about the newcomer.

Viktor kept his arm around her waist as he swept his gaze over the room again. "Your towers are most impressive."

"Thank you," Brant acknowledged. "We hope you think the same of the construction. Many of the features will be similar to our existing towers."

"Will you be giving us the tour?"

Brant glanced at her. "I will accompany you for part of it, but I believe your ambassador will be here shortly."

She nodded and gestured to Melvin. "He has already contacted Sergei."

"I see," Viktor said, the slightest trace of irritation in his tone.

Brant's commlink beeped, and he glanced down at it. "Excuse me just a moment."

When Brant stepped away, Valentina took the opportunity to study Viktor. He still hadn't released her, and she was tempted to pull away before Sergei arrived, but she couldn't risk alienating Viktor. "I'm glad you're here. Nikolai is concerned about the situation. I'm hoping you might be able to shed some light on everything."

"We'll have everything resolved soon enough," he promised, his fingertips brushing under the hem of her shirt. "I may have an opportunity for you to consider when we're finished with our tour."

It took everything she had not to shove him away. Instead, she tilted her head and gave him a playful smile. "Will you give me a little hint?"

He grinned. "I think the anticipation may be more fun."

Valentina wrinkled her nose and pretended to pout. "Very well, but I won't be happy with you if you take too long to tell me."

Viktor chuckled. "I would never risk such a horrible fate."

Sergei took that moment to exit the elevator, and his body stiffened at the sight of Viktor's arm around her. His jaw clenched, but he continued to approach them, the small flame in his eyes even more noticeable in the reception area lighting.

"Viktor," Sergei greeted the other man before turning to her. His eyes softened, and he searched her expression. Valentina took the opportunity to step away from Viktor. She brushed a brief kiss against Sergei's cheek in greeting. "Hello, Sergei."

"It's good to see you again, Valentina," he murmured.

She smiled at him and took a step back, making an effort to keep her face friendly when all she wanted was to get him alone again. "Viktor and I were just talking about how eager we are to see the new tower's progression."

Viktor stepped forward, once again putting his arm around her. "Yes. Valentina mentioned you will be providing us with a tour?"

Sergei's eyes narrowed on Viktor's hand, and his mouth formed a thin line. "I'm surprised you're taking such an interest, Viktor. I believe you once called this sort of thing tedious?"

"Oh, you'd be surprised what I find stimulating, especially where Valentina's concerned," Viktor said with a smug smile. "I thought she might enjoy some friendly company. We've worked together several times over the past few years, especially once you decided to take this assignment. After all, she needed a partner she could rely upon. We've gotten to know each other extremely well."

Sergei paused, glancing at her and his expression became guarded. She kept her face pleasant, but she knew he was no longer acting. If the danger levels had become elevated when Viktor walked in, they were now apocalyptic. Sergei was downright pissed, and it wouldn't take much for his tenuous control to slip. Dammit. She'd need to adjust her tactics to manage both of them.

"I see," Sergei replied in a clipped tone. "If you will follow me, I will show you the construction tower. I especially believe you may like the view from the top."

———

VALENTINA LOOKED around another set of rooms and was ready to hurt someone—probably Sergei for subjecting her to this hell. If she never saw another construction site, it would be too soon. They'd spent the past couple of hours practically counting every single one of the nails he'd painstakingly documented in his reports. "I think we have seen enough, Sergei. If you don't mind, I would like to go over some plans with Viktor. Do you have a private office we can use?"

Sergei paused, a wicked light entering in his eyes. "Are you sure? There's plenty more to see. I think Viktor might find it *stimulating* to see how we track inventory."

Valentina clenched her jaw and thought of a thousand different ways she'd make Sergei pay later.

"For fuck's sake," Viktor muttered. "We were finished two hours ago. Show us to this damn office."

"Of course," Sergei agreed, leading them down the corridor in the direction his office was located. He unlocked the door, and she walked inside, sweeping her gaze around the room. Nothing had changed since she'd been here a few days before and had stolen his notes. Even so, she pretended to look over the diagrams scattered on his desk as though seeing them for the first time.

Sergei walked over to stand beside her and pressed a button on the desk panel. The blueprint populated in three dimensions, and he rotated the view. "This is the completed design, and you can see our progress here." He pressed another button, and the image flickered. They still had a lot more to do, but the accomplishments so far were impressive.

She hadn't had the opportunity to see the full image when she'd been in his office downloading his files. The sight was staggering.

Valentina swallowed, wanting to tell him how impressed she was, but not wanting to say anything in front of Viktor. Sergei had accomplished so much while he'd been away from her. Part of her worried he'd be giving up his dreams to stay by her side, especially in the face of such a promising future. Maybe once they resolved these issues, Nikolai would consider remaining here. Although, she still wasn't sure how it would work with them sharing control.

Sergei pressed another button. "Completion will take a few more months than originally anticipated, but we'll be able to provide homes for many more of our people."

"Yes, these delays are a concern," Viktor acknowledged. "Perhaps someone else should take over to expedite matters."

Sergei's eyes narrowed. "We've had complications due to resource restrictions. Considering the magnitude of this project, such a delay was unavoidable. Nothing like this has been accomplished in almost two centuries."

"Exactly why I'm surprised such a project was put into your hands," Viktor retorted, moving to inspect the rest of Sergei's office. "If you don't mind, I have a private matter to discuss with Valentina. You may leave."

Valentina inwardly cursed. Viktor was doing his best to bait Sergei, and from all appearances, it was working. She blinked at Sergei, sending a silent plea for him to remain calm and trust her. He hesitated, his gaze meeting hers before inclining his head. "As it happens, I have a matter which requires my attention. I will return shortly. Please make yourself comfortable, Valentina." Sergei left the room, closing the door behind him.

Turning back around, she found Viktor watching her. "You were rather unkind, Viktor. You know Sergei has accomplished the near impossible. He's exceeded all expectations."

He raised an eyebrow and moved around the desk to stand beside her. "I'm surprised to hear you defend him. Didn't he leave you three years ago? After you were injured helping him in his last assignment?"

Unwilling to discuss it with him, Valentina started to turn away, but Viktor put his hand on her arm to stop her. "You never saw him for who he really was. I was hoping you would begin to see the truth."

She frowned and looked up into his eyes. "What truth?"

"Only a fool would have walked away from you," he said, searching her expression. "Sergei was different with you than he was with everyone else. He's always been overly arrogant and reckless, quick to anger and violent. He's never had any loyalty except to himself. Leaving you was proof of that."

Valentina sighed. On the surface, it probably did appear that way, but she knew a different side of him. So did Nikolai and Yuri. Unfortunately, she couldn't rightly defend Sergei without arousing suspicion. "It doesn't matter. What happened is in the past."

"Perhaps," Viktor murmured and lowered his hand. "Now, tell me what you know about these missing shipments."

"Not much," she admitted, having already discussed with Nikolai what she would reveal to Viktor. "Part of a recent weapon shipment went missing. Nikolai agreed to meet with a representative from OmniLab to discuss some of the problems with our alliance. The meeting was ambushed, and the same types of weapons were used in the assault. My suspicion is the two are connected."

Viktor's eyebrows rose. "And the attackers?"

"Escaped," she said, letting her irritation show. "No casualties on either side, but the meeting was a failure. We don't have any real leads, except I heard a rumor about another missing shipment a few days before the attack. Nikolai reached out to Peter to see if you had any additional information, and he confirmed this wasn't an isolated event."

Viktor nodded and leaned back against the desk. "Yes. At least three partial shipments have gone missing."

"How many weapons?"

He frowned and rubbed his chin. "From all three? In total, less than a hundred. They were smaller weapon shipments, but we've also had food and medical supplies go missing. Those numbers were much more significant."

Valentina nodded. "Nikolai's ordered a full inventory analysis to see if we're missing anything else too. We should have that information back in the next day or two. As far as the weapons are concerned, your numbers align with ours. We have less than a hundred missing. Combined with yours, the cumulative amount is substantial. Our people are trying to trace the last known location before the weapons disappeared."

Viktor pulled out his commlink and placed it on the desk so she could view the screen. He tapped a button and said, "All three of our shipments left this manufacturing facility. We have confirmed their arrival here." He pointed to a medium-sized facility on the map and then traced his finger to the next one and tapped on it. "Our weapons and other supplies went missing before they reached the next checkpoint here."

She frowned, pulling out her commlink to record the locations. "I will check with Yuri to see if we can trace our shipment to any of those locations. Other than that, do you know if your missing shipments have anything else in common?"

Viktor paused and didn't reply right away. Valentina lifted her head to regard him. "You don't wish to tell me?"

He sighed. "I do, but I'm not sure you're ready to hear the truth."

Valentina frowned, lowering her commlink. "I don't know what to say, Viktor. I would like to hear your thoughts, but I cannot force you to tell me anything."

"Do you still care for Sergei?"

Her eyes widened in shock. "You cannot be suggesting he is responsible for the theft."

Viktor crossed his arms. "I am. All our supplies were en route to provide support to our nearby camps. We were able to trace the missing weapons enough to learn that the recipient has a vested interest in OmniLab. Sergei has the most to gain in the face of a rebellion against the Coalition."

She blanched. "*Treason*? You believe Sergei is leading a rebellion against our people? But why?"

"Power?" Viktor shrugged. "As he pointed out, no one else has accomplished such a feat to build another facility in almost two centuries. As our ambassador, he's here in a position of leadership. Once our residents move in, the balance of power within the Coalition will shift in favor of whomever is operating from this location. The longer he remains in charge, the greater his threat to our people."

Valentina pressed her hands against the desk, needing the support it offered to keep her upright. She couldn't believe what she was hearing. The potential implications were disastrous. "How sure are you about this?"

"Very," Viktor admitted. "Peter has already approached some of the other leaders with his suspicions and put in a bid to take control of the construction. Once it's approved, he will run this tower as a permanent base. That's one of the things I wished to discuss with you."

She swallowed, trying to put her emotions aside and think. If things had already progressed so far, they may have already issued orders to have Sergei permanently removed. Traitors were dealt with quickly and harshly.

Viktor placed his hand over hers. "Peter has authorized

me to extend an invitation to you. He wants you to join his service."

"What?" Valentina managed on a whisper. She'd been blindsided by Viktor's suspicions about Sergei and now he was suggesting she join Peter's service? Peter must be holding far more influence than any of them realized if he was making such a move against Nikolai.

Viktor knew the level of dedication she had to Nikolai and Yuri. They'd all been in the same training class together, and even though Viktor's team had gone their separate ways years ago, she'd been with Nikolai for over ten years. It never dawned on her this could be the opportunity Viktor would propose.

Viktor trailed the backs of his fingers along her bare skin and up her arm. "We work well together, Valentina. With Peter running the tower, he will need people he trusts by his side. No one has ever questioned your loyalty, and this would be a good move for you. There is much we could accomplish together."

He moved in closer, crossing all boundaries of propriety. Her weapons were still within easy reach, but she needed to diffuse the situation without taking it to that level. She'd rather not kill Viktor, especially when he still had information she needed. And that didn't even begin to account for the diplomatic nightmare his murder would cause. Even so, her fingers were itching to draw a very clear line with her knife.

Placing her hand on his chest, she reminded him gently, "Viktor, I swore service to Nikolai. You know I'm loyal to him."

Viktor smirked. "Did you know Nikolai has taken other lovers, Valentina? None of your men have remained loyal to you. Sergei abandoned you. Nikolai will be next. I can offer you so much more."

He pressed himself against her, and she felt his hardness and unmistakable intent. Narrowing her eyes, she lifted her head in defiance. "Do you think I'm just looking for a quick fuck, Viktor?"

"Not quick," he murmured with a cocky grin. "I intend to take my time with you. And afterward, you can join me in Peter's camp, and I can take even more time with you."

"Not a fucking chance," Sergei snarled and grabbed Viktor, yanking him away from her. Viktor whirled around, drawing a knife in one swift movement and lashing out. Sergei pulled his own weapon, and Valentina resisted the urge to swear as the two of them began swiping at each other in a masterful dance of blades. Someone was going to get hurt or killed, and she needed both of them to keep breathing.

She dove away as their fight started getting more destructive. A chair flew across the room and into the wall, where it splintered apart in pieces. Pulling out her commlink, she hit the emergency button letting Yuri and Nikolai know she needed them now. Chances were, they were already on their way and had been from the moment they heard Viktor's accusation.

Viktor hit the desk, Sergei's knife making a narrow slash along his arm, slicing through the tendon. A thin stream of blood began pouring down his arm. Dammit. She dodged to the side again as they moved in her direction. Brant ran into the room and gaped at the two men just as Viktor swiped out and sliced across Sergei's chest, creating a shallow wound. They were more than evenly matched, but she didn't trust either one of them not to kill the other.

"Freeze!" Brant shouted, but they ignored him.

Valentina glanced around the room, considering how best to incapacitate them. Out of the corner of her eye, she caught sight of Brant lifting his weapon and aiming in Viktor's direction. She started to shout at him to stop, but it was too late.

Brant fired. The two men hit the wall and tumbled to the side. Sergei staggered, and horror filled her at the realization he'd been the one hit with the stunning device. She took a step forward as Viktor's blade rushed downward, and he buried it deeply in Sergei's chest.

"No!" Valentina yelled, diving toward Sergei as he collapsed on the ground. His eyes were unfocused and his face slack while blood poured out of the wound. Brant's weapon had rendered him unconscious. She yanked her tank top over her head, twisting it tightly to help hold pressure on the wound. The knife had barely missed his heart, but it had still struck a potentially fatal blow. She didn't dare risk pulling it out.

"Call Ariana," she ordered Brant, still using her shirt as a makeshift tourniquet. If Ariana could get here in time, he might have a chance. Brant pulled out his commlink and began speaking into it rapidly, most likely to Alec or Ariana. She wasn't sure which, nor did she care as long as they healed him.

"Valentina, leave him," Viktor demanded, grabbing her arm and yanking her to her feet and away from Sergei. The blade in his hand flashed, making his intentions obvious. He was still determined to end Sergei's life. "He's a traitor and deserves nothing less."

In one swift movement, she withdrew a knife from her arm sheath and spun around, pressing the point of her blade against his neck. Very little pressure was needed to punch through Viktor's jugular vein and rip out his throat. It was a messy way to die, but she no longer cared who would clean the blood off the floor.

"Move and you die," she warned, a strange, cold detachment settling over her. "Although, if Sergei dies from your actions, I will see your end too."

Viktor froze, blood dripping down his throat from where

her knife had pierced his skin, but he didn't move. Although she ached to check on Sergei, she wouldn't trust Brant to keep Viktor contained. He only needed seconds to finish the job. "Drop your knife, Viktor."

His jaw clenched, but the weapon in his hand clattered to the ground. Keeping her blade at his throat, she quickly disarmed the rest of his weapons and tossed them aside. She continued to hold Viktor's gaze, tempted to drive the blade in and watch the light extinguish from his eyes. She meant what she said: Sergei's last moment heralded Viktor's demise.

From behind her, she heard Brant talking to someone on his commlink. It sounded as though they were giving him first aid instructions.

"If you kill me, your life will be forfeit," Viktor warned, his eyes holding a dangerous glint. "Consider carefully, Valentina. Sergei left you bleeding on the floor while he continued to focus on securing the last facility. I heard that once you were transferred to our hospital, he never even waited around until you woke up. Is Sergei's life worth your death?"

Valentina's eyes narrowed, but she didn't respond. If she could trade her life for Sergei's, she would willingly give it. He'd always held a place in her heart, even when he'd broken it. Having him back in her life over the past few days had shown her just how much she needed him. He was worth everything.

Viktor's eyes widened. "Unbelievable. You *do* still care for him, even after everything he's done." He frowned and added, "Sergei does not deserve your loyalty, Valentina. A rebellion is coming, and he's at the heart of it by supplying weapons to people within the towers. He was the target of the failed ambush, not you."

"You already knew about the meeting with OmniLab," she murmured, only halfway listening. Her attention was on

Sergei's labored breathing on the ground behind her. Brant was still talking to someone, and it sounded like Ariana and a medical team were on their way. She said a silent plea to Sergei for him to hold on just a little longer.

"Yes, but I wanted to know if you would share that information with me. According to our intel, we suspect one of the chairmen authorized the ambush," he admitted. "Supplies have gone missing from several camps, not just ours. Everything can be traced back to Sergei."

Valentina remained silent, the knife in her hand growing heavy as she continued pressing it against his throat. It would be so easy to silence Viktor and punish him for hurting the man she loved.

"I would not continue talking, Viktor," Nikolai warned from behind her. "Valentina has shown remarkable restraint already. I would not have had nearly as much."

Viktor's eyes narrowed at the figure over her shoulder. "Your presence in the towers is somewhat suspect, Nikolai."

Valentina pressed the knife harder against his neck in warning. Viktor inhaled sharply, his gaze darting back to hers. "I do not have any issues with you, Valentina. You can still walk away from this without consequences if you lower your weapon."

"Valya," Nikolai spoke softly from behind her. "Ariana is on her way, but she may not get here in time. Sergei will not survive without assistance. If you are able to help him, you must do so now."

Her heart clenched as a crippling fear ripped through her, and she gripped the knife tighter. The thought of losing Sergei was too much to handle. Something creaked and groaned within the walls as though even the building became enraged by the possibility. "Don't you think I would have already helped him if it were possible?"

Nikolai moved closer, his strong and comforting presence

doing little to combat the cold chill within her. Only Sergei had ever been able to chase it away. "Perhaps, but you will not know unless you try. Love is a choice, Valya. You must choose whether to embrace the healer within you or hold on to death."

"I don't know how," she whispered. Her whole life had been a study of death—how to avoid it for herself and how to give it to others. Her trainers had excelled in that regard. She'd become exactly what they intended, but Sergei had helped preserve parts of the girl she'd once been.

He'd been the one who encouraged that playful streak within herself, always coming up with new games and appealing to her competitive nature. He'd shown her laughter, teasing, and passion were necessary components of life because the alternative was nothing but joyless duty. She'd never felt alive until she'd met the three of them, and the thought of losing Sergei was more devastating than anything she could have ever imagined.

Valentina loved him with everything within her. Her soul was tied to his, and without him, she'd lose one of the most precious parts of herself. It was that part their trainers had never been able to touch because she'd given it to Sergei, Nikolai, and Yuri almost from the moment they'd met. They owned her heart, her soul, her entire sense of self.

"You do," Nikolai urged. "You've always known, Valya. Your ability to take lives has never made us stronger. It was your love that did that. Your love draws us to you, and that's what kept us together. Sergei never left you. He only wanted to find a way to remain by your side."

Nikolai squeezed her arm gently, and she blinked, trying to stop the tears that threatened to escape. Maybe Nikolai had been right all along. Maybe the lessons their trainers tried to instill weren't her strengths. Sergei had helped nurture her softer side, and she'd done the same for each of them, allowing them to keep those parts of themselves untouched and whole. As she held Viktor's gaze, there was no trace of that compassion and gentleness she saw so frequently in Nikolai. There was no sign of the teasing and wicked humor Yuri possessed. Even Sergei's passion, protectiveness, and strong moral sense of righteousness were missing from Viktor's gaze. If Viktor had ever held such traits, they were now buried too deeply for her to even catch a glimpse.

As she studied Viktor, it had never been more apparent that the four of them were markedly different. Even when Yuri and Nikolai took other lovers, they held part of themselves back, not willing to trust anyone too deeply. It was too dangerous for them, and survival depended upon a type of cold detachment. For over ten years, the only ones they'd been able to count on were each other. It was only with each other that they relaxed their guard, embracing their softer sides.

A loud *clang* reverberated from somewhere overhead and water began dripping down the walls. Viktor's eyes widened, and his body tensed.

"I can't cut her off," Brant's voice said from behind her. "One of you needs to talk her down. Now. The pipes are bursting."

Nikolai cursed and wrapped his arm around her waist but didn't pull her away from Viktor. It was as though he knew this had to be her choice. "Calm yourself and focus, Valya. Sergei needs you. Only you have a chance of helping him. Do not let him die without trying."

"Release the knife, Valya," Yuri added, moving to stand beside her. "I will take care of Viktor for you. But I cannot do what you can for Sergei."

Tears streamed down her cheeks, and Valentina nodded, trying to get control of her emotions. Yuri took the knife from her and shoved Viktor toward the door. She turned away, her attention once again drawn to the motionless man on the ground beside her. Sergei was unconscious, the blood stain on his chest growing with every heartbeat. Brant was still holding her shirt as a compress around the knife, but it was doing little to staunch the blood flow. Dropping to her knees, she stroked Sergei's face and whispered, "I don't know what to do."

Brant lifted his gaze to meet hers, a small frown on his face. "I'm not a healer, but I've seen it done. I can try to walk you through it."

"Please," she begged, looking down on Sergei's unconscious form. She was willing to try anything if it would keep him by her side.

"It will probably work better with skin contact," Brant said, instructing her to use a knife to cut open Sergei's shirt. She did, peeling it away from where the weapon had entered his chest. Her heart thudded, inwardly calculating the depth of the knife and cataloguing what she knew of anatomy to determine the scope of damage it had caused. That he was still alive at all was miraculous. It would take another miracle for him to survive the next few minutes.

In a strained voice, she managed, "Tell me what to do."

"Close your eyes and place your hands on Sergei's skin near the knife. We can't risk pulling it out yet or he'll bleed out."

She nodded and did as he instructed.

"You know Sergei better than anyone," Brant said, his voice strangely calm and soothing. "Draw upon your memory of him. Imagine him healthy and whole. You can use your energy to feed it into him. From there, use it to repair him until he appears the same in your mind's eye."

Valentina cleared her mind, ignoring the surrounding noises with the exception of Brant's voice. She imagined Sergei, his gray eyes with the small flame around his iris, his strong jaw, his teasing smile, the strength of his body, and the steady beat of his heart she had listened to only a few short hours ago.

She opened her eyes and looked down at his unconscious form. The reality was all wrong, but at least she knew where to begin. Closing her eyes once again, she focused on the biggest element out of alignment—the wound in his chest. Grasping her energy, she channeled it toward him, trying to force him back together. But healing wasn't the type of gift that could be forced. It was fluid, like water, and like her. She paused for a moment, realizing it needed gentle encouragement, a type of coaxing.

With renewed determination, she teased his energy threads together with hers, laying them to rights with subtle suggestion. She paused in surprise at the ease in which they returned to their origins. His body was perfect and whole on its own, but the damage caused by the knife was unnatural. His energy wanted to reject the foreign invasion. He lacked the tools to repair it on his own, but she could help guide his energy in the right direction.

"It's working," Brant urged. "Keep doing what you're doing, and I'll start removing the knife."

Valentina nodded, recognizing the weapon was impeding her efforts to heal Sergei's injury. As Brant slowly began pulling it out, she fused more energy into Sergei, encouraging his body to correct the damage left behind. Brant would pull it out a fraction, pause to let her weave Sergei back together, and then pull the knife out a little more. It was a slow and tedious process, but healing was a gentle art that required patience—something that frequently escaped her. But she'd learn the lesson gladly, provided Sergei opened his eyes once again.

The minutes crept by and sweat trickled down her face from the intense concentration it required to heal Sergei.

Even with her lack of experience, some unknown instinct within her warned that the man she loved beyond all reason would die if she didn't give everything she had to save him. He'd weakened so much from the injury.

Finally, the weapon was out. Sergei was still weak from blood loss, but she could only offer suggestions to his body to replenish his blood. Apparently, there were limits to this healing ability. It would simply take time for his body to recover and bring itself back into alignment, but she'd given him a good start by repairing the worst of his injuries.

As she ran her hands over his body, she found other damaged areas, where the years and battles they'd fought had taken their toll. She felt each of his ailments as her own, and her love for him demanded she chase away all his pain. Moving to each injury, she healed his hurts before moving on to the next.

"You need to stop, Valentina," Brant urged. "You're doing too much."

Valentina shook her head. There was more that needed to be done, but it was getting harder to focus. She had to do at least a little more. The more she healed, the easier his recovery would become. If someone was targeting him, he couldn't afford any lingering weaknesses.

Ariana's voice sounded from somewhere far away. "Brant's right, Valentina. You can do more later, but you must rest."

"I have to do this," she managed, finding another injury he must have acquired while they were separated. She knew his scars as intimately as her own, each one a roadmap to a painful memory. This new scar had healed a great deal, but it was still raw. She wanted to chase away all his pain, just as he'd tried to erase her own.

"Please, Valya," Nikolai spoke from beside her. "You're pulling energy from all of us."

She hesitated, turning to look at Nikolai and sensing the

strain from him and Yuri. He nodded at her. "We're all connected. You must stop. The worst has been healed."

Valentina immediately released the energy threads she'd been using, unwilling to hurt the other people she loved. She started to stand but nearly collapsed from the effort. Nikolai wrapped his arms around her, pulling her against him. She laid her head against his chest and whispered, "I'm sorry. I only wanted to help him."

"I know," he murmured, pressing a kiss against her hair. "I can feel how tired you are. You should rest, Valya. We'll take care of both of you."

"I cannot lose him again, Kolya."

Ariana's voice was gentle as she said, "He'll live, Valentina. You saved him."

She nodded and closed her eyes, trusting Nikolai and Yuri to watch over her. But what Ariana didn't understand was that Sergei had saved her just as much as she'd saved him. All four of them had saved each other, and she wouldn't trade their bond for anything in the world. They were her heart and her salvation.

## CHAPTER NINETEEN

VALENTINA WAS HOT. A burning flame surrounded her, but it wasn't uncomfortable. In fact, her natural coolness made the warmth more than a little pleasant and soothing. She curled up against the heat source, snuggling against the familiarity of it. Caught between a dream state and wakefulness, she whispered Sergei's name on a sigh.

An arm wrapped around her, pulling her closer. Sergei murmured softly, "I'm here, little dove."

The sound of his voice was enough to make her open her eyes. Sergei smiled at her and brushed the hair away from her face.

Pushing herself upright, she searched for any trace of injuries on him. He remained lying down, watching as she trailed her fingers over every inch of his bare chest. A thin line marked where the blade had entered, and she ran her fingertips along it. If she hadn't seen it for herself, she would have sworn the injury was over a year old.

"You healed me, Valechka."

Valentina lifted her gaze to meet his, the small flame around his iris flaring brightly. She swallowed, emotions caught in her throat at the depth of love in his eyes. "I thought I'd lost you, Seryohza."

He sat up, pulling her into his lap, and wrapped his arms around her. Clinging to him tightly as though if she let him go, he would disappear again, she buried her face against his neck. She couldn't lose him again. She'd never survive it.

"Shh," he murmured, tilting her chin to look into her eyes. She blinked up at him, the internal flame within him flaring brightly. "I love you, Valechka. I haven't spent the last three years away from you only to be separated from you now. You will *not* lose me."

Her throat tightened and she shook her head, knowing he couldn't make such promises, especially in light of everything she'd learned from Viktor. Sergei's life would continue to hang in the balance the longer this threat still lurked out there. Viktor was only the beginning.

"Someone wants to see you executed," she managed, burying her face against Sergei's neck again as Viktor's words came rushing back. "They believe you're organizing a rebellion against our people."

His hand calmly stroked her back. "I know. Nikolai told me. We'll figure it out."

Valentina lifted her head. He couldn't afford to be cavalier about this situation, and she couldn't afford to let him. "It's not that simple. Peter's already gone to some of the other leaders about this. They must be supporting his bid for control of your tower. Otherwise, no one would have had the audacity to order an ambush without a collective order. It was messy but very effective if their intention was to create disarray. Your death would not only have opened the new tower up for someone else to take control, but someone may have also viewed it as a neat fix to eradicate a possible rebellion if they believe you're responsible. I don't know if Peter had a hand in it or not, but I think you were always the target, not me."

Sergei cupped her face. "We *will* figure it out. I will not be parted from you again, and I'm not responsible for what they claim."

Her eyes narrowed. "Did you think I doubted you?"

He grinned. "I would hope not."

"I *know* you would never betray our people," she snapped, pulling away from him and climbing out of bed. They needed to start making plans to figure out who was responsible for the thefts. She'd reach out to every one of her contacts and call in every favor she'd accumulated over the years. Somehow, they'd find a way to clear Sergei's name. "We don't have much time. We need to find the people responsible, or these rumors will continue to spread. If they become too far out of control, we won't be able to contain the situation."

Valentina walked over to the bag she'd brought with her and yanked it open. She'd have to start with Peter and Lena first. She had a few contacts in Lena's camps, but no one within the woman's inner circle. She'd already decided to take on some additional jobs so they could extend the construction timeframe, and this could be a good opportunity to investigate. And if Yuri hadn't killed Viktor yet, maybe they could extract more intel from him. She started digging through the bag for her weapons, but Sergei's hand on her arm stopped her.

"Look at me, Valentina," he ordered.

She turned, lifting her head to regard him. He took a step closer to her. "You've been asleep for many hours. During that time, much has happened. We've already begun investigating based on the information you gathered from Viktor. But there are other factors that changed when you healed me."

Valentina frowned, a sense of unease blooming inside her. "What do you mean?"

Sergei wrapped his hand around the back of her neck, his

touch light but still possessive. He stroked the side of her neck with his thumb, the gesture extraordinarily intimate considering the vulnerability of the location. He was the only one she had ever permitted to touch her like this, and it had been years since she'd last allowed it. A small shiver went through her as she held his gaze, letting him know she trusted him implicitly.

His eyes softened as he searched her expression. "There's something I must tell you, but I don't want you to have any regrets."

"What?"

He moved even closer to her. "Before I say it, I want you to know I wouldn't change any of this for the world. Nor would Nikolai or Yuri."

"Tell me," she urged, his hesitation unnerving her more than anything else.

Sergei sighed. "When you drew upon Nikolai and Yuri's energy to heal me, it somehow changed the bond between all of us. Alec says he can sense the energy connection between the four of us now, even when we tried to suppress it. That's not typically part of his abilities, and he wasn't sure whether he was able to sense it because of Ariana or because our connection has changed." He paused, took a deep breath, and added, "Unfortunately, Brant was also able to detect it. Something about your energy is different, and his shadow abilities don't work quite right around you. I'm afraid most of the Shadows will be able to tell we're bonded with very little effort."

Valentina leaned against the dresser for support, immediately understanding the implications. They were all at risk if this information got out. If one of the Inner Circle breathed a word about their connection and the wrong ears overheard, everything they'd accomplished over the past ten years would be destroyed. Hundreds of lives would be put at risk and entire families would be torn apart as Nikolai's territories were divided amongst the remaining leadership. That didn't even take into account their own fates if the truth was discovered. "We have to leave the towers immediately."

"No," he argued, taking a step closer and caging her against the dresser with his arms. "You burst some of the pipes in the construction tower, Valechka. That, and your ability to heal, has made it clear to all of us that proper training is critical. Nikolai, Yuri, and I are all in agreement in this matter. We cannot afford to leave the towers."

She blinked at him, barely able to get her head around what he was proposing. "Are you saying you want to renounce our allegiance to the Coalition?"

Sergei hesitated. "Not exactly. But we need to reassess our loyalties. Our first loyalty and priority must be to each other and to harnessing these abilities. Duty to everyone else, both the Coalition and the Omnis, needs to come second. If we're going to succeed in our endeavors, we *must* embrace this connection between us fully. We can't hide who we are anymore."

"You know that won't work," she said, turning around to look at the clothing scattered on the dresser. She caught a glimpse of her reflection in the mirror and frowned. Someone had removed her bloody clothing and dressed her in one of Sergei's shirts, but there were still traces of his dried blood on her skin. It was a stark reminder of how close she'd come to losing him. "Our people won't accept it when they find out about the four of us, and the Omnis won't understand our bond. Maybe in time, but not now. I don't see how all of us can stay here without losing everything we've been working toward."

Sergei arched an eyebrow and met her gaze through the reflection. "Would you send a partially trained soldier into battle?"

"It's not the same," she argued. "I agree we need to develop our powers. Almost losing you made that very clear to me. But staying here and not doing anything to prove your innocence would be the equivalent of admitting your guilt. That's unacceptable, Sergei."

"What they think of me doesn't matter, Valechka," Sergei said gently, putting his arms around her. "We must be true to each other. If they don't accept us, that's on them. We'll have a home together regardless of whether or not the Omnis understand our bond. Alec has already promised this to us."

She lowered her gaze, feeling conflicted. It wasn't that easy. After her parents had died, she'd agreed to enlist in the training program in exchange for her remaining family's security. The memory of her younger sister and elderly grandmother had been the driving force behind her desire to do whatever was necessary to guarantee their people's continued survival.

Valentina hadn't seen her sister, Nadiya, in years. She only had childhood memories of a playful little girl with long brown hair and an older woman with wrinkles who had showered her with love. But everything Valentina had done since enlisting had been for them. To her, Nadiya and her grandmother represented the thousands of faceless individuals who made up the embodiment of the Coalition. It had fueled her determination to help find resources, protect their people, and secure their futures. As long as Valentina was part of the group, she was helping her family and thousands of families like them.

"I don't want to leave the Coalition or do anything that might jeopardize my position within it," she whispered, turning around and putting her hands on his chest. "I understand your reasons, but please don't ask me to do this. You know I'll always choose to stay with the three of you, but there has to be another way."

He tipped her chin back to look into her eyes, searching her expression. "You're thinking of your sister."

Valentina nodded. "Yes, but I'm also thinking of everyone else. We've spent our lives trying to protect our people. Your efforts in securing this tower have given us a real chance to thrive. Will you, Nikolai, or Yuri really be able to turn your backs on everything we've built?"

Sergei paused for a long moment, trailing his thumb over her cheek. "No, but it isn't possible to keep our abilities a secret any longer. It *will* come out. Alec has offered to check their archives to see if there's a way to hide our bond, but it will take time. We need to decide upon a course of action while we still have a choice. We have a little bit of time to decide, but not much."

She nodded, knowing he was right. He put his arms around her again, and she leaned her head against his chest, listening to the reassuring sound of his heartbeat. "Will you tell me what else happened while I slept?"

Sergei sighed and tightened his arms around her. "It would have been more expedient to have Viktor killed, but Nikolai wanted to keep our options open. Alec used his ability to make him forget everything that occurred after I came back into my office. Viktor does not remember the fight. He was taken to their medical center and had his wounds treated, so he will not even have the scars to remind him. They released him about an hour ago. He is most likely on his way back to Peter's camp."

She frowned and lifted her head. "He wanted me to leave Nikolai's service."

Sergei's body tensed. "I heard. Nikolai and Yuri are in the other room reviewing the recording of the entire conversation again. They're not happy either. You will not be alone with him again."

Valentina shook her head. "You're missing the point.

Viktor wouldn't have made the offer unless he knew Peter's position was stronger than Nikolai's. He also knew Nikolai had taken other lovers. He thought because you had left me and Nikolai had chosen another, that my loyalty would no longer be with you."

Sergei frowned. "You're suggesting Peter has spies within Nikolai's camp? We knew Regina wasn't the only one, but you must have several people whose loyalty has been compromised."

She nodded, irritated with herself for not catching it. As Nikolai's influence grew and more people swore service to him, it became more difficult to manage all the different working parts. "It makes sense. Nikolai is discreet, but someone paying close attention would have noticed. Viktor also claimed one of the chairmen in the area was responsible for the ambush. It's likely he has well-placed spies within several of their camps too."

"Which chairmen are in the area?"

"Four that I know of—Peter, Lena, Ivan, and Oleg. Peter's been cooperative, but I still intend to investigate him. I have people close to Oleg, so I don't think he's had a hand in this. They would have sent word."

"Lena's never been fond of me or Nikolai," Sergei mused and rubbed his chin. "Peter's not thrilled with me either. I don't know Ivan well except that he's overly interested in OmniLab."

"He is, but his agenda here isn't clear. I may need to take a few jobs in his camp to learn more about what he's been doing."

Sergei frowned. "I don't know if that's a good idea. Everyone knows how important you are to Nikolai, and they may use that as a reason to target you. It might be better to let this play out naturally until we have more information."

Valentina wrinkled her nose. She didn't like sitting on the

sidelines, and patience had never been her strongest character trait. But if information was what they needed, there were ways to get that without waiting. First, she needed to check on the two other people she loved. Everything else could wait.

"I need to talk to Nikolai and Yuri," she said and started to head toward the door.

Sergei chuckled and grabbed her around the waist, spinning her back around and into his arms. "You might want to get dressed first, Valechka. As much as I enjoy you being in nothing more than my shirt and your panties, this new bond is requiring some adjustments on our part. Nikolai and Yuri are in the common room with Lars. If you walk out there like this, Lars won't be able to help but admire your legs, and I'd rather not kill him. My control is not what it should be."

Valentina blew out a breath. Without even trying, she could feel not only Sergei through their bond but Nikolai and Yuri as well. Nikolai and Yuri were currently distracted and growing increasingly agitated about something, most likely her recorded conversation with Viktor. But she intuitively knew if she reached out to them, they would come rushing into the room. She'd always been able to sense them, but it was a little disconcerting how they were now edging in on her thoughts.

Before they focused on anything else, they were going to need to get a handle on things and establish some very clear boundaries. Sergei was right about one thing—their relationships with each other needed to come first.

She nodded, grabbed a pair of pants, and quickly pulled them on before heading out to the common room with Sergei. As she suspected, Yuri and Lars were sitting on the couch replaying the recording of her and Viktor. Nikolai was pacing back and forth, rubbing the back of his neck like he usually did when he was worried. As though sensing her approach, Yuri and Nikolai immediately turned toward her. Yuri shut off the audio and stood.

Her heart thudded in her chest as she gazed at them. Through their bond, a sense of awareness and knowing filled her. They no longer hovered peripherally in her mind. Instead, they were vibrant and individual in her thoughts but somehow merged seamlessly with herself. She was still separate but more interconnected with them than she ever thought was possible. Sergei was right. Their bond had changed somehow. She could feel their energy within her, as though she carried part of them with her. She swallowed, amazed and disconcerted at the sense of completion and rightness in having all three of them here with her. It might not be possible to suppress their connection any longer, at least not using their old methods.

"Valya," Nikolai murmured. She immediately walked over to him, and he encased her in his arms. Even without saying a word, she knew Nikolai felt it too. On some level, he must have known what it could be like between them. That was part of the reason why he'd pushed so hard to bring Sergei back to them.

Nikolai hugged her. "I'm assuming Sergei told you everything?"

"You know he never tells me *everything*," she grumbled against Nikolai's chest. "He only tells enough to tease or annoy me. But he told me our bond has changed. I feel it too."

"You're not mad?" He leaned back to look at her. "We're all much closer now than we were yesterday."

She smiled and shook her head. "No. It's going to be an adjustment for all of us, but having all of you so close is comforting. It feels right, Kolya. This is the way it was supposed to be between us."

Yuri walked over to them. "You do realize we're never

going to be able to get rid of Sergei now, right? We're going to be stuck with him."

She laughed and threw her arms around Yuri. "Good. You two can irritate each other and give me a break." He hugged her tightly, and she leaned against him. "Are you really okay with this, Yuri?"

He ran a hand over her hair. "Which part? Deepening our bond? Or not being able to get away from Sergei?"

Valentina pulled back and swatted at him lightly. "I'm serious. Does it bother you?"

His grin faded. "I love you, Valya. Flaws and all. That wouldn't have changed, with or without a bond. I think there could be a lot of benefits from it, but we're going to have some challenges too. None of us have ever shied away from hard work though, and quite a bit will be necessary in making this relationship between all of us work." He paused, hugged her again and whispered, "No, it doesn't bother me. I didn't have a choice about my birth family, but I had a choice about you. The three of you are my chosen family... even Sergei. But I'll deny it if you tell him I said that."

"I love you too, and I won't say a word," she whispered, blinking back the moisture from her eyes. She released him and gave him a small smile. He acted gruff most of the time, but Yuri's heart was bigger than most people realized.

Lars stood. "Alex and Ariana wanted me to let you know they're at your disposal. They said they'd be more than happy to work with all of you on learning to manage whatever this change is in your bond. Much of it will be finding your balance with each other, but they can offer some suggestions on adjusting to it. Alec also suggested the possibility of asking Kayla to return from the river excavation site. He thinks she might be able to help, too, since Valentina's energy is similar to hers and Ariana's."

Sergei put his hand on her back. "I think we'd all appreciate that."

Valentina turned into Sergei, wrapping her arm around his waist and leaned against him. He kissed her hair and said, "If I didn't say it before, I'll say it now. Thank you for saving me, Valechka."

Gazing up into gray eyes that flickered with smoldering embers, she felt a surge of emotion. Somehow, against all odds, they'd managed to find their redemption and salvation within each other. Nikolai had been right when he said love was what bound them all together and made them stronger. Choosing love had brought him back into her life, and that same love would see them through the dark days ahead. No matter what happened, she'd never lose sight of that again.

She reached up to trace the line of his jaw with her fingertips. The love she had for him was overwhelming and stronger than anything she'd ever known. His gaze softened, mirroring everything she was feeling. It only reaffirmed her decision to do whatever was necessary to ensure Sergei and the rest of her family remained safe. And the best way to do that was to clear his name and hold whoever was responsible accountable for their actions. Everything else was negotiable. Whether they lived here in the towers with the Omnis or on the surface with the Coalition, it didn't matter. Her home had always been with them.

"You saved me too, Seryohza. You all did."

# ABOUT THE AUTHOR

Jamie A. Waters is an award-winning science fiction and fantasy romance author. Her first novel, Beneath the Fallen City (previously titled as The Two Towers), was a winner of the Readers' Favorite Award in Science-Fiction Romance and the CIPA EVVY Award in Science-Fiction.

Jamie currently resides in Florida with her two neurotic dogs who enjoy stealing socks and chasing lizards. When she's not pursuing her passion of writing, she's usually trying to learn new and interesting random things (like how to pick locks or use the self-cleaning feature of the oven without setting off the fire alarm). In her downtime, she enjoys reading, playing computer games, painting, or acting as a referee between the dragons and fairies currently at war inside her closet.

You can learn more by visiting: www.jamieawaters.com